HUNTER'S FALL

"Gripping, emotional and tense, and the book easily swept me up in its events. I look forward to reading more Hunter books!"
— *Errant Dreams Reviews*

"Complex personal histories and a very solid paranormal world add detail and intrigue as beautifully well-rounded characters reach for clarity and survival."
— *Publishers Weekly*

"Terrific."
— *Midwest Book Review*

HUNTER'S NEED

"A Perfect 10! *Hunter's Need* is a riveting tale that I couldn't put down and wanted to read again as soon as I finished . . . Highly recommending you pick up your copy immediately."
— *Romance Reviews Today*

"A sensual and arousing delight . . . Compelling and suspense filled . . . Shiloh has once again delivered a spectacular mystery romance paranormal. This novel had me spellbound from the start."
— *Bitten By Books*

"This is a terrific Hunters romantic fantasy starring two intriguing protagonists . . . Fast paced from the onset . . . Fans will relish this fine entry and seek previous thrilling Hunter tales."
— *Midwest Book Review*

HUNTER'S SALVATION

"A page-turner from beginning to end."

conti

"Scorching hot . . . Everything about *Hunter's Salvation* was mind-blowing . . . Shiloh Walker is truly one of the best writers I've ever had the pleasure of reading."

—*Romance Junkies*

"One of the best . . . Shiloh Walker provides an excellent thriller that subgenre fans will appreciate."

—*Midwest Book Review*

Hunters: Heart and Soul

"Some of the best erotic romantic fantasies on the market. Walker's world is vibrantly alive with this pair."

—*The Best Reviews*

Hunting the Hunter

"Action, sex, savvy writing and characters with larger-than-life personalities that you will not soon forget are where Ms. Walker's talents lie, and she delivered all that and more . . . This is a flawless five-rose paranormal novel, and one that every lover of things that go bump in the night will be howling about after they read it . . . Do not walk! Run to get your copy today!"

—*A Romance Review*

"An exhilarating romantic fantasy filled with suspense and . . . star-crossed love . . . Action packed."

—*Midwest Book Review*

"Fast paced and very readable . . . Titillating."

—*The Romance Reader*

"Action packed, with intriguing characters and a very erotic punch, *Hunting the Hunter* had me from page one. Thoroughly enjoyable with a great hero and a story line you can sink your teeth into, this book is a winner. A very good read!"

—*Fresh Fiction*

Titles by Shiloh Walker

HUNTING THE HUNTER
HUNTERS: HEART AND SOUL
HUNTER'S SALVATION
HUNTER'S NEED
HUNTER'S FALL
HUNTER'S RISE

THROUGH THE VEIL
VEIL OF SHADOWS

THE MISSING
THE DEPARTED
FRAGILE
BROKEN

Anthologies

HOT SPELL
(with Emma Holly, Lora Leigh, and Meljean Brook)

PRIVATE PLACES
(with Robin Schone, Claudia Dain, and Allyson James)

HUNTER'S RISE

SHILOH WALKER

BERKLEY SENSATION, NEW YORK

THE BERKLEY PUBLISHING GROUP
Published by the Penguin Group
Penguin Group (USA) Inc.
375 Hudson Street, New York, New York 10014, USA

Penguin Group (Canada), 90 Eglinton Avenue East, Suite 700, Toronto, Ontario M4P 2Y3, Canada
(a division of Pearson Penguin Canada Inc.) • Penguin Books Ltd., 80 Strand, London WC2R 0RL,
England • Penguin Group Ireland, 25 St. Stephen's Green, Dublin 2, Ireland (a division of Penguin
Books Ltd.) • Penguin Group (Australia), 250 Camberwell Road, Camberwell, Victoria 3124, Australia
(a division of Pearson Australia Group Pty. Ltd.) • Penguin Books India Pvt. Ltd., 11 Community
Centre, Panchsheel Park, New Delhi—110 017, India • Penguin Group (NZ), 67 Apollo Drive,
Rosedale, Auckland 0632, New Zealand (a division of Pearson New Zealand Ltd.) • Penguin Books
(South Africa) (Pty.) Ltd., 24 Sturdee Avenue, Rosebank, Johannesburg 2196, South Africa

Penguin Books Ltd., Registered Offices: 80 Strand, London WC2R 0RL, England

This is a work of fiction. Names, characters, places, and incidents either are the product of the author's
imagination or are used fictitiously, and any resemblance to actual persons, living or dead, business
establishments, events, or locales is entirely coincidental. The publisher does not have any control over
and does not assume any responsibility for author or third-party websites or their content.

HUNTER'S RISE

A Berkley Sensation Book / published by arrangement with the author

PUBLISHING HISTORY
Berkley Sensation mass-market edition / April 2012

Copyright © 2012 by Shiloh Walker, Inc.
Excerpt from *The Reunited* by Shiloh Walker copyright © 2012 by Shiloh Walker, Inc.
Cover art by Danny O'Leary.
Interior text design by Kristin del Rosario.

ISBN: 978-0-425-24837-9

BERKLEY SENSATION®
Berkley Sensation Books are published by The Berkley Publishing Group,
a division of Penguin Group (USA) Inc.,
375 Hudson Street, New York, New York 10014.
BERKLEY SENSATION® is a registered trademark of Penguin Group (USA) Inc.
The "B" design is a trademark of Penguin Group (USA) Inc.

PRINTED IN THE UNITED STATES OF AMERICA

10 9 8 7 6 5 4 3 2 1

ALWAYS LEARNING   **PEARSON**

CHAPTER 1

"THE one thing I wanted him to do was *die*. And he wouldn't. I mean, he had that fucking heart attack and I thought, *finally*, this is over. And what happens?"

Bent over her drink, the brunette smiled a little as she listened to the conversation between the two women. Maybe it was morbid of her—it was definitely a morbid discussion to eavesdrop on, but gloomy bits like that were one of the few things that amused her.

Her name was Sylvia . . . at least for now. She toyed with her glass of wine without drinking more than a sip every few minutes, more focused on the discussion than her drink.

"Oh, come on, Faith. He'll die, sooner or later. We all do, right?"

Faith, a pretty blonde with pretty blue eyes and pretty curls and pretty, plump breasts shifted on her seat and sighed. "Um, this is about *him*. And he's not going fast enough. I'd like him to kick it early enough that I can still enjoy *my* life before I'm too damned old and ugly. Damn it, this wasn't what I'd planned on."

Idiot. Sylvia set her wineglass down and checked her purse once more. The woman was an idiot. That's all there was to it. Shifting around just a little, she studied the friend. The poor woman looked uncomfortable, but she was trying to hide it.

Faith didn't even seem to notice as she leaned in after a quick glance around the bar—it wasn't even a *subtle* glance. "That's why we're here. I'm looking to meet this . . . person. Apparently she takes care of problems."

"Problems?" The friend was looking more and more nervous with every passing second, Sylvia noticed.

Smart girl.

Some people talked about doing stupid shit.

Others actually tried to go through with it. Faith was dumb enough, arrogant enough to try and go through with it.

"Yeah." Faith worked up a convincing little sob. "He hits me. All the time. He doesn't leave marks, because he likes to show me off. But I'm so *tired* of being hurt . . ."

"Faith, you're not . . ." Her friend tried to laugh, but it fell flat. In the end, she just cleared her throat and asked, "What are you talking about?"

A cold glint appeared in Faith's eyes. "Doing what's necessary. And it's not like I can divorce him, either. There's that damn prenup and everything. And if I screw around on him? *I'm* screwed."

"Look, this isn't funny." Her friend didn't just look nervous now; she looked outright sick. "I know you don't much care for the guy, so just divorce him. If you disliked him that much, you never should have married him."

She reached into her purse and grabbed some money, threw it down on the table. "You can sit here and feel sorry for yourself alone. I don't want to—"

Faith snaked out a hand, curling it around the other woman's wrist. "Sit down," she said, her voice cold. "You think I called you just so you could whimper and whine? I need somebody with me tonight and it's going to be *you*."

"I don't *want* to be with you," the other woman snapped, trying to jerk away.

"Tough shit." The smile on Faith's face now was cold. Cold, mean and ugly. "Because if you're not, I'm going to spill *your* secrets."

The woman went white.

"Faith, this is insane." The woman was trying not to cry now. "Just divorce him or something. You can't . . . you're going to . . ."

"I'm just trying to make sure I have a nice, easy life." Faith shrugged, unconcerned. "Just like you have a nice, easy life. It's only fair."

Fair. *Fair?* The absurdity of the conversation was almost enough to make Sylvia choke on the wine. Except she'd actually heard more absurd shit in her long life. After all, she was an assassin—very often, people didn't have good reasons for wanting to see another person dead.

"Fair . . ." Sylvia lowered her glass of wine to the bar and spun around, studying the blonde and her friend. "Life really doesn't have a great deal to do with being *fair*, does it?"

"Excuse me?"

Sylvia James leaned back against the bar and crossed her legs, an amused smile on her lips, keeping a hand on her purse. "I mean, if you wanted to talk about *fair*, we could talk about the fact that it wouldn't be *unfair* to expect a woman to actually *abide* by the vows she took."

Faith went white, and then red. Not quite so pretty now that she was pissed. Sylvia smiled. She was going to make the woman even angrier shortly.

Next to Faith, her friend squirmed uncomfortably. "Hey, lady, we're just . . ."

"You, my dear, were just avoiding a whole shitload of trouble," Sylvia said, resting an elbow on the bar, flicking her a glance before looking back at Faith. "You, on the other hand . . ."

"Bitch, why don't you mind your own business?" Faith narrowed her eyes.

"My own business?" Arching a brow, she slid off the stool and sauntered closer to the table the women shared. "Maybe we should just get down to business then . . . ?" Without waiting for an answer, she reached into her purse and withdrew a small digital recorder, hit the play button.

Faith's voice, recorded two days ago, came out.

And Sylvia didn't need supersensitive hearing to hear

Faith's breath catch as her eyes darted to the recorder and then back up to Sylvia's face.

"Now, Ms. Dwyer, what were you saying about minding my own business?" With one hand resting on her purse, she leaned over the table, peering into Faith's dazed eyes. "You called me. I told you I'd be here. I told you to take precautions. I told you to be discreet. I also told you . . . *no lies*."

She paused and sipped her wine, studying the dark red liquid, desperately wishing it was something else. "Now I've been sitting here for twenty minutes. You weren't discreet. You didn't take precautions. And . . ." She drew her voice out, studying the woman through her lashes, watching as the blood slowly drained from Faith Dwyer's face. "You lied to me."

"I didn't lie." Faith blinked, rapidly working up some pretty convincing tears. "My husband beats me. All the time."

Convincing. But not convincing enough. She reeked of lies. Humans couldn't lie very well. Not to somebody like Sylvia, at least.

More than a century ago, she'd been made into a vampire, and she'd spent quite a few years refining her skills. One of them was learning how to read people—fellow vampires, other freaks in the world . . . mortals. This woman was lying. Vampires could smell a lie the same way a human could smell spoiled milk—lies didn't smell much better, either.

"You're lying," Sylvia said gently. "I'm already pissed . . . don't make it worse. I'll be sending this on to the cops."

"You fucking bitch. You *can't*." Faith stood up, shaking her head. One hand curled into a fist at her side.

Sylvia saw the muscles tensing in her arms and she chuckled, slipping the recorder back into her bag and stepping back. "I'd think twice if I were you—remember what you hired me for. Do you *really* want to try to grab something from me? Or worse, *hit* me?"

Then Faith decided to change tactics. Tossing her head, she settled back in her chair, legs crossed lazily. She studied Sylvia with practiced boredom. "That little thing doesn't prove jack*shit*. Just a couple of voices . . . doesn't even sound like me. Why waste our time? Look, I'll just pay you the money and we call this quits."

"So you can try to hire somebody else later down the road? I don't think so." She stroked a hand up the buttery smooth leather of her cross-body sling bag, patted it. "You see, I have this little problem with women who try to paint men as abusive, when the men aren't. It just makes it that much harder for the real victims, you know. The recording will go to the police . . . as will this." Sylvia pulled another device out of the concealed pocket in her bag, this one a sleek, little digital video recorder.

Sylvia loved that device. She hit a button and after it had rewound enough, she showed the display to Faith. It had captured the blonde's pretty face with crystalline clarity, as well as her voice. It played a few seconds before the recording stopped and then Sylvia hit the record button again, careful to keep it angled away from the friend. She hadn't gotten the woman on video earlier and she wouldn't this time, either.

So far, the woman was only guilty of bad judgment in friends. No reason for her to suffer overmuch for that. "So, Faith Dwyer, wife to the Honorable Justin Dwyer, is sitting here and we just heard her discussing with an unknown party plans to have her husband killed—she was going to pretend to be an abused wife, if I'm not mistaken. Anything to say, Faith?"

"You *whore*!" Faith lunged for her.

Sylvia sidestepped, laughing. "Oh, that was perfect. I bet your husband's lawyer is going to *love* this." She stopped the recording and took a moment to wag the device at her before tucking it safely away. As the woman came for her again, she delivered a quick, easy jab, sending the icy bitch straight to the floor.

Behind her, she heard the bartender pick up the phone and calmly start to dial. She'd warned him earlier there might be trouble. And she'd paid him an extra hundred to keep calm if she had to get . . . physical.

Things had just gotten physical. He'd kept calm and earned that hundred. But it was time to go.

While her friend continued to stare, her mouth open in shock, Faith sprawled on the floor moaning, her pretty blue eyes dazed. Sylvia knelt down at her side and waited until that fog started to lift before she said anything.

"I don't appreciate having my time wasted, sweetheart," Sylvia said once Faith was looking at her. The arrogance she'd seen was gone now, replaced by fear and worry. Good. "You don't want to be married? Listen to your friend . . . file for divorce. But don't lie to get me here." Rising, she went to take a step away when Faith clamped a hand over her ankle.

"You can't go to the cops," Faith said, the fear in her eyes taking on a desperate slant. "I . . . shit. I'll *pay* you, damn it. Just don't tell them."

"Sorry. I don't do bribes or blackmail." She shook Faith's hand away and kept walking.

Behind her, Faith sat up, pushing her hair back. At the sound of the sirens wailing out in the streets, she blanched and shoved upright onto her feet. "I'll tell the cops it was *your* idea," she said. "If you turn that in, you look as bad as I do—since you agreed to *meet* me."

Sylvia paused at the side exit door and looked back, chuckling. "But I was never here, sweetheart. The cops don't even know who to look for."

"I'll tell them. I'll give them your name, your phone number . . . everything."

"My name? My number? Faith, darling . . . do you *really* think either of those is real?" She smiled. It was a lovely, rather disturbing smile. "They've been looking for me for years . . . I'm nothing but a ghost."

Y EARS.
Decades.

But she'd been evading them with ease. Sylvia had learned how to hide when she'd been running for her life, certain the monster who'd created her would change his mind, come looking for her. That never happened, but it had taken years for the fear to fade.

Years before she finally stopped hiding in the shadows.

Before somebody had all but *forced* her to stop cowering in those shadows.

Then, she had to learn to hide for a different reason, as she became a predator in her own way. A killer-for-hire, one who hunted other monsters. Sometimes, people came to her for revenge, sometimes people came looking for justice . . . and she'd learned to hide her trail very, very well.

Hours later, Sylvia let herself into the little apartment that was the closest thing she had to a home. It wasn't leased to Sylvia James—she used one of her other aliases, Alice Sanders. Boring, simple Alice.

Boring simple Alice and Sylvia had one thing in common . . . they only existed on paper. Kind of like the guy in *Shawshank Redemption*. She loved that movie . . . something about it just clicked for her. She'd escaped from the hell that had been her life. Andy Dufresne had escaped from the hell that had been his prison after he'd been falsely accused of murder. Both of them escaped. She had adopted a new persona—or ten. He had adopted a new persona.

Of course, Dufresne had kept his cool a lot better during his imprisonment than Sylvia had.

The "James" part was completely made up. Sylvia, however, was her real name, one she'd chosen for herself, years and years ago. She used it from time to time. She should probably shift away from it again for a while, but that was a problem for another night.

For now, all she wanted to do was sit down, relax with a better glass of wine than she could find in any bar and just zone out. It had taken hours to deal with that nasty mess involving Faith Dwyer. The vapid little bitch—she'd really thought she could hire Sylvia to kill her husband just so she'd inherit? Of course, it wasn't the first time, but it still pissed her off.

"Stupid cow," Sylvia muttered as she headed into the bathroom. She needed a shower. She'd managed to feed, but it had been late and she hadn't had the luxury of being choosy. Now she smelled like the inside of a beer keg. She could blame that on Faith Dwyer, too.

The woman probably had her hands full right now. No doubt she was telling lots and lots of lies, and causing her lawyer many, many headaches while her husband's lawyers rubbed their hands together.

The husband . . . bent over, she paused in the middle of unzipping her boots. She hoped the man hadn't really loved his wife too much. Whether he'd loved her or not, though, this must be one hell of a sucker punch. He might have been wishing Sylvia *had* taken the contract.

But there was just no way.

There were, Sylvia knew, more than a few killers-for-hire who would have taken the job. They killed for the thrill of it, for the hell of it, for the fun of it or for the money.

She didn't operate that way—she killed because it was what she did. She was good at it. But she was selective. Very selective. Abusive husbands, yes. She'd actually killed her first abusive *wife* a few years ago. That had been a head-spinning job, for certain. Abusive spouses were fair game. Abusive parents? Absolutely. Any type of abuser, *if* she knew the abuse was real.

Killing an abuser was one thing that did satisfy her. Others . . . it was just a job. Drug-dealers and other criminals fell in a gray area for her, but if they were involved in areas that could affect kids . . . well, they were playing a dangerous game. No reason kids should have to suffer the risks.

She didn't get involved in political messes, not unless there was another issue involved. Human politics, human concern, she didn't give a damn.

She didn't kill just to kill.

Just like she didn't kill to feed.

A vampire had to have standards.

A killer-for-hire had to have standards.

Sylvia was both, and she'd spend a very long time on this earth—she didn't want to live with any more mistakes than she had to. She kept her standards pretty high, and when somebody crossed her own personal lines, it was at their own risk. That was a lesson Faith Dwyer had learned earlier.

She couldn't say she hadn't been warned, either. Because Sylvia had warned her, when the woman had first contacted her. *Be careful. Don't take risks. Don't tell anybody else about this . . . and do NOT lie to me. About anything.*

Those were the ground rules Sylvia had laid out when she'd made the phone call after the first few e-mails had been exchanged.

Faith hadn't taken the warning seriously.

Pity.

That relaxing glass of wine beckoned, but she knew that if she had the wine, she'd want to do nothing else work-related before she settled down to rest. And she needed to take care of business matters first, and start making plans to move on. She'd been putting it off for weeks, and it was time.

If she didn't get things in motion now, she'd get caught up in another job and then put it off again, and again . . . she excelled at procrastination.

So instead of going for that glass of wine, she settled at her desk to check her e-mail. There were a number of them. Most were from a familiar site—an underground Craigslist for killers sort of thing. She skimmed through them, deleting most without reading more than a few lines. She was, after all, very picky. She wasn't killing some moron's "cunt" of a girlfriend, and she wasn't killing this woman's husband because he cheated on her.

But one e-mail made her go still.

One had images flashing through her mind . . .

A boy. And images of the boy brought other images to mind . . . images of a man.

Alan Pulaski—

That name. Gripping the edge of her desk, she closed her eyes and let the memories dancing in the back of her mind come to her. After a woman's lived more than a few decades, the memory can get chaotic . . . and Sylvia was over a hundred years old.

Missing—

A missing child. Toby . . . innocent eyes, sweet smile . . . there. His face. She had never been able to forget that boy's face. Locking on the memory, she pulled it to the front of her mind and then she looked back at the e-mail, read it through.

The boy's name was Toby. He'd been killed a year ago.

By one Alan Pulaski.

"COME on, baby face." The tall, slim blond brandished a knife as he squared off with the other man. His name was Toronto, and he was known for having a wicked temper, a wicked way with a blade and a smart mouth. He moved, graceful as a dancer, to face a man that outweighed him by a good fifty pounds and topped him by nearly six inches.

He was built like a tank, and he stank of blood, sex and violence.

That pissed Toronto off. A lot. He'd just pulled the bastard in front of him off a woman mere seconds ago. Now she struggled to live and Toronto's partner was kneeling at her side, trying to stop the bleeding.

Curling his fingers at the vampire, Toronto said, "Come on. What are you waiting for?"

The vampire grinned at him, too young and too stupid to realize just how much trouble he was in.

"Get out of my way, fuckhead. You don't know what you're messing with."

Toronto cocked a brow. The boy hadn't been changed long. Maybe a year. He didn't stand a chance against a were like Toronto. "*I* don't?" Twirling his knife, he smiled. "I think it's the other way around, kid."

"You think that knife is going to hurt me?" He flashed his fangs and gave Toronto a menacing look.

Toronto wasn't quite impressed, and he had the feeling the vampire was shocked by that. And the idiot also hadn't given Tor's knife much more than a cursory look. The knife *would* hurt him. It was a custom-made Keltec, one that had enough silver in the blade that it would leave any vamp or shifter all but begging for mercy. It might not *kill* him, but it would definitely hurt. Silver was a bitch.

Yeah, this vamp hadn't been around long, and nobody had bothered to teach him much, either. Toronto could teach him a thing or two. Before he ended the son of a bitch.

"Actually, I don't need the knife." Toronto flung it off to the right with enough force that it embedded itself in the wooden wall, hilt quivering. "I'll just use this . . ."

He lifted a hand, watched the boy's face as his hand shifted.

Claws emerged.

The vampire was every bit as uneducated as Toronto had

thought. *What in the hell is this*? Toronto wondered as he watched the vamp's eyes all but bug out of his head in shock. It was like the vamp had never seen a werewolf before.

A split second later, the young vamp panicked. It wasn't much fun when they panicked. Still, Toronto hadn't done it in the name of fun—or at least not entirely. He'd been looking for information, and he had gotten a little bit.

Lately, more and more Hunters throughout the country were reporting incidents like this. That wasn't good. A shitload of random, violent occurrences. Too much bloodlust, too little control. Too many who seemed to have lost all humanity—and that wasn't how it was meant to be. Most vamps and weres had a sense of who could get through the Change intact, who couldn't. They weren't to be touched if they couldn't live through it . . . or come through it sane.

Bad things happened when monsters thought they could do whatever they wanted without fear of consequences. Like what this fucker had done. Grabbed some poor woman off the streets, assaulted her and fed.

After he'd finishing dealing with the feral, he turned back and saw his partner Kel cradling the woman. The vampire had his hand, palm sliced open, over the wound in her throat in an attempt to save her life—the blood could close the wound, keep her from bleeding to death.

If she wasn't too far gone.

She wasn't bleeding anymore, but she was too still. Too pale.

"Is she going to make it?" Toronto asked.

"I don't think so." Kel gave him a sad look. "We were too late—she's fading too fast."

Toronto gave a short, single nod and looked away. She'd lost too much blood. Fuck. Yeah, bad things happened with monsters, all right. "It happens that way sometimes."

Kel swore under his breath viciously. "Happens, huh? Fuck that."

"We can't save everybody," Toronto said, jerking one shoulder in a shrug. He came closer, staring at the woman's pale face. Her heartbeat was faltering, her skin taking on a waxen cast—that spark of life was already gone. She wasn't going to make it. It was an ugly, bitter knowledge they'd have to carry.

Kel swallowed, a muscle working in his jaw as he stared at the woman's face. "Yeah, and you're okay with that?"

"It doesn't matter if I'm okay with it or not." Toronto slanted a look at Kel. "It just is. We can either accept it . . . or go crazy fighting it. But . . . no. I'm not okay with it. It fucking pisses me off. And that won't help her, either."

Kel continued to stare at her, his eyes glowing. "I could . . ."

Toronto knew what he was planning even before he said it. "I wouldn't, kid." He crouched down, studying the woman.

"But it would save her."

"No." Toronto reached down and took the girl's limp, cooling hand. "She'd either die in the transition or she'd go feral. You don't want to save her only to have to kill her, Kel."

"You don't *know* that."

"Maybe. Maybe not. That's not my area, right? But you know." He paused and then asked quietly, "What's your gut saying, Kel?"

Kel's furious glare was answer enough. He knew. She wasn't strong enough to survive the Change. Not everybody was.

It only took a few more seconds.

Toronto pretended not to see the faint glint of reddish tears in Kel's eyes. He pretended not to notice the ache in his own chest, too.

No. They couldn't save everybody.

Hell, some of them were hard-pressed to save themselves.

He'd been trying to save himself for a good long time. He was still trying. And failing.

THIRTY minutes later, he delivered a sad, solemn Kel back to the enclave, where the young vampire's wife waited.

They would have been back sooner, but they had to do some cleanup, including burning the vamp's body and taking care of the blood at the site. It was all over the damned place. They had to spread a specially made bleach compound everywhere to keep human cops from finding anything funky in the blood left by the vampire. None of them needed the mess that would happen if the oddities in vampire DNA came to light. Or shifter DNA. The chemical turned everything to sludge and no tech alive could harvest anything useable from it.

Toronto's world was nothing like some of the stuff people watched on TV—his kind weren't coming out of the closet any time soon. Humans weren't ready to deal with vampires or werewolves. Especially not when it was a crapshoot as to who would emerge sane . . . and who would emerge a monster after the Change. The monsters were executed. Plain and simple. It might not happen right away—sometimes it took a little while for that thread of sanity keeping the monster in line to snap.

But once it did . . . well, execution was the only option.

This vamp's creator should have seen that monster looming inside him. It hadn't been a quiet madness Toronto had seen. No, that fuck had been laughing and gleeful about his bloodthirst, delighting in the way he'd hurt that poor woman.

Toronto and Kel left her broken body back there in the alley.

Her family deserved to know what happened to her, deserved to have something to bury.

He wished he could do more for them, but giving them that answer was something—he knew what it was like to live without answers . . .

A dark, empty maw danced in the back of his mind, tormenting him, along with the ghosts of his earliest memories.

You'll have to learn to control that, boy. But you'll do well enough.

He's going to go feral . . . I'll put him down . . .

And always, that brutal, vicious hunger . . .

As the edginess crept up on him, he slid away from the others and made his way to his rooms. It took him fifteen minutes to clean up and change his clothes, five minutes to pack a bag and then he slid out the door.

He didn't leave a note, didn't let them know he was leaving. Rafe, the local Master, would be *pissed*.

But he had to get away for a while. Had to breathe. Sometimes, he thought he was going to come out of his skin if he had to stay here . . .

CHAPTER 2

"Toronto . . . as in Toronto, *Canada*?"

Nessa snuggled against Dominic's back and smiled. "Yes. Toronto." The wind tried to tear her hair out of the tight braid and she knew she'd be spending a great deal of time brushing the snarls and tangles out later. Her bum would be sore, too, after hours and hours spent on a motorcycle.

But that was fine; it was worth it. She was pressed up against her lover's back, his body warmed by her, and just now, he had his hand covering hers.

"Why the sudden inclination to go to Toronto?"

"Just a feeling," she said, sighing. She opened her eyes, staring off into nothingness. Memories rose, whispering into her mind. A broken body, one that had taken all of her skill to heal. A shattered mind, and although she'd been able to heal the physical damage, the memories, the soul, everything that he had been . . . *that*, she hadn't been able to save. The vicious pain echoing through him as he struggled with the weeks and months of fever and pain that came after his attacks.

He had been a nameless, broken child when she'd found him.

Now he was called Toronto—he'd claimed that name all

those years ago, because they'd needed to call him something. Some part of him had hoped they'd discover his hidden past.

It had never happened.

And now, Toronto had gone back to the city where they'd found him—the city he'd named himself for. Back to the place where he had been born . . . in a twisted sort of way. He'd been like a babe, born into the body of a youth, not quite a man, but close. He'd already had the instincts of a fighter—she suspected the early years of his life hadn't been easy, but his mind had been a blank slate. His past was lost to him, yet he seemed unable to let it go and he went back, time and again, as though hoping he would find some loose thread that would connect everything together.

Best to leave that past alone . . .

His past was a sad, unhappy road, she suspected, one she couldn't pierce. All she knew was that he'd been wrapped in shadows, shadows so thick, they had all but choked him. His past had placed him on the path that had damn near killed him. Whatever those shadows were, he should just let them go. They no longer mattered to who he was now. If he could just accept that and let it go, he'd be happier for it.

Not that it was likely to happen. She could even understand it.

Her past hadn't been an empty pit, but she certainly hadn't been able to let it go, even when she'd wished she could. Even when she'd tried. The past had a way of bogging a person down, and sometimes, the harder one tried to fight it, the harder it was to let it go.

Something from that past is about to reach out and bite him—

A shiver raced along her spine. Sometimes, the knowledge she had well and truly sucked.

I T had been nearly fifteen years since he'd let himself come back here.

Fifteen years. Not bad. For a while, Toronto had come back almost every month. Then it had been every year, and finally, he'd been able to stay away for longer stretches.

This had been the longest he'd ever gone.

But once he hit the city, Toronto found himself following the same path he always took. The alley where he'd been found wasn't an alley anymore—he couldn't even get to it, unless he wanted to walk through the middle of a busy store. Which he did. It was maybe thirty minutes before it would close. People stared at him strangely, but that was nothing new. Head bowed, senses alert, he waited . . . waited for . . . what?

Toronto didn't even know anymore.

"Why do you keep doing this?" he muttered.

But he had no answer to that.

This place held no answers for him. It never had. It didn't add to the riddle of his life, but it sure as hell didn't bring any solutions, either.

Evading the throngs of people, he made his way to the area that was close to where he'd been found. Even with a building standing over it, he knew it was the right place. He'd know it in his sleep.

Not because he remembered. Nessa had led him here, and he'd come back time and again—he'd watched as they'd constructed the building, even, and he'd considered tearing it apart, brick by brick.

There was a wall in the spot, barring him from getting as close as he'd like. That was where he stopped. Closing his eyes, he pulled those foggy memories from the depths of his subconscious. His first memories. Before that . . . nothing. Just blackness.

He remembered nothing of the night he'd been found. Nessa had taken him back. Walked him through the night, again and again, for those first few years. He could see it through her memories, but it was like having somebody tell him about something they'd experienced. It didn't feel like *his* life.

She'd been old, even then.

She hadn't moved like it, though. And she hadn't been alone. Two other Hunters had been with her. Another witch, and a vampire. The boy Toronto had been lay in a pile of broken bones and bloody flesh—the were virus had already

been working on him. It should have killed him. But as the
fever burned through him, the virus healed him, keeping
him alive until Nessa found him.

It couldn't heal everything, though.

The shattered mess that was his skull, and his scrambled
brain . . . everything he'd been, all of that was gone.

She'd sent the vampire after the wolves while the witch—
a man—had carried the boy.

Away from the alley where Toronto had both died and
been born.

"Sir?"

Hearing the nerves under the voice, Toronto lifted his
head and saw the security guard staring at him with a mix of
bravado, nerves and fear. Instead of waiting for the standard,
Can I help you please leave now, he just turned on his heel
and walked out of the store, following the path of faded
memories to the next spot.

Near the edge of the city, he paused, dragging in the stink
of something nasty. It was faint, and old. Vampire. It had a
familiar edge to it, though. Familiar enough that it made
Toronto think the vampire had come through the city more
than once. More than twice . . . revisiting his old hunting
ground the way Toronto came back to haunt these streets?

He didn't know, and just then, he didn't care. He'd send
word up the line. Somebody would have to start patrolling
through here more regularly. Toronto felt the buzz and burn
that indicated more paranormal creatures; as the human
population boomed, so did their kind. They kind of went
hand in hand. Made it damn hard to keep hidden sometimes.

Pushing problems of work, of Hunters, of monsters to the
back of his mind, he continued his walk outside the city. The
old place was still in one piece, still in decent condition and
he knew that if he walked inside, he'd find there wasn't a
speck of dust, not a thing out of place.

It had been more than a hundred years since he'd finally
emerged from the fevered Change . . . in this very house. It
was empty now. But he still heard the echo of her voice, the
echo of his own.

His first clear memories had been of her—Nessa. Agnes Milcher. An old woman who looked frail and was anything but. She had been there through the nightmares, had been there as the hunger ripped through him, had cooled him as the fevers raged.

She hadn't been alone. There had been others with her.

He's going to go feral, Agnes—he's too young. Watch yourself. A woman's voice.

No. He shall be fine. He's strong. I feel it. He'll need food, something big and bloody should do the trick. Mary, could you . . . ?

A pause. Followed by a woman's low, disbelieving voice, *You want me to hunt . . . for him?*

Well he needs to eat, doesn't he?

A man's voice. *I can bring him something.*

Then there were long moments of silence, and he'd tried to fight past the fog that wrapped around him. The hunger, so thick, so strong, tearing into him with dagger-sharp teeth.

He had to eat—had to—

Then his first glimpse of the woman who would be like mother and grandmother. His first friend—faded blue eyes, peering down at him. He hadn't seen the kindness in those eyes, then. Hadn't been able to recognize the power either. He'd just seen . . . meat. Felt the hunger tearing into him, his mind going blank.

The next thing he knew, he was hovering in midair, tearing at his throat and struggling to breathe, while the old woman stood a few feet away. The younger woman watched him with disgust and pity in her eyes. *I told you he wasn't going to pull through. I'll put him down, Nessa.*

But when the woman had reached for her belt, the other one had smacked at her hand. *You'll do no such thing, Mary. He's fine. Look at those eyes—he's quite lucid. No feral wolf could just hang there like that, waiting. Listening.*

Wolf—

What had she meant . . . and then he heard the growl. Like it came from deep, deep inside.

You'll have to learn to control that, boy. But you'll do well enough.

Control.

Shit.

Yeah, he'd learned to control it well enough. She hadn't let him out of her sight until she was certain he could.

It had taken months, and he'd spent most of them here.

From hooded eyes, Toronto stared at the little house, more of a cottage than anything else, searching for some answer. But, as always, there was nothing.

I T was midnight when he finally left the city itself, staring at it from over the water. It sparkled with light, spread under a sky of black. But he didn't see those lights, didn't see the massive skyscrapers, the CN Tower as it jutted into the velvety black night.

Eyes locked on those long-gone memories, he tried to pierce the fog of his past. But there was nothing there.

Back then, the were virus had still been viewed as a curse, and he'd been bitten only days before the full moon. There was a cyclical thing to the bite, and more than a little bit of magic. The science-minded people suspected the reason weaker weres *had* to shift around the full moon was because they all believed they had to. The virus caused a hormonal spike and those hormones built in their system and needed release—almost like a climax—and that release was needed on a regular cycle. So much shit was built up about werewolves and full moons, there could easily be deep, racial memories that were tied to the shift. Because they thought the Change came with the moon, it did.

Stronger weres could resist it longer. The stronger the were, the longer he or she could go without shifting. Likewise, the easier they could shift. There were more theories tied to complicated shit like *viral loads*—speculating that Master weres were created when they received a bite from either another Master, or from numerous wolves.

Toronto's existence seemed to support that. Those theories speculated that if a victim survived the bite, which wasn't likely, the most plausible outcome was that the victim would go feral—a loss of control, usually accompanied by a loss of sanity. Always followed by death, because ferals were executed. If the victim *didn't* go feral, he had a very good chance at being a high-level shifter, probably a Master.

Toronto had been bit by five werewolves—bitten, chewed on and played with, from what Nessa had told him. For those first few months, death and madness had chased him with a passion.

The fevers had hit hard and fast. Followed by rages ending in blackouts. Sometimes he woke in bed. Other times, he woke up restrained. And all the while, Nessa had been there. *You'll get through this, boy. We'll pull you through . . .*

Each time the hunger, the madness tried to take over, she'd been there. She'd kept him from dying. She'd pieced his broken body back together. But she couldn't do shit for his shattered mind.

There was nothing she could do about his lost memories. He'd tried to find the missing pieces of his life, but he'd never even been able to find a name.

He went by Toronto, because that was where he'd been found. For the longest time, he'd hoped he'd find some clue to his past and didn't want to get used to a real name.

After all this time, he knew it wasn't going to happen— this was just rote. And he couldn't stop it. Couldn't stop hoping. Couldn't stop half wishing something would trigger those lost memories, or that somebody held the pieces of his lost past. Couldn't stop wishing that something, *finally*, would make him feel whole.

Best to leave that past alone, Nessa had told him, more than once. *Stop looking for answers that do not exist . . . why torture yourself so?*

"Just a glutton for punishment, old woman," he murmured into the night. Hours bled away as he stood there, staring out over the water at the skyline. By morning, he'd have to leave. But he'd give himself the night. One night. Alone—

Or perhaps not. He wasn't terribly surprised when he felt the presence that whispered *witch . . .*

He recognized her. But she wasn't alone. There was another scent on the air, one he could have done without. He'd heard Nessa had finally found her own piece of the past, in the form of a lover who had died and somehow found his way back to her in a new life. Toronto personally didn't have any real problems with Dominic. But the other vampire was a reminder that he'd left responsibilities behind.

Toronto was supposed to be taking more care with those responsibilities.

But instead, he was here again.

Here, thinking selfish, dark thoughts and trying not to feel jealous over the fact that Nessa had found that missing piece of her soul. With Dominic, of all people. He never would have expected that one.

As they drew closer, Toronto shoved a hand into his pocket and pulled out a pack of gum. "Sometimes a man just wants to be alone," he said conversationally.

"And sometimes, you just want to brood, even though it's not good for you," Nessa said brightly.

Her voice, crisp with the sounds of England, was altogether too cheerful. But when she hooked her arm through his and slanted a look up at him, he saw the sympathy in her eyes.

"I thought you weren't going to come back here so often," she said softly.

"I haven't." He blew a bubble almost as big as his face and then popped it, mostly just to annoy her, watching as she made a face at him. "It's been fifteen years. That's a pretty good time-out, don't you think?"

Without waiting for her to respond, he shot Dominic a look. "And look at you, all mated up and happy. It's a good look for you, kid."

Dominic just stared at him.

Toronto huffed out an exasperated sigh. "Here I am, trying to be nice to him, even."

"Yes, you were." Nessa beamed at him, looking as pleased as if she were a teacher and he'd presented her with an apple on the first day of school.

Was it foolish that it made him feel absurdly proud, even as it embarrassed him? Scowling, he shifted his gaze over to the water. "The two of you . . . didn't see that one coming." Curious, he glanced at Nessa. "How did you know? Was it like *wham*, some sort of click and you just knew? Did it take longer?"

"Yes . . . and yes." She glanced at Dominic and then back at him, a faint smile on her face. "There were all sorts of *clicks*. But it took a while, too. Mostly because I tried to mess things up. But that's neither here nor there. Why are you here, Tor?"

"Not like I got anything better to do." He bent over and scooped up a rock, hurled it into the water—it almost made it to the opposite shore before it touched the surface. "Hey, what should I get you for a wedding present? I could always buy you some garlic to keep the vamps away, right?"

Nessa rolled her eyes. Dominic's response was to reach up, cup his hand over the back of his wife's neck. "Please tell me we didn't spend all this time driving up here to deal with this basket case."

"Well, he is my favorite basket case." She rose on her toes and pressed a kiss to Dominic's jaw, lightly patted his chest. "He can't help it, usually. He could stop being less of an ass sometimes. If he changed completely, he wouldn't be Toronto, would he?"

"That wouldn't be a loss," Dominic muttered.

Toronto sighed and continued to stare out over the rolling black waters before him. The moon was a high, gleaming circle in the sky—it was full—casting its light down on the world, reflecting off the water. It was hypnotic, lovely . . . he could almost imagine he heard it whispering to him. He should shift . . . run, let the wolf have his way, but the wolf would want to *run*, and *hunt*.

Toronto was here to search for answers—the wolf didn't care.

He'd like to pretend the lunar cycle had something to do with his edgy mood, but he could do better than this if he had to.

It had nothing to do with the lunar cycle, nothing to do with the changes the werewolf virus had wreaked on him all those years ago. In short, it was just him. Him being a basket case, an asshole. All of it.

"Nessa, stop worrying about me," he said softly.

"I can't." She moved to stand at his side, nearly as quiet as a vampire herself, quieter than any shifter. He heard her, but didn't move. When she reached up and rested a hand on his shoulder, he wished he would have, though. "I can't stop worrying about you, lad. You're a friend. I worry about my friends. And . . ."

"And what?" He slanted a look at her, scowling as he saw her eyes darken. He knew that look.

She might not look like the sweet old matron who'd saved his ass all those years ago—and that had been such a deceptive appearance—but damn it, she hadn't changed that much. That look didn't mean good things.

But she didn't answer.

"Damn it, Nessa," he snapped, his voice edging low and rough.

"You might want to watch how you talk to her, Lassie," Dominic warned, taking a step in his direction.

"Or what, dead man?" Toronto shot him a derisive look. "You haven't been without a pulse long enough to take me, and we both know it."

Dominic smirked. "Well, if push comes to shove, it's not *me* that you need to worry about it." He closed a little more distance between them, his eyes flashing in the night. "But that doesn't mean I'm going to let you talk to her that way."

"Dom . . . don't." Nessa rested a hand on his chest, staring in Toronto's direction. "It's not like I'd let either of you go at it, and that's another thing you both know. If push did come to shove, I'd have you both on the ground, begging for mercy."

Dominic covered her hand with his. "I don't care to listen to Furface talking to you like that."

"Hmmm. Well, Furface is having a bad night. We all have them, don't we?"

Toronto hated the sympathy he heard in her voice, hated it enough that he was willing to pick a fight with a witch who damn well *could* put him on the ground, if she so chose. "Yeah, well, instead of standing there talking about me like I'm not here, why don't the two of you fuck off and let me have my bad night?" He let his wolf show in his eyes as he flicked his gaze to Dominic before he looked back at Nessa. "I'm sure the two of you are still having a lot of fun tearing up the sheets and all that jazz. Leave me the hell alone, old woman."

The scent of anger lit the air around them—Dominic's. Dominic was pretty strong for a vamp less than two decades old, but he was still young. He couldn't handle Toronto.

Nessa, though, Nessa would leave his head ringing. That would stop any pitying talk. Except, of course, she knew exactly what he was after.

"Don't even think of it, wolf." Nessa's voice, cool and sharp with warning, wouldn't have been enough to get through to him.

Right then, he was so desperate to get them both away from him, to stop that infuriating pity, *nothing* would get through to him. But when he tried to take a step forward, he found he couldn't and there was an unseen, warning *hand* around his neck.

Witches. Strong ones were a pain in the ass. They manipulated the elements the same way others could flip a light switch, and the stronger they were, the easier it was to manipulate said elements. Nessa was the strongest witch alive.

"Fuck, Nes—"

That was all he got out before she tightened her grasp. "Do stop, Tor, my dear," she said, sighing. "You're pissing Dom off and trust me, while it would be great fun to watch the two of you wrestle around like buffoons, that's not why I'm here."

She peered at him, her big blue eyes narrowing. "So, if I let you go, are you going to behave yourself? As best as you know how, at least?"

He glared at her.

The unseen "hand" around his neck tightened and he tried to suck in a desperate breath of air. Damn it, she hadn't gone and forgotten he still needed to *breathe*, had she? Black dots started to dance in front of his eyes.

"Toronto, you have always been so bloody stubborn." The hand loosened, and he sagged, sucking in desperate draughts of air.

"And you were always so damned determined to mother me." He shoved his hair back and glared at her. His throat ached, damn it. "Mother me and then do crazy shit like fucking trying to *strangle* me. What in the hell do you want, Nessa?"

"Oh, do be quiet." Nessa shot Dominic a warning look. "Really, Toronto. If I'd wanted to strangle you, there would be no *try* to it, and you well know it."

With the blood still roaring in his ears, Toronto struggled to hold on to his control, but every second made it harder. The wolf inside him started to stretch, rolling around inside his skin. *Out . . .* the wolf whispered. *Let me out . . . let me run. Let me hunt . . .*

"What do you *want*?" he snarled.

Something about the way she stared at him made the wolf still. Toronto's blood ran cold and his heart shuddered inside his chest. "Darkness . . . you know it's part of us all, don't you, Toronto?" Nessa eased away from Dominic to stand at Toronto's side, staring out over the river.

"All of us?" He tried to force himself to smile. "You don't have a lick of darkness in you, old woman."

A faint smile curled her lips. "You know, it's terribly amusing to hear that from you, when *I* look younger than *you* now." Then she slanted a look up at him. The look in her eyes was . . . awful.

Something he'd never thought to see from her, something he never *wanted* to see from her. Something too close to a monster peered at him from her lovely blue eyes and he watched, with his heart racing, as that darkness leeched away, replaced by a grim, bleak sadness. "We all have darkness, Toronto. Mine is a burden I'll have to bear for all my days, I fear. You . . ." She closed her eyes. "Your darkest days are in your past, Toronto. Let them stay there. Leave it alone."

"You know more than you've told me," he said, and it wasn't the first time he'd said it. Closing his eyes, he thought, *Will she tell me this time?* But he already knew the answer. "When are you going to tell me?"

"Leave it alone," she said again, her voice gentle.

Leave it alone? If only it was as easy as that. He wished he could—

Something raced along his spine.

It was faint, but unmistakable.

Sighing, he opened his eyes and slanted a look at Nessa. She felt it, too. He could tell just by looking at her. She stood with her head cocked and a frown on her face. "Hardly what we need right now," she murmured, absently toying with the end of one braid.

"What?"

Dominic, it seemed, was too young to feel it. Turning away from the river, Toronto said, "Call is going out. We need to batten down the hatches."

"Batten down the hatches?" Dominic lifted a brow.

Nessa moved to him and hooked an arm through his. "There's going to be a need for us soon."

"Us . . . us, who?"

She answered, but Toronto tuned it out. His mind was focusing on the fact that he needed to go back to Memphis. But that wasn't where he wanted to be.

Or where he belonged. Of course, he didn't know *where* he belonged. Actually, that wasn't true.

He didn't belong anywhere, and he hadn't for quite some time.

CHAPTER 3

"Look who decided to grace us with his presence."
Toronto should have known that coming back in the daylight wouldn't prevent the Master from going for his throat.

Plastering a blank expression on his face, he paused on the steps and glanced over to the office. It wasn't even close to dusk, maybe four in the afternoon. But Rafe was a Master vampire, and he wasn't a weak one, either—that came with some perks. Sometimes those perks involved being able to rise well before sunset. Didn't mean he'd be able to go for a tan or anything, but he wasn't a slave to the rising and setting of the sun, either.

Which meant Toronto had to face him.

He shoved his hands in the back pockets of his jeans. "Hey. Sorry I took off." There. Did that cover it?

"Sorry." Rafe stroked a thumb down his jaw and nodded. With deceptive laziness, he sauntered out of the darkness of his office into the brightly lit hallway. Sunlight fell through the window to dance across his face as he crossed to the stairs. Rafe didn't so much as flinch.

"You're sorry. You disappear, leave one of the younger Hunters alone after a bad fight and you're sorry."

Something itched inside Toronto—stretching, spreading. The wolf inside him didn't like having to answer to *anybody*. His wolf was every bit as strong as the vampire before him—they both knew it. Toronto didn't *have* to serve here. He chose to.

But it wasn't about strength.

Toronto had decided to settle in one place and that came with rules to follow. He wasn't about to challenge Rafe for the land—he didn't *want* the damn land. He just wanted to stay in one place for a while, and why not here? Especially seeing as how he had people to hassle on a regular basis.

But it came with giving in at times, and giving in, plain and simply put, sucked.

Swallowing the growl that rose in his throat, he cocked his head to the side. "I had to leave."

"Why?"

This time, he even had a logical, although not particularly honest, answer. "I didn't shift last full moon. You had problems here, remember?"

The problem had come in the form of a stray shifter who'd somehow found his way into Rafe's land the night before the full moon. They suspected they'd interrupted a near attack. Toronto, being the oldest shifter in Rafe's enclave, had been put in charge of the stray.

Rafe stared at him, his near-black gaze unreadable. "You took off because you didn't shift last month."

"I took off to save you the hassle of dealing with my cranky ass," Toronto said, shrugging. "It wasn't going to be an easy few days for me, and you're always yelling at me to take it easy on your little flock. Since it wasn't likely, I took off for the full moon."

"I'm not buying it." Rafe smiled. He mounted the steps, one hand trailing up the banister. "After all, the full moon was just last night. If it was that bad, you'd want more time. But here you are. "

Toronto scented the anger, but he didn't care. If the

vampire was that mad, he could kick Toronto out. Didn't matter much to him, one way or the other. He'd returned to the enclave, offered an apology—as far as he was concerned, he'd done what he needed to do.

"You know why else I'm not buying it?"

Sighing, Toronto leaned against the railing and crossed his arms over his chest. Staring up at the ceiling, he said, "I don't much care, but I guess I'm going to hear anyway."

"You don't *care* if I ask you to go a little easy." Rafe stopped on the same step where Toronto waited and stared at the were. "That's where the problem is. If I bought this bit, that would mean I have to believe you actually are learning to obey orders and not constantly turn the rest of my Hunters into chew toys."

"I only did that once. With Dominic. And he asked for it," Toronto pointed out. Dominic had been an asshole, damn it. Was he supposed to apologize, *again*, over that? "And besides, that was almost two years ago."

Rafe didn't look impressed. "You take off whenever the hell it suits you. And you never let anybody know. What in the hell do we do if you're needed and *you're not there*?"

"I'm here now, aren't I?" Toronto said. This time, he couldn't quite keep the growl from his voice. "And it's not like I don't *know* when I'm needed. Something's in the air, right?"

"Yeah. And you're good at knowing when there is a need. You're here now, but you ignore the fucking rules and screw how it looks to everybody else." Anger flickered in the depths of Rafe's eyes, red behind black glass. "If I had *anybody* in my house other than Hunters, you know the kind of hell you'd be causing me?"

"Oh, for fuck's sake—"

But even as he started to explode, he stopped. Damn it.

It sucked that the bastard wasn't wrong.

What sucked more? Toronto *was*.

Leaving the enclave in Memphis had been necessary.

Coming back had been necessary as well, for different reasons.

Now he was stuck there, waiting for those reasons to make themselves known as he slowly went out of his mind.

As added company, in addition to his normally dark thoughts, he had Nessa's words to torment him now as well.

Your darkest days are in your past, Toronto. Let them stay there. Leave it alone.

Leave it alone . . . best to not *know*? He couldn't understand it. What would it hurt for him to know who he was, where he'd come from? He just didn't get it.

But that was Nessa for you—she practically defined *cryptic*.

Even if she did have her reasons for keeping her knowledge to herself, it made it damn hard for those around her.

Setting his jaw, he met Rafe's eyes. "I had to leave," he said again, keeping the growl from his voice, and as hard as it was, he forced the edgy temper back as well. "I apologize, but I can't explain any more than the fact that I *couldn't* be here."

For a long moment, Rafe stared at him. "Maybe you need to think about it for a little while and decide if you *want* to be here, Toronto. I need that commitment. Or I need you gone."

Toronto didn't know how to respond to that. He didn't necessarily *want* to be here. But he didn't really want to be anywhere. He gave Rafe a short nod and headed up the stairs, his skin prickling and hot.

Whatever had pulled him back here, it would reveal itself soon.

But would it be soon enough?

S YLVIA had only had a few hours the night before to devote to researching the couple who wanted her to kill Alan Pulaski. Sunlight wasn't something she could fight—once the sun rose, she went down, and it didn't matter if she wanted to or not.

Since she didn't particularly like collapsing where she stood, she'd stopped fighting and accepted it.

When she woke, she got back to the job—of course, that was *after* she started putting things in motion to get that move done. It didn't take long—she already had a framework set up and all she had to do was get the ball rolling, which meant she had the entire night to focus on the job, and the entire night to make her decision.

But she already knew she would take the job.

Sometimes, she would spend a few days researching a mark, sometimes a few weeks . . . a few months. However long it took to be sure. She was picky, very picky about the jobs she accepted—she didn't like living with mistakes. But the moment she'd seen Alan Pulaski's name, she'd known she would do this. Killing a murdering, pedophilic monster wouldn't be a mistake—it would be doing the world a favor.

The killer from Memphis, Tennessee, never should have been released from jail. Mortal justice, she thought, was seriously lacking.

She'd do this job, find justice for his victims and be quite pleased with herself.

Pulaski's string of crimes had come to light over the past year—crimes that had stretched back for quite some time. A teacher, a friendly looking bastard who worked with kids, he was one of the guys people never would have suspected of committing the crimes he was eventually arrested for.

But he had. He was arrested. Then he was let out on bail . . . a few weeks ago. Placed under house arrest pending his trial, he'd been keeping quiet, staying in his home.

Then he escaped.

His ankle bracelet was found busted a few miles from his home and he hadn't been seen since.

In the time since his disappearance, apparently more evidence had been found on his property—not in the main house, though. He'd been a well-off son of a bitch and on his estate, there was another house, one that hadn't been checked out during the initial search . . . for whatever reason. Maybe they hadn't known about it, maybe it hadn't been included in the warrant, Sylvia didn't know.

But in that house, the police found enough evidence to put Pulaski away for the rest of his natural life. Hell, if they'd seen *that* evidence, he probably wouldn't have been released on bail. If they found him, he'd go away and this time, he'd probably stay locked up for a good long time.

If they found him.

If they didn't fuck things up.

She didn't really trust mortal justice.

And the people who wanted to hire her didn't want him *found* . . . they wanted him *dead*.

Sylvia could give them that.

And then she would disappear for a while. Lay low.

Still, she didn't contact the family right away. She needed to finish up her research. Although there was no doubt in her mind that Pulaski needed to die, she needed to know more *about* him. Needed to connect all those sick, twisted dots and try to understand the mind of this particular monster, who had preyed on children and broken them.

Sylvia understood brokenness. She'd seen what happened when one took a child, warped a child, twisted a child, broke a child . . .

A face flashed through her mind . . . a boy. It was the reason she was taking this job.

Toby—his name was Toby . . . and it was his parents that had written to her. She didn't know how they'd come to find her, but she understood what had motivated them to look for a hired killer.

After all, the ghost of a dead child was one of the reasons she had *become* a hired killer. And he had looked a lot like Toby . . .

I'm sorry—his voice was a ragged cry in her mind.

"Don't," she whispered, brushing it off. Had to keep focused in the here, in the now. On *these* children—they were all connected.

By one Alan Pulaski. As she focused on her target, revulsion flooded her.

Staring at the picture of Pulaski, she let the anger fill her, ice her pain away until it was numb. Then she let herself study the victims. Toby, first, because he was the most heartbreaking.

From the first time she'd seen Toby's picture, he'd called to her. Blue eyes. A kind smile. A handsome kid. One who made her remember things she shouldn't let herself remember.

She'd spent too much time following that story in the papers, in the news, watching the reports about how he had gone missing. Good kid, bright and kind. Had done volunteer work through his church, worked with younger students.

The kind of kid parents probably hoped to have, she imagined.

And then every parent's nightmare had happened . . . he'd disappeared.

The last person who had seen him alive had been his teacher . . . Alan Pulaski. There was suspicion, of course. But he was a *nice* man . . . surely nobody could think he had anything to do with it. Outrage had torn through the community.

Then it settled down, while the boy's parents continued to search and hope and wait.

Then another boy went missing, months later. She hadn't been around when that one happened. But she could remember wishing she'd decided to do some nosing around on her own. Screw the bit about not getting involved in mortal affairs.

She couldn't undo the past but she could damn well do something now. Sylvia remained bent over the computer, studying as much information as she could pull up about her intended target and his known victims.

As she researched, she didn't make notes. That was dangerous. Leaving behind a trail was one sure way to trip herself up. Besides, she didn't need to make notes. She stored all of the information she needed in her mind. What she wouldn't give, though, to have a way to take the knowledge of this man out of her mind when it was over. Removable knowledge, perhaps—know what she needed to know, for as long as she needed to know it. Once she no longer needed it, she could be done with it.

Pity that it wasn't possible. She could get rid of those bad memories that always crept out to trip her up at inopportune moments.

Once the bumbling cops who had the case finally connected the dots, the evidence had piled up hard and fast. She accessed computers files—breaking several laws, but nobody would ever know, much less track it to her—and the images she saw, the reports she read were enough to have fury snarling inside her, a chained, massive beast.

Yet somehow, Pulaski'd managed to make bail. The legal jargon in the court reports wasn't anything she hadn't had to decipher before. It came as no surprise. Still, it was still enough to leave her lip curling in a sneer.

Bastards. Bunch of sniveling, idiot bastards.

Absently, she stroked a hand down one of her blades, her fingers itching. When she found this one, he was dead. So very, very dead.

Monsters didn't deserve anything but death, and she didn't care if they were monsters of the human variety or the nonhuman.

A face flashed through her mind.

A man who had promised her a new life, a sweet life . . . a man who had lied to her. He'd been human. She'd believed him. And she'd been a fool. Then there'd been another man . . . one who hadn't been human . . .

Both of them had hurt her in ways she'd never thought possible.

I'll get you out . . . The voice whispered from her subconscious, but she shoved it down. No time for that now. She had a job, a monster to hunt.

Couldn't do that if she let herself fall into a pit of memories, could she?

All of that should be locked away, in the past where memories belonged. Right now, her mind needed to be focused on the damn job.

She took a deep, steadying breath. The feel of oxygen moving in and out of her rarely used lungs was calming. When she opened her eyes, she made herself stare at the other boys, not just Toby. Studied the other victims.

Four boys dead, and all of them could be connected to Pulaski. Plus, others who'd been caught on video—no telling what had become of *them*. After he'd disappeared, a more detailed search had been conducted—not just of his house, but of the property surrounding it—and they'd found where he liked to play with his victims.

The videos—shit, the videos.

Those were the things she'd like scrubbed from her mind. She'd seen too many awful things in her years to be easily

affected, but still . . . pity, grief and rage swam through her.
Yes. Very often the monsters in the world were human.

Sylvia didn't have any problem at all hunting that breed
of human.

CHAPTER 4

Y OU'LL *be fine, though, lad. You will. Just wait and see.* Nessa had told him that, time and again.

He was still waiting. So far, he didn't see *fine* coming any time soon.

Sometimes he did okay. After more than a century, for the most part, he dealt with it, not having any past to look back to, any memory of a family.

Plus, after more than a century, he *had* a past . . . one he'd built. He should focus on that more. Think more about the friends he had. Granted, the good friends were few and far between. Toronto was a prickly, abrasive son of a bitch at the best of times and he knew it. He liked it that way. People were just easier when he kept them at a distance.

He did have those friends, though, and they were close enough that he could almost call them brother, sister.

But there were times when those black, empty years crept out to haunt him, a screaming void that wrapped around him and wouldn't turn him free. Tonight was one of those nights.

He lay there in his bed, staring up at the ceiling, edgy, restless, his skin practically crawling with it, and the void in his mind was a black hell while instinct hummed under his skin.

What are you doing with this life of yours?

Why are you here?

Why did you live?

It wasn't just because he was meant to be a Hunter. He wasn't even that good of one. He refused to lead. He hated to follow. He questioned every damn thing, hated authority and most of the time, sheer boredom drove him more than any inborn desire to protect. That wasn't how a Hunter should be and he knew it.

But if he wasn't called for this, then why had he survived that attack?

He should be *more* than this. But whatever in the hell he *should* be, he didn't know. And too often, he didn't care.

His brooding reverie was interrupted by a pounding fist on the door and he closed his eyes, wishing he could shut the rest of the world out today.

"Go away," he said, keeping his voice flat and level. He didn't need to yell to be heard, not when the person on the other side of the door was a vampire.

"Problems."

In response, Toronto lifted a hand and flipped off the vampire on the other side of the door. Not that Kel could see—he might have vampire hearing, but he didn't have X-ray vision.

Apparently, he didn't need it.

The door opened a few seconds later and Toronto tried to decide if he wanted to waste the energy and knock the idiot boy out of his room, or just continue in his brood. He had a pretty good groove going. He wanted to continue it.

"Rafe needs you."

Forgetting his earlier resolve to try and push a little less was as easy as blinking an eye.

"Tell the *Master*," Toronto said, his voice mocking, heavy with derision, "he can kiss my ass."

Kel's brows arched. "It's your funeral, man." Then he sauntered out of the room, not bothering to close the door.

Toronto glared at the vampire's back for a moment, but he

didn't care enough to get up and shut the door, and he lacked the motivation to knock the kid around. Because if he did that, he'd have to deal with Kel's wife, Angel.

He'd rather avoid that.

The girl was spooky.

Very spooky, and worse . . . she knew it.

Kel wasn't worth dealing with Angel, and the aggravation wasn't worth throwing off the brood he had going.

Less than two minutes later, Toronto felt the cold edge of a Master vampire's anger chill the air, and he rolled his eyes. When Rafe appeared in the doorway of his room, Toronto just flung an arm over his face.

Going one-on-one with Kel wouldn't do more than irritate him.

Going one-on-one with Rafe would irritate him, but it would also require a bit more concentration and would probably entail some pain. Actually . . . Toronto lowered his arm, popping one eye open to study Rafe. A good, dirty fight didn't seem like a bad idea.

"I'm tired of this fucking shit," Rafe said, his voice terse and abrupt. "I told you—just *hours* ago. If you want to be here, then you'll damn well *be* here. If not, you'll damn well get the hell *out*." He paused, and then added icily, "I suspect it's not a matter of want with you. You don't give a flying fuck."

The slash of the vampire's rage cut through the air, a cold, heavy punch, but even as Toronto readied himself for that down and dirty fight he really, really wanted, Rafe turned on his heel and stalked away.

That was it.

"What the . . ."

Over his shoulder, Rafe said, "Make up your fucking mind. Either you're here to be a Hunter or you're not. If you're *not*, get out and get out *now*—I'll make it simple. Decide. *Now*. Or the next time you and I have this conversation, it's going to involve serious bloodshed. You won't keep challenging me this way."

Feeling a little deflated, and maybe, okay, yeah, a little

guilty, Toronto climbed out of bed. Snagging a pair of pants
from the foot of the bed, he tugged them on and lingered by
the bathroom long enough to splash some water on his face
and brush his teeth.

The face in the mirror hadn't changed much over the past
century. He'd been attacked when he was in his teenage
years. By the time he hit his late twenties, his body had hit
full maturation and the aging process had stopped. Back
then, it had still been called a curse. Now they knew it to be
a virus, one that warped and mutated the genes until they no
longer resembled anything human.

Werewolves and shapeshifters aged, but it was a slow
process and the stronger the creature, the slower the aging
process.

Toronto was pretty damn strong.

His hair was pale blond, almost white blond and he wore
it long, kept it tied in a queue at his nape. His eyes were a
pale, silvery blue, rimmed with a deeper blue. More often
than once, that pretty face had thrown people off balance,
unless somebody looked deeper.

Although werewolves healed with amazing speed, he
wasn't without scars. Some remained from the attack that
had made him a were—bite marks on his arms, chest, thighs.
Others were from his life since the attack, a nasty slice down
his left pectoral from a silver blade, another low on his belly.
There was only one that was likely from his forgotten mortal
years—a messy affair on the back of his right forearm, a
jagged line that somebody had ineptly tried to stitch closed.

Scars aside, he had a handsome face, and he knew it.
Handsome, bordering on pretty . . . but there was something
that lurked just behind the eyes. A wildness that even more
than a century couldn't curb, and the body belonged to a
warrior, a fighter.

Right now, he was a fighter looking to rumble, and the
one chance he'd had of a decent fight had been denied. But
he couldn't really be pissed about it, either—he had screwed
up. Again. And there was the icy anger he'd heard in Rafe's
voice that wasn't about him. Toronto's fuckheadedness was
just part of it.

A heavy weight hung in the air, one he realized he would have sensed already if he hadn't let himself get so caught up in his own problems.

Heavy—almost oppressive.

It all but choked the oxygen out of the air.

Rubbing the heel of his hand over his chest, he padded on bare feet toward the Master's office.

*H*UNTERS.
Memphis was lousy with them. The feel of them was an itch on her spine, but she ignored it. Once she'd decided to take the job, she'd driven the four hours to Memphis to start getting a lay of the land and the Hunters weren't going to stop her.

Technically, they *couldn't* . . . unless she went around breaking laws.

She wouldn't, either. She had a job to do and she'd see it completed, come hell, high water or holier-than-thou Hunter types.

If she needed incentive, she had it in the form of a photograph tucked inside her back pocket.

Not that she really needed the reminder. His face was one she'd never forget. Actually, *none* of the boys Pulaski had taken were likely to be forgotten. Four kids, lost.

Four kids who deserved justice; Sylvia could give it to them, and all she had to do was find his trail.

She'd be a lot harder to dodge than the police, too.

She'd have to move quickly—in, out—assuming he was in Memphis.

If she'd done her homework right, the local Master here was Rafe, a vampire. He was a Hunter—no big surprise there. On the rare occasion a non-Hunter set up an official territory, it was usually somebody who was on good standing with the do-gooders of the freak world.

Mostly, Sylvia didn't have much issue with Hunter types as long as they stayed out of her way. She'd much rather a Hunter get a Master's call than a non-Hunter. Hunters didn't go feral—it was like they didn't have that ability to break inside them—they somehow maintained that much needed humanity.

Or maybe they just didn't have that innate cruelty. She knew all about that innate sense of cruelty. It was something she'd seen in both mortal and non-mortal. That was one reason she made a very, very good living. She got paid for killing cruel sons of bitches.

The Hunters did it out of altruism. She did it for a paycheck.

No, on a professional level, she didn't have a problem with Hunters, as long as they stayed out of her way. They served a purpose and kept things under control when the monsters would have turned mortals into their personal play and feeding ground.

But personally, Sylvia didn't like them and she didn't want to have to deal with them, especially not when she was on a hunt of her own.

Master vampires were territorial bastards, and rumors were that Rafe, the local Master, was more of a bastard than most—he wasn't going to tolerate having a murdering pedophile in his territory, but if she knew Hunters, he'd want to turn the man over to mortal authorities. Hunters did interfere with mortal issues, but when it was likely the matter would catch attention, they often let the mortal cops take the reins, guiding things like an unseen puppet master. Keeping in the shadows, not drawing any undue attention—after all, none of them wanted any of the mortals to know about them. Sylvia understood it. Attention to their kind was bad.

Letting monsters like Pulaski live was worse.

"In. Out." She prowled around the house, keeping her distance, searching for signs of life, signs of the cops, signs that anybody might be watching her.

All she needed to do was find Pulaski . . . and get the hell out.

CHAPTER 5

Toronto hadn't even entered the office when Rafe's gaze cut to him. The Master's eyes were black, icy with anger and something else.

"No time for you. If you haven't made that decision—get your brooding ass out of here. Actually, if you haven't made it, that's decision enough and I still want you out and gone," Rafe said.

The abrupt tone of Rafe's voice, coupled with the fact that they now had an audience, teased the edges of Toronto's temper and he had to work to keep the fire down. He had agreed to serve Rafe when he came here—either he abided by the rules or he left. Although the people serving under Rafe were the good guys, too many of them had predators' instincts, and those instincts only worked *together* when a certain sense of order was followed.

They had order, they had rules, they all got along better. Usually.

Though Toronto liked to jerk Rafe's chain, for the most part, he respected that sense of order.

"I'm here, aren't I?" he snapped, his voice harsh, edged with temper.

"Yeah." Rafe's eyes narrowed. "You're here. And just like always, you're being an asshole. Either lose the attitude or get the fuck out because I don't have time for this *shit*."

Toronto's hand closed into a fist. Part of him wanted to say *Fuck it* and just leave. Or just give into the burning rage, the wildness inside him—have that bloodshed Rafe had promised.

The other part, though, was louder. And for the first time in what might have been forever, he felt the temper ease back, felt the edginess settle down. He wouldn't do this. He wouldn't.

You'll have to learn to control that . . . Hell. Nessa hadn't just been talking about the hunger.

"I'm here—my decision was made." Folding his arms over his bare chest, he leaned one shoulder against the doorjamb.

Rafe stared at him, his black eyes glittering. And then he gave a short nod. This was it, though. He and Rafe might be at a fragile truce, but Toronto needed to come to peace with the monster inside him, or he'd have to leave.

If he left, he would no longer be able to call himself a Hunter—he wouldn't deserve it. That whole *lead, follow or get out of the way* thing. He wouldn't lead, so that meant he'd have to follow . . . or just stay the hell out of the way.

If he stayed and answered the challenge Rafe had put out, he'd be done as a Hunter as well. He was supposed to be one of the good guys—whether he won or lost the fight with the vampire, he'd be done.

A good guy didn't go for somebody's throat just because he was having a bad day.

Toronto wasn't going to go that low. Eyes hooded, he watched as Rafe lifted up a small device from his desk. The lights in the room dimmed and a screen descended from the ceiling.

Rafe liked his gadgets.

An image flashed across the screen.

It was a boy—human, probably twelve or so. It was hard for Toronto to judge the ages of human children sometimes. He had bright eyes, though. An infectious smile.

"His name was Toby Clemons," Rafe said, his voice flat, his eyes unreadable. He didn't look at Toronto, didn't look at anybody. Just stared at the screen. Anybody who didn't know the guy might have thought he didn't feel anything— he could have been discussing the weather for all the emotion he showed.

But those in the room knew otherwise. They sensed the rage Rafe barely held in check.

"He was twelve. He was killed by a scum-sucking piece of shit who had a predilection for pretty, preteen boys. This sorry bastard's name is Alan Pulaski."

A couple of the Hunters in the room muttered—the name was familiar. Pulaski's case had sent shockwaves rippling through the city once his crimes had come to light. The depravities had left many people reeling. And he'd somehow gotten out on bail. *House* arrest, as if that made a difference. He was still *free*. And *alive*. Dead and ripped apart would have been the most ideal resolution.

"He was confined to his house. Nobody ask me *why* they let that piece of shit out when he should have rotted in a hole for the rest of his life. Pulaski skipped out, managed to get out of the ankle bracelet they'd put on him. That was found smashed apart a few blocks from his house. So far, mortal police aren't having much luck finding him."

Lindsey, one of Rafe's younger wolves, sat with her back against Rafe's desk, staring at the image of Toby's face. The werewolf's dark eyes were like obsidian ice in the paleness of her face. "I take it we aren't listening to this for kicks. You know where this scum-sucking piece of shit is? Can we have a race? Whoever gets him first gets a pizza party or something?"

She flicked her black hair out of her eyes and despite the light tone, a storm brewed in her gaze and thundered in her blood. They could all scent it.

Rafe paused by her feet, bumped the toe of one booted foot against her thigh. "You get him, sure, I'll order you a pizza. Shit, I'll buy you a damned pizza parlor. But there's more to it than that." He pointed the remote at the screen.

The image changed, now showing a young man, probably in his midtwenties.

He looked like a fucking schoolteacher. A preacher. A doctor. Somebody *safe*, Toronto thought, absolutely disgusted. Golden brown hair cut in that hip, shaggy fashion, a friendly, affable smile on his face, dressed in the clean-cut clothes of a well-off but not exactly rich American male.

The other image was his mug shot. Not quite so appealing.

But he didn't look like a monster.

Then again, most of the monsters didn't really *look* like monsters half the time.

"This is the scum-sucking piece of shit. His name is Alan Pulaski. He was one of Toby's counselors at a youth retreat last summer." He paused, and the icy edge of his rage danced across the air like the first kiss of winter. "There was video found in the house after his disappearance. I'm not going to inflict that on any of you. There is no doubt of his guilt—well, not in our minds. We know how lawyers in the mortal world like to twist things, but they've got enough evidence to hold him solid and his running really screwed things up. Once they get him back in jail, he'll go away. For a long, long time."

A sinking feeling hit Toronto's gut.

They had no problems dealing with scum-sucking pieces of shit on their own. Sometimes, sure, they turned things over to mortal hands, but not all the time. Certain bastards just needed to be dead and in Toronto's opinion, this was one of them.

What was Rafe up to?

Once more, Rafe pointed his remote at the screen. Three more young boys flashed on the screen. "Video of these boys was also found in Pulaski's house. If they are dead, their families deserve to know what happened. If he dies, they don't get that. Life can suck bad enough—most of us know that. Living your years without any sort of closure, that's a level of hell all its own," Rafe said, his voice quiet.

Toronto blew out a disgusted breath. Shit. Shit. And double shit. There was nothing, absolutely nothing, Rafe could have said that would have hit him on a deeper level.

Absently, he reached inside his pocket, hoped there was

some gum in there. There was—one half-smashed piece. He popped it in his mouth and half-choked on it two seconds later as another image came up on the screen.

Damn . . .

Absurdly, he found himself thinking of what he'd flippantly said to Nessa only the day before.

Was it like wham, *some sort of click and you just knew?*
There were all sorts of clicks.

All sorts of clicks? That made a lot of sense to Toronto, because just looking at the picture of the woman on that screen was making everything inside him *click . . .* and a few things roar.

She was vampire. Toronto recognized that instinctively, even though nothing about her physical image actually gave that away. He just knew.

She was also the sexiest damn vampire he'd ever seen, despite the lousy, grainy image.

"And this is our final complication. Her name is Sylvia James . . . or at least that's the name she is using now. She's something of a mercenary, something of a bounty hunter and something of a pain in the ass," Rafe bit off, although a blend of amusement and respect glinted in his eyes. "Authorities tend to frown on her methods—a lot of her targets end up dead. Very dead. She's very good at evading capture, very good at evading detection. The cops don't have shit on her. She is, in short, excellent at her work."

Over by the wall, there was a low, soft chuckle. It came from a petite blonde who spoke with a lazy southern drawl. Her eyes were a soft blue and though she hunted, she was more at home fussing with the house than kicking ass. She did enjoy the occasional ass-kicking, though.

Which was good. Her name was Sheila, and she was Rafe's wife. Any woman married to him would have to know how to kick ass, otherwise he'd run roughshod over her.

"Yes, authority types do frown upon vigilantism," Sheila murmured. Then she winked at her husband. "So try to keep the smile out of your voice in front of the kids, okay? And try not to drool much more."

A faint smile curled Rafe's lips. "I'm not drooling."

Rafe might not be, but Toronto almost was, even as his mind was dancing around the fact that this woman was a mercenary. They definitely had a few of them among their kind. Most of them steered clear of the Hunters, which wasn't a surprise. As long as they didn't cross the line, the Hunters wouldn't mess with them. But if they ended up crossing each other's paths, there would be problems.

A bloodbath waiting to happen.

For that reason, mercenary types and Hunters tended to avoid any sort of close contact. He might not mind risking that close contact in this situation, though, especially since he was still feeling all those weird little *clicks*.

Want . . . the wolf inside him whispered. *Want* . . .

Yeah, boy. Me, too.

She was a looker. The image showed her stats, even a rough guess at her weight. Five feet five. One fifty—she'd be compact and curved, he figured. A powerhouse of curves and muscle. Shit, he *was* about to drool. Her hair was dark, as dark as his was pale. The image wasn't clear enough to show the color of her eyes, but he'd guess they were equally dark. Something about the set of them was faintly exotic, a slight slant.

She had a wide, lush mouth, and he wanted to feel that mouth under his, then he wanted to feel it at his throat as she fed from him.

Shit.

His cock pulsed, throbbed.

As his hunger started to color the air, several sets of eyes shifted his way, curious, then moved away.

"According to my info, somehow Toby Clemons's parents got news of Sylvia James. I don't know how. She's fairly discreet, expensive as hell—the Council has a file on her, but she's always played within the rules—doesn't do anything that would make them come down on her. She's got a name in the human world, if people know where to look."

"I guess the parents wanted him dead badly enough that they figured out where to look," Lindsey muttered. As Rafe glanced at her, she shrugged. "I can't say I blame them."

Rafe didn't say anything, but the look in his eyes said he

didn't, either. "Of course, money isn't an issue for his folks. They are, to put it lightly . . . loaded, but word has it, there are certain jobs that James will do for free."

Lindsey shifted on the ground, looking slightly miserable. "She's trailing after the perv who killed their kids and you want us to stop her, don't you?"

Rafe hit the remote, and the image changed once more. To the three boys. Nobody in the room moved. The wave of anger and agony was enough to choke them. Most of them would never have kids—were females didn't carry to term easily. Vamps couldn't breed.

Children were precious . . . and this bastard had slaughtered them.

"No," Rafe said, his voice tight and angry. "I don't want her stopped—I'd happily let her kill him." His gaze locked on those nameless, lost boys. "But those boys' parents? They deserve closure, too. She can't kill him if there's a chance we can find out what he did with those other boys." Then he knelt down in front of Lindsey. "But if it makes you feel better . . . I wasn't going to let you go out on this one, anyway."

She scowled at him.

"We've got James pegged at over a century. I don't think she's Master level or I likely would have sensed her when she came onto my land. Still, I'm not taking chances—there are some who can cloak that and I won't risk her being one of them. All of you are now on alert—watch for signs of her. An older one has to handle this Hunt." He caught a lock of her hair and tugged. "But I'll order you a pizza before I head out."

Toronto shoved off the wall. "I'll go."

Rafe paused, those black, black eyes narrowing. Although an uneasy truce might have been reached, the Master didn't look too fond of that idea. "You'll go," he echoed, his voice flat.

"I'm better-suited." He hooked his thumbs in his pockets, kept his voice level.

"Better-suited." Rafe ran his tongue over his teeth and then he glanced around the room. "You all, head out."

The rest of the Hunters left, a heavy, weighted silence wrapping around them.

"One reason, Tor," Rafe said quietly. "Give me just one reason why I shouldn't boot you out of here."

"I'm the strongest Hunter you have at your disposal, for one," Toronto said, although they both knew that was an obvious answer . . . and it was also something that could be easily rectified. All Rafe had to do was ask for more Hunters and he'd get them. Granted, he may not get another Master as strong as Tor. Not many of them were willing to serve. Most of them wanted to lead or just fly solo. But he could get stronger Hunters and they both knew it.

"Not enough." Rafe called him on it, shaking his head. "Kel can hold down the fort for a while and Lindsey, Josiah, they may never be Masters, but they aren't weak. Dom already volunteered to help for a while if I need him—one phone call and that means I'll have both him and Nessa here. You're not needed with that kind of firepower."

It burned Toronto's ass to realize that he'd been enough of an ass to deserve a dismissal. Not just today, but often. Very often. It burned, it tore at him, and pissed him off . . . and left him shamed. He'd failed. The one thing he could do, he'd failed. He wouldn't keep doing it. It stopped. Now.

And there was no way Toronto was letting anybody else go after that woman. In the back of his mind, the wolf kept growling, pacing, muttering, *Mine . . . want . . .* All very Neanderthal, but Toronto's wolf was a rather basic, primitive thing. He wasn't going to try and modernize the thing, especially when he really, really understood that *mine, want* instinct. As long as Toronto didn't let those Neanderthal instincts rule what he did, it was all good, right?

"I'll offer my apologies," he said, his voice harsh and tight. "I've been an asshole and I'll apologize.

"But I'm going to disagree—you *do* need me. If this woman needs to be tracked down before she kills her target, your best bet is a day-walker, somebody who can track her while she sleeps. That would be me—I'm your best tracker. I don't need to sleep much and you know it. I can take as long as I need to, even if she leaves Memphis—you can't. This is your territory and you're needed here. I'm your best choice."

"And I can trust that hot temper of yours?" Rafe asked, tossing the remote from one hand to the other.

Toronto's instinctive reply, *Well, I haven't pounded you bloody yet, have I?* leaped to his lips and he bit it back. Instead, he looked at the images on the display. Innocence stared back at him. Innocence broken, destroyed . . . killed. And their families . . . left without answers. Had he left behind a family like that?

It was something he'd never know, and the pity he felt for both the children and their families, the rage he felt for what had been done to them, tore at him, and he felt the burn of something he hadn't felt in too long.

He could fix this.

Damn it, he could fix this . . . get those answers for the families. He could never have them for himself, but he could get closure for them. And after that—he could maybe see to it that Pulaski suffered an unhappy, painful accident.

"You don't need to worry about my hot temper. I can do what needs to be done for those boys," he said softly. "And if there are three, there may well be more. They deserve answers."

On silent feet, he moved to stand in front of the screen, so close that the faces on it blurred—it didn't matter. They were burned on his mind. He lifted a hand and let it hover above the screen and then he turned, met Rafe's gaze across the quiet room.

"You don't know what it's like to not have answers—to live your entire life with that ache inside you." The growl was back in his voice, but this time, it had nothing to do with temper, nothing to do with rage. Stripped raw and bare, he said gruffly, "I do."

CHAPTER 6

R AFE wasn't surprised when Nessa and Dominic arrived on his doorstep not long before sunset. Although he was jealous, he'd never admit it. Not in a hundred years. At least not around Agnes Milcher—no. Ralston. They'd married. She was known as Agnes Ralston—Nessa Ralston.

There were benefits to being married to a freaky strong witch, Rafe knew. Studying Dominic's face, he glanced out at the sinking sun. He could take some rays, but only some. Out and traveling around the daylight? Different story. "Kind of early for you to be up and crawling around, isn't it?"

Nessa patted a hand against his chest as she came inside, Dominic grinning, his teeth a brilliant white flash in his face. And although Rafe hadn't voiced his envy, his friend already knew.

"We were in the Bahamas a few weeks ago," Dominic said. "I watched the sun come up over the ocean."

"Jackass."

Nessa chuckled. Then she stopped in the middle of the brightly lit foyer, her head tilted to the side, wisps of blond hair escaping from her braid. "He's not here."

Dominic frowned at her. "Who?"

"Toronto. He's gone." She turned to face Rafe, a solemn look in her blue eyes. "You didn't set him after the mercenary, did you?"

Rafe didn't bother asking how Nessa knew about Sylvia James. This was Nessa. He'd be more surprised if she *didn't* know. "Is that a problem?" Something in her voice made a sliver of cold run through him.

Nessa sighed. Then she closed her eyes, pressing the tips of her fingers to one temple. "It would seem that wolf finally found a way to let his past catch up to him."

K EEPING her attention split between watching her back and searching for her target slowed her down. Sylvia's first spot was Pulaski's home. Not that she expected to find him there, but she could always hope.

It was empty, and as much as she'd hoped to find clues, or a glaring neon sign to point the way, there was nothing.

Since she couldn't find a glaring neon sign, she checked her iPhone and followed that instead. She'd done a search for areas where she'd find those with particular tastes in Memphis, and that meant another drive.

She might not find him there, but maybe she could find somebody who knew him.

It always started like this, these vague sorts of chases. Little bits of nothing, until she finally had something.

Sylvia suspected she'd been chasing little bits of nothing for a while.

Before she climbed back on her bike, she sent an e-mail to a contact. She wanted an idea of Pulaski's history—a background search that she couldn't run without risking tipping off the police and the like. It could be done, but she wasn't as interested in learning tech as some, so she let others do it.

All it would cost her was some cash.

Once she had that request sent off, she got on her bike and paused, lingered. That vague, itchy sensation still lingered low on her spine but it wasn't too bad.

Nobody was trailing her. Yet.

Hunters all over the place, but nobody at her back.

"Let's just hope that holds," she muttered.

T ORONTO figured the best way to find a hired killer would be to track the hired killer's prey. He needed to keep the scum alive long enough for Rafe or one of the other vamps to get the information they needed about the rest of the victims from Pulaski, which meant finding him before Sylvia James did.

He had a few advantages on her.

He knew Memphis.

It wasn't his town, exactly. That would imply it was home, and it wasn't. But he'd been living here for quite a while and he knew the place. Sylvia, though, she wasn't from around here. If she had been in the area long, he would have known. Rafe would have known. They would have crossed paths.

Which was why the mercenaries tended to keep their distances from Hunter types. As long as mercenaries didn't go over a certain line, Hunters didn't worry about them. They had their hands too full dealing with the ferals to worry about other shit, but some of the mercenaries traipsed just a little too close to that line.

He'd almost found himself bending too near that line a few times, but he'd always managed to pull back.

Rafe didn't think he could control himself around Pulaski. Toronto got that. His temper was nothing if not explosive and he didn't always bother trying to control himself. The irritating thing for people like Rafe was that they knew he *could* control himself. He just rarely did. He let his temper lead him around.

Just like you have since the day you woke up . . . you might have learned to control the violence, but are you really that much better?

Pushing that irritating voice aside, he crouched down on the roof of a building. Down below, Beale Street was alive with action. Pulsing and throbbing with life, lust and laughter, and below, there were licks of anger, aggression, apathy.

The smell of liquor was strong in the air, along with the smell of food. He caught the sharp edge of drugs but ignored it. He had another job today and besides, if these idiots wanted to waste their short, fleeting lives rotting their brains out on something that would eat those brain cells and those fleeting days, let them.

He'd only step in there if he saw drugs being peddled to kids.

Then he'd step in and shed blood before he was done.

For now, he was looking for somebody.

A familiar head of wiry red hair caught his eyes. A satisfied smile curled his lips and he rose to a half crouch and then leaped. It was a three-story jump down and he landed with his knees flexed, the impact as minimal to him as if he'd jumped off a curb.

The man was gone by the time he moved into the crowds of Beale Street, but that was fine. Toronto knew where he was going. It was a little dive just around the corner where the strippers looked younger than they were, where the clientele was just a few steps up from the scum-suckers and nobody wanted to talk to anybody.

They would, though.

Especially Bobby Prescott.

Bobby Prescott and Toronto had a special relationship.

Toronto hated the sick little fuck and wanted to kill him.

Bobby knew this, and he wanted to live. He was a werewolf, but his abilities were weak—he'd barely survived the Change and now he spent the night of the full moon locked in a cage because he didn't trust his control.

But that wasn't the worst part.

He had a weakness for pretty boys—*boys*, in the most literal sense. His particularly favorite age was right about fourteen. But he'd managed to keep that weakness to just dreams, and as long as he looked like he was able to control it, Toronto wouldn't kill him. Toronto's unhappy responsibility was making sure he watched Bobby, and closely.

Bobby's fear of Toronto worked to keep him in line and right now, it might work to help get some information about Pulaski if there was any to be found.

Toronto made it to the bar without Bobby scenting him. If the lesser wolf had caught his scent, Bobby would have been half-mad with fear.

But the second Toronto pushed through the door, the game was up.

They were the only non-mortals in there and although Toronto could mask his presence pretty damn well, Bobby was a werewolf—weak, but still were.

At a table off in the corner, Bobby sat rigidly, eyes on the floor.

Gazes skittered toward Toronto and then away. Unlike Bobby, they didn't know what he was. They just recognized trouble. He ignored everybody in there, including the pseudoboys dancing on the stage. They'd be legal, he knew. Probably just *barely* legal, but barely was enough—it had to be.

Sauntering toward Bobby, he caught the back of a chair and gave it a glance before he sat down. "Your taste in entertainment hasn't improved, Bobby," he said.

Bobby ducked his head, hunching in on himself.

Toronto leaned forward, resting his elbows on the table, staring at the top of Bobby's bowed head. "You been being good?"

"Yes." It was a high, tight whisper. "I . . . I swear. I come here. I have—well, a friend. It works."

"A friend." Toronto checked the air. The wolf wasn't lying. "How old is the friend?"

"Twenty. He works here. This is how we met."

Still being honest. Good enough. Still, he couldn't let Bobby think he was getting complacent. Laying a hand on the table, he did a minor shift. Judging by the way Bobby's scent changed—sour, acrid fear—the other man could see Toronto's altered hand just fine and he didn't like the look of the elongated fingers, the black claws. It was a freaky sight— that was the whole point.

"Look at me, Bobby."

As the other man lifted his head, Toronto smiled. "You remember what I said I'd do to you if I even *thought* you were going to slip, right?"

"Yes . . ." Bobby blinked his eyes rapidly, trying not cry.

"You're not going to slip. Are you?"

"No."

"Good." Pulling the wolf back inside, his hand reformed, shaping itself back into a human one—it was like water flowing over his skin. Bones popped, breaking as they realigned. It wasn't a painless process, but he took it without blinking or looking away from Bobby. It was part of what made him a Master were—that ability to change at will, to think past that pain, to handle those minor shifts. "Now. Let's chat."

Bobby blinked. "Ch . . . chat?" The words came out a bare squeak.

"Yeah." Slumping in the chair, Toronto reached inside his coat, pulling out a picture. He threw it down on the table. Even touching it made him want to vomit. "Know this guy?"

Bobby went white. "I had nothing to do with anything he did, Master, I swear. I—"

Master—hell. That annoyed him. It wasn't a title given just out of fear. It came with responsibilities—responsibilities too close to those Rafe carried. And while Rafe might be the local paranormal badass, he wasn't wolf. Toronto was. Here, the wolves bowed to him, whether he wanted it or not.

He lifted a hand and Bobby's chatter cut off in midstream. "I didn't ask if you had anything to do with it. If you had, I'd already know, and you'd already be scraping up your guts off the floor in hell." He flashed Bobby an ugly smile. "I look forward to the day I can send you there. But that's not why I'm here. I want to know if you *know* him."

"I . . ." Bobby's eyes wheeled around and he leaned forward. "If I talk to you in here, and they see, nobody will let me back in."

Toronto leaned forward as well. "And if you don't talk to me, I'm going to reach under the table and slice your balls off, right here and now. They'll grow back before the paramedics even hit Beale Street, but you'll hurt like a bitch. Then I'll do it again, and again, until you tell me what I need to know."

A panicked whine escaped Bobby's throat and a faint glow sparked in his eyes. Fear rolled from him in waves.

"Oh, please." Toronto rested his chin on his fist. "Do it. The moon was just yesterday—you probably have enough juice in you if you get scared. And if you lose control in here, I can finally kill you—can't have you being a danger and all."

Bobby wilted, his head falling forward to hit the table. "You're such a bastard, Toronto. Don't you get it? I *need* this place. It . . ." He paused, swallowed. "It keeps me in control. I can't lose it."

A bastard . . . He should have been pissed. He could kill this pussy in under three seconds and the werewolf still had the nerve to call him a bastard. But he heard the naked desperation, sensed it. Maybe Bobby did need this.

Maybe it kept him from going back to what he'd almost been.

Years ago, after his attack, Bobby had found his . . . urges . . . strengthened. He'd always liked his lovers young and pretty, but the Change intensified *everything*, it seemed, and it had done the same to Bobby's preferences. Young and pretty wasn't enough, not unless they were *too* young.

Toronto had found him outside a middle school. The lust coming off of him had been strong, but he hadn't done anything. Toronto had watched. Had waited. Had stalked.

But Bobby hadn't broken—he'd fought it. So Toronto let him live. He'd never once tried to cross that line. After Toronto put the fear of God, death and blood into the weak wolf's mind, the wolf had stopped doing the shit that was playing havoc with his faulty control and *tried* to get better. Fear was apparently his motivator.

And this place was Bobby's release valve.

Stroking his tongue along his teeth, Toronto made a decision. In a voice so low no mortal could hope to hear it, he said, "You've got my number. In ten minutes, you're to leave here. You're to call me. You're to tell me every *fucking* thing you know. And if you don't, I suggest you go kiss your pretty little toy good-bye, because in twelve minutes, I'll be back and I'll kill you. There won't even be skin left when I'm done with you—do you hear me?"

Bobby nodded morosely. "I hear."

"Good." Rising, he shoved back from the chair, letting the infamous edge of his temper show through. "You sorry little shit—I ought to beat you into the ground. Tell me, damn it."

This time, he raised his voice so that everybody could hear.

Bobby glanced up—surprise flickering in his eyes, followed quickly by understanding. Then . . . relief. Before it could morph into anything else, Toronto snarled at him silently, flashing teeth and letting his wolf gleam in his eyes. He wasn't doing this for Bobby—it was to prevent any future victims. If Bobby truly did *need* this place, Toronto wasn't cutting off that need.

"I can't tell you what I don't know," Bobby said. The stink of the lie flooded the air around them, but nobody else would have been able to tell.

"You expect me to believe that?" He glanced around, his gaze lingering on the stage where a couple of the dancers hesitated before continuing their routines. He had all sorts of attention now. That was fine. "You sick bastards all seem to flock together, from what I can tell. You all like them pretty and young. *Too* young."

"Everybody here is legal," Bobby said, that whine slipping into his voice once more.

"Legal." He sneered once more, but this time, he directed it at the crowd, keeping any sign of fang and flashing eyes hidden. "Maybe legal—they just pretend otherwise."

Shaking his head, he turned on his heel and stalked out the door. Once he was outside, he pulled his phone out. He figured it would be roughly seven minutes before Bobby left the club. If he left right away, it would be *too* suspicious. If he waited much longer, he'd be pushing it too close. Bobby was many things, but he wasn't stupid.

E YEING the joint in front of her, Sylvia sighed. She spent way too much time in shitholes like this, she decided.

The little strip joint off Beale Street appealed to those with seriously weird tastes. She wasn't sure of the best way to approach anybody just yet. The customers, the clients, they were all male. She couldn't pass for male, no way, no how.

Blowing out a sigh, she moved along the sidewalk, studying the building, glancing down the alley that ran alongside it. *Hmmm.* She pursed her lips and pondered her options. An employee, possibly. Wait at the side door and . . .

Her skin prickled. A scent that made the hunger within her burn in her caught her nose.

Scowling, she jerked it under the choke chain of her control and skimmed her gaze along the crowd, searching for whoever had caught her attention. Then she did a double take—the one person that drew her gaze had just come striding through the doorway of the club.

That wrong sort of club, if she had any hope of filling this sudden, burning hunger.

Everything about him was long, it seemed.

Long, pale hair, worn pulled back in a queue. Long, lean face; long, lean body; long, almost poetic hands. She watched as he pulled out a phone and glanced at it before turning away from her and striding off down the street, moving with an eerie, unearthly grace.

Inhuman.

Animalistic.

Werewolf . . .

He sensed her in that exact moment, which surprised the hell out of her. Most vampires developed an unusual ability as they aged, and some developed several of them. Sylvia's main skill was the ability to hide herself.

Vamps gave off vibes. She simply suppressed hers. It was a handy skill for a paid killer, especially since half of her targets were non-mortals.

But he'd still felt her.

He hid it well, but she felt his awareness all the same, heard the telltale quickening of his heart—it only lasted a few seconds before he controlled it. Impressive control, too. He moved out of the ebb and flow of people, and if she hadn't been concentrating so completely on him, she never would have seen him as he slid into the shadows, all but becoming one of them.

Oh, she did like how he moved.

Even people like them—the non-mortals—had to learn how to *move* like that and it wasn't something that happened overnight, or even in a few weeks or months. He had that easy, sinuous grace of somebody who knew his body, knew his surroundings.

She could just barely see him now, standing still as death in the shadows. He shouldn't be that hard to see, damn it. He was pale—he was a blond white dude, nice and tanned, but hell. He shouldn't blend with the shadows so easily. He might as well be one of them. Nothing about him moved— he didn't even seem to breathe, although she knew he needed to. Warm-blooded creatures still needed oxygen.

She made the bad mistake of looking into his eyes, and her breath caught. Blue. Soft, pale blue. Almost gentle. But there was nothing gentle about him. She knew that as well as she knew her name. Nothing gentle or soft.

And she appreciated that. She had no room for gentle or soft in her life, not even for a few moments. Sylvia wanted him—for those few moments.

Seconds ticked away as they stared at each other. Those seconds bled out into minutes and then a sour, acrid stink filled the air. Fear. *Musky* fear.

Resisting the urge to cover her nose, she searched the crowd from the corner of her eye and saw somebody else come out of the club just moments later. Another wolf. He didn't move quite so well, and when he saw the other man, he stumbled to a halt for a brief second before he kept on moving.

The blond wolf continued to watch her. There was something about his gaze that unnerved her. A lot. Even as need clenched through her middle.

He continued to watch her and then abruptly, he winked. And turned away.

She might have gaped. But then she realized what he was doing. He was following the other guy.

Instinct demanded she do the same.

* * *

STARING at her made things *click* again.
    Damn it.

It was one thing to see a woman and *want* her. It was another to see a woman and feel like he had to have her . . . or die trying. Throw in the complications he had and Toronto had a mess all around.

She was quick, he had to give her that.

Sylvia James might not call Memphis home, but she had sure as hell arrowed in on the right area pretty damn fast.

Toronto couldn't decide if he was irritated or amused as she started trailing him. She didn't make much of an attempt to hide herself. There wouldn't have been any point, and she probably knew that. Since he was already aware of her presence, hiding from him would be a lot like trying to hide an elephant in a ballroom full of world-class dancers.

Pointless, and a waste of time.

She'd done a damn good job of hiding her presence until she was all but on top of him, and he was impressed. But he felt it now—a strange void. All he had to do was lock on that and he felt it *more*.

She was about a quarter mile behind him when his phone rang. Far enough away that she wouldn't hear Bobby, and that was good enough. She'd hear *his* voice, he figured, but the voice on the other end of the line was a different story.

"Should I just meet you?" Bobby asked as Toronto came on the line.

"No. We stay moving. Don't circle back, either."

No response.

"What do you know about Pulaski?"

"Personally, nothing." Toronto had to strain to hear the nuances in the man's voice—cell phones were all well and good, but sometimes the reception sucked and crowds made it that much worse. But he didn't detect anything of a lie in Bobby's voice. And Bobby was too interested in living to lie to Toronto.

"You better have something to tell me," he warned softly.

"Nothing that I can say for certain is true." Bobby paused and then in a low, rushed voice, added, "There are rumors about this deal—sort of like a prostitution ring. I've heard he likes boys from there."

Toronto narrowed his eyes. "There are all sorts of prostitution rings in Memphis, Bobby. You're not being helpful."

"This is out of a school, out in Cordova. Some of the teachers even know about it."

F ury had a scent to it.

It could be hot and metallic, or hot and woodsy, like a forest fire just starting to burn.

This was a forest fire and it flooded the air around her with such intensity, she wouldn't have been surprised to see the air going red with flame. She moved into the shadows and started to run, keeping her pace to a mortal speed.

It was the werewolf. She had no doubts about that.

She just knew.

What had him so angry . . . ?

She came around the corner just in time to see him lowering a phone. Narrowing her eyes, she stared at him.

He turned around and his gaze connected with hers.

Once more, that jolt ripped through her. Want. Need. Burning hunger. He was closer now, less than thirty feet away and she could all but smell the warmth of his skin, all but feel it warming her own. Her fangs throbbed in their sheaths, aching to lower themselves and press against flesh.

As he started toward her, she flexed her hand.

He was sexy as hell, with that warrior's body and angelic face. Something about him flipped every switch she had, but still.

She had to be careful.

The whole damn reason she was stuck in this life was because she'd once trusted a pretty face.

It wasn't happening again.

R afe wasn't going to be happy.

They had much bigger problems than the sexy vampire coming his way.

Much bigger.

But the vamp still needed to be dealt with, and they still had to handle Pulaski. Oh, the fucking joy.

He had to get his brain focused on those problems and away from Sylvia James, but damned if that wasn't hard to do. In the back of his mind, his wolf was growling, rumbling under his skin and whispering, *Want . . . want . . .*

She was even better in person.

Staring at her made the blood in his body hum. His cock throbbed, burned. *Hurt.* A faint smile curved the lush pink of her mouth, left him wondering what she was thinking. Then somebody came tumbling out of the bar next to her, spilling bright lights of blue and red onto the sidewalk, and Toronto had a better idea.

As the rainbow of lights flickered off the blade she'd concealed in her left hand, he studied the crush of people around them. It wasn't as crowded here as it was just a few streets over on Beale, but it was still crowded enough.

Not the ideal place for a fight. He'd done it before and managed to avoid human casualties, but he suspected that Sylvia James was a different breed from what he was used to. Ferals fought to live, so they could kill—by nature, most of them weren't always clearheaded. Sylvia, like him, was a trained killer. *She* would be clearheaded. It would make a difference.

He hunted the ferals.

She hunted for money.

In the end, he'd win, because he was stronger.

But he didn't want to have to fight her. He wanted to have sex with her—down and dirty sex, maybe up against a wall, in the light so he could watch her. Then on a bed, her body under his, or over . . . his hands tangled in that dark, silken hair.

"You know, most men would at least bother to introduce themselves before the guy starts picturing the woman naked," she drawled, coming to a stop eighteen inches away.

Toronto smirked. "That's bullshit. We see a woman, we frequently picture them naked. We mess with the names when we want to actually think about getting them in bed.

Some of us, at least." He skimmed a look over her body, taking in the sleek muscles, the powerhouse curves. Then he focused on her face again, smiled slowly. "So. What's your name?"

She laughed. "Oh, you're smooth. Too bad I'm only in town for a little while."

"Business?"

"Hmmm." She cocked a black brow at him. "Am I interrupting something important? You sounded sort of aggravated on the phone."

"You like listening to private conversations?"

With a lazy shrug, she sauntered around him. Toronto tracked her movements by watching her reflection in the window of the nearest bar. As she circled back around in front of him, he checked her knife hand. Still in the left hand, tucked out of sight so nobody would see it unless they were looking for it. She was very, very good.

He was just better.

"Just curious. You're a pretty high-level wolf. It's got to take something serious to get you mad. The tough ones are supposed to have mad skills in the control department." She smiled again and this time, it was touched with a glint of devilishness. "I've always wondered if those mad skills translated over into other areas."

The air between them heated, and Toronto was hard-pressed not to close the distance and press his mouth to hers, see how she tasted. But if she was going to try and pull that knife on him . . . shit, another complication. He really, really wanted a taste of her, but he didn't get naked with women who tried to kill him.

Toronto didn't have a lot of rules, but that was one of them.

Still, he wanted to touch her. Reaching up, he toyed with the ends of her hair. She stilled, that particular stillness unique to vampires. She didn't breathe, didn't move. Yet there was a strange sense of life, awareness to her. Her eyes, so dark they were nearly black, locked on his and he took another chance, reached up and laid his hand along her throat, his thumb resting in the notch at the base of her neck.

Her skin, silky and cool, warmed under his touch. He wanted to feel that happen along her entire body.

"So." She watched him from under hooded lashes. "After I finish my business, maybe I could meet you somewhere."

S YLVIA couldn't believe she'd actually said that. But she wasn't about to take it back.

He continued to watch her, his gaze strangely hooded. He didn't look at all worried. At all concerned. Probably hadn't realized she had a blade in her hand. A werewolf with as much power as he had banked inside him wasn't going to stand there and let somebody hold a knife that close without reacting in some manner.

"That probably won't work," he said, quietly, his eyes shifting down to linger on her mouth for just a moment. Then he sighed and stroked his thumb along her throat. "A pity, Sylvia James."

She tensed and before she could stop it, her heart banged against her rib cage, once. Hard and fast. Already in motion, she jerked up her knife.

But he was faster—*so* much faster. And she knew.

Hunter—

The blade was in his hand and he stood five feet away. "If you try to kill Pulaski, I'll have to stop you." He eased farther away, moving into an alley at his back, away from the press of people.

Sylvia curled her lip at him. "Fucking Boy Scout. Don't you know what he did?"

"Yeah. I know." Something flickered in his eyes, a flash of rage. Gone within a blink. "If I had my way, I'd spill his guts all over the place and I'd do it in a way that he'd live long enough to suffer. But . . ."

"If you breathe so much as a word about human laws, *I'll* be the one doing the gutting."

He grinned at her.

"Bloodthirsty. In more ways than one. I admire that in a woman." Then the grin faded, and once more he stood there staring at her with solemn, serious eyes, his face grim. "You can't kill him. He can't die . . . yet."

Something in his voice whispered down her spine and made her still. Narrowing her eyes at him, she moved deeper into the alley. *"Why?"*

"Because there are still victims missing—bodies that haven't been recovered. Their parents deserve to have bodies to bury."

Sympathy stirred inside her as she thought of the boys she'd uncovered in her research. Yeah, she wanted to find answers for all of them. But she'd promised Toby's parents she'd get justice for their son . . . and she'd do it. Pulaski had to die.

She'd accepted a contract. She'd complete it.

"That's not my concern."

She expected to see disgust in his eyes. Disapproval.

All he did was shrug. "I figured that would be your view on it. Which is why my priority is getting to him before you do." He threw her knife into the air, caught it. Over and over, until the blade was just a silver blur above his hand. "Pity for you . . . the sun will rise in about a couple of hours. While you're in your coffin, I'll be out hunting. So unless you find him tonight . . ."

She curled a lip at the coffin comment. She'd spent about as much time in a coffin as *he* probably had. And he knew it. "You have to sleep sometime."

"I never did sleep all that much." He smiled at her. And then, he hurled the blade. She held still as it buried itself into the crumbled concrete at her feet.

Bastard. The blade would need to be sharpened again.

She lifted her gaze just in time to see his booted feet disappear out of her line of vision. He was already halfway up the old, rusted excuse for a fire escape.

To follow or not to follow . . .

Except she didn't have time.

He was right about one thing.

She had to go to ground soon. And he could search around the clock. He'd have to rest sooner or later, but Masters came with higher power levels. Sylvia was a mean-ass vampire and she knew how to kill. But she wasn't a Master. She'd never be a Master and sunlight was still a fatal—and she meant *fatal*—weakness for her.

Damn it.

R AFE was out of the house before Toronto even cleared the drive.

"Unless you're bleeding from every bodily orifice or you've turned him over to mortal cops, you get your ass back out there," Rafe snapped.

"Bigger problems than the mercenary," Toronto said, shaking his head.

"*Bigger* problems than the fact that she's out there hunting for him and you're not?"

"Source says he might have connections to a prostitution ring . . . a kiddie ring—a bunch of high school kids." Toronto crossed his arms over his chest and waited, watched as Rafe's eyes flickered to red and then back to his normal black.

"Go on."

"It may or may not be connected to a local school. Highbrow area, too, over in Cordova." Toronto relayed what Bobby had told him, hitting the highlights. "He thinks a few teachers are involved, but he doesn't know the names."

"You're sure?"

Toronto tugged the band from his hair absently. The pale strands fell forward to frame his face as he stared at Rafe. "Positive. This guy isn't one who would lie to me."

"Shit, you mean you got a real friend somewhere around here?"

Toronto snorted. "No. What I have is a weak, sniveling werewolf who knows I'd rather rip his guts out than look at him. He won't give me an excuse. Lying about anything, even jaywalking, is about all the excuse I'd need with this guy."

"Are you too close to a line, Toronto?" Rafe asked softly, his eyes narrowed.

"No. Trust me. Even you'd be hard-pressed with this one, your mercifulness."

Rafe blew out a breath, doubt written all over him. But he nodded. "Okay. Go on. Get back to finding Pulaski. We'll get to work on this other problem."

"How do you plan on doing that?"

A faint smile curved Rafe's mouth. "I actually have the perfect plan."

CHAPTER 7

I T had been more than a dozen years since Kel had come
to Rafe.

His wife, Angel, hadn't been with them quite so long.

And she wasn't a Hunter.

Sheila sometimes referred to Angel as a "hot mess," and
Rafe figured that was about as good a description as any.
The woman wasn't vampire, wasn't mortal. When she was
only nineteen, a vampire had forced their blood to mingle,
and it had altered her on the most basic level. But even before
that, Angel hadn't been normal.

She and Kel had met when they were children. From
what Rafe had heard, she'd known she'd marry the boy the
moment she'd seen him. Weird, yeah, but explainable, he
thought. The other stuff . . . how Angel had known there was
danger coming. How even after Kel's disappearance, she'd
known he still lived. Everybody else had given him up for
dead, but she'd dreamed about him . . . not just *dreams*, but
times when it was like she was echoing his life. His hungers.

Not vampire, not human and she couldn't make herself fit
back in the mortal world, even if she wanted to, which she
didn't. Three days ago, she'd come to Rafe and told him he

needed to find a way to make her fit in *this* world. Kel had nearly gone ballistic. He was a vampire, he was stupid in love with his wife and he was terrified of something happening to her. She wasn't strong enough to handle a vampire, wasn't fast enough to go head-to-head with shapeshifters.

But Rafe could understand her need for something *more*.

This couldn't be any more fitting for her if they'd hand-picked it. Because of the blood-sharing between her and the vampire years earlier, Angel hadn't aged much since college. She had a young face, almost too young—her eyes changed that, but Rafe suspected she could act rather well. She could hide those old eyes if she wanted.

She was also pretty as hell, and according to what Toronto had learned, the ring wasn't just for boys. It included girls, too. Apparently they preyed on a certain type of kid—or teenager. Angel would pretend to be just that.

He found her in the gym, going through a workout with Lindsey. For the past few years, she'd been training hard and she was getting better all the time. She usually went back and forth between training with her husband or Lindsey, and she'd picked up tricks from both the vampire and the werewolf that would surprise even some of the non-mortals. He had to admit, she moved pretty damn well.

She probably couldn't take down a vampire, but she'd never be a mortal's victim.

He watched them for twenty minutes, until he saw Angel staggering from a blow she took to the head. Then he called it quits. He needed her coherent and he'd seen her fight enough to know she wouldn't really care if Lindsey pushed her into unconsciousness, not if she healed before her husband returned from his nightly patrol. And she would, another weird side benefit of that altered blood.

"Enough."

Lindsey caught his gaze and grinned. "Hey, we're safe. Kel's gone for a few more hours—he's got the western grid side tonight."

"I need to talk to her." Grabbing a towel, he tossed it to the blonde standing at Lindsey's back. "You want to shower?"

Angel shrugged. "Not unless you want me to."

Rafe shook his head. "Come on. Let's talk outside."

They were a little less likely to be overheard out there. And he'd be more likely to feel Kel coming in time to wrap things up. That way, both he and Angel could figure out how to present this matter to the young vampire.

Because that boy wasn't going to be pleased.

Rafe knew that much. Even as he knew Angel was going to be delighted.

H E pegged it right.

Angel's eyes were glowing and she looked more animated than he'd seen her in a long time. The only thing that dimmed that enthusiasm was when he said, "We'll have to find a way to explain this to Kel. Without him trying to kill me."

"Don't worry. If he gets too scary, I'll protect you." She gave him a faint grin.

Rafe smiled. "I'll take you up on that."

Kel wasn't going to be able to kill Rafe, although if he got pissed enough, he might try. But the person who could get through to that one was Angel. She was the only one he always, always listened to.

The blue of her eyes shifted, darkened to midnight. "He's on his way. And he knows something is up."

Rafe cocked a brow at her. She shrugged. "He feels it through me."

Well, that may or may not be a good thing. If he felt it through her, then at least Kel would know that Angel wanted to do this, that she wasn't being put up to it.

And it didn't mean jack in the end, he knew.

Five minutes later, a furious vampire stood in front of Rafe, his eyes glinting with rage and fangs flashing as he snarled at him. "You actually want to send my *wife* into the middle of a sex ring. Have you lost your *mind*?"

"I want to send a woman who is more than capable of taking care of herself to investigate a problem. We need to know what's going on. She's the only one we have who can pull it off, Kel, and you know it. These are high school kids."

Rafe raked his nails down his face and pointed to it. "Do *I* look like I can pass for a high school kid?"

Kel curled his lip. "Send me."

"And what are you going to do? Pretend that you're in night school or something? You need to be able to get in the school, move with the crowds. You can't leave the house during daylight hours—you can't even drag your ass out of bed before five yet. How are you going to help?"

Kel glared at him and then spun around, staring at Angel. "You can't do this," he whispered, his voice soft, pleading. It wasn't an order.

All of them knew that. It was a plea that came straight from the soul.

"I have to," Angel said gently. She glanced at Rafe.

He nodded and slipped out of the room. Shutting the door behind him, he sagged against the wall and sighed. This responsibility shit *sucked*, he decided. He hated it.

T HE look on Kel's face almost broke her. Sighing, Angel reached up and cupped his face in her hands, staring into his eyes. She had to make him understand, though. She was fading away here, bit by bit. She couldn't exactly pursue some die-hard career—for one, she looked too damn young for most people to take her seriously. For another, in about five or ten years, people would wonder why she never seemed to age and she'd have to move on to another job or something before people started wondering *too* much. Picking up something just as busywork didn't cut it because she wasn't about to invest the time in something she didn't love.

The one worthwhile thing she did was volunteering at various places, but that could only take up so much time.

The rest of her days she was here . . . doing nothing.

As she had ever since she'd found her way back to Kel. It had been enough, for a while. And he was enough, to keep her heart happy. But it wasn't enough in the long, empty hours when he wasn't there, when he slept . . . and she couldn't.

All those long empty hours when all she could do was

volunteer under a name that wasn't her own—lying about who she was, or putter around the gardens, or shop, or read.

She was losing herself, losing her mind, bit by bit and it didn't have to be that way.

She could be *more*—she *should* be more. And this was her chance. She just had to make him understand that.

"I'm dying inside, Kel," she said softly, hating herself as she saw him flinch, as she saw the pain her words caused him. "You seem to think that all I'm to do with my life is hang around here and do the grocery shopping, screw around in the garden . . . and it's driving me insane. I *need* to do something."

"You *do* something—hell, you spend four or five days a week volunteering at hospitals and shit."

"Yeah. For a couple of hours. And I show people to this floor, to that floor. Don't get me wrong—that helps. But Kel . . . I'm *wasting*." Stroking her thumb over his lip, she studied his face. "Is that all I'm meant to do? Direct a person to the elevator that will take them to the fifth floor? Plant pretty flowers? Go buy more shoes that I hardly ever wear? You . . . you *do* something with your life. I barely exist."

"And what if you get hurt?" he demanded, curling his hands around her wrists. "You know what that would do to me?"

Moving forward, she pressed her lips to his. "Probably the same thing your getting hurt would do to me. Yet I live with that fear every time you leave. And you leave here to go on patrol five times a week. You come back bruised, you come back battered, you come back covered with blood. And I still let you go. I don't make you pretend to be what you aren't."

"I'm not *human* anymore, Angel." His lashes drooped, shielding his eyes from hers. Awful, terrible thoughts flooded his mind—and although he tried to block them, she sensed them anyway. They left him shuddering, half-sick, and her heart wrenched in her chest.

Part of her wanted to say, *Okay, I'll tell Rafe I changed my mind—I won't do this to you.*

Instead, she waited while those thoughts circled through

his mind, as he fought with them and then finally looked back at her. Something half-desperate glinted in his eyes. "I'm not human, Angel," he said again. "I can't break the way others can."

She eased back, staring into his eyes. "But I'm not exactly human anymore, either . . . am I?"

CHAPTER 8

Sᴙᴠɪᴀ didn't know how she'd caught the attention of the local do-gooders and she didn't care, in the long run.

What she had to do was find Pulaski.

Okay, she was making a *minor* adjustment. She could kill him after she dragged the information out of him. If it took a quick mind-fuck, so be it. She'd forced information out of her targets before.

She could do it again.

An uncomfortable prickle nestled at the base of her spine, but she shrugged it off. It had nothing to do with anything the Hunter had said. It was just . . . well. Shit. It wasn't even because it was the *right* thing to do. She'd already been pissed off because of what Pulaski had done. Hell, pissed off didn't touch it. Infuriated, sickened, disgusted . . . and her heart had ached for those lost children.

Finding answers wasn't going to change the outcome of her job, right?

No. It wouldn't change anything, so why not do it?

Yeah, she'd get that information from him.

Then she'd get him done. All nice and neat. *Before* the

Hunter caught up with her, because if he caught up with her, he would stop her.

The cold hard fact was that she wasn't any match for him.

They were two completely different classes, and it wasn't even so much that he was a Hunter.

She'd met weaker-level Hunters before that she could have handled. This guy wasn't one of them.

And why did he have to be a Hunter anyway . . . hell, even if he *was* a Hunter, she could have had fun dancing with him . . . if she had met him away from here. Off this job.

Hunger rubbed through her body in a sweet, burning ache, teasing her skin, making her fangs throb with the memory of his scent. How would he have tasted? She didn't know. She didn't feed from non-mortals often. She didn't think she'd ever fed from a Master were. It was supposed to be one hell of a kick.

"Don't think about it now," she muttered as she settled deeper into the shadows. She was waiting for the door to that club to open.

She could remember the acrid stink of that fear from earlier—it had been like a cloud, and she'd taken it apart, bit by bit until she knew all the layers, all the traces.

Most vampires didn't rely so heavily on scent, but Sylvia had long since come to accept she was about ready to max out in the power department. So she'd made the most of every ability she had at her disposal—she'd honed them, fine-tuned them until each one was a weapon or a tool of its own.

Strength. Speed. Her refined senses. She wasn't a Master, but she had mastered her skills.

There was somebody in that club who smelled a lot like the man the Hunter had been trailing. Either very close friends . . . or lovers. Most likely lovers. They were together often enough that they wore each other's scent like a second skin.

It was entirely possible that what one knew, the other knew.

Since she doubted she could get to the one the Hunter had

been trailing without his knowledge, she was going to focus on the other.

It was another forty-five minutes before her patience paid off.

A skinny, pretty boy dressed in denim shorts and little else came out, a cigarette in hand and a troubled look on his face.

"Hey." Sylvia waited until his gaze swung her way. "You got another cigarette?"

He gave her an absent smile. "Sorry . . ."

Their gazes locked and he went mute, the cigarette falling from numb fingers, his mouth slack.

Sylvia caught the cigarette, careful not to break the connection between their eyes. "I need to ask you some questions. Answer me and you can go back inside. You won't remember."

"Answer you and I can go back inside. I won't remember," he echoed.

"That's right. I'm looking for a man." She pulled out a picture and showed it to him. "Do you know this man?"

Lashes flickered. Something angry swirled below the hypnotic web she'd cast over him. "He's a sick fuck. He likes to hurt little kids."

Considering what she'd seen in the club earlier, she was a little surprised at the depth of the rage she felt in him. Okay, maybe she'd been a little too quick to judge. "Do you know where I could find him?"

"He likes hitting the raves somewhere down by the river—they move around a lot. Some of the little idiots there don't realize how much trouble he is. We've tried to put the word out, and since he was arrested, more people are careful." He blinked then, looking around puzzled.

Sylvia pushed harder, watching as he sank back into the web. "Have you seen him recently?"

"No. I steer clear of people like that. But I've heard he's not been around as much—found a new way to get his kicks. Someplace over in Cordova." He rambled off an address. "I think that's it. Somebody's house. People party there, but they keep it quiet. Rich bunch of freaks. I heard he has a new boyfriend, too. Another rich freak, but this guy's not from here."

"Okay." Sylvia smiled at him and handed his cigarette back, watched as he stared at it in bemusement. "Walk back inside. You've already forgotten talking to me."

I⸀T took her another twenty-five minutes to drive to Cordova, a few more precious minutes to stash her bike. Precious, precious time.

The dawn was edging ever closer, and she wanted to scream.

Frustration chewed at her as she took a deep drag of air in—she'd have to come back here again, because the scents flooding the air were a *mess*. Too many scents to process in the short span of time she had.

The area was huge, sprawling out over several miles, and although she could move fast, she had to hold herself to a human's pace, giving herself time to pick through the layers upon layers of scent.

If she wanted to make sense of it all and find this needledick in the haystack, she needed to focus her hunt and not search blindly.

Which meant she likely wouldn't get it done in one night.

"And what if the Hunter gets him first?" Just the thought sent a spark of frustration twisting through her. Sylvia didn't fail on her jobs. She saw them through.

And shit, failing *this* one wasn't an option. Not with Toby's face haunting her thoughts, a young ghost.

Pulaski seemed to have disappeared without a trace—he hadn't been seen, hadn't been heard from, and she suspected the Hunters weren't having much luck, either.

No way of knowing that for sure—it was just instinct, but she trusted those instincts.

Where was the Hunter now?

If he'd had a good line on Pulaski, he wouldn't have wasted time talking to her earlier. So he was probably doing the same thing she was, spinning his wheels and chasing dead ends for now. She didn't *think* he was following her—it was a vague possibility she'd kept in mind. She'd done as much to confuse her back trail as she could, but there was no way she could guarantee it would work with a Hunter. Especially a were.

Why did there have to be a Master were here? And *why* was there a Master were here? The local head hotshot was a vampire. *He* should have been the one tracking her, right? Vamps and weres were all territorial bastards and Masters were more so—why were two Masters so close together?

Maybe he wasn't a Hunter . . .

Nah. That wasn't likely. She needed to quit worrying about him, focus on the job. Already the feeling of the night had changed, and there wasn't much time left. Dawn wasn't quite peering over the horizon, but it wouldn't be long.

Sylvia closed her eyes, blocking out everything around her as she focused on the night, on the scents, on the ebb and flow of life.

She might not be able to scent-track quite as well as a wolf could, but she had one advantage. She could feel *life*. And weres all but vibrated with it. Now that she had his particular vibe, so to speak, she should be able to get a better lock on him if he was anywhere near.

His particular vibe . . . damn. She'd really like to have his particular vibe, in a particular way. Her skin hummed just thinking about it and once more, she had to block the idea out.

Dawn edged closer by the time she finished doing a fruitless search, skirting around the lushly landscaped lawns, keeping to the shadows. Inside some of the houses, people were already shambling around. The scent of coffee began to perfume the air, the sounds of a shower here and there.

"Time to go," she whispered.

It was on the way *out* that she caught the drifting scent of *something*. Faint. Coming from the east. Up several streets. Maybe as far as a mile away. And although she didn't have much time left, she couldn't resist the lure of those scents.

There was blood. But it didn't draw her—it was tainted with fear. Pain. The entire air was thick with it. And sex—

Shit. "How can humans not *feel* this?" she whispered as

she edged closer. Only a few blocks away . . . she continued to filter her way through the layers of scent—a lot of people. Some of them had come this way. Often. Some faded and went off in different directions.

Sylvia stilled in the shadows, crouching down as she let her brain process the tendrils of scent more, letting her mind form a picture. She could see it. Some of the scents were the same, but layered, older, covered with new. People visiting the same place, over and over. And then other scents were new, just barely there.

And sex—under all of it was sex. Heavy and hard, coupled with violence.

Orgy.

That's what she was trailing. The fading stink of an orgy. But it hadn't happened tonight—

Exhaustion snuck up on her, grabbing her around the throat like a fist.

Shooting a look at the horizon, she groaned. So caught up in the trail, so determined to find *something*, she'd let the dawn creep *too* close. Rising, she looked at the slim, simple watch she wore.

The sun would pierce the horizon in forty-two minutes.

If she was lucky, she could stay awake for forty-four.

Unfortunately, the place she'd found to stay was thirty miles outside of town.

T ORONTO kept catching her scent.

All over the damn city, which was ridiculous considering how big Memphis was. She'd been all over downtown, crossed back and forth over the river, spent quite a while on Beale Street—shit, she'd gone back to the club, too.

But she'd spent most of her time prowling around outside of Memphis—near Cordova. Why in the hell wasn't he surprised? He followed in her tracks, unsettled by how strong her scent still was. He'd missed her by minutes, and the sun was up. Not by much, just a sliver of it, barely visible through the trees and over the houses.

A car engine caught his ears and he moved into the

darkness of a nearby yard—plenty of shadows, there. He waited until the car passed and then he moved back out, keeping out of sight as he followed the trail of her scent.

No big puzzle why she'd pushed it so long, either. Although damn, he hoped she was one of the vamps who could take some sun, considering just how *long* she'd pushed it.

The stink in the air was enough to have the wolf in him wanting to pull back. Blood, fear, violence, rage. All of it left him twisted in knots and he wanted to find a nice, clean, icy-cold river to swim in. Might help. Hell, a dip in the Mississippi would make him feel cleaner.

None of this was new, though, whatever she'd been tracking; unless she'd gotten lucky, he doubted she'd nabbed—

Her scent trail stopped.

Tor groaned, stopping in front of a house and staring at it. The trail stopped *here*, but he could still smell her.

The house *looked* empty. Judging by the For Sale sign in front, he suspected it damn well *should* be empty.

But it wasn't. He could feel the vampire now, in the same way he'd felt her earlier—a strange little blank spot on his senses, and the more he focused, the more aware of her became.

Inside—she was inside. Apparently she hadn't left in time to make it to wherever she was staying and she'd had to find safety.

Rafe's enclave was eight miles away. She could have made it there and *technically*, she could have asked for sanctuary. No surprise she hadn't done that, though. Rafe would have given it to her—Tor had seen the respect in the other vamp's eyes when he talked about the mercenary—but he also knew the boss wasn't going to let the woman out to kill her target, either.

Shit.

Why did it have to be so complicated?

Stroking his tongue along the inside of his teeth, he told himself to walk away. He had an entire day to search the city. It was summer. The days were long. She was trapped inside for all those long daylight hours.

Turning away, he made it two steps.

And then he was whirling back around and running to the house.

S HE'D entered through the back. There were tracks from a bike—motorcycle? Oh, man, he liked that image. That sexy, sleek little vamp perched atop a shining, black and chrome machine. A real motorcycle, he knew. It wouldn't be a toy, not for her.

He didn't see any signs of it. A quick trip around the perimeter of the yard showed why. It was behind the little pool house, tucked out of sight. He didn't find her there, though. The small building had four windows, and there was no way a vamp could escape the bright light of day.

No, she'd be in the house.

Crouching down, he eyed the back door, searching for signs that she'd picked the lock. There weren't any, but he knew she had. There was also an alarm, but obviously, she hadn't set that off or he wouldn't be the only one poking around the house.

Wasn't hard to figure one's way around locks and alarms, not if you had the time. Vamps and shifters had plenty of that.

CHAPTER 9

*G*IVE *credit where credit is due*. Rafe had to give Angel credit. She'd done the high school senior bit to a *T*. She'd managed to make herself look even younger. Innocent. Sweet. Not necessarily typical in this day and age.

"You sure that's the right look?" he asked, studying the dress. "You're looking for information on a sex ring, not the good girls ring."

Angel lifted a brow. "You trust me to do this or not?"

"Yes." Rafe sighed.

"Then let me do it." She skimmed a hand through her hair and then waggled her fingers, showcasing the rings that sparkled there. "I'm not taking off my wedding ring. It's unusual enough that it doesn't *look* like a wedding ring and I don't have an engagement ring. I figured if I paired it with a bunch of rings, it wouldn't look weird."

Rafe stared at her hand and then back at her face. "Please tell me you're not asking my opinion about your jewelry."

"I'm not." With a wide grin on her face, she pointed out, "I'm just letting you know that I'm not taking off my wedding ring." She rubbed the tip of one finger over the gold band inlaid with Australian opal and continued to watch him, amused. "Although, now that you've let me see how much the idea terrifies you, I'll be sure to ask for your advice at some point in the future."

"Shit, you're a brat. No wonder Sheila likes you so much." He shook his head and settled behind his desk, reaching for a file there. It held a number of illegal, forged documents. False transcripts, a false birth certificate, Social Security card, the works—everything Angel would need to get into high school. "So, you think you'll have any trouble with playing a student?"

"Academically or socially?"

"Either," Rafe said bluntly. "I need you to pass as a student on all accounts. The teachers have to buy it, the students, *everybody*. Teachers, probably administrative staff are involved in this. If even *one* wrong person gets suspicious—"

"They'll start thinking that maybe I'm a cop or something." With a dramatic sigh, she said, "They'll shut things down, or move things, or something else. We'll have a hard time tracking them down, which means you all can't go and do terrible, bloody atrocities to them and make them pay for using kids." She sat in the seat across from him, her blue eyes level. "Rafe, I don't think you get just how easily I can pick up a thought."

She cocked her head and then said, "Somebody just came inside. You probably know who it is, just by their scent. I can tell you it's Lindsey, and I can also tell you that she is going to go upstairs—she doesn't want to see anybody, talk to anybody, look at anybody. She's upset . . . angry."

Rafe frowned. He knew that—he'd caught the subtle variation in the scent, but the werewolf wasn't hurt. He also had a weird ability to tell when things were of a personal level, or something that would affect the Enclave—the small group of Hunters he ran. This was personal. Therefore, none of his concern.

"I don't need to know why she's angry," Rafe said softly.

"No. You don't." Angel smiled sadly and shrugged. "Neither do I. And I shut the door. But the *doors*, so to speak, are just *open* for me. I have to close to them, or the thoughts are there for me to read."

"Are mine?"

Angel just stared at him.

Narrowing his eyes, Rafe asked again.

Resting an elbow on the arm of her chair, she propped her chin in her hand. "You know, that brooding glare bit tends to lose its impact after a few years of living with brooding males. You do it. Dom did it. Kel does it—and I sleep with him. It's nowhere near as intimidating when you're sleeping with a brooder."

"How in the hell can you read my mind?" he demanded. He was a Master vampire, coming up on a hundred and fifty years. Angel was just barely above human, she was just barely *thirty.*

"I don't know." She shrugged. "It's probably because of what happened to me. I'd say if it wasn't for that—if I hadn't had vampire blood forced down my throat—it wouldn't be possible. But my blood isn't the same—*I* am not the same. I heal faster, I'm stronger than I should be. We already know this. Only makes sense that my gifts changed as well."

Shit. Rafe knew all of that. He'd just never made the leap to thinking she might be able to read *his* mind. "How long have you been able to read the minds of vampires?"

"You mean other than Kel's?" With an unblinking stare, she studied him. "I've always been able to read his. Even when we were kids. The rest of you . . . it was just vague murmurs, at first; about two years ago, I guess. You were first. Your voice is the loudest—I guess because you're the strongest."

"I—no. Shit." Shoving back from the desk, he stood up and turned away, staring out the window. This wasn't a concern. It couldn't be. Hell, it *might* even come in useful.

"It very well could. Especially if I need to speak to you."

"If you can shut the damn door, Angel . . . do it," he growled.

"Yes, sir."

He didn't have to look at her to know she was smirking. Damn it, he really needed to do something with her. He didn't know *what* but he needed to do something. "Okay. Let's get back on target."

There was a knock at the door and Rafe turned. "Come on in, Kel." He watched as the younger vamp prowled into the room. Suddenly, the phrase *This will not end well* kept circling through his mind. He pushed it aside.

This would end *fine*. Angel was the one most suited for the task. Okay, out of the men and women he had? Angel was the *only* one truly suited. Kel looked young, but he couldn't go out in the daylight without developing third-degree burns all over his body within moments of seeing sunlight. Lindsey looked fairly young, but she had about as much subtlety in her as a bull in a china shop. She was a great Hunter. As an investigator? Not so much.

Angel was it.

Besides, although Kel didn't see it yet, he might even get to play, too, probably. But they'd worry about that later.

"You get how this has to play out, right? You're looking for leads, information. If something sets your mental alarm off, I want to know. You do *not* place yourself in danger."

Angel rolled her eyes, toying with the strap of her backpack, slung over one slim shoulder. "Yeah, Rafe. I got it. One of your pet humans is coming by to pick me up—she's going to act like my mom. She's in sales and she travels a lot. An absentee sort of mom, and my dad's *way* out of the picture. We've got all the forged crap, fake transcripts from my last so-called school." She paused and sent Kel a flirtatious look, fluttering her lashes. "And you gave me permission to mention a boyfriend, although we don't know if he'll show up much."

"Boyfriend?" Kel muttered, combing his fingers through her hair. "I'm back to being a boyfriend?"

"Well, she can't be married. She's a high school senior," Rafe pointed out. Then he glanced back at Angel. "One of my pet humans?"

She grinned at him. "What else do you call them? You snap your fingers, they all come running."

"You act like there is a platoon of them. And I'll have you know . . . this is a local witch, thank you."

From the doorway, Sheila said, "He had to leave behind the platoon of human pets when we married. And only one or two have ever figured out what he is. He doesn't keep a bunch around here to feed on, and there aren't enough vamps in the house that he needs to do that, anyway."

Kel turned around, his eyes burning hot, his mouth a harsh, narrow line. "You're sending my *wife* off to someplace where there's a suspected sex-slave ring and you all are talking about human *pets*. She's teasing me about being allowed to have a *boyfriend*. What's wrong with this picture?"

"Kel . . . I'm going to a *high school*. Filled with a bunch of mortals." Angel moved closer to her husband, her moves graceful and easy—sinuous.

She didn't move like a mortal anymore, Rafe thought. He'd already pointed that out to her and he hoped she'd remember to watch it. She would, though. That was Angel. She didn't forget the small details, the big details, *any* details. Another reason why she was perfect for this.

"A school," she said again, leaning in and pressing her lips to his. "I can handle a bunch of schoolkids."

Kel sighed, skimming a hand back over her hair. "It's not just the kids I'm worried about. But they can be mean sons of bitches nowadays."

"They've always had the capability to be mean," Angel said. She brought up her hand, resting it on Kel's chest. "Listen, I'm not some tough vamp who can leap tall buildings in a single bound, and I may not grow fur once a month, but I'm not exactly helpless. You *know* that."

"I'm pretty sure it's Superman who leaps tall buildings, Angel." Kel closed his eyes, lowering his head to press his brow to hers. "I know. Shit, if you *were* helpless, I'd find a way to keep you from going, even if I had to tie you up while you slept."

Angel laughed. "Baby, if I was *helpless*, you never would have fallen for me anyway."

"Hmmm. There is that."

Across the room, Rafe eyed them, debated on interrupting, but then Sheila caught his eye, nodding subtly toward the door. Rolling his eyes, he slipped out of the office along with his wife. "I still need to talk to her," he muttered. "And they are in there cuddling."

"You're just jealous. You still have all those big, bad boss things you need to do and I'm going to have to hit the sack soon. You wish you could be cuddling right now." Sheila smiled, hooking her arm through his.

He stopped and spun her around with enough speed that she crashed into his chest. "Who says I can't cuddle?" he murmured, dipping his head and slanting his mouth over hers. He pulled her close and whispered against her lips, "I love you, Belle." She was his belle . . . his southern belle, his lady . . . his only love.

"Hmmm." She hummed under her breath and opened for him. "You better be careful. If you go getting all mushy on me, I'm going to drag you to our room and you won't finish that talk with Angel . . . and you'll feel better if you do your hovering."

He stiffened, slowly lifting his head to glare at her. "Hovering?"

"Yeah." She patted his cheek, an impish smile on her lips. "It's cute, though. Big, broody, bad Rafe. Worrying about sending his people out."

Behind him the door opened. Still glaring at his wife, he stepped back. "You're a brat," he said, keeping his voice pitched low.

"Yeah. I know. Go on. Finish your . . . you know." She made a shooing motion at him.

Resisting the urge to grin, he turned back and saw Kel standing with his hand on Angel's shoulder and a grim look in his eyes. He met his vampire's gaze first. "She can handle this, you know," he said quietly.

"Shit, I know that." Kel skimmed a hand back over his short, dark hair and then glanced at his wife, his thumb stroking over her flesh. "She can probably handle it better than I can."

"Probably?" Rafe and Angel said it at the same time.

Kel grimaced.

Shifting his focus to Angel, Rafe said, "We've gone over everything." Angel didn't sleep much—he thought she might

need even less sleep than he did—and they'd spent most of
the night getting her ready. They were doing this in a rush,
even calling in tech support—the computer geniuses back at
Excelsior had hacked into the school system's computer
records to get the transfer in. Everything looked all nice,
legal, official. Another hacker with serious skill might be
able to uncover the deception, but it would take some doing.
The Hunters had some of the best tech, and the best minds,
around.

Rafe wasn't waiting to do this the slow way. Not if there
was any shred of truth in what Tor had heard.

"Stop worrying, Rafe." Angel tapped her brow. "I got it
all up here."

He'd been able to let her use her psychic gift to connect
their minds, and what he wanted her to know, she *knew*. It
was locked in her mind. No forgetting it, and no need for
notes or anything else.

Her abilities far surpassed anything he'd ever be able to
do, as far as the mind went—although he could seriously do
without her having the ability to read *his* mind. Her gift had
so many layers and complexities, it was bizarre, and he was
just now starting to realize how useful she might be. No, not
could be. *Would* be.

"You'll be careful." Crossing his arms over his chest, he
studied her face.

Angel examined her nails. "Well, I considered just storming in there and demanding at the top of my lungs, *Who is
the fucking pervert responsible?* Following up with a brutal
one-on-one interrogation of every person I met, but I didn't
think that was the best way to handle this."

Sheila snickered. Then she slid a hand down his arm,
linked their fingers. That gentle touch said a thousand things.

Closing his eyes, he blew out a breath.

He was doing the right thing. More, this was the *best* way
to do it.

Outside, he heard a car's engine—too close to be anybody but the witch coming to collect Angel.

Too late to back out now.

And it wasn't like he really had an option.

"Stay safe," he said quietly. "And find me something."

Angel gave him a smile. "Oh, I won't find you *something*. I'm going to bring you back a damned gold mine. You'll see. Just give me a few days."

CHAPTER 10

T HE house was stuffy.

It had that closed-up, stifled feel of a house that had stood empty for quite some time.

It also had her scent.

Toronto stood inside, his eyes closed as he breathed it in. Damn, she smelled good. For a long, long moment, he stood there, just wrapping himself in it . . . and wishing there was some other thing that had brought her to Memphis. Or maybe something that had led him to her outside of Memphis.

Anything but this.

"It is what it is, though," he muttered, forcing himself to shake off the exotic, sensual spell of her scent. Opening his eyes, he took a long, slow look around. He was in the kitchen. There was a door across from him, and there was a scent-path right to it. He followed it and found that it led to a basement.

That wasn't where she was, though.

Weird. That was exactly where he would have figured she'd go. A basement made the most sense for a vampire, after all. All nice and tucked away from the sun, less chance of catching rays through the windows as the shadows shifted and changed during the day. Easier to find the darker shadows.

Still, this was a big house. There would be other places.

She might be laying in wait for you, buddy. Just because the sun was up didn't automatically mean she would fall down in a dead sleep. Plenty of vamps could stay up awhile after the sun breached the horizon, and she had some years behind her. More than enough to have developed some resistance to the heavy, heavy call of sleep.

But each room proved empty and he continued tracking that scent-path through the house. It was on the third level that he finally found the next place where she'd stopped. A narrow, simple door tucked away at the end of the hall. He opened it and found a set of stairs that led *up*.

An attic?

What kind of fricking vampire chooses an attic *to bed down in?*

He stared upward, not entirely liking the idea of climbing the steps one at a time—she'd have the high ground. Okay. So he wouldn't take them one at a time . . .

He tensed his muscles, leaped—

And landed in a crouch at the top of the steps, braced and ready.

It was something of a letdown to see . . . nothing.

Just a brightly lit room painted a sunny yellow, with white trim. Simple blue curtains covered the windows. There were bookshelves tucked against the walls, and just more empty space.

And . . . a closet. Frowning, he stared at it. It was against the northeast wall. Little sunlight would get in as long as the door wasn't opened and then it wouldn't be much. She was over a century old—she should be able to take a little sun. It was probably safe enough. But a closet?

On silent feet, he padded across the floor. With each step, her scent grew strong. And his blood pulsed hotter, his heart raced faster. She was in there . . . he could feel her. In there. Tucked inside that coffin of a closet . . .

Caution fell away as he reached the door and jerked it

open with an almost savage twist. A bright slice of sunlight fell across the floor and he stared as it hit her hand. A brilliant, hot stain of red spread across her skin almost instantly. "Fuck."

He slammed the door shut. But with him on the *inside*.

He'd burned her . . .

Just a sliver of light managed to penetrate inside the gloom of the closet and it didn't reach her with the door shut. Safe—she'd been safe until he opened the door.

Reaching into his coat, he pulled out a small, powerful penlight and flicked it on. She hadn't even stirred. Most vampires above the midlevel power range would wake up with that sort of threat in their immediate area. They'd wake up around *him*. Sunlight. Both. They might not be able to fight well, but they'd try. Stronger vamps could put more into it.

Fuck, he should have been more careful . . . he hadn't heard her stirring, should have thought—

Enough with the should-have's, he told himself silently. She couldn't take sun. He'd fucked up. End of it.

Guilt twisted inside him as she continued to sit there, silent as death and just as still, although when he shifted the beam of light toward her hand, he saw that the burn was already melting away. She'd burn easily, but that minor of a burn would also heal fast, as long as she'd been feeding regularly.

Her hair, black and silky, fell around her shoulders. Crouched by her side, he reached out and caught a lock of it between his fingers, rubbing it back and forth. "I'm sorry," he whispered softly.

But there was no answer. Nor had he expected one.

Fuck.

Why was this woman getting to him so bad?

C ONTRARY to mortal myths, vamps didn't *die* when the sun rose. They just slept.

And with sleep, came dreams.

Her dreams were too often dark, and twisted. But rarely did they travel down this path . . . at least not for years.

But even as Sylvia tried to pull away from them, she found herself more and more trapped.

Trapped . . . and as the dreams pulled her in, it was every bit as much memory as dream, and they held her captive.

"He'll pay ya a lot. You don't make as much money here as he'll pay you."

Standing downwind of the grubby youths, she eyed the money. They'd followed her as she left home that evening, and to her surprise, one of them had approached her. They were young—too young. And someone was using them.

One of them was a sullen little thing, with cruel, cunning eyes that watched everything. He kept watch as the other talked business. And he did know how to talk business. He held out money, brandishing it as though he knew how much she needed it.

"Who is he?" she asked quietly, staring at the bills for a moment before looking back at the child.

"You can find that out later."

His friend came up to mutter in his ear, shooting her a look and then glancing at the money, eyeing it like he wanted to grab it and run. But he didn't, just moved back to his spot and continued to look around, quick darting little glances. A watchful, distrustful thing.

"You gonna do it or not?" the other boy demanded. "I ain't got all night."

She swallowed, trying to decide. Something inside told her that she should not do this. But if she did this job, she was that much closer to freedom . . .

Already the boy held more money than she normally saw in one week, much less one night.

"How much more money?" she asked, forcing the unfamiliar words out as she accepted the bills and tucked them away.

He grinned at her, a knowing glint in his young eyes. Now both of them watched her and the knowledge in their eyes shamed her, hurt her deep inside. But she did not look away. She would do what she must. Staring at the boy in front, she waited.

"He says that depends on how good you are. But he said

he'd pay ya fifty dollars, at least. He wants you to wear the blue thing."

"Blue thing . . . ?" she echoed.

"Yeah. Like that. But blue." He waved toward her silk kimono.

She glanced down and then back up, nodded. "I accept his offer."

"Good. I'll come back. Take you to him later tonight."

As the two boys turned away, she thought of the money he'd given her, and the money she would earn. He had given her twenty dollars. And later, he would give her fifty more. It was the most she'd earned since she'd been forced to turn to this.

Forced to sell her body. All because of a lie. Sold the promise of a happy, better life.

With an apprehensive look around, she took a few of the bills and stashed them in the small slit she'd made in one of her sleeves. Soon it would be enough money that she could run . . . she could be free.

T HE dream shifted. Trapped in the prison of her body, trapped by the sun, Sylvia longed for the freedom to weep. To rage. Even to simply wake. But all she could do was relive those days from so long ago.

. . . free . . . I'll never be free . . .

"I'm sorry. I didn't think he'd try to keep you. He . . ."

She did not look at the boys standing on the other side of the bars. Bars—he'd locked her behind bars.

Now those two boys were there, and while the quiet one remained ever silent and watchful, disgust and distrust still in those young eyes, the other one cried. "I'm so sorry." He paused and swiped the back of his hand under his dirty, runny nose and continued to watch her with beseeching, sad blue eyes. "He's never tried to keep a girl before. He just wants to fuck 'em and then he lets them go."

"Please leave me alone." She sat on the floor, wearing nothing but the cotton shift one of the maids had brought her, and it barely covered her bruised, battered body. She

had nothing now. She hadn't her clothing, hadn't her money, not even her dreams of freedom from her "husband."

"I'm sorry," the boy whispered again.

His friend grabbed his arm and tugged, whispered softly, "We have to go before he catches us."

"I can't. I have to tell her . . ."

"You have to tell me you are sorry," she said, pinning the boy with a hard stare, ignoring the other one. Rage throbbed inside her. Rage over what had been done to her. Rage over what would still be done. The man who had raped her would do it again. She'd seen it in his eyes . . . in his cold, cold eyes. He was a man who liked to hurt. She could live with that. She had been hurt in many ways over the past two years.

But she had never expected this—to be locked away. Like an animal. Deep inside, she knew she would never leave this place. Not alive. Her dreams of freedom, of having a life, they were all gone now.

"You do not know what sorry is," she said, shaking her head.

"Lady, please . . ."

She shook her head. "Do you know . . . I came to America two years ago. I came as a photograph bride. I was to marry a man who owned a shop." A sad, bitter smile curled her lips. "He owned no shop. He was not even from Japan. I had been tricked, my family had been tricked. He has twelve of us 'brides.' And he makes us sell ourselves. I was saving up enough money to run away." She sighed and closed her eyes. "I was almost there. My . . ." She paused, foundering for the unfamiliar word. "There was something inside me that tells me I should not listen to you, boy. That I should stay away. But I wanted the money, so I could go run away sooner."

Shifting her gaze, she stared at the bars. A prisoner. Completely and utterly trapped. "Now, I am more prisoner than ever."

A sniffle came from the hallway.

"Do not cry in front of me, boy," she whispered, shaking her head.

*A year ago, two years ago, she wouldn't have dared
speak in such a manner. But the girl she had been—that girl
was dead. Through her lashes, she said softly, "Do not cry
in front of me. You are the reason I am prisoner in this
place."*

*"I know." He wiped the tears away, leaving clean streaks
on a grubby face. "I'll find a way to get you out. I don't care
if it takes me years."*

*He stared at her, like he waited for something—absolution?
Understanding?*

She had nothing to offer the little monster.

Averting her face, she stared at the wall.

"I'll get you out. Even if it takes years. Even if it kills me."

I'LL *get you out . . . even if it kills me . . .*
     Sylvia came awake with tears choking her and the bit-
ter taste of regret heavy on her tongue.

Scrubbing her hands over her face, she groaned. "Why?"
she muttered. But she already knew the answer to that. Seeing a picture of Toby was all it had taken—he reminded her
so much of the boy who'd led her to the vampire. She'd spent
those weeks hating him. But he hadn't known.

All those old memories, trying to choke her.

That poor, pathetic kid. He hadn't been a monster . . . and
his determination to help her *had* killed him. Him, another
boy, all because of her selfishness, her stubbornness, her
anger.

"No." She slammed her head back against the wall and
whispered, "You did that."

"Stop it. Shit, you have to stop this." Shoving away from
the wall, she went to swipe her hands over her face.

That was when she realized it . . . she hadn't noticed it
right away because the dream had been choking her, keeping
her from thinking. But she *should* have noticed it.

There was a scent in the air—one that wasn't her own.

Warm. Male. Not new, but not old.

Hissing, she jumped to her feet. That scent was *on* her.
On her hand. That scent—the werewolf.

He'd been in *here*. With her. Her gut churned and she stared at the floor. The strip of light coming under the door was nonexistent, even to her eyes. Night had fallen. Reaching for one of her blades, she caught the doorknob. Listening.

He was out there, and she was in here worrying about old dreams and old humiliations and nightmares. He was *out* there, damn it. She could hear his heart beating.

Lubdublubdub.
Lubdublubdub.
Lubdublubdub.

The heartbeat was about twice as fast as a human's. He was close, but not on the other side of the door. She flexed her fingers, wondered if he was there to try and kill her. No. That idea didn't seem quite right. Judging by the scent, he'd been in *here*—in the closet—hours ago. When the sun was up. If he really wanted her dead, he could have just opened the door and hauled her into the light of the room. Enough sunlight would have flooded the area that she'd be toast. Hell, for that matter, he could have just destroyed her heart or taken her head.

If he'd wanted her dead, why not do it that way?

Unless he was actually a fair player—Boy Scouts and do-gooders tended to do that, right? But she knew Hunters didn't have a problem taking out vamps while they slept. They were about exterminating problems, not a fair fight. If they'd decided she needed to go . . .

Okay, so he's not here to kill me.

Why *was* he here?

Only one way to find out. Sylvia drew one of her throwing knives—one of the smaller ones she could hide in the palm of her hand. He wouldn't be able to see it, although she still didn't know if it would do her a hell of a lot of good against him.

Wouldn't stop her from trying.

Squaring her shoulders, she pushed the door open, braced herself. The attic room was empty—she'd known it would be. Still, his scent was strong. Very strong. A silvery band of moonlight fell in through an open window and she stared at it before following it along the floor to the open window. She'd slept until moonrise. Shit. Why had that happened? She never slept that late anymore. She couldn't take sunlight, but generally by twilight, she was up and moving.

Also, she hadn't left that window open.

Stroking the edge of her knife with her thumb, she eased her way into the darker shadows of the room.

Even before she saw the moonlight shining off his pale hair, she knew.

He was down there, in the backyard, waiting for her. And damn it. He'd hauled her bike out. Bastard. He was leaning against it, leather stretching over those long thighs, a black T-shirt clinging to his lean chest. He had that blond hair pulled back in a neat tail at the nape of his neck, and he looked good enough to eat. In many, many ways.

Her fangs pulsed.

Lower, much lower, other things pulsed. Because she knew he'd be aware, she figured she'd hide one hunger within another. Standing in the open window frame, keeping her knife hand free, she murmured, "Oh, *look*. It's Meals on Wheels."

He grinned at her. And then he leaped. Sylvia fell back, moving away from the window even as part of her wished she could stand there and just watch him move—

She pulled another knife, but didn't bother hiding that one. He'd go for the one she'd left in open view, she hoped.

He came through the window, almost silent, a grin on his lips, his blue eyes glinting with humor. That hot, rich scent of his flooded her head and suddenly, she had to swallow. It was that, or start drooling.

"Delivery service." She waggled her knife at him. "I like that."

"That mouth of yours ever get you in trouble, Sylvia?"

She shrugged lazily. "A time or two. You know, I don't like strangers touching my bike." Actually, she didn't like *anybody* touching her bike. "What's your name?"

Instead of answering, his eyes dropped to her knife. "You know, if you greeted the real Meals on Wheels that way, we'd have a problem."

"Well, since you're not actually on the menu, it's not an issue." She eyed him narrowly. He wasn't armed. Or at least, he wasn't holding any weapons. He probably *had* weapons. He wouldn't go out to Hunt without them. But he wasn't holding any. She could see his hands, open. Empty. Unlike hers.

Although, *hello*, he was a werewolf—in a matter of seconds, he turned into a fucking weapon.

"I hadn't exactly *planned* to be on the menu." He slanted his gaze to hers, a slow smile curling his lips. "But if you're hungry . . . just put away your blades."

Blades—

Shit. He was good.

Sighing, she tucked them away. He wasn't here to fight. If he was, they'd already be at it—she'd be bloodied, battered, and hopefully, she could at least mark up that pretty face of his a little before he killed her. Still, she was pretty certain that wasn't what he wanted out of her.

"Would you just go away?" she said, combing her hands through her hair. She needed a shower. She needed to change. And she was thirty miles away from the place she was renting. "I've got a job to do."

He lifted a wrist. "Are you hungry?"

Sylvia couldn't have been any more surprised if he'd sprouted a second head. That hunger tried to grab her by the throat, but she'd mastered it long ago. Still, she found herself staring at that wrist, the exposed veins for a long, long moment, almost mesmerized.

"If you're hungry, go ahead." Toronto cocked his head. "I've fed vamps before. It's not like I'll miss a half a pint."

Her belly all but cramped with need and her knees got weak just thinking about it. What the hell . . . she wasn't *that* hungry. She'd just fed last night. She could go another day before it should be *this* bad. Wary, she eyed him. "Why? Why would you feed me? You should all want me out of the territory."

"Well, for one"—he watched her, that light of amusement still in his eyes—"it's considered polite to make sure new . . . visitors don't go hungry. After all, hungry people sometimes go looking for food in the wrong place. We can't have that.

Besides, you and me? Tonight, we've got a killer to track down."

We . . .

"Not unless it's snowing in hell." Sylvia glared at him. A killer to track down? With a fricking Boy Scout? No. Way. No way in that frozen, snowy hell.

"Check the forecast, baby." He lowered his hand and sauntered forward, his gaze dropping to rest on her mouth. "Did you smell me on you when you woke?"

"I'm starting to think the crap about Masters having wicked control is just that—*crap*. Otherwise, I don't think I would have woken with your scent on me. Men with control don't go pawing sleeping women."

"Oh, I've got control." He dipped his head.

She held her ground, curious. He breathed in her scent, and when a groan rumbled out of him, she felt a strange warmth rush through her. Oh, this wolf was not good for her peace of mind. Not good for *her* . . . he was starting to make her *want* things, and this was only the second time she'd seen him. Not just sex—if all she wanted was sex, she wouldn't get that curious little twist in her heart when she looked at him.

This was much more than just craving sex; how was that even possible, anyway? She'd seen him *twice*. In under twenty-four hours. It was insane . . . and it was very real. She wanted to see his hair free, falling around her as he moved over her. She wanted to feed from him as he rode her. Wanted to feel his teeth on her flesh, breaking it—

"You keep thinking whatever you're thinking and I'll have you naked and wrapped around me in ninety seconds," he whispered. "And I still haven't told you my name. After all, we really should know each other's names before we fuck, right?"

Oh, she was in so much trouble here. Jerking back, she gave him a narrow glare and wished there was something, *anything* she could do to control her body's response to him. Anything to keep him from reading that response. She might as well waste her time wishing the sun wouldn't rise.

"I said it once, I'll say it again," she whispered, her throat dry. "Get the hell out. I've got a job to do."

"No, Syl. *We* have a job to do."

She stilled at the sound of her shortened name on his lips. "It's Sylvia," she said huskily. "Sylvia. Not Syl. Not any other name. Sylvia. And *we* don't have a job."

"Okay." He shrugged, unconcerned. "Think about it. It makes more sense. What *we* need is information from Pulaski. What *you* want is to complete your contract. The two things don't have to be mutually exclusive." He reached out, toyed with a lock of hair.

She watched as he wrapped it around one finger, around and around. Then he let it go, the backs of his knuckles brushing against the curve of her breast. "Like your Master is going to go for that."

"My Master . . ." He chuckled. Scratching his chin, he tipped his head back and studied the ceiling. "That's a funny thing. Let me put it this way. If I produce the results he needs, I don't think Rafe's going to give a flying *fuck* what happens to Pulaski. Not officially."

"Not officially? What in the hell does *that* mean?" She sneered at him. "You Boy Scouts are all about your damn rules."

"Boy Scouts?" He started to laugh. He ended up leaning against a wall, he laughed so hard. "I'm a Boy Scout? And I'm all about rules? Please. Pretty please, if you ever meet Rafe, you have to tell him that."

"Oh, like you're *not*?" Crossing her arms over her chest, she tapped her nails against her arm and eyed him. "If you're not all about rules and being Boy Scouts, then why in the hell would you all *do* the shit you do? It's not like you do it for glory or anything."

"If we don't . . . who will?" He eyed her curiously.

"So it's altruism?"

"No. It's . . ." A far-off look crossed his face and then he shrugged. "Somebody has to be willing. If it's not us, I guess it's nobody. And that's just not an option." He paused then asked softly, "Do you really want to live in a world where nobody stops the monsters, Miz James?"

Where nobody stops the monsters . . . Images flashed through her mind and the remnants of the dreams from the past day rose up to choke her. "Oh, go fuck yourself," she snapped. Spinning away from him, she went back to the closet and snagged her pack. She needed to get out of here. Fast. Once she got to her bike, she could keep away from him. Even a were couldn't keep up with a vamp on a Harley, right?

Bending down, she grabbed her bag. When she turned around, he was there. Her breath caught in her throat as he crowded her up against a wall, his body blocking her in, one arm resting by the wall near her head, the other coming up to rest lightly on her hip.

Too intimate—

"Listen, Sylvia . . ." He dipped his head and once more breathed in her scent. "We need to get something straight. You're not . . . aw, hell. You smell so good."

As he turned his face into her hair, she shuddered. "Okay. I'm glad we got that straight, wolf. I smell good—glad we got that nice and squared away. Now. Can you give me some space?"

"No." He pushed his thigh between hers.

Shock flooded her. *Heat* flooded her. "What . . ."

"My name is Toronto," he whispered against her ear. "Say it."

"Tor . . . Toronto?" She tipped her head back, frowning. "That's a . . ." *Hated place. I hate that place, I hate that place, I hate that place . . .* "Weird name."

"Yeah. So what? Say it again. I want to make sure you remember it. Because sometime very damn soon, I'm going to be inside you, Sylvia." The last words were spoken in a growl against her lips.

"Toronto." She opened for him even as she reached up and jerked the band from his hair.

CHAPTER 11

Dark. Mysterious. That was her taste. Like the night. Something exotic and sweet. Stroking his tongue along her lip, he waited until she'd curled an arm around his neck before he took her mouth in a deeper, rougher kiss.

Her fangs were down. He teased one of them with his tongue. Hot satisfaction burned through him as she shuddered. *Meals on Wheels*—she'd thought she'd been being insulting when she'd said it. She didn't know much about wolves. Much about Hunters for that matter. He didn't mind feeding vamps—so long as it was *his* decision.

It could save lives. Beyond that, vamps could make a bite pretty damn pleasant, especially if it was a female partner. And when it was a woman he wanted in bed?

She didn't know it, but he had every intention of feeding her at some point. He'd wanted it from the first moment he'd seen her, just as he'd wanted to feel that lushly curved body under his own. She'd just moved up the timetable. As she started to rock her hips against his, he eased back, falling on the control she'd taunted him about.

Yeah. He had control. He just didn't always choose to *use* it.

Tonight, though, and for the next few days, he'd have to.

Lifting his head, he stared down at her, her swollen mouth, her eyes—when she was hungry, they glowed with a strange, silvery light, almost like they were flecked with a hundred tiny stars. Lovely . . .

Lashes swept down, hiding her eyes. He watched as she took one deep breath, then another.

As she did that, he pulled his hand from her waist, lifted it. She was trying to ease away as he sank his teeth into his wrist.

She froze as the scent of blood flooded the air.

He pulled her back against him, turning her so that her back was against his front. "Feed," he whispered against her ear. "You need it, I think."

He'd explain why later.

She hesitated, and he pushed his wrist closer.

It wasn't until she covered his bleeding wrist with her mouth that he did the other thing he'd been dying to do . . . he slid his hand down the front of her body and cupped the heat of her in his palm.

She arched against him with a startled cry.

"Feed," he whispered again, rubbing the heel of his hand against her.

I T was a shocking, almost brutal assault on her senses. His blood—she'd never had *anything* like it. It was almost orgasmic, just that.

But then he reached between her thighs, covering the aching heat of her sex, Sylvia came apart. Wave after wave pulsed through her, battering her senses. It was a damn good thing she didn't *have* to breathe, because she couldn't. As he stroked her, as his blood flowed into her, he continued to mutter to her, his voice a low, husky rumble in her ear.

Then it was over, another shock to her senses. She clutched at his arm, unable to stand. Her head spun, her body pulsed and she felt . . . *alive* . . . almost too alive. Drunk, even. But she couldn't *get* drunk. God knew she'd tried over the past century, especially those first few years after she'd managed to escape—

No—

A hand stroked her hair, and she forced herself to open her eyes, swallow. The wine-rich taste of his blood lingered on her tongue, an addictive one that she already wished she'd never had. She didn't think she'd ever want to feed from another for as long as she lived.

She might hate him a little bit for that. Hell, if she was smart, she *should* hate him for what he'd just done . . . except she wanted to strip off her clothes and beg him to do it again. And then she wanted to strip his clothes away and do it to him, and . . .

Shit.

Behind her, his body was hot and hard, cradling her with surprising gentleness. His hand continued to stroke her hair as he touched his lips to her shoulder. "I wanted to let you feed from my neck, but I had a feeling if we did it that way, I'd end up on top of you for the rest of the night. We've already lost too much of it."

"Quite possibly. You know . . . I should hit you for doing that." Sylvia closed her eyes.

He rubbed his lips over her shoulder. "I'll let you if you want to take a shot. I can even say I'm sorry . . . should I?"

"No. Because I'm not sorry you did it, you jerk." Sighing, she shifted her gaze to the window, staring out into the night. "I never sleep this late."

"That's . . . probably my fault."

She frowned at the odd note in his voice. Shrugging away from him, she moved to stand on the other side of the room. "Perhaps you should explain that."

"How old are you?"

She made a face at him. "You know, vampire or not, some might still consider it rude to ask a woman how old she is."

"How old are you? Our research puts you at over a hundred. Your skill level seems to go with that. But I don't think you're particularly strong." He paused, waiting. When she didn't say anything, he sighed and glanced at the closet. "I opened the door while you were sleeping. It was only for about two seconds and sunlight hit you. You burned. That's probably . . ."

Why I'm so tired. She'd used resources healing the damned burn. Damn him. "Look, I just don't take sunlight as well as others." With a brittle-edged smile, she added, "You should have seen me as a mortal."

"You don't take sunlight well." He lifted a brow. "You're not newly turned. But you can't take two seconds of day? Again, how old are you?"

Sylvia set her jaw. She'd be damned if she answered. "You know, how old I am is hardly any of *your* business. Now, while I appreciate the delivery service, I need to get to work."

She kept him in her line of sight as she edged around the room to get her bag. He seemed like he was going to push the issue. Apparently he decided on pushing another issue instead.

"Look, sweetheart. I've already told you . . . we're doing this together." He caught her arm, his thumb stroking along the sensitive skin inside her elbow. "You probably know as well as I do, you can't exactly beat me. So how are you going to stop me?"

"You always this overbearing, Toronto?"

He grimaced and shoved a hand through his hair. "Usually, I'm about ten times worse. Consider yourself lucky I'm trying to be nice to you." After a glance around the floor, he reached into his pocket and pulled out a band, tying his hair back once again.

"So. Do we do this the easy way or not?" He stared at her, eyes watching her closely.

She was tempted to tell him to shove off. But Sylvia had worked pretty damn hard to build her self-worth back up. If she pushed him, they'd end up doing this the hard way. She couldn't win against him, not without a lot of dirty tricks.

"I have to finish this job," she said quietly. How could she make him understand that? She *finished* jobs. Especially jobs like this. It wasn't just a matter of pride. It was . . . it was part of her. She had to finish the job. And even aside from the fact that she didn't leave jobs unfinished, she couldn't walk away from the memories of this one.

She closed her eyes, and she saw Toby, and she thought of another boy. One from so long ago—another who'd died because of a monster. She *had* to find Pulaski. Had to stop him. If he didn't die, if she didn't know he would stop, the nightmares wouldn't stop.

In a low voice, he said, "If we find him alive, once I get what I need from him, he's yours."

Sylvia averted her face—she couldn't keep looking at him. For some reason, she *wanted* to trust him, even though that was the absolute last thing she should do. She didn't trust anybody. Ever. It was a rule of hers. She'd stopped trusting people after the last one had screwed her over and landed her in this living nightmare that was life as a vampire.

A weak vampire—one who burned with even two seconds of sunlight—

"Why should I trust you? How can I trust you to hold up your end of the bargain?"

"Because I said I would," he said, his voice flat. "I'm giving you my word."

"And just *why* should that mean jack to me?" She planted her hands on her hips, glaring at him. "I realize half of the freaks in this world think you guys are saints and the other half is terrified, but I don't fall into either camp. I trust somebody after they've *earned* it. Why *should* I trust you?"

He reached out and snagged the front of her shirt, moving so fast she barely had time to evade his grasp. Judging by the glint in his blue eyes, she decided it would be better to not bother just then. Besides, being pressed against that body wasn't a hardship. "How about we put it this way, sweetheart . . . I'm telling you that you can have him, and you can either just take a chance on that . . . or I'll haul you to the Enclave and just lock you in one of the isolation chambers. You'll get out when I decide you can come out."

Even though the thought of being locked up was enough to send fear ripping through her, she'd be damned if she showed that. Sylvia rose up on her toes and put her face in his. Baring her fangs at him, she snarled, "Just try it."

"Oh, you know I can do it." His voice was low, menacing and soft, but his hand oddly gentle as he stroked it back through her hair. "You'll bloody me. I'll hate having to do it. But you know I can. So why push it?"

* * *

SOMETHING dark and painful moved through her eyes before she hid it. Toronto hated himself for putting it there. He knew what had done it, too. Up until he'd mentioned the isolation chambers, she'd been fine. Pissed off, but fine. Not afraid. Oh, there had been some fear, but nothing like that screaming, silent hell.

She clamped it down, got it under control—it barely even had time to change her scent. He wondered at that. A fear that wild, that strong . . . it usually showed, and lingered. Unless a person had learned in painful, painful ways *not* to let it show.

I won't do that again, he promised her silently. Reaching up, he toyed with a lock of her hair, wondering how to undo the damage he'd just caused. "We can do this working together. I don't want him—I just need that information. And I imagine you're a clever woman. You can probably figure out a way to kill him, leave the body so he's found . . . without it being tracked back to you. That way the families of his victims get that final closure."

Her lashes flickered.

He tugged lightly on her hair. "Don't act like you don't feel pity for them." He continued to toy with her hair, not looking into her eyes, giving her a few minutes to steady, to think. To decide. "If you didn't feel pity, you wouldn't take jobs like this for free."

That did it.

She smacked at his hand, jerking away. "You don't know jackshit about the jobs I do."

"Don't I?" Smiling, he rubbed his knuckles along his jaw and leaned back against the wall near the open window. "Prove it. Tell me you're taking the money they offered you for this job. It's not like they can't afford it."

They could . . . Toby Clemons's folks were loaded. Seriously loaded.

Sylvia just glared at him.

"That's what I thought."

Sooty black lashes fell to shield her eyes. "I don't think I like you very much," she said, sighing and reaching up, gathering her hair in her hand.

Distracted, he watched as she twisted it around and around, piling it in a loose knot on the crown of her head. "Yeah, you do." She seemed to like him, though. A lot. Which was actually something of a surprise. A lot of people wouldn't mind at all if he disappeared from the face of the earth.

"Arrogant bastard," she muttered, a faint, reluctant smile curling her lips. She held the mass of hair with one hand and reached into a pocket with the other. A few seconds later, she had a couple of neat little sticks jammed into the ebony locks, holding the knot in place. Slanting a look at him, she said, "You ought to know that I'm tempted to tell you *no*, just for the hell of it, just to see what you'd do, just to give you grief."

Hearing the unsaid *but*, he cocked a brow and waited. And thought about going over there, pulling those sticks out of her hair, just to see it all come tumbling down around her shoulders. Damn, that hair. He loved it.

"But . . . I get the feeling you're serious about letting me have Pulaski. And I think we could do this better together. So, fine. We'll do it together." She sauntered toward him, her lush mouth an unsmiling line, her eyes glinting with an unholy light. "But I'm warning you, Hunter . . . screw me over and I *will* make you bleed."

Two seconds later, he felt a prick. And he realized she was better than he thought. She'd distracted him, all right, using that lovely body and that gorgeous hair. She'd palmed a knife again, and this time he hadn't noticed. *Shit*, she was dangerous.

And not just because she currently had that thin sliver of a blade pressed against his cock, either. Crooking a grin at her, he drawled, "Oh, come on, sweetheart. You really want to make me bleed *there*?"

"Right now, I want you to bleed in so many ways and in so many places, I can't even begin to list them." She stepped back and then he watched as she took the blade and sheathed it.

Narrowing his eyes, he studied the sheath—it was one of her fucking hair things. Sticking a knife in her hair was just plain stupid, but that little blade was sheathed. And nobody would think to look for it there, either. With a sly smile, she stuck it into her hair knot and grabbed her bag. "Come on, Hunter. Let's get this done."

"I've got a name," he said mildly.

"Yeah. A weird one."

S HE followed him down the stairs, carefully checking for any signs she might have left. There wasn't anything. If he'd left anything when he'd come in earlier, that was his own damn fault.

He could worry about his own ass.

That very, very fine ass . . .

Scowling, she jerked her gaze away from that very, very fine ass and focused on his back instead. Nice back. Leanly muscled. Not bulky though. It was possible for shifters to bulk up—she'd seen it. It was freaky and required a dedication to pumping iron—usually in the seven-, eight-, nine-hundred-pound range, but she didn't like that kind of mass on a man anyway.

He looked . . . well, like what he was. A leanly muscled wolf in human's clothing. That skin he wore was the disguise. Once they reached the kitchen, she pushed around him and said, "You know, if you damaged my bike, I'm going to damage you."

"You're so violent . . . I love it." He followed her outside, but before she could get to the bike, he did, using that wolf-quick speed and resting a hand on the handlebars. "I'll push it out."

"I can get my own bike," she said, glaring at him.

"Yeah, and until I'm *on* the damn bike with you, I'm pushing it. You don't trust me . . . I don't trust you, either. I definitely don't trust you not to try and take off without me."

Sylvia had to admit. It *had* occurred to her, more than once, although she'd brushed the idea away almost immediately.

She'd *said* she'd work with the jerk. She didn't go back on her word. Glaring at him, she shoved him back from her bike. Or she tried. He didn't move. "Look, pal. I said we could do this together. Now will you back *off*?"

"So you can try to get on it and take off?" He leaned over the bike, pressed his nose against the curve between her neck and shoulder.

Sylvia shuddered, but all he did was breathe her in.

"You know, I think I'll back off. And part of me even hopes you try to run. You know what will happen if you do? I'll chase you . . . ever been chased by a Hunter, Syl?"

"Don't call me Syl," she said hoarsely.

He ignored her, rubbing his cheek against the sensitive flesh of her neck. She needed to push him away. Really. That was what she needed to do. Instead, she just stood there. "You haven't been chased by one of us. You've done a damn good job staying out of our way," he rumbled, his voice taking on that deep, low rasp. "But you couldn't do it this time. Know what they say about a Hunter and his prey?"

He bit her.

Sylvia slammed a hand against her bike. If she hadn't, she just might have collapsed to the ground, a useless puddle of flesh, want and lust.

"Once we get your scent, we never stop." He lifted his head, staring down at her with eyes that glittered. Eyes that burned. Eyes that glowed. "And Sylvia . . . I've got your scent all fucking *over* me."

Her heart beat hard and slow inside her chest. Stifling a groan, she whispered, "Is that a threat, Hunter?"

"No." He cupped her chin in his hand, stroked his thumb over her lip.

"It's a promise. And I think you and I both know that I don't plan on sticking a knife in you. I want something else entirely." Pressing down against her lip, he held her gaze with his and then asked gruffly, "So . . . are you going to try and run?"

She was tempted. Wildly tempted. For several reasons. He made her nervous . . . and she didn't like it. He made her needy . . . that wasn't so bad. And while she might have enjoyed the chase, she was more inclined to run just to get the hell *away*. Because he was complicating her life all too much and he'd only been *in* it for less than a day. And in a matter of days, he'd likely be out of it.

Sylvia didn't need complications.

Blowing out a sigh, she turned her head. "I've got a job to do. Anything else has to wait . . . including jerking your chain."

"So you'd run to jerk my chain?"

Sliding him a look, she muttered, "I get the feeling I could have a lot of fun jerking your chain."

CHAPTER 12

"You've got people after you."

Alan Pulaski rolled onto his belly and smiled at the man on the bed. He felt half-drunk. This was . . . intense. He'd had no idea life could get this fucking *intense*. "Yeah. I know." Of course, he had people after him. He wasn't worried . . . they couldn't find him.

Not now.

A hand, hard and brutal, came down on his flank with bruising force. "You should be a little more aware."

Pouting, Alan stared at his lover. "What's the problem? The cops haven't found me yet. They aren't very likely to. Nobody knows *you*. Nobody knows about you. Nobody knows I'm here, and it's not likely I'm going to go to the grocery store or anything." He giggled insanely at the thought.

The grocery store . . . well, he'd always enjoyed that place. But still, he knew he had to be careful. He wasn't going to go out *advertising* himself for crying out loud.

A hand fisted in his hair and jerked him up. "I'm having fun with you, but if you start being stupid, that's not going to last."

"I . . ." Alan swallowed, fear filtering through the near-drugged feeling that had wrapped around him for the past few weeks. "Look, I'm not going to do anything stupid. I'm not going anywhere, not talking to anybody. How can anybody find me?"

Shooting for a smile, he slid a hand down, wrapped it around the man's cock. Squeezed. Watched as the man's lashes dropped. He squeezed, tighter . . . tighter. "I'm not going to be stupid. I'm just going to be here. Right here. Until you're ready for us to be elsewhere."

The hand in his hair pushed downward. Alan went. He'd please the man. Later, the man would please *him* with their games. And maybe he'd even bring him another little toy. He found the best ones.

H E rose from the bed, leaving Alan sleeping behind him.

They needed to leave.

It had to be handled with care, but they needed to leave.

Alan didn't realize what was coming after them, but he did.

He'd felt that strange, hushed silence for the past two nights, and it had kept him trapped in the house like a little rabbit cowering in a field, hoping the hawk wouldn't find him.

It pissed him off, but he rather enjoyed life, so he'd cower. He'd be pissed off. He'd live—and he'd make sure Alan did the same.

His latest lover was a stupid son of a bitch, but Alan understood *pain*.

And pain was something he had to have . . . since Alan could give it to him, Alan would get some leniency.

But they couldn't linger any longer.

He'd had a feeling this was coming, so preparations had been in the works all day. No more time to waste.

S HE'D been riding motorcycles off and on for decades. Her first bike had been an Indian—a 441. Sylvia had loved it . . . damn, she'd loved that one. It had died a brutal death, though, when she'd been pursuing one icy piece of work in 1949. Since then, she'd had a number of other bikes, Indians, Harleys, a couple of Ducatis, but she had a fondness for the Indian.

For the past three decades, she'd spent a decent amount of free time restoring bikes. The new bikes were fun, but there was just something about the classics. She knew them inside and out and it was almost as much fun for her to build one as it was to ride one—almost.

Riding, for her, though, was a solitary thing. She didn't like to share—hell, she didn't even like to be *around* people.

So why was it oddly easy to be around him? Easy . . . and erotic. Having Toronto sitting so close up against her back was driving her mad, making it almost impossible for her to concentrate on what she needed to be doing.

His hands, those long-fingered, poetic-looking hands, rested on her hips, fingers splayed down to touch the tops of her thighs, another distraction she just didn't need. As she took a left on the road up ahead, he asked, "Are we looking for something in particular?"

"Yeah. Use your nose. Tell me when you smell it." It was in the air, but it was faint, fainter than last night.

"I already smell it. You want to tell me why we're tracking it?" He leaned forward, dipping his head a little so that his chin rested on her shoulder.

Close . . . man, he was just too close. Did he have to sit so close? She wanted to groan. At the same time, she wanted to cuddle even *closer*, sink against the warmth of that lean, powerful body and feel his arms come around her. Instead, she kept her body rigid as she replied, "Because I think we need to. You wanted to work together, so work with me."

"I *am* working with you." He laughed, humor heavy in his voice, his fingers kneading her hips. "Come on, it's not like I'm demanding you turn around and head somewhere else, am I? I'm not growling at you to follow my lead or anything. And actually . . . I had a source tell me that Pulaski had a rich new lover. Even indicated this general area."

Sylvia glanced around, eyeing the subtle gleam of golden light behind arched windows of etched glass, the look of rough-hewn stone or aged brick, all the carefully manicured lawns. "Rich guys, yeah. You'll find them here." Something vague and uncomfortable started to itch along her spine. She didn't like it . . . odd, slippery, familiar—

Frowning, she brought the bike to a halt at a stop sign and turned off the engine. "Something's wrong," she said quietly.

"Yeah?" He kicked a leg off the bike and moved to the sidewalk, looking around. His head fell back and he scented the air. "There's blood in the air, but it's old. A few days, at least. It's coming from the same place as the sex, the sweat."

"I smell pain. Misery." Shaking her head, she looked at him and said, "How can your Master have something like that going on so close to his house?"

"Do me a favor—quit calling him my *Master* like I'm his dog or something," Toronto said, his voice just barely above a growl. Then he shoved a hand through his hair, shook his head. "The blood I smell, it's all human. We're not omnipresent, Sylvia. Not all-powerful. Memphis has got one hell of a paranormal population and lately, it's getting bigger. We've got our hands full just keeping *that* under control. When we *know* something bad is going down, we'll do what we can, but our main concern has to be our own kind. If they get out of control, the humans are screwed."

She stared at him, the stink of rage and anger so thick, so heavy. Then she shook her head and turned away. "We need to walk," she said quietly. "Let's find a place to stash the bike."

"There." He pointed across the street.

Sylvia narrowed her eyes before glancing at the house. "I'm not just leaving it in somebody's drive."

"It's not just somebody. It's a local witch. I'll tell him you're leaving it. The bike will be fine." He flashed a smile and there was something decidedly twisted in it. "Don't worry, it will be completely safe. I want to ask him what's going on around here anyway. This is the sort of thing Rafe would want to know about. And there's no way this guy didn't know."

* * *

THE door opened, revealing a brunet with cool gray eyes and a polite smile. It never wavered as he looked from Sylvia to Toronto, but she caught the slightest change in the air. Fear.

He was afraid.

It wasn't her that bothered the man, though.

"Paul."

Toronto didn't wait for an invitation to enter.

Sylvia didn't have much choice. At least the guy didn't shut the door in her face. She suspected that had more to do with Toronto, though, than her.

And the invite didn't come. Frustrated, she stood there as Toronto prowled around the foyer, pausing by a long slim table set under a mirror. The mirror was set in an old oak frame and looking at it made her itch. She had a hard time looking away, though.

"Don't look at it too long, sweetheart," Toronto said, glancing at her over his shoulder. "It's spelled—he uses it to try and catch bits and pieces of a person's past, of their secrets."

Sylvia hissed and jerked her gaze away, but not before she saw the echo of something in it—no. Not an echo. A face . . . *her* face. But not as she was now. Snarling, she shot the witch a look. With a flick of her wrist, she dropped one of her blades into her hand. Oh, she was going to cut him for that. Cut him wide open—

"This mirror," Toronto whispered, reaching up to touch his fingers to the smooth surface. "I wonder if it could tell you much about me."

The witch watched Toronto with expressionless eyes. "It won't because I don't allow it. I told the Master I wouldn't practice against the Hunters. I wouldn't break the laws. I've kept my word." He flicked Sylvia a look. "And I haven't broken it. She's no Hunter."

"Hmmm, but she's with me. That means no tricks, witch." Toronto reached up and trailed his fingers across the surface. "And I have to wonder, just how well are you keeping to your word? There are things going on here that we really should have known about, Paul. I think you even know what it is."

Lashes swept down, shielding those gray eyes. "Human affairs belong in the human world. You shouldn't concern yourself with them. Our worlds do not belong together."

"He's lying about something," Sylvia said quietly.

Toronto smiled. "I know."

"H E didn't tell you anything."

Sylvia stormed along at Toronto's side, disgusted. Damn it, five minutes with him and the witch would have told *her* something.

"I don't need him to tell me anything. I can find the place myself, and Rafe will get him to talk—he's already en route."

"And what if he leaves before Rafe gets here?" Sylvia asked, staring at the house. It made her hurt, she realized. Deep inside, like a sickness. Made her ache, and left her skin all tight and itchy. As she raked her nails over her flesh, Toronto reached out and caught her wrist.

"Don't. It's just a side effect of his magic, whatever protective spells he has on the place. But the more you react, the harder it will hit you—think of it as magical poison ivy." With that, he let go of her wrist and glanced back at the house, a mean smile twisting his lips. "And don't worry. He's not going anywhere soon. Witches don't heal as fast we do."

Arching a brow, she waited, but he didn't elaborate. "Rafe has to be the one to handle this from here on out. It's his territory and this shit isn't tolerated. Our kind know that. This witch might not be the only one involved—there were others, most likely. Once he finds them, he'll clean them out."

"Clean them out. As in kill them."

Toronto pushed the bike into the driveway, off the sides out of the shadows. "You think he should live?"

"It depends on how involved he is," Sylvia snapped.

"Hmmm. How involved." Toronto turned and pointed off to the east. "I figure the house we're looking for is roughly a quarter of a mile that way. Paul is a witch of pretty decent strength. From what I know about witches, a low-level witch would feel the disturbance from as far as five miles off. Either the power would seriously fuck up the witch's head, his power, his life . . . or he was waiting for it."

"Waiting for it?" She glanced back at the house.

"Torture is a power surge." He came to stand a few feet away. "If it wasn't disturbing him, then that means he welcomed it. Since he didn't report it, that means . . ."

"He wanted the power surge."

"Why else do you think he was keeping so quiet?" He had a weird look in his eyes as he stared up at the house, something that made the hair on the back of her neck stand up. "He was feeding off it. And although I can't find the trail myself, I bet if a witch started looking, we'd find that he might have been hiding this somehow."

"Hiding it." She narrowed her eyes, staring at the house as the pieces began to shift into place. As they did, it painted a picture, one that made her burn with fury. As the hunger grew, so did the rage. "He was hiding it—so close to you, so close to the people who are supposed to be able to *stop* this, but you couldn't stop *him*. What fucking good are you?"

When he didn't answer her, she whirled around and glared at him.

His blue eyes swirled, spiked as their gazes locked, but that was the only sign of emotion—the only damn flicker.

"Well?" she demanded. Stalking closer, she glared at him. "You're supposed to stop this. Why didn't you?"

"We didn't know—*I* didn't know. But we're stopping it now."

"We?" Sylvia shook her head. "No. Not *we*. I'm working a job and it's not fixing *your* fucking mess."

She would have turned away but his hand caught the front of her jeans, hauled her close. "Sweetheart, in case you haven't noticed, your job and this mess seemed to be pretty closely involved. And you're either working this with me, or you're *not* working it."

"Let me go." Her heart slammed against her ribs as she stared into his blue eyes, and she tried to figure out just what it was about him that made that useless bit of flesh react so strongly. Just what was it about him that made *her* react so strongly? Yeah, he was a bigger, badder predator, but she'd *killed* bigger, badder predators before. She did it by being smart. Sylvia wasn't so certain that would be the case here. Those lazy smiles he flashed hid a burning intelligence— she'd seen it gleaming in his eyes.

This mess aside, Hunters weren't exactly known for being slackers.

More, though. It was more than that.

You just want to jump his bones.

Okay, there *was* that. She definitely wanted to jump his bones. That was an image that had planted itself inside her head and just wouldn't let go. But she wasn't doing this.

Reaching down, she curled her fingers around his wrist and pulled. To her surprise, he let her go. "I don't want to work with you. I don't want to have anything to do with this mess you've let happen." She turned her back on him, on the house that whispered of a power that made her skin itch. And a mirror that had showed her a ghost. "I have a killer to find."

"And we'll find him together."

She could argue. And take that much more time to track Pulaski down. She'd taken too much time already.

"M Y first day as a student and I have homework out of my butt." Angel lay across the bed, staring at the math problems and wishing she was just a little less obsessive. A little less anal. Because then she could just not worry about the work.

But if she did something, she did her best. And that included being a student.

"Ugh."

She was halfway done when she felt him. And a smile curled her lips as she felt his frustration—they were in a witch's home, and Kel hadn't ever been inside. He was a vampire—he needed an invitation, and since it was a witch, there were specific wardings on the house anyway.

It had been a weird thing to discover there was actually truth to the threshold and invitation legends about vampires.

A home *was* a place of safety . . . or at least, an apparent place of safety. After a period of time, a person's very presence sank into the ground and became a static spell on its home. A spell of life, so to speak. A *thing* of life.

Vampires weren't of the same breed anymore and that threshold spell didn't recognize them. For them to pass inside that first time, they had to be invited.

There were ways around it. Every damn thing came with loopholes, it seemed. If somebody hadn't been in a house very long, it wasn't a home, and it didn't offer the same protective aspects. If somebody wasn't there very often, the same deal went. And older vampires were better at "camouflage"—pretending to be something they weren't. Even alive.

So while Angel lay upstairs, doing the schoolwork that she really didn't need to do, her husband was downstairs knocking on the door and dealing with the witch's inquisition.

By the time he made it upstairs, Angel was grinning ear to ear.

And he was scowling.

Bunch of stupid-ass bullshit, why the hell do I gotta . . . shit, she's beautiful . . .

She looked up at him through her lashes and smiled. Kel stood in the doorway, his dark eyes locked on her face, dark hair spiked and disheveled. He'd been running his hands through it again. He did that when he was distracted or irritated. Or both.

He was so damn pretty. Before he'd been bitten, his skin had been a light gold and the more time he'd spent in the sun, the deeper it had gotten. Now it was a strange shade between ivory and gold, stretched over a long, lean body that was just a little too skinny. He'd never change. He'd been bitten young. The two of them had been in college, and his Change had halted him forever.

But he was still beautiful. To her, he was perfect.

Even with that grim look in his eyes and the frustration she could see written all over his face, hanging around him like a cloud.

Propping her chin on her hand, she smiled at him. "You

know, if you're nice to me, I might let you talk me into making out. But we have to be quiet . . . my mom's downstairs."

Kel came inside and shut the door. "Screw being quiet." He stripped off his jacket and tossed it on the chair.

Her heart fluttered as he came for her.

S HE made him ache.

Not just physically, but in his heart, in his soul.

As he moved to the bed, Angel pushed onto her knees, a smile curving her lips, while her gaze heated. "You in a mood, Kel?" she asked softly.

"You're here. I'm here. Damn straight I'm in a mood." Sliding an arm around her waist, he pulled her against him. "I want you naked."

"Hmmm. I can do that."

"So can I." He reached for the hem of her shirt, stripping it away. "Pretty, pretty Angel."

White lace dotted with red cupped her breasts. Nice. But in the way. He opened the front hook and tugged the straps off, tossing the bra to the side. "You weren't there when I woke," he said, kneeling down and raking his teeth down the curve of her breast. "I didn't like it."

"I know." Her hand came up, curled over the back of his neck. "I'm sorry."

"I hate this." Frustration, fear for her burned inside him. Impatient, he dealt with her jeans and panties and tumbled her back onto the bed—it was a simple affair of white painted iron, with a blue comforter and white pillows. Nothing like their bed, the heavy, oak four-poster they'd picked out together. He wanted her back in their bed.

But as he levered himself up on his elbows and stared down into her face, he saw her eyes. He could hate it all he wanted. But she needed this. A fist wrapped around his heart. "You better stay safe, Angel," he whispered.

"I will." She stroked a hand down his chest, tugging at the cloth of his T-shirt. "You're still dressed."

"I know." Biting her lower lip, he muttered, "But you're not and that's good enough for me."

Angel chuckled, slipping her hand lower. Freeing him from his trousers, she watched him from under her lashes as she wrapped her fingers around his cock and stroked. "And what if I want you naked?"

"Then I'd say you better be the one in a mood next time." He shifted between her thighs and pressed against her. "I don't want to wait."

"Then don't."

Their mouths met. As he sank inside her, she sighed and her arms came around him, tight and strong.

And for the first time since he'd woken that day, he felt complete.

CHAPTER 13

"HOUSE is empty."

Toronto had the feeling Sylvia was biting back something pithy as she shot him a look. "Yes. I noticed that."

"Most of what I smell around here is human." And it wasn't even that easy to smell that. Frowning, he rubbed his nose and had to fight the urge to sneeze. There was something in the air, and if he tried to drag it in, filter through the scents, he'd end up gagging. "I can't tell if there's anything else or not."

"Hmmm."

She didn't sound terribly interested. She'd already been checking the air in the same careful way he had. She'd also been checking the windows, searching the grounds. Just like he was doing. Sylvia didn't wait for him, she didn't ask his thoughts—she very much didn't want to be working with him.

But then again, they'd already established that fact.

Too bad.

Barely into this Hunt and he was getting bad vibes. There

was a connection between this place and Pulaski. They already knew that. But what was the connection between Pulaski, this place and the witch?

Abruptly, Toronto caught the sharp edge of a scream, cut off after not even a second, off in the distance.

Sylvia heard it as well.

It made him smile. Slanting a look to the west, he said, "Rafe's got our witch now."

"You sure it's him?"

"Yeah."

She stared out into the night, her eyes unreadable. "What will he do to the witch?"

"Knowing Rafe? Whatever it takes." He shrugged. "It's what I'd do."

She slanted a look at him and to his surprise a faint smile curled her lips. "Good."

Thirty seconds later, a text popped up on his phone. *We have him. I'll let you know when I get more information from him.*

Not *if. When.*

Rafe would get it. It might involve removing body parts and other bloody crap, but Rafe would do what he had to do. The sad thing with witches . . . they wouldn't grow those body parts back. Maybe it wouldn't come to that and Paul could just die a quick death.

He texted Rafe back the address of the house. *Find out who owns this place. There's a connection here. If he won't talk and give up names, see if Ex can send a witch. One of ours can probably track this back to anybody connected.*

Without waiting for an answer, he tucked the phone away and looked back at the house. Rafe wouldn't like it, but if Paul didn't—or couldn't—give the right answers, they might need a witch to help untangle this. Toronto wasn't going to be able to track for shit here.

"What in the hell is with the scents here?" he muttered, crouching down on the ground. He went low, until his nose was just a few inches above the closely cropped blades of grass. It was stronger there, but only faintly. A trace of something.

Chemical.

"What are you doing?"

"Trying to figure out why my nose isn't working." He flicked her a glance. "What do you smell?"

"Human. And something that smells almost like mint."

"Nothing else?"

Sylvia jerked a shoulder. "Nothing else. What do you smell?"

"Something I don't get. Yeah, it's not mint. Close, but not quite. Chemical, almost. But again, not exactly. It's like it's . . . eating the scent." He took another scent of it, rolling it around on the back of his tongue, but it just lay there. He couldn't name it, couldn't place it. Couldn't even understand it, although his wolf didn't like it. That mintlike scent was the strongest and he couldn't get past it to pull the other scents apart.

"Eating the scent."

"Yeah." Rising, he shrugged restlessly and prowled around the grounds once more. He still needed to go inside, but that was going to be a damned waste of time, too. Just like out here. "It's not covering it up. You know that nasty crap people spray in the air to hide a smell? That covers things up. This isn't covering it. There's something that's been *erasing* a scent. Eating it. Whatever. I smell just the faintest trace of something."

From the corner of his eye, he could see her watching him for a minute. Then she shrugged and turned away. "Sounds like Febreze for werewolves."

"Febreze." He frowned. That . . . that wouldn't work.

Unless—

No. Not right now. He tucked that puzzle in the back of his mind. Something to think about later. Right now, they had to finish up here and get out before they were discovered.

Maybe they'd luck out and find something.

If not, they still had several hours left of the night. He'd just see where Sylvia led them. Once she was down for the day, he'd follow his own leads. He'd need some sleep soon, but an hour or two would do for now.

"Come on. Let's head inside."

She stared at him. "I doubt I'll be able to enter."

"And I bet you will. Whoever owned this place . . . it wasn't a home."

S YLVIA's skin hurt as she pushed her way over the threshold. Physically *hurt*. But she made it over and stood there, shaking, her head bowed, as she waited for the reaction to pass.

"It always hit like that?"

"Harder, probably." Toronto rested his hand on her shoulder. "You okay?"

"Oh. Just peachy." *Just peachy keen*. She shrugged his hand away, reminding herself she didn't want to be here. She wanted to be very elsewhere. Well, she'd be here if it had something to do with Pulaski, but she didn't want to be here with Toronto.

"Just keep moving. The more you're on the move, the less the house will fight you. It doesn't have much resistance in it anyway or you wouldn't have made it through the door," Toronto said.

She nodded and forced herself to take that first step. Then another—shit, it was like wading through quicksand. The very air seemed to drag at her, pulling her back.

Yet each step got easier and by the time she'd made one circuit around the kitchen, that odd resistance began to melt away, like ice under the spring sun. As she slipped into a short hallway that led to a formal dining room, she just felt faint dregs, like something from a nightmare.

"We need to find out who owns this place," she said quietly.

"I'm already working on it." Toronto padded across the plush silver carpet, pausing by the big window that faced out over the backyard. Moonlight shone down, painting the world in streams of silver light.

Room after room came up empty.

Room after room, she smelled human. Just human. And the stink of blood, which had led them here. Although it hung in the air, she didn't see so much as a drop anywhere. Considering the pale décor—all silver and whites—the blood would have stood out rather glaringly.

"The smell of blood in the air is thick enough to choke on," she said as they climbed to the third floor.

So far, all of the rooms were empty. Not even appliances had been left. Only the shades and the curtains. She hadn't seen so much as a stray eyelash, a scrap of paper.

"Yeah." Toronto grunted. "It's all human, though."

She knew that. He might know scent, but she knew blood. And one thing was really, really weird. "If there was that much blood being shed around here . . . why haven't we seen even a drop?"

Blood and sex. That was what she smelled, and the two of them didn't go neatly together. The smells permeated every damn room of the house. Blood would have spilled *some-where*, she thought. They couldn't be that neat, could they?

Was it possible?

She didn't know.

"Okay, we need to think it through," she said, shaking her head. "If there's something that's covering the scent—"

"It's not covering it. It's *erasing* it," Toronto cut in.

"Covering. Erasing. Whatever. You can't track it. If it's doing that to *some* of the scents, why not the human scent?" She frowned, hands on her hips as she studied the room.

"Easy. Whoever it was that wasn't human hasn't been here in a while—they did this and then left and haven't come back. The others have." He continued to prowl the room.

Eyeing him, she asked, "If you walk in enough circles, do you think the walls will start to talk or something?"

"Wouldn't that be handy?" He flashed her a toothy smile and then stopped, completely still. His lids drooped low over his eyes and his nostrils flared. "I smell . . ."

They both heard it—a faint brush of sound, the scrape of a shoe over concrete. Yards away. But in front of this house.

She dashed for the stairs.

Toronto didn't bother for the quiet approach. She heard glass shatter before she'd even managed to clear the first flight. And by the time she was outside, he had a man dangling from his hand, the mortal's feet a good twelve inches above the ground.

"Sylvia, can you grab his mind?"

As the mortal struggled to get enough air to breathe, she glared at Toronto. "And if the answer is *no*, what are you going to do?" she demanded.

Toronto smiled. "His smell is all over this place. What do you think I should do?"

Slanting a look back at the mortal Toronto held, Sylvia eyed him narrowly. He stank with fear. Yeah, his scent was familiar. And recent—matter of fact, it was one of the stronger scents. Like he'd been inside the house within the past day or two.

"Do you know something?" she asked him softly, moving closer.

"Let go of me," he squealed.

Something massive and dark rolled through the night. Sylvia closed her hands into fists, her nails tearing into her skin. Blood—her own—scented the night air. Focusing on that, she ignored the fear Toronto brought to the night. It was something the high-level weres could do—inspire fear—mind-shattering fear.

Shit. She'd faced that once before, but it hadn't been from a wolf on his level. She really didn't want to have that directed at her, she decided. Not at all.

The human hadn't stood a chance.

He was sobbing, nose running, and as she watched, he pissed his pants.

"Try asking him again," Toronto said quietly.

"Do you know anything about what happened in this house?" Sylvia said and this time, she pushed at his mind.

His sobs quieted. The frantic struggles of his body eased and he whispered, "Yes."

Toronto flicked her a glance. "So you can grab his mind."

"I never said I couldn't." Mortal minds were often very

malleable, and when they were afraid, much more so. Taking control of this guy's mind was like taking candy from a baby. "We're too easy to be seen here."

Toronto moved them into the shadows. "You'll have to make this quick. We were probably heard."

"We?" She smirked. *He* had been heard—going through the glass like some actor in a B action movie. Still, he was right. They needed to be quick. "You listen for cars." Focusing her mind and her attention on the mortal, she asked, "Where did the people who lived here go?"

"Nobody lived here." The man's eyes were glazed and he stared at Sylvia like she was his world.

"Okay, the people who owned it. Where did they go?"

"I don't know. I don't even know who owned it." With that rapt stare still on his face, he tried to pull away from Toronto's steely grip. Unsuccessfully. So instead, he just stared at her. "You're so beautiful. Your skin, it glows."

Sylvia ignored him. "What do you know? What happened here, and who was in charge?"

"Sex. We fucked here. I don't know who was in charge. I heard the name Kit—if you were enough fun, Kit might like you. Everybody wanted to be liked by Kit."

"Why?" She tucked that name away. Kit—male? Female?

"Because those people got special stuff. Kit got the youngest ones, or the virgins. All the best." His pupils constricted and he licked his lips, staring at her mouth. "I wanted a virgin. A young one who'd fight me. So I came. And I paid—"

"A virgin?" Sylvia asked quietly. "How young?"

"As young as he could get her. Are you one of Kit's? Your skin . . . you've got the most beautiful skin." He was panting now, staring at her neck, her cleavage, and she could smell his arousal on the air.

It turned her stomach. "Do you know where Kit is now?"

"Kit isn't from here. Has a place outside of town, or north of here. I can't remember. Nobody ever said. Kit's got money and likes to play, likes to party. The rougher you play, the more likely Kit will like you. So I play rough and I pay a lot to do it. There was supposed to be another party here, but then we got the call that the parties were stopping." He made a weird, rough sound low in his voice. "I don't know anything else about Kit. I want to touch your skin."

She smiled and then closed the distance between them. "Did you hurt women here?"

"No." Staring at her, mesmerized, he licked his lips. "There weren't women. I wanted younger . . . they were all teenagers. And yeah, I hurt them."

The rage inside her grew. As her fangs extended, Sylvia grabbed the back of his head. Still holding his mind with hers, she jerked his head back and sank her teeth in.

"Sylvia—"

Over the man's rigid body, she stared at Toronto. *Stop me.* She dared him with her eyes. She wanted to rip the man's body apart with her bare hands. A virgin—that was what he'd wanted. A young one. And so he could get what he'd wanted, he played rough. Paid to do it, even.

Toronto stared at her and judging by the flicker in his eyes, he was mad about something.

Sylvia didn't drain the bastard, as much as she wanted to. They didn't have time for that—it wasn't a fast process, emptying a human body of blood. Lifting her head, she let him go and watched him hit the ground, weakened by the hold on his mind and the blood she'd taken.

She sliced her palm and covered his bleeding neck. Healing it took only a minute, but it was a minute they could hardly afford.

"The cops are coming—I hear the engines." Toronto held out a hand.

She accepted and rose, kicking the bastard in the kidney. He cried out. "You won't remember this," she warned him, slowly uncurling her psychic hold on him. "You'll forget. But you're going to tell the fucking cops what you've done here."

"Shit, that's going to screw with Rafe's investigation," Toronto muttered.

She arched a brow. Then, with a sigh, she kicked him again, hard enough to hurt, but not hard enough to break anything. "You'll tell them in a week."

She didn't know if it would hold—her mental hold was

better than her other skills, but she wouldn't bet the bank on it lasting. Looking at Toronto, she said, "That's the best I can do. He can't do this again, but we don't have time to deal with him."

Toronto held something up. It was a wallet. "Oh, don't worry. I plan on paying him a visit or two . . . that's assuming Rafe doesn't track him down first."

CHAPTER 14

"I'M surprised you didn't try to stop me."

Toronto shot her a look as he pushed her bike out to the street. "Stop what?"

"Stop me from biting him."

He snorted. "I don't know why you'd want that fuck's blood in you, but I'm not going to protect somebody like that. If we'd had the time, I would have turned him into a piñata and beat the shit out of him until his skin ripped and his bones fell out like candy."

"That's . . . an image." She smiled a little before she could stop herself. Thinking through what he'd said, she let the image she had of him realign a little. He wasn't just about playing by the rules—and if he was, then the rules he had were so far pretty incomprehensible to her. Things to think about later, when they weren't in the middle of moving quickly, quietly and calmly before any cops saw them.

Pushing her mind back to the image he'd called up, she pictured him doing it. Thought about doing it herself—stringing up that son of a bitch who had dreams about raping a child. Yes. She would enjoy whaling on him like he was a piñata. "I have to say, I don't think we could actually make his skin split and the bones fall out like candy, though."

"I would have fun trying." He glanced down the street, although they couldn't see the other house from here. "We need to go."

"Where are we heading now?"

"Someplace where we might find some answers." He gestured to the bike.

It wasn't until he climbed on behind her that she realized she hadn't been tempted to take off without him.

She told herself it was because she wasn't interested in having a Hunter chase her down.

But that wasn't entirely true . . . she wouldn't mind a bit if he decided to chase her. He'd catch her, she knew it. And she was starting to think that would be a hell of a lot of fun.

Which only made things too complicated . . . they had no time for fun, and this definitely wasn't the place for it.

"WHY are we back here?" Sylvia stared at the club, her belly twisting as she thought of going back inside there.

Her visit here before hadn't exactly been fruitless, but she didn't see herself finding a lot more information here. And going back in that place left her . . . uncomfortable.

"Information." Toronto sighed and pulled his hair back. After he did that, he pulled out something metallic and pink from his pocket.

As the scent—sugary and sweet—drifted upward, he held out the mangled pack of gum toward her. She eyed it narrowly and then shook her head, watching him as he popped a piece in his mouth. A werewolf who chewed Hubba Bubba. Weird.

"What kind of information?" she asked, making herself look back at the club.

"The kind that might have to do with somebody who sells kids. This place sells the fantasy. I don't like it, but it's legal and it . . . fills a need." He shrugged restlessly. "Some fucks have that need and as long as they don't cross the line, we can't do shit about it. But if these people know about the fantasy, maybe they've had a few people come looking for the reality."

He slanted her a look. "After all, somebody pointed you in the direction of that house. I'm figuring you found them here . . . you were here last night, I know."

Sylvia rolled her eyes at him.

"So people here know something. We'll see if we can't get more."

"If the kid I spoke with knew more, I would have known more." She thought of the young man, his anger. "He told me everything he knew."

"We aren't looking for the kid. We're looking higher up this time." Toronto pushed the pack of gum back into his pocket and nodded toward the alley. "Come on. We'll go in through the back. I suspect management will be more likely to cooperate if we aren't seen."

"Management? We're talking to management?" As they slipped into the alley, she pushed her hands into her pockets. "You looking for a new line of work, Toronto? You're pretty, but I don't think you're young enough."

A thin smiled curled Toronto's lips. "Probably not."

"How old are you?" She eyed him curiously.

He shot her a look. "I'm not sure."

Caught off guard, she stumbled in her tracks. "You . . . you're not sure?"

"Yeah. I was changed more than a century ago, but I don't know how old I was before I was changed, so, there's no telling." As they reached the door, he said, "Now why don't you focus on that job you're so worked up about?"

Frowning, she went to glare at him. But all she got was his back—his very rigid back. He'd already forced the door open and was disappearing inside the gloom.

Somehow, she'd hit a sore spot.

Odd. She hadn't thought he'd have them.

He didn't go far. The door he stopped in front of was plain and unassuming, unmarked, and if she hadn't done this sort of thing in the past, she didn't know if she would have thought to look here.

But she wasn't at all surprised when he opened the door to reveal a slick, posh office that would have rivaled the designs of some top-level executives. As the man behind the desk looked up, surprise flitting through his eyes, Toronto held the door open for her. She sauntered inside and made a show of looking around. "Wow. Selling little boys must pay well."

"Excuse me." The mortal gave her a blinding, disarming smile. "Do we have an appointment, Ms. . . . ?"

She just smiled and sat in the chair in front of his desk. It cupped her body like a glove, soft and comfortable. Crossing her legs, she propped an elbow on the arm of the chair and watched Toronto. This had been his call—how was he going to play it?

As Toronto shut the door, the man's eyes shifted away and if she hadn't been used to reading mortals, she wouldn't have seen it. He hid it well. But he knew Toronto. And he didn't like him. His shoulders stiffened minutely, then relaxed. Something flickered in his pale brown eyes, but was gone almost as quickly as it had appeared. With a genial smile, he studied first Toronto and then Sylvia. "I'm afraid I'm at a loss. Did we have an appointment?"

"Nope." Toronto came farther into the room, long black coat swirling around his ankles, his blue eyes locked on the man's face, and although that face should have been too damn pretty to look so fucking scary, he did it. Eyes like ice, a decidedly wolfish smile and an expression that said he was ready, willing and able to cause a lot of trouble.

He sank into the chair next to Sylvia's, his pose deceptively lazy, legs stretched out in front of him, hands linked across his belly. "But we have one now, Mr. Markland."

"I'm afraid you've got the wrong man, my friend. My name is Ben Muccino. Benito, actually, but that's a mouthful." He smiled once more, that same winning smile. Although this time, it looked a little frayed around the edges.

"No, it's not. It's Benjamin Markland—born in Chattanooga, 1975 to Beth and Charles Markland. Mom and Dad still live there—they are very proud. Think you are an executive." Toronto glanced around and his smile took on a derisive slant. "I guess you are, seeing as how you run this joint. Running a strip joint still counts as management, right? And you make a pretty penny, selling fantasy and all."

A muscle jerked in the man's face, and Sylvia watched as he took a deep, slow breath. "What do you want . . . money? I won't be blackmailed. I'm not doing anything illegal here." He curled his lip and shot both of them a dark look. "People like you, you see in black-and-white. Life isn't black-and-white—it's all shades of gray. If there weren't places like this, then the people who need these fantasies? They'd go looking for their own—they'd *make* their own."

Toronto cocked a brow. "Is that how you see it?" He shrugged. "That's fine. You say to-may-toe. I say to-mah-toe. You see this as all fucking kosher. I see it as a disgusting enterprise where kids who are barely old enough to be called adults act like kids so men old enough to be their daddies can sit in the dark and jack off while they fantasize. That's fine. It's legal . . . and nobody gets hurt." He smiled thinly and added, "Trust me . . . I've been watching."

"I'm aware." Ben leaned back, his eyes narrowed on Toronto's face. "Hassling one of my customers. I saw. I wasn't pleased. If you do it again, I'll call the cops."

Toronto burst out laughing. "Oh, please. Spare me." He leaned forward and said, "You go ahead and do that. They'll come out here to look for me. And I'll wait for them."

The smile he gave Ben was one that would have given grown men nightmares, Sylvia thought. To Ben's credit, he didn't look away, didn't blink.

"After all, I'm a law-abiding citizen. Can you say the same for all of your . . . clients?"

A hiss escaped him. "I don't think I like you, Mr. . . . ?"

"Don't worry." With a friendly smile, he leaned back in the chair. "Not many people do. And as to your customer? You can say Bobby and I go way back, and he's got . . . problems. I'm sort of his probation officer."

Ben's lids flickered. "Probation officer. I wasn't aware Robert had a criminal record. If he's violating the conditions of his parole—"

"I said *sort of.* I help keep him in line, let him know when he's close to slipping. And I'm there to jerk him back in line if he thinks he might slip, or if I see it happening." Something dark moved through Toronto's eyes as he watched Ben. "You know what happens when somebody with the wrong kind of hungers slips, don't you, Benito?"

At that, the man went white.

"Get out," he snarled, shoving upward. But the cool, collected man was gone.

In his place stood a man who was scared and *pissed*. And there was hell in his eyes. Glaring at Toronto, he said again, "Get out *now*."

"I can't." He continued to watch Ben, his eyes unreadable. "They slip sometimes. Even those who try not to, don't they?"

Ben swallowed.

Sylvia felt sick to her stomach. She could hear the poor guy's heartbeat, all but taste his terror . . . and his humiliation. "Tor . . ."

He ignored her.

"Sometimes, they don't care if they slip, though."

"I don't let those in my house," Ben said, his voice raspy and low. He leaned forward, desperation and defiance in his eyes. "I made this place to help, you stupid son of a bitch, don't you get it?"

"I think I do." Toronto rose from the chair, slid his hands into his pockets, and the menace in the air faded.

Sylvia didn't even know how he did that—sucked all of that back inside him. It shouldn't be possible, but he did it and he managed to stand there like some easygoing dude who didn't have the ability to turn deadly in a microsecond.

"I think I get it better than you realize. And I just realized something . . . you hate them." Toronto glanced around that sleek, sexy office and then looked back at the man with pity in his eyes. "You hate this place, you hate this job, you hate what you do and you hate those 'customers' out there more than I do. You just hide it."

Ben stilled. Then, he closed his eyes and turned away. "Who in the fuck are you? What in the hell do you want?"

"I'm looking for somebody." Toronto glanced at Sylvia.

She reached into her pocket and drew out Pulaski's picture,

rising from her chair. Like she was approaching a wounded animal, she eased up to the desk. When Ben tensed, she simply waited until he turned to face her. "This man. Do you know him?"

Ben's face darkened. "Alan Pulaski. I don't know him, never have. But his kind wouldn't have been welcome here." He took a deep breath and then looked up, studied Sylvia for a long moment before shifting his gaze to Toronto. "There are varying degrees of men who fantasize about children. There are those who will offend, those who will hurt. And then there are those who have the fantasies . . . but they control the urge, never cross the line. I opened this place to give them a safe place to indulge in those fantasies."

"What if indulging them here tempted them to go over the line?"

A dark smile slanted the mortal's face. "I'm good at recognizing that, too."

Violence had a scent. She wondered what had inspired the rage she sensed within him. But they'd intruded on enough of his secrets. Let him keep this one. "So you've never had him in here."

"He wouldn't have been welcome. I would have made sure he realized it, too, should he ever try to come in." He gave them a cold smile and Sylvia decided that the mortal had a pretty decent freaky thing of his own—if she'd been human, that look in his eyes might have scared her. *Just what do you do*, she wondered, *about those who cross the line?*

Ben reached up and straightened his tie, smoothed the lapels of his already impeccable suit. "Was that all?"

"No." Toronto took the picture and handed it back to Sylvia and as easy as that, nudged her back into the passenger seat. "There is a . . . group of people who are getting a little heavy into their fantasy shit. I don't think it's fantasy anymore. Getting into hurting their partners and most of the partners are kids. I don't know if the kids are volunteering in exchange for money, if they are being forced into it or what. The only name I have is Kit, and it was happening at a house in Cordova. It's been shut down now, or maybe moved. Do you know anything about it?"

Ben looked away. "I can't say if I've heard the name Kit or not—you hear a lot of names in this business and it's best if you just forget them. But I did have somebody ask me if any of my boys would be interested in making extra money— they said 'anything goes' and I won't let my boys do that. If they go into it on their free time, I can't stop them, but I won't tell them, I won't mention it to them and I won't let them be approached on my property." He shrugged rest- lessly and moved over to the bar. "I hope you don't mind— actually, I don't care if you mind or not. I'm having a drink. I'm not offering you one." He splashed something into a glass—judging by the smell, it was whiskey, potent and expensive.

As he turned, he lifted it to his lips and sipped. "I can't say if any of them were approached off property. But if they went, it must not have been too bad. I would have heard."

"Are you sure?"

He glanced at Sylvia and then nodded. "Yes. The men here . . . they trust me. I make sure of it. And none of them have been hurt. That's another thing I watch for. I take care of them. It's my job."

Those last words were spoken with deep, intense passion. Sylvia felt an unexpected lurch in her heart. This man had been through hell. She had a bad suspicion about just what had happened, but it was his private hell. She understood all about private hells, too.

"Is that all?" he asked, his voice dismissive.

"Yes." Toronto reached into his pocket.

"If you pull money out of that pocket, I'm going to cut your hand off," Ben said, his voice neutral. Cool.

Sylvia smiled. She hadn't expected to like anybody she met in this place. But she decided she might like Ben. He had balls.

Toronto laughed. "Okay. I won't pull out money. How about a card, though? If you see or hear anything about more of these parties, I'd appreciate if you'd let me know."

Ben watched with impassive eyes as Toronto approached the desk and laid the card down.

Hunters. Carrying business cards. Handing them out to

unsuspecting mortals. Shit, the world was a weird place, Sylvia mused.

"Why should I?" Ben asked after staring at the card for a long, silent moment.

"Because I think you have a good idea what happens when 'anything goes,' " Toronto said, his voice gruff. Too gruff.

Sylvia tensed and chanced a look into his eyes. But they were perfectly normal. A little too intense and that in and of itself was spooky, but they weren't all glow-y and that was good.

"Once I find out who is responsible for these . . . parties," Toronto continued. "I'm going to stop them. And I'm going to hurt the people responsible."

Ben picked up the card, studied it. Then he tucked it inside his pocket and nodded. "I'll think about it. If I hear anything."

CHAPTER 15

"How did you get all that dirt about him?" Sylvia asked once they'd hit Beale Street. It was quieter now, and she knew what that meant. She didn't have much time.

"I've had it for quite a while." He slid her a look and shook his head. "And no, I'm not telling you. He had a hellish time when he was a kid. Leave him alone."

She made a face at him. "I wasn't going to go give him the third degree or anything." Sympathy twisted in her heart, but she shoved it aside. No time for it now, no room for it. "You can tell he's got hell trapped inside him. If it was that bad, maybe somebody needs to pay."

"The guy did pay. Little Benito snapped when he was fifteen and killed him. It was his mom's little brother. Nobody knew. But Mom and Dad stood by him, even after the rest of his family tried to blame the kid."

"Everybody tries to blame the victim," Sylvia whispered.

"Sometimes even the victim." Toronto stared off into the night. "I've known about it since he started running the place. He's not doing anything illegal—the men who strip there *are* of age. They just don't look it. If it makes it easier for some to control whatever fucked-up fantasies they have?

Fine. And it makes it easier for me to keep an eye on a problem of mine."

"A problem?"

"Yeah." He sighed grimly. "The were I was talking to the other night—weak-ass son of a bitch. The Change does bad things to people. Can warp the hell out of them. He'd always liked them young—the pretty-boy college type was his favorite. But the Change made it worse, twisted him."

"The Change usually doesn't make them want things they didn't already want." She stared off into the night.

"It can warp the mind something awful, though. Especially if it's somebody who never should have been turned to begin with—Bobby shouldn't have been. But feral wolves don't care. They just attack. That's a different problem, for a different night. We need to talk to some of Ben's dancers. See if any of them were approached. By who. Where. See if they have names." He pulled out his phone. "I've got a list of them actually. Although it will be easier to hit them tonight. You can do the whammy on them. I'll just make them piss their pants. Both can make them talk, but I'd prefer the subtle approach."

Sylvia glanced at the sky. "No time tonight. I need to get back to my place."

He watched her for a second and then said, "And that's . . . close?"

Sylvia just stared at him. He smiled. "I didn't think so. I've got a better idea. I know a place—we use it sometimes when we have . . . guests."

"I don't want sanctuary with the fucking Master," she said, curling her lip at him. She needed to be away from him. Very desperately. "I have a place."

"I'm sure you do. But if it's outside the city . . . and I bet it is . . . then you're wasting time traveling that we could be using to investigate." He shrugged and said, "And it's not sanctuary at the Enclave. This is neutral ground—Rafe doesn't own it, but it's vamp-outfitted. You can sleep safe from the sun, and it's only three miles from here. So as soon as you're able to be out tomorrow night, we can hit the streets."

Shit. Shifting her eyes away from him to the dark streets,

she scowled and resisted, barely, the urge to kick at the ground. He wasn't lying—she'd know if he was. And shit, she'd already figured there was a vamp-safe haven somewhere around here. Most decent-sized towns had them, and if there was an established Hunter presence, it was pretty much a given.

It made sense—of course, that was part of the problem. He was making sense, he was easy, or easy enough, to work with. And damn it, they were spinning their wheels.

"Fine," she muttered. "But it's just for tonight."

He smiled at her. The light glinted off his eyes, making them impossible to read. But still, it was enough to send a shiver down her spine.

"SHIT. How many dancers does he *have*?"

Sylvia was *tired*. Vamps weren't prone to headaches but she felt like her head was about to split into a hundred pieces.

A hand came up, brushed against the nape of her neck. "He rotates between twenty or so. Most of them are going to school and shit and he watches their hours. We've only got one more."

"Twenty?" She frowned at him. "I've only seen thirteen." Thirteen—had to pry open thirteen minds, hold them steady and then release them. No wonder her head was killing her. This was more mind-twisting shit than she was used to.

"I talked to some earlier while you slept." He shrugged as they jogged down the steps and headed north.

"You talked to some earlier." Narrowing her eyes, she caught his arm and glared at him. "I thought we were working this *together.*"

"We are." Toronto crossed his arms over his chest, his blue eyes glinting with something that just might have been the edge of temper.

She stared right back. *Come on, wolf.*

"You had to sleep. I rested for two hours—that's all I needed. Did you want me to twiddle my thumbs and pretend we're not trying to find a killer?"

"Smart-ass." She started to walk once more, long angry strides. What if he'd found him? Would he have . . .

"I would have tied his sick ass up and delivered him to you," Toronto said quietly. "I made you a promise. I don't plan on breaking it if I can help it."

"Wow." She rolled her eyes and muttered, "*That* is reassuring."

"You want guarantees, and I can't promise them. For all we know, the bastard is dead in a ditch somewhere—and if he is, I hope something ripped his dick off and choked him with it first. But if we find him alive, I plan on keeping my end of the deal."

Stopping on the sidewalk to look at him, she studied his face. That pretty, pretty face with those impossibly blue eyes. "Okay, then. Let's finish this up."

"Y ou." The boy was the last one on Toronto's list, and the minute Toronto had appeared on his step, he looked nervous. "I've seen you."

Toronto lifted a brow. "Yeah? I hear that. Maybe I got a familiar-looking face."

Sylvia bit back a snort at that. He had the most *un*familiar face she'd ever seen. When the dancer looked at her, she smiled.

He didn't bother smiling in return, just shifted his gaze back to Toronto. "No. You've been at the club. I've seen you talking to one of the guys there. He's scared of you."

This isn't going well. Sylvia had no doubt Toronto was picking up on the kid's fear the same as she was—if he had too much fear, she'd never be able to grab his mind without damaging him. Fear left marks. Pushing in front of the were, she caught the kid's eyes—shit. He wasn't a kid, not really. But she had a hard time looking at him and thinking *adult*.

Especially as that fear grew larger, and larger . . .

"Hey, we're not here to cause you any problems. We just need to find somebody," she said. When he looked back at her, she reached out, caught his mind, but gently. *Calm down . . . we're not going to hurt you. Calm down . . .*

Just a little of the fear receded. Somebody had done a number on him.

Reaching inside her pocket, she pulled out the picture of Pulaski. "We need to find this guy. Do you know him?"

At the very first look, his face went white. And he started to scream.

"S HIT."

"Yeah." They stood outside, watching as an ambulance drove away.

The man had shattered. One look at Pulaski's picture and he had broken. Now he was being taken away, his mother in the ambulance with him as he lay there, all but catatonic.

"Any idea what was done to him?" Toronto asked quietly.

"No. I can't pick up on thoughts well. All I could tell was that he was afraid, and he has been for a while. Somebody hurt him." She tugged the picture out of her pocket, staring at it with distaste. One more sin to lay at this bastard's feet. "I don't know if it was him or not."

"He's too old for Pulaski. I've got him at twenty-two."

Sylvia sighed. "He barely looks old enough to shave." Her heart hurt for him and she wanted to kick herself . . . she'd done that. One look at this picture and she'd reduced that kid to a screaming, terrified mess.

"You didn't do it."

Through her lashes, she stared at Toronto. "Didn't I?"

"No. You didn't." He took the picture from her, tucked it back into her pocket. Curling his fingers in the lapels of her jacket, he tugged her closer.

She thought about pulling back, but instead, she let him, until they were standing just a breath away. "You didn't," he said again. "Maybe it brought the memories to the fore, but they were already there and it looks like they were choking him."

"If he wanted to hide from it, he had that right." Her own memories sought to choke her often enough, rising out of the dark at the worst moments. She could understand the need to hide away from them.

"As broken as he is, if he doesn't deal with them, he'll do

something desperate . . . you can see it in his eyes, all but smell it on him."

Troubled, she stared down the street. They were lost in the shadows, hiding away while they watched over the boy they'd just terrified. It bothered her, she realized. A hell of a lot more than she wanted to admit.

"We can try to rationalize it all we want," she finally said, shaking her head. "But we hurt him. Maybe the memories were already there, but we were the ones who cut him open and forced them out."

Pulling away, she started down the street. "And it was all for nothing, too. Not that it would be any easier if we'd found out anything, but if we'd learned *something . . .*" Shit. She didn't know if it would have helped or not. The one thing she did know—those screams would haunt her. For a long, long while.

A s she mounted her bike, Toronto caught up with her. He looked as grim-eyed as she felt. "We lost the night," he said.

"Really? I hadn't noticed." Shit, her head was killing her. A wave of weakness swamped her as she swung her leg over the bike, but she ignored it. Nothing that wouldn't ease after a decent feeding; there was bagged blood at the safe house. Yum.

A hand came around her arm, steadying her. "You're beat. You pushed yourself too hard with the mind thing, didn't you?"

"No." *Yes.* Jerking her head toward the bike, she said, "Get on. We need to move. I want to feed before I crash for the day."

"I think you should crash with me."

"No." She clenched her jaw, ignoring the feel of him along her back. "I don't think I should. The vamp safe house worked fine." It had been fine—technically. A room the size of a small bathroom, a small cot. It had been like a damn cell, but it did the job.

"My place is better . . . and it's closer. You wouldn't have to do bagged blood, either. If you're feeling so lousy you're swaying, you need a better hit than bagged blood can give you anyway." He leaned forward, resting his chin on her shoulder. "We're going to my place."

"I'm pretty sure I didn't go and turn over my free will to you," she drawled. *Hell, no.* That just wasn't an option. She was having a hard enough time just keeping her distance from him, trying not to stare, trying not to wonder.

And now he expected her to be *alone* with him? And feed from him? *Again?*

Just the thought of it was enough to make her want to start drooling. *No, no, no—*

"It's got nothing to do with free will." Still sitting there, his chin on her shoulder, his hands on her hips, he turned his face into her hair. "You need a place for the day. I've got a place . . . and it's not at the Enclave. You need to feed, and you'll do better if it's something other than bagged blood; we both know that. It's just common sense. You're a sensible type, right?"

I used to think so. But if she was *sensible*, she would have found a way to avoid being on her bike with a werewolf who made her head hurt, who managed to make her undead heart pound and who also made her toes curl. Sensible vampires stayed away from troublesome things like that.

And yet here she was, about ready to go stay at his place. Worse, she was all but salivating at the thought of feeding from him again. It wasn't *just* the hunger doing it, either. Feeding was rarely intimate for her. But it had sure as hell been intimate with him.

As his lips brushed against her neck, she shivered. "Do you really need to think it through that hard? A lousy meal and a room that's not much bigger than a closet, or you can come with me, sleep in a real bed after you've had a real meal . . ."

No. Sighing, she pulled away from the curb. "Sometimes, you really make me want to hit you."

"Only sometimes?" He squeezed her waist. "Hell, that means we could be like the best of friends. Most people who know me want to hit me all the time."

"Give me a few more days." Although if she had her way, she'd speed up time and just get this job *done*. Before she got too attached to him. He was already too easy for her to be around—and that was something that just never should have happened.

"Where in the hell do you live? I'm tired."

S OMETHING had her pulling away from him. He wanted to find it and hurt it.

He wanted her to explain it to him, so he could fix it for her. Instead, he stayed quiet as she drove, giving directions when she needed to turn but otherwise holding his tongue.

What am I doing?

He had no clue—none at all.

She was tired. She needed to feed. This made plenty of sense and yeah, Toronto knew he could argue that with anybody. But it had nothing to do with logic, and everything to do with the fact that he wanted her with him. At his place.

Where he could feed her, then tuck her into a bed and . . .

Stop it before you go thinking crazy stalker thoughts, he told himself.

Except he was already feeling slightly crazed over her. He didn't get like this over women. He liked sex, liked it a lot, but that was generally all he wanted when he was attracted to a woman.

Sex barely touched the surface of what he wanted to do with her, although that was definitely part of it. Touching her, stroking away whatever had brought the unhappiness to her, holding her until it all faded. Feeding her . . . fucking her. Then starting all over again.

And *none* of that was what he needed to be doing. Markland's dancers had been a bust—except this latest one. Toronto wasn't going to go adding to his misery, but there were other ways to get answers. He could start with that.

But instead, he was going back to his place.

CHAPTER 16

"Turn here."

A strange, heavy silence had fallen during the drive. It was a lovely one, even though the last few miles over the unpaved, rutted mess of a road were rough as hell. Still, it was a pretty drive, yet Toronto was just about certain Sylvia was completely unaware of it, maneuvering her bike completely on autopilot.

She was sad.

And hurting. He decided he didn't like that. It bothered him, on a lot of levels. Even the wolf wasn't happy. It rumbled within him, pacing and uncomfortable, but unsure of how to act.

Comfort wasn't something that came easily to him. It didn't want to come at all, but he couldn't stand to see her so sad, so full of pain and misery.

Reaching up, he cupped her cheek. "What hurts you?"

She looked away. "Nothing," she whispered. Gently, she nudged his hand out of the way and climbed off. "I've got some clothes stashed in my bike, but I'll need to go back to my place at some point or do laundry."

So that was how she wanted to play it. The misery was

still there, dark in her eyes and twisting his heart into knots. Climbing off the bike, he studied her averted face.

"You can wash whatever you need to wash here if you want," he said.

As her gaze cut his way, he grinned at her. "And if you feel like it, you can do mine. I never did like messing with laundry."

"Are you trying to make me want to hit you?" she asked conversationally. "Trying to be an ass?"

"Nah." He shrugged. "That comes naturally." There wasn't as much misery in her eyes; he decided it had burned off under the irritation. Much better. "Although if you want to go a round or two, we could. I wouldn't mind."

"Yeah. I bet." She grabbed a bag from her bike and then headed toward the house.

"It could be cathartic." As she slid him a sidelong look, he smiled. "Get rid of some of that tension—hot and sweaty action has a way of doing that."

Sylvia snorted and this time, when she looked at him, there was a glint of heat and humor in her eyes. The misery, wherever it had come from, was gone. "Don't worry, wolf. If I feel like getting hot and sweaty with you, I'll let you know."

I live for the day, he thought. Both he and the wolf inside him watched her with want.

*C*ATHARTIC . . .

Hell. *Cathartic* wasn't exactly the thought that came to mind when she thought of getting hot and sweaty with him.

And she wasn't thinking of fighting him, either, although that could be an experience.

No, when—

When? What in the hell am I thinking . . . when? If—if I get hot and sweaty with him, it's not going to be a therapeutic thing. As he opened the door and stepped aside to let her enter, she even tried to pretend she really hadn't made up her mind to sleep with him.

She was lying to herself—and she could happily continue

to do it for the next little while as she moved through the house. It was huge—she'd already seen that and the first look had also let her see enough to leave her scowling. Lots of big windows, lots of open spaces . . . where was she to sleep?

"There are rooms deeper inside the house."

Turning, she looked at him, saw him leaning against the doorway, the moonlight shining in to frame him, dancing along the hollows and planes of his face, turning his pale hair to silver. "Rooms?"

"For you to sleep." He shoved off the wall and held out a hand. "Come on."

Sylvia eyed the hand he held out—she didn't need to hold his hand to be shown around the house, did she? But was she so desperate to keep him from touching her that she couldn't accept it?

Yes.

That was an easy enough question to answer.

Damn it. *If we get hot and sweaty . . . if . . . if . . .*

Screw it.

It was going to happen, and as she stood there staring at him, she decided she wanted it to happen *now*. Because then she could relegate him to the sidelines, where he belonged. She could stop obsessing over him.

Life could go back to normal . . . right?

Placing her hand in his, she smiled. "Lead on."

The room he led her to was in the depths of the house, completely enclosed. Yet it was designed in a way that kept it from being anything remotely cagelike. As she moved past him into the room, she couldn't help but pause and stare. A huge oak bed, set on an elevated platform on the far wall, dominated much of the room. It was covered with a comforter that gleamed with colors of dull rust and gold, and those same colors were echoed in the pillows on the bed, in the art on the walls, in the sofa that waited in the small sitting area. That space was on the lower area, complete with a mini-bar, what looked like an electric fireplace, a huge, flat-screen TV and a coffee table. A small bookshelf was there as well.

Against the eastern wall there was a door, and she made her way over there, opened it and checked inside. A bathroom. There, she found one window, facing the heavily wooded area. Just under it was a huge tub that was almost big enough to swim in.

Turning, she lifted a brow. "You must have a few vampy friends that you really like if you have a setup like this."

"Sometimes somebody needs a place to crash." He came forward, his eyes resting on hers. "You know how we are. Not all of us play very well together and we need room. This is where I go when I need space. I figured it couldn't hurt to have the extra rooms, just in case."

He caught a lock of her hair and twined it around his finger. "You'll be able to sleep here."

"Yes." It shouldn't be such an erotic thing, seeing him play with her hair. But as he continued to do it, she felt that hot little ball of want in her belly flare hotter. Brighter.

Tossing her bag down, she reached up and wrapped her hand around his wrist. Under her thumb, she felt the strong, steady beat of his pulse. "Thanks for the room."

"Hmmm." His voice was a low, rough growl, and under her touch, his pulse raced harder. Then he moved closer, until his body was just a breath away from hers. "You need to feed."

"I'll let you know when I'm ready, wolf." Leaning in, she pressed her lips to his, nipping his lip lightly. "You won't be seducing me, Toronto—no grabby hands this time." She planned on being the one to grab him.

He hissed out a breath, his gaze turbulent . . . a summer storm.

The sight of it made her smile.

"I need a bath," she murmured, turning away.

If she was going to jump him, she planned on cleaning up first.

I T was frustrating as hell, he decided, to have a woman only a couple of dozen yards away, sitting in a hot tub full of water, a woman he wanted like he wanted to breathe, and knowing she'd laugh at him if he tried to go to her.

You won't be seducing me . . .

She meant it.

No grabby hands—

Shit. She'd given him the back off and he had to respect that. Until he could get her to change her mind.

About the grabby hands thing, the seducing her thing, because damn it, if he didn't have a taste of her, he'd lose his mind.

"You already have," he muttered.

Determined to distract himself, he grabbed the phone and put in a call to Rafe while he went about making himself something to eat. If he couldn't sate one hunger, he'd sate the other. A quick rundown about what had happened and he threw the name Kit in there.

"The only Kit I'm familiar with is a werewolf in Chicago—married to the Master there."

"No. It's a male—he's involved in this somehow."

Rafe was quiet. "Okay. We'll start looking around."

That managed to take up a whopping three minutes. Scowling, he stabbed at his steak as he flipped it over the grill. It was still rare when he was finished with it and that was how he wanted it. If he hadn't had Sylvia here, he would have gone hunting for his meal—he ached for it, but he didn't think it would do his seduction efforts any good if he went and ran down a deer and then tried to seduce her.

Not that she would be very surprised. She was a damned vampire.

But he was going to play the gentleman, eat his damned steak and then pretend to be a nice host—

Shit. This was going to try his control like nothing had done in years. Grumbling under his breath, he dumped the steak on a plate and cut into it, eating at the counter and trying to figure out the best way to handle Ms. Sylvia James. So far, they were working together okay. Right?

Two nights in and they hadn't tried to kill each other. She hadn't tried to strangle him or anything. That was practically a record. Sadly, he brought out the worst in people and had been known to provoke them after only a few hours. Usually on purpose, so he could be on his own once more. He liked working with her, though.

And they were slowly finding out information. The problem was they weren't finding it out fast and while he knew it worked that way, he could see the echoes of demons in her eyes. Something was pushing her hard on this case and he didn't know what.

Every now and then, he caught a glimpse of something in her eyes—something dark and achingly sad. Like earlier. It wasn't just sympathy for Pulaski's victims, although God knew, that would be enough.

There wasn't a level in hell hot enough for monsters like that one. Of course, Toronto had no problem trying to think up perfectly painful, brutal deaths, even knowing they wouldn't be bad enough.

But first they had to find him and figure out what he'd done with his victims.

Hearing a footstep, he looked up as he popped the last bite of the steak into his mouth. And he almost choked when he saw her standing there. Dumping the plate on the counter, he grabbed a glass of water he'd poured earlier and gulped it down like he was dying of thirst.

She was wearing one of his shirts.

Fuck, what was it about a woman in a man's shirt, anyway? How could they look so good in a stupid T-shirt?

"Hey." She leaned against the wall, a sly little smile on her lips, her hair hanging in damp, clinging ropes around her shoulders and back. "I guess I should have asked you, but I needed a shirt. I don't usually pack pajamas."

"Ah . . ."

Pushing off the wall, she shrugged a shoulder and said, "Can't really wander around here naked, right?"

Naked. She couldn't wander around here naked? Skimming his eyes over her lush curves, the sleek muscles, he met her eyes. "If I say I want the shirt back, does that mean you'll wander around naked? If so, I'm very tempted to tell you that you can't have the shirt."

The smile on her mouth widened. "Can I get some water?"

"Sure." Water. He needed to get her water. And then he needed to get his hands busy. Otherwise he was going to think about trying to touch her, even though she'd told him to back off. He had to go about this differently. Had to actually work at the seduction thing, and he'd probably have to work overtime since she was determined that he *wouldn't* be seducing her. As he grabbed a glass, he noticed that his fingers were shaking.

This woman had him shaking.

This is bad. He had to get a grip.

After getting her some water from the fridge, he turned around and held it out. Was it his imagination or was there a devilish glint in those liquid, dark eyes? Her fingers brushed his as she accepted the glass and that slight touch sent a burning jolt through him.

Hell. He needed to get some distance between them and try to wrestle his body back under control.

Try. Turning around, he gripped the marble counter with one hand and tried to yank his body back under the chokehold of control, the one he had to use on nights of the full moon when he *couldn't* shift—that iron control that he could command, when he needed it.

But he was failing.

Hell. He needed to get out of here. Out of here, away from her . . . clear his head. He'd shift and go for a run. A good hard run would help. It always did. Taking the edge off was the best thing for him. Actually, that needed to be the first thing he did—

Mind made up, he forced himself to let go of the counter so he could gather up the dishes from his meal. Still not looking in Sylvia's direction, he rinsed the few dishes off and put them in the dishwasher. He had somebody come out once a month and clean for him, but that didn't include doing the dishes.

Cleaning up after himself was a necessity, even if he was suddenly in a mad hurry to get out of there. Werewolves, like other shifters, like the vamps, tended to be pretty fastidious. It was a side effect of having overly sensitive noses.

"Can you go ahead and feed? I need to go for a run and I won't be back before the sun rises." He kept his eyes focused on the mundane chore of straightening up, although it really didn't require that much attention. If he was looking at his hands, he wasn't going to be looking at her, though, and he needed to avoid looking at her. Especially since she needed to feed . . . *fuck*.

There was a whisper—a familiar one—of cotton against flesh.

Turning his head slightly, he watched something black and soft fall to the floor.

His T-shirt.

His heart jumped into his throat, lodged there for about five seconds and made it impossible to breathe. Then it settled back in his chest, beating about two hundred beats a minute, he figured as he shut the dishwasher, still staring at the puddle of black cotton on the floor in front of him.

His palms were sweating as he lifted his head and stared at Sylvia, standing eighteen inches away, wearing nothing more than her damp hair and that devilish, cocky little smile.

"I don't get seduced," she said quietly. "I might decide to seduce somebody, or I might just decide to have wild and crazy sex with them. But I don't get seduced."

She closed the distance between them and reached out, trailed her fingers along the front of his shirt. "You still want to go for a run, Toronto?"

He couldn't speak. For the life of him, he couldn't say a damn word.

So instead, he gathered that dark, silky hair in one hand and slanted his mouth over hers. As she met his kiss, he wrapped his free arm around her waist and hauled her against him. Naked, her skin still warm from the bath, she fit him perfectly, those amazing curves aligning next to his body like she'd been made for him.

He growled against her lips as she rocked against him.

"I thought you said no grabby hands," he muttered against her mouth.

"I wasn't being completely honest . . . I planned to do plenty of grabbing. I just wanted to do it my way." She pulled back a fraction, staring into his eyes, clear challenge written on her face. "Is that a problem?"

She was in his arms, naked. "Hell, no."

"Good." A pleased smile curled her lips as she stroked her hands along his waist, then dipped them under his shirt, pushing it up as she went until she could strip it away completely.

As it fell to the floor by the other one, she eased back, staring into his eyes for a long moment before lowering her gaze. Toronto held still as she lifted her hands and curved them over his shoulders, stroking down, her fingers learning the planes and ridges of his body. When she reached the small ring piercing his left nipple, she paused. Lifting a brow, she touched it, tugging it lightly. "Silver, Toronto?"

He shrugged. "I got bored one night."

"So you pierced yourself with silver. You trying to poison yourself?" She continued to toy with it, her skeptical gaze lingering on his face.

"I'm too strong for that little bit to poison me." He grinned at her, trying not to react while she played with the ring. It shouldn't feel that damn good, he knew it. But while he was too strong for the ring to poison him, that bit of silver piercing his flesh did make him damn sensitive there and it was almost painfully erotic to have her tugging on it like that.

"So you did this because you were bored?" A wicked grin curved her lips. "You get bored a lot? What else did you pierce?"

Her gaze dropped low and a visceral, blistering punch of heat raced through him even as he instinctively winced. "Not there, sweetheart." Although if it felt like that when she toyed with it . . . ?

Besides, if he had silver piercing his cock, he couldn't put it in her body. And he planned on having his cock inside her very, very soon. Reaching up, he covered the piercing with his hand, nudging her fingers aside. "I should take it out."

"Nah." She pressed a kiss to his chest and murmured, "I like it. Silver won't bother me much unless I'm stabbed with it or I get it stuck inside me."

Toronto lowered his hand, flicking a glance to the ring. No. It wouldn't stab her, but . . .

"Stop worrying." She bit him lightly, then touched her fingers to one of the scars on his chest. "Silver?"

"Yeah."

He had a lot of scars, she realized. A lot. Frowning, she studied what looked like bite marks marring his arms, his chest—they'd healed, but the indentations from teeth still lingered. "Wolf attack," she whispered.

"I'm a were." He shrugged.

But there were so many bites—shit, he looked like they'd tried to turn him into a fucking chew toy. Forcing it aside, she continued on her study of his scarred, beautiful body. One scar in particular didn't seem to match . . . it wasn't silver-made, she didn't think—just didn't look right. Rubbing her thumb along the ridged, uneven line, she slid him a look, quirking a brow at him.

"Can't tell ya there." He grinned and added, "I'd have to kill ya."

"Cute." Leaning in, she pressed her lips to his and scraped her nails along his belly.

He jumped, caught her wrist. "Hey."

"You're ticklish."

Before she could do it again, he caught both wrists and whirled her around, shifting so that he had her arms pinned behind her back. "No tickling," he muttered, dipping his head to press his mouth against the curve of her neck. The scent of her, warm and sweet, flooded his head and he growled, desperate for more. Moving her wrists to one hand, he boosted her up onto the counter, keeping her hips at the edge.

He flicked a look at the clock. Too little time left before dawn. Forty minutes, tops.

Not enough time . . .

"Let my hands go," she said, twisting against his grip.

There wasn't any fear in her lurking under her voice. But he remembered the fear he'd sensed on her before—all at the mention of the isolation chambers. Keeping his voice light, he loosened his grasp and said, "No more tickling."

"I'll stop. For now . . ." Her hands came up and he stilled as she went for the band that held his hair back.

As it fell down around his shoulders, she said, "You really should be shot for having hair like this, you know. Guys just shouldn't have hair this beautiful."

He gathered up her hair, as dark as his was pale. "Mine's just hair. Nothing special about it. Your hair, though . . ." He wrapped the dark, shining mass around one wrist and used it to arch her head back. "Your hair is beautiful. I've thought about holding it like this, seeing you on your knees . . ." He grinned at her.

"Pervert." She reached down and stroked him through his jeans. "If anybody goes on their knees today, I think it should be you."

"Hmmm. That's fair." And he heard her surprise as he did just that, tugging her closer to the edge of the counter and nudging her thighs wider.

Tight black curls covered her sex, and there were already beads of moisture there. He tasted her there first. She slammed one hand against the counter, her body sagging backwards. As he used his tongue to part her, she whispered his name, a low, broken rasp of sound. Then he licked her— hot, rich and wild.

With teeth and tongue, he worked her close to the edge. He wanted to feel her climax, hard and fast, and then again, slow and easy. But he was too aware of the coming sunrise, too aware of her. Once he felt her body tensing, once he felt her moving closer and closer to that edge, he stood and gathered her in his arms.

"Bed," he whispered as her lashes lifted so she could glare at him. "We finish this in bed. Because I plan on having you at least twice before the sun rises."

"We'll have each other," she said.

And once they reached the room she would use, she made good on that promise. He went to lay her on the bed, but she rolled to her knees and made quick work of his pants, stripping them away and then pulling him down, nudging him onto his back.

There was a challenge in her eyes, one that all but dared him to say otherwise.

Hell, she was out of her mind if she thought he'd have any problems with her riding him.

He'd ride her . . . later.

As long as he got a taste of her. And another. And another—

She came down on him, settling one knee on either side of his hips. He reached down, curving his hands around her, gripping that round, perfect ass as she curled her fingers around his cock, held him steady.

And as she took him inside her, she watched it . . . as he watched her.

"Look at me," he muttered, tugging on her hair, guiding her gaze to his.

"I am looking at you," she teased, but the lightness in her tone was forced—he felt it, tasted it. She paused, teasing the sensitive skin of his cock with her fingertips. "This is you, right? And it's a nice piece of you, too . . ."

"Sylvia," he growled.

Her gaze swept up to meet his. And he felt some icy, lonely part of his heart soften at the look in her eyes. A look she hid almost immediately. Vulnerable . . . something soft, something gentle, something that made him think she was about as alone as he was.

"That's it," he whispered, sliding his hands up her back and hooking them over her shoulders. He tugged her down so that her upper body was pressed to his. "I want to see you . . . feel you. Touch you."

S HE wasn't much for seductions, but this . . . this was worse. It wasn't a seduction. It was deeper, something more. Something powerful. It terrified her. A seduction could be purely physical . . . This left her stripped bare.

And she couldn't turn away. Couldn't pull back.

As she rocked against him, her heart ached, skittering into a slow, irregular rhythm. Cupping his cheek in her hand, she stared into pale blue eyes.

He swelled inside her and she cried out. Her fangs pulsed. Ached.

Then, as though he sensed that other hunger was raging out of control, he cupped the back of her head and guided her mouth to his neck. "Bite," he growled against her neck.

And the damned wolf, like he knew what it would do to her, *he* bit her, sinking his teeth into her shoulder, hard enough to hurt, hard enough to draw blood . . . hard enough to drive her mad.

"Tor . . ." She shuddered.

His hand pressed the back of her head again and she struck, sinking her teeth deep, deep into him, instinctively seeking out not the vein, but the areas around it, intent on drawing it out as long as she could.

The orgasm slammed into her and she couldn't scream.

His arms tightened around her and beneath her, his body stiffened and arched, one long, lean bow—then he started to move faster, driving himself deep inside, his cock pulsing, swelling.

And his blood—

Oh, his blood . . .

Beneath her chest, she felt a vibration. Growling. He was growling. Disoriented, she made herself lift her head, licking the blood from her lips. And she found herself staring into eyes that glowed and swirled. Power came off him in waves—all that power, he'd kept it banked.

And now, it wrapped around them both like a heavy, warm cloak.

"Syl . . ." he rasped.

Then his eyes closed, and a long, racking shudder took his body.

As he climaxed, she sank down against him, her brain whirling, her body humming.

Damn.

If that was what sex with a Master was like, she needed to be careful . . . She tried to tell herself it was all about what he was.

But even as she did, she knew she lied. It was him. It was all about him. And she had a bad feeling she was already developing an addiction to him.

CHAPTER 17

"Knock, knock . . ."

Toronto heard the voice.

He recognized it and once he took a deep breath, he even recognized the scent.

What really threw him was the fact that he hadn't heard her coming *before* she'd got to his front door. She was quiet. She wasn't *that* quiet.

Swearing, he climbed out of the bed and grabbed his jeans. Behind him, Sylvia sat up, her hair spilling over one pale shoulder, framing her face. She was flushed, thanks to his blood pounding through her system, and she was beautiful and perfect and damned if he didn't want to fall right back into bed with her.

"Somebody's here," she said, her face strangely blank.

"Yes. A friend." He jerked his jeans on and headed out into the hall.

"Not my friend."

He wasn't surprised when Sylvia joined him thirty seconds later, wearing jeans and a T-shirt, her breasts naked under it. No bra. But he saw the knife in her hand. Sighing, he said, "She's not a threat, sweetheart."

"She got here without *either* of us realizing it. She snuck up on us. That's a threat," she muttered, shoving her tangled hair back from her face.

"No. That's just Angel." He caught her arm and pulled her to a stop. "Trust me. Angel isn't going to hurt you, try to hurt you, or anything. But she's . . ." He paused and tried to think of the right explanation. "Angel's kind of weird. She was attacked when she was a kid, survived it. But she was kind of different before that."

"Different how?"

"You'll see." It was a good thing she'd fed, though. Angel sometimes had a disturbing effect on vampires.

S YLVIA had spent months as a prisoner after she'd been changed. Hell, not a prisoner. A *slave*. A thing. He'd reduced her to nothing but a thing, starving her for so long it had affected her on a basic level—it was why she wasn't as strong as some vamps, why she couldn't take as much sun.

He'd had fun, knowing he was toying with her and damaging her in a way that would leave her vulnerable. But she hadn't been the only one. He'd had other . . . toys. One of them had been a girl. She'd been younger than Sylvia, probably only fourteen or fifteen when he'd gotten ahold of her, and whatever atrocities he'd done to her had frozen her forever at that stage.

She hadn't been a vampire, nor had she been human.

And she'd . . . smelled so good. So unbearably good. Sylvia had spent weeks across from that woman-child, with the hunger all but driving her mad, and the promise of the sweetest meal . . .

She knew if she had gotten out, she would have killed the female. Not out of any desire to harm her, but because she wouldn't have been able to control herself. But then one day, the strange woman had pissed him off. Sylvia had listened to her tortured screams for hours as he methodically, and slowly, killed her.

In all the years since then, Sylvia had met perhaps two

others who had been like that girl and she'd kept a very, very wide berth. But now, as she trailed along behind Toronto, she caught that first whisper of scent. Wine-rich and intoxicating. Hunger burned inside her, even though she'd already fed, and fed well.

She tensed when he reached for the door and as he opened it, she saw him slide her a quick glance. If she hadn't been watching for it, she wouldn't have seen the muscles in his body tense.

The door opened, revealing a slender blonde. She was average height, maybe five foot six, and she looked like she belonged on a basketball court in a cute cheerleader uniform, shaking a pair of pom-poms or something, Sylvia thought. *That's it, focus on the inane—anything but how damn good she smells.*

Anything but how easy it would be to lunge, grab, feed—

A smile curved the blonde's lips. "Probably not as easy as you think, lady."

Sylvia blinked. She hadn't said a damn thing.

"Nah. You don't have to." The girl reached up and tapped her temple. "I'm just a little bit psychic."

Sylvia fell back a step, the burning hunger turning to ice.

"A little?" Toronto echoed. "Saying she's a little bit psychic is kind of like calling the Mississippi a little bit of a crick." He cocked a brow at the girl and then looked back at Sylvia. "It doesn't seem that vamps have any natural immunity to her abilities, either. I'd think if you don't project too loudly, it might help, but I don't know."

"It helps." Without waiting for any kind of invitation, the woman sauntered inside, her hands tucked inside her back pockets, her eyes locked on Sylvia's face. "Makes it a little more of a murmur. I can ignore murmurs a lot easier."

"Why don't you just ignore it *all*?" Sylvia snapped.

"For me, it's a lot like trying to not hear the music some idiot kid is blasting at maximum volume as he drives down the street." She shrugged. "I tune it out for the most part, and after I'm around somebody for a while, I can mostly filter their voices out. But newer people . . . it's not so easy."

Sylvia lifted a brow. "Try harder."

"Angel . . ." Toronto slid between them when the woman might have said something.

Angel? Sylvia rolled her eyes. What a name.

She tried to ignore how close he was standing to the woman now. Too close. Sylvia frowned, edging around the room and watching the two of them. He was smiling at the girl—a weird smile, too. Something that looked torn between amusement and frustration. She didn't like it. Not at all.

"What are you doing here?" Toronto asked.

"A couple of things." She shrugged absently, her gaze roaming around the room. "Rafe had Josiah go out to that house."

"Josiah?" Toronto frowned, then nodded. "He went to check the scent thing, didn't he?"

"Yeah. Apparently it's all messed up. Josiah was almost delirious with joy—he hasn't been that happy since they cancelled *Buffy the Vampire Slayer*. He's running some samples from the yard and the house, but basically, it's used to cover scent—actually, it *erases* scent. Some sort of plant base is in it—he thinks it's in the mint family. There are some enzymes in there that he thinks are responsible for erasing the scent trail, although he hasn't gotten that detailed yet. He said it will take a few days to get anything final, but any evidence that we might have found? You can thank the mystery chemical."

Sylvia watched them, mystified. Mystery chemicals. Enzymes. Plant base. Shit. This was like watching *CSI: Vampire Unit*. Or the Horticulture Unit.

Angel shot her a grin and then looked back at Toronto. "You asked about somebody named Kit."

"Yeah. Did Rafe know something about him?"

Angel shrugged a shoulder and brushed past Toronto, sauntering into the living room. She came within a few inches of Sylvia—close enough that the hunger started to whisper inside her once more. Hot and sweet. *One taste . . .*

Sylvia scented the air just once, felt her control trembling. As she did so, the blonde looked her way. A smile curved her lips and if she wasn't mistaken, those blue eyes glowed.

"You can handle it," Angel murmured.

"Arrogant little bitch." Sylvia shook her head.

Angel just shrugged. "You live with vamps, you get an idea what they look like when the hunger is riding them hard. You also know which of them are close to the breaking point. You aren't. You just think you are."

Sylvia stilled. "Keep your fingers out of my head."

"I'm not in your head. All of that is written in your eyes." Angel smiled and then settled on a chair, crossing one leg over the other.

"Angel . . . what does Rafe have to say about Kit?"

"How would I know?" Angel shrugged. "I didn't ask him. I just talked to Josiah earlier."

Toronto closed his eyes and muttered, "I don't need another crazy cryptic chick in my life." Without explaining that comment, he sat on a chair across from Angel and rubbed his hands over his face and then focused on her face again. "Come on, Angel. Help us bumbling simpletons out. I'm not connecting the dots here. Are you here about Kit or not?"

"I am." She rested her chin in her hand and grinned at him. "But Rafe doesn't know anything about him. For that matter, I don't. I was back at the house—heard Lindsey mention the name and I wanted to . . ."

Her voice trailed off and she leaned forward, her gaze unfocused.

"Angel?"

Sylvia moved deeper into the room. The tension in the air was almost electric—she could feel it, all but taste it. The hairs on her arms, the back of her neck stood on edge and if lightning had started to crack outside, it wouldn't have surprised her.

Drawn inside by some force she couldn't name, she found herself sitting on the table just a few feet away from Angel. Then the blonde closed her eyes. Sylvia frowned, rubbing her arms. She was cold for some reason. Very cold—

Angel opened her eyes. And that blue held an eerie, eerie glow . . .

She touched Sylvia's arm and Sylvia hissed as electricity

crackled between them. "There's a connection," Angel murmured. "It's there. I can't find it yet."

Her eyes met Sylvia's—the jolt from it rocked Sylvia clear to her toes. "Some of us change with age—it doesn't always have much to do with the Change. We can't blame all our failings on that." Her lashes drifted low for a moment, a harsh sigh escaping her. "Some of us break . . . because we break ourselves. We let failures, fears, all of it fester inside until it's a poison that turns to madness."

And then, she rose from the chair, walked past Sylvia, past Toronto, headed for the door. At the door, she paused and said, "But there are others who become more. We become better." The eerie glow left her eyes and she turned away.

"Wait!" Sylvia shot to her feet, rushing for the other woman.

Angel closed the door behind her.

"I said, *wait.*"

But Toronto caught her arm before she cleared the room. "Let her go," he said. There was an exasperated look on his face as he stared after the blonde.

"She knows something, damn it," Sylvia said, jerking against his hold.

"Not yet, she doesn't." They listened as the van outside started up. "Something's probably coming to her, but it's not like doing math with *two + two*. She's doing a puzzle and a third of the pieces are still missing. She'll get the big picture, but for now, she's got to go on the few pieces she has."

I T was harder than hell to concentrate that day.

Angel had no intention of screwing this up and she knew she needed to focus—there was a lot riding on this, and not just because it was her first chance to prove to Rafe that she could be useful around the Enclave. That was a minor concern, in the scheme of things.

Kids were being hurt.

People had died.

And all of it was tied to this place—she'd felt that the minute she stepped inside. Others were hiding it and that painted a bigger problem—it took power to hide this kind of stuff from a Hunter, and that spelled bad things. Rafe's control of the land was being threatened, being tested and if he couldn't prove he could hold that control, the other predators around here would rise up against them. There would be bloodshed. Lots of it. And if it happened *here*, it would happen in other places.

Personally, that mattered to Angel because her husband was one of Rafe's lieutenants. She also didn't like the idea of her friends having to go to war, didn't like the idea of the mortals who'd get caught in the middle.

But her brain was clogged today—it kept spiraling down a path of memories that wasn't her own. She saw a newspaper. An article about a dead child—Angel recognized him. One of Alan Pulaski's victims—Pulaski, the man Toronto was hunting. Other dead children. Then a longer spiral, like a dark vortex, sucking her back through time and then she was trapped, chained in a room, while the hunger tore into her and a boy stared at her through a series of bars.

Locked. Locked in a room while a boy stared at her and cried.

There was another boy with him.

Familiar—the boy looked familiar.

I'm sorry . . .

I'll get you out . . . die trying . . .

And screams—long, tortured screams. Guilt, and misery—

". . . any time today?"

A slight vibration jerked her back to the here and now. Angel looked up and saw the teacher staring at her. It was "Tank" Edwards. Mr. Edwards, she was supposed to call him. He taught the honors English course and she'd decided from the get-go she didn't like him—he'd checked out her ass as she left the classroom yesterday.

"I was asking if you knew the answer." He gave her a faint smile and then shifted his gaze away. "Perhaps—"

Angel heard the echo of the question he'd asked drift from the mind of the student next to her. She could have just stayed quiet. It didn't matter if he thought she was a slacker, and hell, she *had* been drifting off in la-la land. But she smiled at him and answered. The slight flicker in his eyes betrayed him.

Then he patted her shoulder. "Very good."

That light touch—

She had to fight not to tense. Not to react. Not to puke.

She'd been straight-up honest when she'd told Sylvia that most people were just too loud for her to block out their thoughts. There were others, though, who had a natural resistance to psychic skill. Their thoughts were on a quieter frequency. Before Angel had been bitten, before her body had undergone whatever weird physiological changes, those quieter frequencies would have likely been silent.

She heard them now, but it took physical contact and sometimes all she got was a rush of images, a blur that didn't always make sense.

That was what she got from Tank Edwards.

And as he moved past her, continuing with his random little questions, Angel sat there and tried to puzzle through what she'd picked up.

Very little was clear . . . but there was a man. One she recognized. He had somebody with him, and as that image solidified in her mind, Angel felt a few more pieces settle into place.

Time. She needed a little more time to let that image settle.

It was almost ready to form a whole.

Sighing, she bent over the book in front of her. She had a feeling Rafe . . . and Kel . . . wouldn't be happy with her. They'd wanted her to keep her focus *here*. Only here.

Not exactly my fault this thing is flying off in five different directions, now is it?

"H E's a jerk, isn't he?"

Angel looked up from her locker.

The redhead next to her smiled.

"Who?"

She rolled her eyes. "Mr. Edwards. He's a jerk."

Angel shrugged. "I've met worse." Then she wrinkled her

nose and said, "Although I think he might have been looking at my ass yesterday."

"Just don't ever stay after for tutoring. He'll check out your tits. And good luck trying to mention that to the staff. You get marked as a *problem child.*" She opened her locker and switched out her books. "I'm Rachel, by the way. I sit a few seats behind you."

"Angie." She pretended to think. "We're in French together, too, right?"

"Yep. At least that teacher isn't a sleaze."

Angel laughed. "Seems like they got them at every school."

Rachel sighed. "We've got more than we need, that's for sure." Something shifted in her eyes but then she smiled, shrugged. "I just stay away from the creeps."

You didn't stay far enough, did you?

Angel wanted to grab the girl, hug her. Something had happened to her. Something dark and awful . . . and when she'd tried to talk . . .

"Hello, Rachel."

A woman emerged from a classroom at the side.

"Hi, Ms. Braddock," Rachel whispered.

Braddock. Angel tucked that name in the back of her mind, even as she pretended to blithely ignore the woman—the look of her bothered Angel. She couldn't even say why. She just made her . . . itchy. Rachel was terrified. Still not looking at the woman, Angel hooked her arm through Rachel's. "So you think we could eat lunch together? I haven't really met anybody yet. New schools really, really suck."

Rachel stood there, like her feet were frozen. And Angel suspected it was because they were—the girl's very *thoughts* felt frozen. Frozen . . . and blurred. What the hell . . . Deliberately, Angel gave her a sharp psychic jab. It was something only another psychic could sense and the woman behind them was no psychic. She was *something*, but not psychic.

Rachel blinked, her gaze unfocusing and then refocusing on Angel's face. She smiled and then said, "Sure."

Angel glanced up, as if just noticing the teacher. "Hi!"

She gave the lady a bright, vacuous smile and then, after slamming her locker shut, they started to walk.

The farther they got from the woman, the less clouded, the less iced, the girl at her side felt.

What the hell . . .

"So." Angel smiled over at Rachel and asked, "Is there anything we can eat here that isn't completely toxic?"

As they rounded the corner, she glanced back.

The woman, Ms. Braddock, was still standing there. Watching.

Good. Angel could use a better look at her face. It gave her a better focus. It just made it that much easier to get a better lock.

CHAPTER 18

T RAPPED . . .

"I know where he keeps the keys."

She looked at the boy, uncaring. She cared even less now than she had a month earlier. It had been a month of hell— endless rapes, beatings . . . and worse.

They were no longer in California. He'd dragged them across the country, kept them locked up at all times. They were in Toronto now; and she was in hell. Trapped in a small cell, starved . . . little more than an animal. A desperate, desperate animal.

But the boy did not seem to realize it. Nor did he seem to notice the changes in her. He only stood there, watching her with pleading eyes, his surly friend at his back. *"Please, Sada—"*

"Boy, do not speak my name." She closed her eyes, wishing he would just leave. It was so hard to sit still with him there. Of late, even being around the women who brought her food and bathing water caused her pain. Caused such an awful hunger inside her.

She stared at him and saw blood.

As though realizing the danger, the boy at his back curled a hand over his friend's shoulder. *"We need to go."*

"But I have to tell her, Sol! I have to let her know—"

"You already tried." Although the two boys were likely of the same age, this one was bigger and stronger. He had older eyes. Wiser. Or perhaps he just wasn't as likely to trust anybody. He stared at Sada with an intent, watchful look in his eyes and as her gaze shifted to his, she saw the warning there.

Stay away, he warned.

She looked away, resting her head against the wall. As if he need worry. She had no way out of here.

So completely trapped—

"S HHH. . ." Toronto lay there, rubbing his hand down her back.

Whatever dreams were bothering her, they must be monstrous—usually a vampire's sleep was a little more placid than this. They weren't without dreams, but their bodies tended to conserve their energy for rest, leaving them almost trapped in the cage of their mind.

It took one hell of a dream to break that.

She tensed, her spine a long, rigid bow. Pressing his lips to her brow, he wished he could find a way to take those nightmares. They all had to live with them and he wasn't any more disposed to let somebody's nightmares get to him. But then again, he'd never lain in a bed with Sylvia James before . . . and she had already proven that she could tangle him into knots.

She threw out a hand, clenched into a fist. Catching it, Toronto brought it to his lips. "Rest, Sylvia . . . you're safe. Nobody's going to bother you here. You're safe." Still stroking her back, he continued to murmur to her until the tension drained from her body.

"I DON'T exactly have a witch *handy*, Angel," Rafe bit off, glaring outside. It was overcast, hot and humid as hell. It didn't much bother him, but it made people cranky and tempers short, which always made their work more fun.

Once they got through September, things would get easier, maybe, but he couldn't even think about that—he had bigger problems to deal with than hot tempers and stupid actions. He had to fix this fucking problem first, because if he didn't, there was going to be a lot more violence happening once the non-mortals around realized what had been happening here.

There was also the problem of the Council—they didn't like it when shit like this happened, and it had happened under his watch.

And now he apparently needed to call them up and request a witch? That was just the icing on the cake.

"You need to get a witch," Angel said again.

"So you've already told me . . ." Rafe let his voice trail off, but Angel didn't elaborate. Hell, he'd already pried all the information out of Paul's mind—that witch had caused problems, all right. Rafe had suspected he would, but he came in under the "peaceful existence" promise and as long as he'd sworn to abide by the laws of the Council, Rafe hadn't been able to touch him.

He'd broken those laws—a fact he very much regretted now.

"Look, we've got a witch involved already in custody—I've picked his brain apart and other than the fact that he threw a camouflage over things and had a few phone calls with some vamp, he hasn't done much, doesn't know much." Rafe stared out into the night, his skin crawling all over, his head itching. "Why should we get a witch here?"

"There's more going on," Angel said, her voice soft, but even over the phone Rafe could hear the certainty. "There's more . . . and I don't know if I'll be enough to untwist it. If you're looking for hard-and-fast answers, I can't give them to you. I just think a witch has a better chance at unraveling this."

From the doorway, he heard Toronto's voice. "Good call."

Rafe closed his eyes, unsurprised. He'd known the other Hunter was there. "Tor, I'll be with you in a minute." Although he didn't really want to know why Toronto was agreeing with Angel—the two of them were supposed to be working with two different things. "Angel, I'll call up to

Excelsior and see what happens—if they shoot me down, that's it. No promises."

As he hung the phone up, he turned and met Toronto's gaze.

"You know if you tell them we need a witch, they'll send one. They aren't going to shoot you down."

Rafe just stared at him.

Toronto shrugged. "Fine. Be a hard-ass."

"That's a laugh and a half, coming from you," Rafe muttered, shoving a hand through his hair.

"True. But, still, it's not like I'm wrong. We need a witch. A decent one can untangle the muck from Paul, plus maybe track down where this is all coming from. And if Angel thinks we need one for her problem? All the more reason." He paused and then added, "But you'd have already thought of all of that. So what's the problem?"

"The problem." Rafe sank down into the seat behind his desk, folding his hands over his belly. "The problem would be this . . . all of this is happening on my land, and I can't fucking stop it. Not without help. That's the fucking problem."

He'd fucked up. He'd lost control of his territory and people were getting hurt.

"You're not God," Toronto said quietly. "We've got a lock on it now and we'll fix it. It's the best we can do. None of us are perfect."

"The best we can do." Rafe stared at Toronto. Abruptly, the fury in him surged to the forefront and he rose to his feet, sent his desk flying and stormed across the room. In Toronto's face, he snarled, "I've got a fucking pedophile who likes to kill kids somewhere in my territory and I want him dead . . . but I can't kill him, and so far, we're having trouble even finding him, or you wouldn't be here. There's some sort of fucking sex ring going on a few miles away from here . . . and I didn't know jack*shit* about it until you told me. And that's the *best* I can do? If that's the best I can do, do I really belong here?"

He whirled away, stalking to the door.

The sound of Toronto's quiet voice made him pause. "If

you're going to let this knock you down without a fight, then maybe you don't."

"Don't you have a job to be doing?" Rafe closed his eyes and wondered where in the hell that cocky, irresponsible son of a bitch he'd been fighting with for *years* had disappeared to. The *last* thing he needed right now was for Toronto to be talking him down, damn it.

"Yes. And I'm trying to do it." Toronto pulled a mangled pack of gum from his pocket, popped a piece into his mouth. "It seems to me you've got a job to do, too. There's a mess to clean up here, Rafe. We both know it. So do we clean it up, or do we sit around here and brood and moan about how we've fucked up?"

"We didn't fuck up," Rafe swore and turned around, facing the werewolf. "*I* fucked up. I'm the Master."

"You're *the* Master. But I'm every bit as strong as you, and you know it. If there was something that off, I should have sensed it, too. Now we need to figure out why we didn't. And fix it." Toronto blew a bubble, and just to be annoying, he snapped it loudly before flashing Rafe a wicked smile. "So are you going to brood and moan? Or deal?"

Rafe narrowed his eyes at him. "You're such an asshole."

"Yeah." He shrugged.

"The witch you sent me after—he doesn't have much to do with anything. He camouflaged and got his rocks off on the power high, but that's it." Rafe rubbed his hands over his face before meeting Toronto's gaze once more. "There was a vamp involved—he told me that, but he doesn't have so much as a fucking name. The vamp called him, every time, warned him when something would go down so Paul was ready to cover. The most Paul ever got was a number, in case there were 'problems.'"

"Like us?" Toronto grinned.

"Yeah. Like us." Rafe turned back around, studied the devastation of his office. The desk was solid, sturdy oak. It would be fine. But hell. It looked like a tornado had struck the place. "Speaking of problems, why are you here instead of there being a problem for Pulaski?"

"Don't worry. I plan on being my normal, problematic self very shortly. I've just been thinking . . . wondering if maybe there isn't some sort of connection. One that goes deeper than we realize. Not just Pulaski getting boys from the kiddie ring from time to time, but all of it." He studied Rafe, his eyes shrewd. "Angel was out at my place, talking about shit. We've got a pedophile who disappears into the wind. Witches hiding magic they shouldn't be able to hide from us. All this crazy shit, that tells me there's something else going on. Things are connected, Rafe. I'm starting to feel it in my gut."

Rafe scowled. "Having Angel out at your place doesn't count for much. It's Angel, for fuck's safe."

"That's true." Toronto shrugged. "It may not count for anything."

As their gazes met, Rafe felt it, though. That low-level burn. Shit. He was lying to himself if he tried to believe this wasn't any sort of connection. And Toronto knew it, too.

"WAKEY, wakey . . ."

That voice was an annoying, nagging buzz in Sylvia's ears. She didn't want to *wakey, wakey*.

She wanted to *sleep*. Needed to sleep.

The sun's pull was still a drug in her system and she couldn't fight—

A wine-rich scent flooded the air.

Sylvia cracked one eye open, then the other and adrenaline tried to flood her body. It did burn away some of the sleepy fog in her brain, but not all of it. Sylvia didn't know how much fight she'd have in her for the next few minutes, but the woman sitting across her from wouldn't need *that* much.

After all, Angel was still mostly human—how much trouble could she be?

A smile flirted around Angel's mouth. "You'd be surprised." She used a piece of gauze on her arm and Sylvia scowled as she realized the blonde had cut herself.

"Are you *insane*? Cutting yourself around a sleeping vamp?"

"Hey, it got your attention, right? I needed you awake."

"And if I'd decided to need *you* as a good morning snack?" Sylvia felt the pulse of her fangs as they throbbed in their sheaths, and the heady scent of the girl's altered blood was almost too much of a temptation. The girl was *nuts*. Just plain crazy. No other explanation.

"Oh, I could have handled you."

Sylvia was tempted to teach the girl a lesson. Altered blood or not, the girl was *not* a vampire. Foolish, stupid little idiot. How had she survived this long, in their world? Clueless. She was *clueless* and she had no *idea* how easily she could be broken.

Sylvia did.

"The ones you knew had been starved. Mistreated. Weak. New in their skin." Angel leaned against the wall, still smiling. "I'm not new in my skin."

"You're a young fool," Sylvia said quietly.

"I'm not one who was locked away, starved, mistreated." She shrugged, that pretty blond hair floating around her shoulders.

Shit, she looked like a china doll. She lived with monsters. Granted, those monsters played by the rules, but she was going to get hurt. Badly hurt, if she decided to keep screwing around.

A CHINA doll?

Angel knew how to keep her emotions from showing. Physically, emotionally. Living with the monsters, as Sylvia called them, had taught her pretty decent control. She'd had to refine that control early on, thanks to all those nagging voices in her head, but the monsters had made it even more crucial.

Especially since she was married to one.

Nothing like being married to a vampire and knowing he sometimes picked up on stray, random thoughts when the two of them slipped into dreams . . . and he realized that one of his friends had walked past you and thought . . . *fuck, she smells like dinner.*

Angel did smell like dinner to vamps, even more than most humans. It happened after a vamp forced his blood on a human—almost enough to induce a Change, but not quite. She was altered now. Vamp bait. And the more she could control herself around the monsters, the better. Because that meant her husband was less likely to get into a nasty little fight with some of his buddies because they were a little too into the way she smelled. Not that they'd act on it, but still.

She had good control.

And she also had damn good reflexes—the only warning she had was a flicker, but it was enough. Rolling to the side, she drew the custom blade she'd taken from Kel's stash.

Sylvia's eyes lingered on the blade before she looked up.

"I'm not the helpless one you saw die all those years ago," she said quietly from five feet away.

Sylvia's muscles didn't even tense. This time, it was harder to evade and Angel felt the ghost of Sylvia's fury, and an echo of worry, and grief. Shit. *Maybe I should stop pulling the tiger's tail*, she decided. Sighing, she came to a halt and lifted her hands, keeping the blade ready. She didn't think she'd need it, though. "Look, I'll stop fucking with you. You got poison inside you, you know that, right?"

Sylvia was only a foot away when she stopped.

Staring into those dark eyes, shimmering with an eerie silver glow, it took all of Angel's control not to let the fear show. Fear and predators—not a good mix.

Slamming it into submission, Angel held Sylvia's gaze. "I can't help that I can see your memories, any more than you can help having them. But that's not entirely why I'm here . . . I met somebody today who had a run-in with your man, Pulaski. It was enough that I caught a few more blips—this time with Pulaski in it. I can help you find a house where he and his lover have been. You might find some answers there. But we have to go now."

"In case you haven't noticed . . . the sun is still up," Sylvia said. A sneer curled her lip and she looked at Angel like she'd just as soon wipe the floor with her.

Angel had no doubt the woman could. Angel would do her damnedest to bleed her.

But Sylvia was a vampire, and Angel needed to remember she wasn't dealing with a Hunter. Sylvia didn't have the stop button a Hunter would have and she didn't operate on the same playing field.

If she was *smart*, she would have waited until Toronto arrived.

Except when things finally settled into a cohesive picture in her mind, her thoughts had come together and focused on one person.

Sylvia.

She had ties to this . . . very strong ties.

Angel waved a set of keys. "I've got a van. You're awake and moving. All you have to do is to get to the van . . . which I have practically pulled up to Toronto's little escape route." She smiled. "He's had to house vamps before, get them out in the middle of the day. I even have something you can cover yourself with. You won't get a bit of sunshine on your lily white skin."

"What did you have in mind?" Sylvia tossed her another scornful glance. "Throwing a blanket over my head?"

Angel bent over and grabbed the pile of velvet from the floor. "I'm a little taller than you, but this will cover you." She handed Sylvia the cloak and grabbed the book-laden backpack from the floor.

"What's in there . . . garlic and crucifixes?" Sylvia frowned as she let the cloak unfold, falling in a luxurious tumble to the ground.

Glumly, Angel glared at the backpack. "No. Worse. It's homework."

Sylvia flicked her a puzzled glance. "Homework . . . ?"

"Yeah. You get to go out and kick ass and they stick me back in school. Life just isn't fair, ya know that?"

T HE cloak did a damn fine job covering her from head to toe.

She'd wanted to leave Toronto a note, but Angel had

vetoed that idea with the simple words, "I'm not exactly sure where we are going."

Sylvia couldn't explain just *why* she was okay with following this crazy woman-child, but something in her gut whispered she needed to. It wasn't wise. It wasn't smart. And the skin on the nape of her neck crawled—a certain warning. But she had to do it. There were secrets in the girl's eyes, secrets that Sylvia needed to understand.

Plus, she'd mentioned Pulaski. And Toronto trusted the strange woman. That shouldn't matter so much, but it did. *He* shouldn't matter, but he did.

"He'll follow us."

Sylvia looked up and met Angel's gaze in the rearview mirror. Bright light spilled inside—although none of it reached Sylvia where she sat, she still flinched, turning her face aside. Another hour, she thought. In another hour, the sun would set and she could rest easy about being out here. "Who will?"

"Lover boy." Angel flashed her a smile. "Tor will catch our scent. He'll be on our trail in no time."

Sylvia cocked a brow, unsettled by how easily the woman followed her train of thoughts. And she'd been trying to think *quietly*. "And this matters . . . why?"

Angel shrugged. "You don't strike me as the type to trust anybody. I get that sitting back there doesn't mean you trust me, but I figured it might make you feel a little better if you knew he'd be on the scene shortly."

"The scene?" Smirking, she rested her head against the back doors of the van. There were no windows in the back, nothing that could let the sun in. She was safe, secure—at least as secure as she could be hurtling down the interstate at eighty miles an hour with a mortal who dashed in and out of traffic with little regard for the speed limit, laws and the various semis crowding around them. "You going to college for criminal justice or something?"

"No. I'm in *high school*. Well, not technically. They put me in the school where they think some of the sex ring stuff is going down. I'm looking for pieces of the puzzle to hand

to Rafe so he can go after the sons of bitches doing this."
Angel grinned. "I'm working undercover."

Tapping her fingers restlessly on the steering wheel, she
continued, "That's where these pieces in my head came
from. There was this . . ."

Sylvia narrowed her eyes, staring at the back of Angel's
blond head. "This what?"

"Never mind." Angel flicked her another look. "That's
Rafe's turf. You want the Pulaski son of a bitch, right?"

"Riiiiight . . ." Sylvia drew a blade from her boot, absently
stroking it with her thumb. "Now you have me puzzled,
being one of Rafe's and all. Shouldn't you be trying to keep
me *away* from him?"

"Oh, Pulaski isn't there—this is all just another piece of
my puzzle. And I'm not one of Rafe's. My husband is."
Angel darted across the interstate.

Sylvia closed her eyes as people around them laid on their
horns. The girl was crazy—just plain crazy, the way she
drove. Like she didn't care if she lived or died.

"So we're going someplace where Pulaski stays? Or to
find somebody who knows him?"

Angel shrugged again. "I don't know that yet. It's not
clear."

"*What's* not clear?"

"The picture in my head . . ." Angel sighed. "It's almost
there. But not quite."

CHAPTER 19

Toronto knew the minute he pulled up to the house it was empty.

Angel.

Shit.

What in the hell was Sylvia doing running around with Angel? Swearing, he debated for a split second on whether or not to put in a call to Rafe, then decided against it. Rafe had been babysitting Angel for too long. The girl knew what she was doing.

If Angel went searching for Sylvia, it was for a reason.

Although what in the hell those reasons were, Toronto was clueless—might have been nice if she'd clue him in, too.

Had to be something important. But, he was bothered by the scent of blood in the air.

Angel's.

Shit. What in the hell . . . ?

The buildup of electricity in the air was enough to have his wolf snarling. Sighing, he headed for the chest of weapons he stored. He'd only made it about two feet when Kel appeared in his living room.

"Do me a favor. Don't teleport into my house without letting me know first," he advised as he crouched in front of the chest. Kel had picked up that handy little skill early. Too early.

"Why was Angel here and why do I smell her blood?" The single-minded obsession, however, wasn't anything new. Kel had always been focused completely on his woman.

"I don't know." Toronto pulled out a modified Glock and loaded it. Hollow silver bullets in that one. The baby Glock had regular bullets. He added a couple of knives, ranging from just a little larger than his palm to almost as long as his forearm, tucking them into various sheaths. "It's not my job to keep up with your wife, Kel."

"Toronto . . ." Kel's voice was a low, deadly whisper.

Rising, Toronto met the vampire's stare. It was hard, cold and held a lot of power for a vampire as young as he was. Under it, Toronto saw the fear and because he did, he didn't let the threat he heard in Kel's voice trigger the anger whispering just below his skin. "Listen, kid, I don't know. But your wife isn't an idiot. She came looking for the merc I'm . . . working with."

"Merc." Kel's eyes narrowed. "James. You're not supposed to be *working* with her. You're supposed to be getting your hands on Pulaski."

"My best bet of getting my hands on Pulaski is working with her."

"And if she kills him?"

Toronto smiled. "We've made a deal about that. Now are you going to come with me while I track her and your girl down or are you going to stand there and yap the night away? If you're yapping, have fun talking to the walls." With that, he slammed the chest shut.

Once he was outside, he tipped his head back and checked the air. Not as easy to trail them once they'd gotten into the van, but he could do it. If it had just been Sylvia, it would be harder. If it had just been Angel, it would be harder.

But the two of them together . . . especially since Angel had decided to go and do some bleeding in his house . . . and she hadn't covered the wound all that well.

Toronto wasn't drawn to blood the way vamps were, but he sure as hell could use it to track. Eyes closed, he dragged the scents deep inside, let them rest on the back of his tongue.

"She was still bleeding when they left," Kel whispered.

Toronto opened his eyes and looked at the younger man. "You better lock it down if you want her found right now. Otherwise the stink of your anger is going to get in my way."

Kel flashed fang at him, eyes glowing in the coming twilight. But then he closed his eyes and took a deep breath. Once he looked at Toronto, he wore a mask that was almost human and had managed to shut down the fury flickering inside him.

"Find her."

"WE'RE here."
Night had fallen.

Actually, it had fallen quite some time ago and Angel had driven through the darkness without speaking much.

Now they were parked in front of a house overlooking the rolling waters of the Mississippi. "Wonderful," Sylvia said quietly as she slid out of the back, studying the house. "Just one question . . . where is *here*?"

"A little outside of New Madrid, Missouri."

"Missouri." Sylvia stared at the house as foreboding settled over her shoulders like a cold, slippery cloak. Two hours driving. "Okay, you want to tell me why we drove about a hundred and twenty miles? There's nobody *here*."

"I know." Angel slanted a look at her from under her lashes. "He's gone. So is the guy he's with. But he was here. I don't know what you're going to find in there, but you needed to come here."

"Shit." Sylvia popped her neck and looked back at the house. "No wonder Hunters don't like you psychics. You're irritating as hell."

"Yes." Angel's eyes held a far-off look. "The boys . . . who were the boys, Sada?"

* * *

S^{ADA-}
     He was screaming.
     She could hear him—
     Those desperate, desperate pleas were faint though. It was like she heard them through a dream. Through somebody else's ears, perhaps.
     Although considering how her heart raced, how her heart thundered in her ears, it was hard to believe she could hear anything. Hungry, so hungry. It was a ravenous beast in her belly and it had been for days. Weeks—
     And then all was silent. Sated, replete, she rested.
     But her blissful peace did not last long. A low, pleased laugh drifted through the small room that was her prison and she jerked upright, staring out into the hall at her captor. He watched her with cruel, cold eyes, and on his mouth, there was a cruel, cold smile.
     "I warned him," he told her.
     She swallowed. The taste of blood lingered in her mouth and she could have shuddered—it was so sweet, and already she craved more.
     "Warned who?"
     "The boy. But he wouldn't stop trying to get down here." He glanced at something on the floor.
     And although she wanted to fight the urge to look, Sada couldn't stop herself.
     A scream tore from her throat as she saw him lying there. The boy.
     Pale, still . . . and his throat was a ragged, bloody mess.
     She lunged for him while out in the hall, her captor laughed.
     Then he swore . . .

$"S^{ADA?"}$
     "Don't call me that," Sylvia whispered, shrugging Angel's hand away.
     Sada no longer existed. She'd died that day in the cell. Those blue eyes haunted her. The promises to help. Pleas for

forgiveness—now *she* was the one who wanted to beg for forgiveness, except she didn't deserve it.

"You were starved."

Ignoring Angel, she stormed toward the house. It smelled of vamp. Cool, musky and of the earth. And there was something more, too. Death. Blood—coppery, old and thick with fear. People had died here.

"You were starved, all but driven mad with hunger—tortured. You were a new vamp. You can't be held responsible for what happened."

"Yes." Sylvia stopped on the steps and turned, staring at the woman standing there in the moonlight. "I can. I don't buy into this '*it's not my fault, somebody forced me to, it's my mother's fault, it's my father's, the little blue elephant made me do it*' crap. *I* did it. I wasn't strong enough to control the hunger and I broke. I killed."

"*You* were tortured," Angel said quietly. "By a monster."

"We're *all* monsters." Sylvia curled her lip.

"Not all."

"You actually believe that." She stared at the woman, wondering if there had ever been a time when she'd been like that. This woman actually believed there was something good inside those who'd ceased to be human.

"Yeah. I do." Rocking back on her heels, she shook her head. "If you were just a monster, you would have spent the past century or whatever you've got under your belt killing. Hell, you would have come after me earlier. But you didn't."

Angel shifted her gaze past Sylvia's shoulder, staring at the door. "You want to find Pulaski, you're going to have to face something from your past. You up to that?" Then she turned. "I need to go. This will be easier without me here, I think. You don't want me seeing all the shit that's going to go through your head, and you're not going to be able to block it out."

By the van, she paused. "Tor's on his way. You got maybe a half hour. If you don't want him seeing you when you find it, you better hurry."

"Find what?" The question came out in a faint whisper.

Sylvia had no doubt the woman heard. But Angel apparently wasn't in the mood to answer.

Looking back at the house, Sylvia stared at it as foreboding wrapped her in its icy, slippery arms. Suddenly, she wanted very much to run. Forget the damn contract, forget that she'd given her word. Forget about the way Toby's face haunted her. Forget her damned job and just *disappear.* Spend a few months relaxing on some night-dark, warm beach and sleeping the days away.

Face something from your past . . .

What in the hell was she supposed to face?

Walking up the steps to that house was one of the hardest things she'd done in quite a while, and she didn't even completely understand *why*. It was an empty house. She wanted to tell herself it was because Angel had gotten her worked up. This was just a house . . . that was all, right?

Set on a knoll overlooking the river, made of wood and glass, it should have been a pretty sight. Huge windows dominated the place and in the daylight, all of that glass would sparkle under the sun. At night, a person could look out one of those many, many windows and stare at the expanse of the sky and stare at the stars.

Looking at it made her think of hell and suddenly, she *wanted* to wait for Toronto. She didn't want to go in there alone. Not at all.

Brainless idiot—you've known him two days? Three? And now you can't seem to even walk in a house by yourself.

Tugging out one of her blades, she whispered, "It's not that I *can't*." She just didn't . . . want to. Angel had gotten to her.

But it wasn't going to stop her. Neither was the stink of vampires, blood and painful death—it clung to the house, a nasty miasma that felt like it was sinking into her very pores. Ignoring it, she stood in front of the door and steadied herself, braced herself.

She could do this.

Hell, Angel could even be *wrong*. The worst part of her past was *dead* . . . Harold, the man who'd made her, was dead. The bastard who'd tricked her into coming to America was dead. The boys . . . yeah. They were gone, too—that poor, brave little fool who'd tried to help her, and his friend.

Just what was left that could haunt her?

"Quit stalling."

The door was locked. Her fingers trembled as she pulled out her lockpicks and went to work. It took nearly three times longer than it should have and by the time she heard that telltale click, she was almost ready to just break the door down. Yet as she pushed it open, she knew that would have taken more than just a kick or two. The door was too heavy—reinforced. Eyeing the doorframe, she saw more telltale signs there. Somebody had done some serious work here.

Vampires hadn't just settled down here for a night or two. This was a home to one, a safe place.

The reinforced door was just one sign. The walls were reinforced as well, and although there were all those lovely windows, the outer rooms were small, long and narrow, almost like a walled-in wraparound porch. Moving deeper into the house, she studied the inner rooms taking up most of the space—none of them had windows. A weird layout . . . unless the owners had issues with sunlight.

Once those outer rooms were closed, a vampire could wander these inner rooms all day long and not have to worry about burning. Assuming, of course, the vampire was strong enough to rise during the day. Sylvia usually didn't rise more than an hour or so before sunset.

A whisper of power still lingered in the air. Whoever had lived here was stronger than she was—strong enough that the buzz of his power still hadn't completely faded.

There was a familiar scent, too, one that tugged at something deep inside her. Familiar, but not—she couldn't quite place it.

Strangely, it made her hurt, although she didn't know why. It hurt, and it made her want to run. *Then get this done—get it done and you can run as fast as you want, all the way back to Memphis if it will make you feel better.* With that promise to herself in mind, she continued through the house, peering into rooms, searching for whatever it was Angel seemed to think she'd find here.

Boxes were neatly stacked in many of the rooms. Packing up. Or packed, rather. The boxes just needed to be moved.

She poked through a few of them, frowning. Books. A lot of them. Movies. Upstairs, she found more boxes—this time, it was clothes, neatly folded away.

Making her way back to the lower level, she stood there, breathing in the scents. Blood. Death. Not fresh. Where? Aimlessly, she roamed through the house, tracking it to where it was the strongest. In the hall. But nothing had died *here*—somewhere else . . .

Frowning, she studied the table placed at the end of the hall, just under a mirror set in an old oak frame. That mirror . . . oh, no. No. A fist grabbed her by the throat. Shit. Shit, no—

"*W*HAT *do you think of my guest wing?*"
         Sada tried to jerk away from his hands—she could get away. She could. Up the stairs, and then through that hidden door . . . the mirror. It had been behind the mirror. She did not remember much, but she remembered that, through the blood and the pain and the humiliation.

But his hands were so strong. So cruel and so strong. Memories flashed through her mind—those hands, ripping away the silk of her kimono, holding her down. No . . . she could not think of that now—she had to get away, had to . . .

J ERKING her mind back to the present, she closed her eyes.
         It wasn't the same mirror. It wasn't.

And he was dead.

She'd planned to go after him—had even gone so far as to hire out for more help, because she knew she couldn't take the man who'd made her. But he'd already been killed.

Rumor had it he'd been done by one of his own vamps—somebody else he'd made. It was sweet justice in Sylvia's mind, but one she'd wanted for herself.

The mirror. Shit, that mirror . . . it couldn't be his.
Face something from your past . . .

Setting her jaw, she stormed toward the table and threw it aside. It hit the wall in the room to her right with a crash, the crystal vase on it shattering into shards. "It's nothing. You're freaking over nothing." She lifted a hand . . . and felt a faint draft.

Closing her eyes, she swallowed.

No.

She lifted her hands, feeling along the wall behind the mirror. When her questing fingers hit a small notch, she could have screamed. Instead, Sylvia pushed.

The door of the hell house where she'd been made had opened with a rough, grating noise—the sound of stone rubbing on stone. Here, there was barely anything, just the soft, almost inaudible whine of electronics whispering inside the wall.

As the mirror and the false wall disappeared into a recessed area, lights came on, illuminating the stairwell.

And the stink of death, blood and pain grew stronger.

Sylvia sagged to the ground, staring down those steps.

T ORONTO brought Sylvia's bike to a stop at the start of the driveway. The scent trail on the drive had gotten faint, but it wasn't hard to figure out they had stopped here.

After all, Angel was parked there in a van, sitting in the open door with one knee drawn to her chest and a smile on her face.

Toronto hadn't even completely stopped the bike when Kel was off and moving. Good thing, he figured. This way, Sylvia wouldn't see he'd had somebody riding on the bike with him. While Kel was busy kissing his wife, Toronto let himself take in the night . . . and he didn't like the feel of it at all.

Tension gathered inside him, edgy and hot, tightening his muscles, sharpening his senses. Things were getting ready to happen. He could all but taste it in the air.

He slanted Angel a look after Kel finally let her come up for air. "Kid, you know Rafe will have your hide if he knows how much you're poking around in things."

"I'm not worried." She moved her shoulders in a lazy shrug, her fingers toying with the front of Kel's shirt. "Besides, this mess is connected. I can almost see it my head."

"I already figured that much out." Toronto flashed her a wide grin. "And I'm not psychic. You losing your touch already, sugar?"

She stuck her tongue out at him. "Hey, I just gave your girlfriend a very big piece of the puzzle, Tor. You should say thank you and go find her."

"What piece?" He shifted, trying to see through the trees, but all he could make out was the bend of the driveway, what might be a house.

"Head on up the drive. Find her. You'll start to figure things out. And you'll find him soon." She pulled away from Kel, a wicked look in her eyes. "You know, you two have a long drive ahead of you. Maybe you should let us take the bike back. You all can have the van."

"She'd kill me—just have Lindsey head wherever with it. I'll call her . . . make plans to meet up later, if you're that certain we'll need it." Catching a hank of her hair, he tugged on it and then he shot Kel a look. "Make sure you floss tonight, Kel—gotta take care of those fangs and all."

Kel stared at him balefully as Toronto took off down the driveway.

"I DON'T like him touching you," Kel muttered, wrapping an arm around Angel from behind and tugging her back against him.

"That's probably why he does it. He's just messing with you." She pressed a kiss to his arm. "He's different. Head isn't quite so . . . wrapped around himself."

Kel snorted. "He's as self-involved as he ever was."

She made a face. "It's not that. And he's not exactly self-involved. He's locked up in his past and can't seem to cut those threads, but it's not choking him the way it was. He's seeing others better than he usually does."

* * *

Nice house.
     Bad vibes.

That was all Toronto could think when he rounded the bend. Perched on the edge right above the water, it all but screamed money and power. It was also empty, except for Sylvia.

She was in there, somewhere.

And she was hurting. Pain, sorrow, joy and pleasure, all emotions had a way of scenting, coloring the air. And right now, the pain and fear was like a death shroud.

Drawing one of his blades, he held it close against his body, ready. He was pretty sure nobody was here . . . but that ball-busting little bitch wasn't going to let just anything push her to fear. He could shift if he had to, but that would whisper through the air, a silent warning—he didn't plan on giving *any* warning if he had to attack.

He ticked off the details as he went inside.

The door wasn't locked—that was probably Sylvia's handiwork. Door built to withstand a tank, practically. Solid walls. Vamp house. Cleverly disguised. Shallow outer rooms, light-safe inner rooms. Nothing set up to look like a prison, either, the way some vamp houses were laid out.

Whoever this was, the person had money, and he liked comfort.

Toronto scented the air, but the only person who'd been in this house recently was Sylvia.

And she was close—

There.

Sitting at the end of the hallway, staring down what looked to be a flight of stairs.

Still as death, pale as milk. And trembling.

"Sylvia?"

She didn't move.

Closing the distance between them, he checked each room he passed—caution, caution . . . but there was nobody there, damn it. What the hell was going on?

Once he reached her side, he touched her arm and waited until she raised her eyes to his. "Sylvia, baby, what's wrong?"

Her gaze lifted to his, and he saw something he knew very, very well . . . the shadows of old ghosts. Sighing, he slid the blade he carried back into his sheath and then settled beside her, touching her cheek. "What hurts you?"

"Toronto." She blinked, a dazed look coming over her face.

She frowned, shaking her head. "I didn't realize . . . shit. Stupid. I'm not being careful." She went to get to her feet, but he reached out, caught her arm. "Shit like this can get somebody like me killed."

"I think your body would have warned you if it had been somebody other than me." He figured she'd pull away, but to his surprise, she didn't. She closed her eyes and slumped over, burying her face in her hands. Shoulders bowed, she started to quiver.

Shit. *Don't let her start to cry*, he thought, helplessness flooding him. Stroking her back, he stared down the steps while the wolf in him started to growl and pace. Whatever it was that had hurt her, it was here. So he just needed to find it, tear it apart and everything would be better, right?

"What's wrong, Sylvia?" He leaned over, wrapping his body around hers and pressing his lips to the back of her neck. "You know . . . I can't kill whatever it is until you tell me."

She made a strange sound, halfway between a laugh and sob. "I can kill my problems just fine on my own, thank you."

"But I'll feel better if I kill whatever's hurting you." He nuzzled her neck. "And you can watch."

"You can't kill memories." She sighed and lifted her head, staring down the stairs. "I was made over a century ago . . . in a place far too like this." She shifted her gaze to the side and the haunted look in her eyes tore at his heart. "Made, then locked away, starved for the first few months. You want to know why I'm weaker? Why I can't take sunlight? The bastard who made me crippled me. It wasn't enough that he tortured me, that he raped me, that he stole my life . . . he had to make me so weak, it was a miracle I was able to survive as long as I have. Those first few months, I didn't even feed once a week."

Rage snarled through him, tearing into him with jagged, poison-tipped claws. He'd hunt . . . and he'd kill—

"There's a mirror," she whispered. Swallowing, she eased away from him and stood up, beckoning until he came to stand beside her.

And he watched as she pushed on the side of the door. When it slid out, they were staring at what look like a wall, one that held a mirror. Beside him, she jolted, like she'd been jabbed with a silver blade.

"He had one like that. It hid a room, as well. That was where he kept me for the first few months. While he starved me." Her lashes swept down, shielding her eyes from him.

"Who?" he demanded. The bastard had known what he was doing—depriving a newborn vamp like that was no different than depriving a human child. It weakened them.

Yet she'd survived. Pulled through and made herself a fighter in her own right.

"Who in the fuck was it?" he growled when she didn't answer right away. He had to know, because he was going on a fucking Hunt right now—no. Shit. He couldn't right now. Pulaski had to be dealt with. A child killer couldn't remain free, but then, he'd go on a Hunt and that was all there was to it.

But he needed a name. Or a city. Something. He could go further back and pry into the details of her past without her help, but it would make it easier . . .

"He's dead." She slanted a sad smile at him. Reaching up, she touched his lips. "Were you going to track him down and do bad things to him, Hunter?"

"Yes," he growled. He caught her wrist and pressed a kiss to the inside of it.

"Doing your job?"

"No." Now he bit the soft pad at the base of her palm, then tugged her close. "I want him dead because he hurt you, tortured you, he did something he knew would damage you and he left you with fear in your eyes even after a century. I don't like seeing you afraid." He closed his eyes and shoved the rage down. It couldn't help now. She was wrestling with memories. She needed him to be a nonasshole, so he could help her with that. Taking a deep breath, he faced the mirror again. "Somehow I don't think seeing a mirror would put you back in this spot."

"It's the same mirror." She grimaced and reached up, touching her fingers to it. "It's the same damn one, I'd swear on it. And the way he used it to mark the area he hid—it's the same. Even the mechanism to open the door. I knew the moment I saw it."

She swallowed and the sound was painfully loud. Stroking her back, he studied the mirror—he could break it. Easily. Even if he did believe in luck, what was seven years to a werewolf, right? "Perhaps one of his people."

"Yeah. He liked making vamps." The echo of pain lingered on her face as she rubbed the heel of her hand over her chest. "He liked torturing them even more."

She sent him a sidelong glance. "There was a woman there . . . for a while. She smelled like Angel. He killed her not too long after he changed me. I remember the smell of her blood . . . it was . . . like a drug." Pausing, she took a deep, steadying breath. "A strong, powerful drug. If I could have gotten out, I don't know what I would have done."

"Gotten out." Still staring at the mirror, he processed that. Easier to look at the mirror than her—if he wasn't looking at her face, seeing that fear in her eyes, it was just a little easier to control the fury raging inside. "He kept you locked up."

"Yes. In a room not much bigger than a closet." Shooting him a quick glance, she moved away, shoving her hands through her hair before linking them behind her neck. "For the longest time, after I was away from him, I spent months, years running. Finally, I found a place to stay . . . a house I'd bought in Massachusetts. I made my own vamp room. Nothing fancy—just a simple, inner room with no windows and a door that faced north. And I stayed there. I left long enough to feed. Then I went back. All I wanted to do was feed and hide. Feed . . . and hide. Forget about those months with him."

"How did you get away?"

"He got bored with me, and let me go." She shrugged and

returned to stare at the window. "He'd already turned me. Broke me. Made me into a monster. What more fun could he have with me?"

The words, so flatly spoken, ripped a hole in him. Crossing the room to stand near her, he pulled her back against his body and pressed his mouth to her ear. "Syl . . . you're not a monster."

"You don't know what he made me do." Sylvia bowed her head, staring at the floor. "You don't know what I *let* myself do . . ."

Was it any worse than what *he* would have done? he wondered.

"I was a teenager when I was bitten." He turned her around and lifted her chin, stared into her eyes as he spoke. "Five weres attacked me."

In the mirror, he saw her blink, watched as her face went blank, then watched as understanding bled into her eyes. "Did you say *five* weres?"

"Yeah. Five. They left me dead in an alley, my head split—brain scrambled." He shrugged and added, "The years before that are lost to me. I don't know who I was. What I was. If I had family . . . none of it. The woman who found me was a Hunter. And the first thing I did after she saved my life, nursed me through the fever, all of that . . . ? I tried to rip her throat out."

"Five—" She shook her head, her tone faint. "I didn't think it was possible to survive if more than a couple bit you. The virus is too high."

"If I hadn't had pretty much the strongest healer around on hand to nurse me through it, I wouldn't have made it." He shrugged. "And when the fevers got bad, she was still there. When I almost went mad from it all and tried to eat her? She was still there."

"You tried to eat her."

He grimaced. "It was driving me mad—the hunger, the need for meat. That was what she was—I looked at her and saw meat. It lasted for months. And she stayed with me anyway. And then one day . . . it was easier, I could breathe, I could think. The next day, it got better, and then the next . . ."

He shrugged, staring at the wall past her shoulder without seeing it. "Eventually the good days outweighed the bad and I no longer looked at every breathing thing as a possible meal. I could control the hunger. But if it wasn't for Nessa, I wouldn't have pulled through. I was on the edge of turning feral—the madness was trying to eat me up inside from almost the minute I was attacked. If she hadn't been there to help me through it, I would have been put down." He reached up and touched her cheek, stroking the pads of his fingers along the soft, silken skin. "You didn't have anybody there to guide you—you were locked up, made a prisoner, tortured . . . and you pulled through sane. You're not a monster, baby."

*N*OT *a monster—*
      She wanted to believe that.
   But she couldn't.
   Curling her lip at him, she knocked his hand away and turned back to the mirror. "You pulled through because you're destined to be a tried-and-true do-gooder. That's why you pulled through, Hunter. Me? It was just luck, but that doesn't mean I'm not a monster." In the mirror's reflection, she met his gaze and asked softly, "What if I told you I'd killed a child? If I told you that my maker threw some poor, stupid kid in there and I killed him? Would you still say I'm not a monster?"
   "I'd say it's a miracle you didn't snap completely—he'd starved you." Toronto shrugged. "Then I'd ask if he'd made the child bleed first—if he'd pushed you to bloodlust first, all he did was aim a pointed gun and pull the trigger. He made you into a weapon and used it. You stopped giving him control all those years ago. Don't give it back, not even to a memory."
   She stared at him. "Didn't you hear me?" she demanded. "I killed a child! Fuck, you're a Hunter, you ought to just kill me *now.*"
   "I heard you." He came up and dipped his head, murmured in her ear, "You're not the first vamp who was pushed

into bloodlust. The question is this . . . did you learn to control it? Yes. You did. So you can't be controlled anymore. Will you let that bloodlust control you again? I think the answer is no. We don't kill because of one *break*, especially when somebody was tortured. We go after killers, monsters and murderers. We don't go after victims, unless the victims have become monsters themselves."

He nudged her aside and started poking around the mirror. "Since you're feeling sorry for yourself, I'll go downstairs and look around. Then I'm heading out. I've got an idea of where we need to go now."

*F*EELING *sorry for myself*—
She watched, her jaw hanging open, as he fiddled around with the mirror. "Jackass," she muttered. "I'll do it. You're not even clo—"

The door opened with a whisper.

As he shot her a look, she glared at him and then pushed past him. "I'll have you know, I'm *not* feeling sorry for myself."

Jerk. Who in the hell did he think he was?

That burn of anger managed to carry her all the way down the stairs. But once she reached the lower floor, she froze. Cells. Rows of them. Each one not much bigger than a closet . . . and each one had bars in place of a door. "I guess he's into the retro look," she said quietly.

"Looks like a dungeon."

"It is." She closed her eyes, recalling the endless nights, the hunger, the pain. "It looks like the place where I was made. It was a dungeon as well. Although sometimes I was certain it would be my crypt."

"It wasn't. This one won't be." He stroked a hand over her shoulder and then surveyed the room. "And I can make sure of that. I'm going to have the place torched."

"Torched?"

"Yeah." He paced around, eyes half-closed, as he breathed the air in. "People died here. He brought victims here, bled them, killed them . . . and he made a vampire here, too. You smell that?"

"So you're burning it."

"Not me. That would be too fucking dangerous. I'll have the Council send a witch, somebody who can bring the fire, then shut it down before it spreads past the house. Whoever built this place won't ever use it again." He turned and looked at her. "So get what you need from here—look around, if you need closure. Hell, if you want to trash the place or go punch that fucking mirror, do it. Do it fast. We need to get on the road."

She clenched her jaw, tempted to tell him to shove it. What if she needed more time?

We don't have time . . .

Taking a deep breath, she turned and studied each cell, walked in front of them. There—she smelled that faint scent. Death, then the faintly stronger scent of vampire. The second vampire she'd smelled earlier. She hadn't caught that. Yeah, a new vampire—she could still smell the scent of him as a mortal.

"While I'm totally flattered that this has you so hot under the collar, have you forgotten we have a monster to catch?" she asked him as she finished her circuit around the room, coming to a halt in front of him.

"No." Stroking his hands down her shoulders, he lowered his head, pressed his brow to hers. "There's a connection between all of this . . . Angel wouldn't have brought you here if there wasn't. She wants Pulaski found, the same as we do. And I was already thinking there was a connection."

She frowned and looked back around the cell. "A connection between this place and Pulaski?" What in the hell was he . . . wait. Shit. *No.* Shit. Staring at the cell, she whispered, "Can you tell how long ago the vampire was made here?"

"Not long. No more than a month, I don't think."

She met his eyes.

"Right about when Pulaski went missing." She closed her eyes. The ankle bracelet had been found broken . . . "A vampire could easily break the ankle bracelet they put on him."

"Yes."

"Shit." The monster that was her fury started to roar inside her head as she thought about what vampirism could do to somebody who was already a monster. Already terrible and perverse. "If he was made into a vampire . . ."

"Then we find him and kill him." Toronto lifted a brow. "That's all there is to it. You wanted him dead anyway—this just makes it that much more urgent. We need to go. Are you done?"

With the bitter wave of fury and fear riding her, she turned in a slow circle, studying the underground room. It would have been hell, she knew. People would have died here, knowing this was the last thing they'd see—that nobody was coming for them, that nobody would save them.

"Angel said there was something here I needed to see. I don't know if this is it, or if there's more." Stopping, she stared toward the cell where the vamp had been made. "All I'm finding are bad memories. I don't see anything that will help me find Pulaski."

She didn't tell you that you'd find Pulaski, something inside her whispered. *She just said you'd find something . . .*

Yeah. She'd found something all right. A reminder of hell on earth. Setting her jaw, she turned to look at Toronto. He wasn't looking at her, though. He was staring off at nothing in particular, a distant look on his face.

"Don't worry. I already know where to look."

CHAPTER 20

S HE woke to hear screaming—

Rolling off the bed, she landed in a crouch. A bed—
wait, what? She hadn't fallen asleep on a bed—she'd fallen
asleep next to one, shielded from the rays of light that might
come in through the curtains.

What the hell? Fuck it. She already had a blade in her
hand and was staring around, trying to get her bearings.

The bed made sense—she was in a hotel room. And it
definitely wasn't the hotel she'd fallen asleep in earlier. It
was nicer, for one. And cleaner. Newer. *Louder*—

It had that fake rustic thing going and was a little nicer
than some, but still a hotel room. And the screaming was
coming from just outside the windows. Unconsciously, a
snarl pulled her lips back from her teeth and her fangs slid
down. Rising, she made her way to the windows. Faint light
streamed in from underneath, but it was faint. Her internal
clock told her that it was still day. The sun was still up,
although not for long.

Easing the curtain aside, she flinched as she saw the light
pouring in through skylights. Her eyes watered at the bright-

ness, but it was indirect—she could do indirect light. What in the world . . .

Suddenly, the screams made sense.

Screams. Laughter. The air was heavy with the scent of chlorine, burgers, pizza.

A water park. Somehow, Toronto had managed to get her to one of those weird water-park hotels. With a frown, she turned back and studied the room. The only windows were the ones at her back, opening up not to the outside where direct sunlight could pour into the room and leave her with a nice, crispy burn, but to the water park. No direct sunlight.

She didn't remember getting here, but she wouldn't.

They'd stopped driving about twenty minutes before dawn. It had been one of those little cheap, roadside motels, the kind of place she hated and tried to avoid, because she was never sure she'd be safe there.

But she'd been fine staying there with him. Because she knew she *was* safe with him.

She checked the time. It was after seven. She didn't have that weird, unsettled feeling that she sometimes had when her sleep had been disturbed or when she hadn't been able to settle for fear of the sun.

Hearing something at the door, she turned just as he opened it. In one hand, he held a box of pizza. She eyed the pizza enviously. Those things always smelled so good. She could swipe a small taste of the sauce, but anything more than that would make her sick.

He lifted a brow at her. "You're awake."

"Nah. Just sleepwalking. Dreaming about pizza and big hotels. Because I'm pretty sure I went to sleep in a rinky-dink one." Spying the water on the table tucked up against one wall, she went and grabbed herself a bottle. She needed to feed. Water would help the thirst, but she really needed to feed.

She barely managed to twist the cap off before he was there.

"You probably need to feed, don't you?"

Wrinkling her nose, she brushed around him. "I'm pretty sure mind reading is a vampire thing, not a wolf thing."

"Hey, some of the close-knit packs can sense each other's

thoughts. It's not really mind reading, but it's pretty close." He came up behind her, one arm sliding around her waist as he draped the other arm around her upper body.

Sylvia sighed and rested her head back against his shoulder. It should have felt stifling, to be held like that. Pinned back against his body. Instead she felt . . . wanted. Treasured. His lips brushed against her temple and he murmured, "You didn't feed that heavily from me the other day. Have you fed well recently?"

"It's been a few days. I'll find somebody tonight before we—"

He lifted his hand, exposing his wrist. "I'm somebody."

"You don't need to feed me." Even thinking about it had her fangs pulsing. Staring at his skin, at the faint tracery of veins underneath, she willed herself not to move, not to breathe. It would be so easy to get used to this . . .

"I like doing it. You need it. I kind of like taking care of you, when you let me." His blond head lowered to her neck and he nuzzled her there, whispered, "Besides, it also makes me hotter than hell. Why don't you make me hotter than hell, Syl?"

"Don't call me Syl." Still staring at his wrist, she tried to think of reasons *not* to do this. Other than how easy it would be to get used to it. It wouldn't *hurt* him. Wolves healed too fast, and that included blood. She'd have to drain him half-dry before it would do him much damage, and vampires just didn't need that much.

Slicking her tongue across her lips, she dipped her head, pressed her mouth to his wrist. She couldn't think of one good, solid reason that wasn't an excuse. It wouldn't hurt him, she needed to feed . . . and he wanted to do it.

"You're getting too easy to have around, Hunter," she muttered, as she stroked her tongue across his skin.

Salty. Warm. Male.

A low, rough growl rolled through the air. Tension spiked. The arm he had wrapped around her waist stroked downward, resting on her hip. Kneading the flesh there, he nudged himself against her and said, "You're the only person I've ever known who's ever called me *easy* to have around."

She laughed and then, forgetting about everything else, sank her teeth into his flesh.

HE'D fed vamps more times than he could recall.

It wasn't his favorite thing to do, but he'd lived for more than a century. For close to nine decades, he'd served as a Hunter—years he'd spent with vamps. Vamps, just like weres, just like witches, could get hurt. When a vamp got hurt, the vamp had to feed. Although he was an ass of the highest degree, he wasn't going to let a fellow Hunter suffer if he could help.

Up until Sylvia, feeding was generally just a responsibility . . . and on rare occasion, something he'd indulge in with a lover.

With Sylvia, though . . . he could come to crave it. It could become a need . . .

The feel of her tongue brushing against his flesh, just before her fangs pierced his skin. Then the pleasure—

Growling, he buried his face against her hair and rocked his hips against the scrap of silk that covered her butt. He'd stripped her jeans away when he'd put her to bed and now he was damn glad. Pushing his fingers inside her panties, he sought out the slick heat between her thighs. She stiffened and then sagged, her mouth still pulling on the wound at his wrist.

When her fangs pierced his skin a second time, he grunted and pulled his hand out from her panties, tearing at the silk until it shredded under his hands. "You . . ." She lifted her head.

"Don't stop," he muttered, catching sight of her flushed face in the mirror hanging across the room. "That feels almost as good as it did when I fucked you."

"You tore my panties," she muttered, lowering her head back to his wrist. She licked at the closing wounds like a cat.

"Yeah. I can buy you more. Do it again." He nudged his wrist closer to her mouth as he used his foot to bump one of her ankles over, widening her stance.

"You want me to drain you dry or what?" She laughed, teasing his skin with the tip of one fang.

"You won't." He reached between them and tore at his zipper, at the button of his jeans, swearing when his fingers seemed to get too damned clumsy on him. Finally, he managed, and the cool kiss of air on his aching flesh was almost torture. Then it *was* torture as Sylvia continued to play with him, taunting the skin inside his wrist with her teeth and tongue.

"Witch," he rasped.

It wasn't until he pressed the head of his cock against her that she stopped toying with him. As he pierced the snug, wet heat of her sheath, she pierced him . . . driving her fangs deep as he drove his cock straight into her core. She shuddered while he fought against the howl building in his throat. Not here—fuck. Not here. One hand flexed, shifted and he swore as he saw the black flaring on the tips of his fingers.

He didn't lose control like that. Not unless he felt like it. Sucking in a desperate breath of air, he grabbed the ragged bits of his control—waited until he thought he could move without shattering.

And then he started to rock, stroking her slowly. The slick wet tissues of her sheath gripped him, milked him. Sylvia twisted against him, rolling her hips backwards.

With a shudder, Sylvia pulled her mouth from his wrist and dropped her head back against his shoulder. The soft moan that fell from her lips made his heart race, and the look in her eyes had something deep inside him twisting almost painfully.

Damn it, she got to him. Got to him in ways he couldn't even begin to explain.

Staring at her reflection in the mirror, he rolled his hips against her bottom, listened as she moaned again. Still holding her gaze, he placed a hand on her belly, stroked it up until he cupped one breast in his hand, watching her face, watching as her lips parted, as her lashes fluttered down.

Her skin was silken-soft, warmed from his blood, from his touch. Her nipple pebbled as he brushed it lightly. He couldn't get enough of her . . . the brief time they'd had in the dawn hours at his house hadn't been enough. This wouldn't be enough.

Eternity wasn't enough.

He angled her chin around, lowered his head and took her mouth. She opened for him and he growled as she bit his lip. Even if they forgot about the rest of the world and stayed in here for the next year, it wouldn't be enough.

But all they had, for now, was this . . .

Too much. She felt surrounded by him, flooded by him. His hands raced over her body as he moved inside her with small, rocking motions—just enough to push her right to the edge of climax . . . and keep her hovering there. Too much. On the knife's edge of pain and pleasure. It was too much.

Twisting her hips, she tried to take it deeper, faster. Toronto growled in her ear, a wordless order. And she did it again. Flooded with the taste of him, surrounded by the feel of him, it was *too much—*

Then he moved, and they were on the floor. Head spinning, she slammed her hands down to brace herself as he held her hips in his hands and reared back, driving into her with bruising, glorious force, and she cried out, her eyes closing.

Again, again—his cock throbbed, swelled inside her, the head stroking over sensitized nerves and then he slid his hand around, pressed the tip of his finger to her clit.

She shattered, falling to pieces.

The only thing that kept her from completely losing her mind was the realization that he was falling with her—he was with her. A low, eerie noise, something caught between a howl and a growl ripped through the room as he stiffened.

Dark, hot bursts of color exploded before her eyes as he fell forward, catching himself just before he would have crushed her body into the ground.

Stunned, devastated, she shook in his arms and he held her. Twisting around, she slid her arms around him and held him tight. Against her cheek, she could feel the racing of his heart.

Nothing in her life had ever felt like this. Sylvia hadn't even realized it was possible to feel like this.

It terrified her.

CAREFULLY, she peeled away the cheese and then swiped her finger through the tomato sauce. With a blissful sigh, Sylvia popped it into her mouth and closed her eyes.

Toronto eyed her as he chewed his way through his eighth piece. "You know, I can figure out another way for you to try that."

"Pervert." Wrinkling her nose at him, she sighed. "That's about all I can do anyway. Maybe another taste in an hour or so before we leave."

"No can do." He finished his piece and grabbed another. "We're leaving in ten minutes."

Sylvia snorted. "Sorry, blondie. You need to check the time. I can't leave for another hour, at the earliest."

"Yeah, you can. I had a van brought in. Your bike is in storage back at my place by now."

Narrowing her eyes, she echoed, "Storage?"

"Yeah." He rocked back on the rear legs of the chair, holding a half-eaten slice and watching her with a closed expression. "We're wasting time, only being able to move half the day. Nobody drove the bike. You have my word on it. It was loaded into a truck, taken to my place and left there. We've got a van where you can sleep in the back. I only need a couple of hours of sleep every few days, and if I have to, I can go a week. Having to stop every time the sun breaks the horizon is slowing us down and we still have another eight hours of driving ahead of us, not to mention I don't know how long it will take to pin this bastard in his lair once we get there."

He paused, took another bite of pizza as Sylvia digested all of the information.

Clenching her jaw, she said, "And just where is *here*? You still haven't told me that."

"North. We've got more driving to do still."

"North," she muttered. Hell, *that* was descriptive. She was two seconds away from demanding a more definitive answer from him, but she'd be snapping at him over the wrong thing. She'd rather fight with him over . . .

Hell. He made sense. Glaring at him with anger simmering inside her, she wished she could just tear into him, but he fucking made sense.

If he'd been an asshole about it and just barked at her instead of being *sensible*, she could have torn a strip off his hide.

"You had no right to move my bike without asking."

"True." He shrugged. "But I was trying to speed things along. I figured your main interest was in finding Pulaski . . . right?"

Shit. How did she answer that? Tell him that she was paranoid about who touched her baby? Make it seem like that was more important than finding Pulaski? It was just a motorcycle. She had four others, and it wasn't likely anything would even happen to it.

Hell, it wasn't even *just* about the bike. It was the way he was . . . moving in on her. The way it felt almost natural to be working with him. The way it felt almost natural to *be* with him. It was the way he terrified her when he held her, because it felt so damn right, so damn natural and it was going to leave a giant hole inside her when it ended. And it would end . . . how could it not?

He was a Hunter. She was a mercenary. They didn't mix.

Hell. She couldn't think about this now. She'd think about other shit. Stupid shit. His high-handed shit. Anything but the way it was going to hurt when he left. When she left. Whichever it came to be.

"Just don't make a habit of this," she muttered, turning away from him and storming into the shower. She was going to have to wash up using the hotel's crap, she thought, seizing on anything to get worked up over. She hated hotel brands—

And all of that irritation deflated when she saw the black toiletry case from her bike sitting on the counter.

She really, really wished he'd go back to being the thoughtless, arrogant asshole he was supposed to be. Her life would be so much easier that way. It was going to be a bitch as it was to walk away from him already. But if he kept doing nice things like this, and if he kept being so reasonable about other things, and so fucking good in bed . . .

And then there was the way he'd gotten so fucking pissed when she'd told him what had happened to her. When he'd said he couldn't kill whatever had hurt her if she didn't tell him . . . a weird thing to get the warm fuzzies about, but . . . hell. Everything about him got to her.

And she had a feeling it was too late to stop things—she was already too wrapped up in him. This was going to end in heartbreak, she realized. She'd gone all this time with having her heart broken.

Then some cocky, smart-ass werewolf Boy Scout came along and blew that straight to hell.

Slamming the door shut, she leaned back against it and covered her face with her hands.

Damn it.

T ORONTO listened as the door slammed, tried not to let it get to him.

It needed to be done, right? He stared at the door, wishing he could see through it, wishing he could figure her out, understand her better . . . and failing.

Miserably failing.

Shit. Closing his eyes, Toronto thought the past day through, tried to figure out how he could have, *should* have done things differently.

Did they just keep wasting time? No. That wasn't an option, and he was pretty sure Sylvia wouldn't argue that point. She had to see that this made sense, right? Why should they stay tucked up inside when he could damn well drive and make up some of the time they lost each time the sun rose?

Fuck. Maybe he should have just waited in that shitty little no-tell motel and run everything by her . . .

Hell. Was that it?

Toronto didn't know how to work with people that well. When he did work with somebody, it was always a Hunter, and usually somebody weaker than he was—leaving him in charge. A Hunter on a job had only *one* focus—the job. Just that, and there were unspoken rules.

Move hard, move fast. Period.

"But she doesn't get that," he muttered, dropping his half-eaten slice of pizza back in the box. He probably needed to eat more—skipping sleep was one thing, but weres couldn't slack on the calories. The appetite was shot, though. Grabbing a napkin, he wiped his mouth and his fingers.

Okay. So that could be the problem. Maybe. She didn't get how he worked, he wasn't used to having to explain things and they just weren't meshing well on this part. Workable, right? He'd been treating her like she was one of the other Hunters—and a subordinate. He'd made all the calls.

To her, that probably felt like she was being cut out. It wasn't that . . . exactly.

Sylvia was weaker than he was, and that wasn't likely to change much thanks to what had been done to her right after her Change, but she'd survived. She'd become a fighter in her own right, and she'd done all of that on her own. Without the security he'd always had, without the network of friends or an Enclave, and no Master to watch out for her.

She'd earned her place. She wasn't his equal in power, but she'd damn well proven her worth as a warrior.

He dumped the trash and went to the sink in the little kitchenette, washing up his face and hands. She'd earned her place, was used to doing things on her own and she probably felt like he was pushing her into the dark or something. He needed to apologize, right?

This compromise shit was a hell of a lot more work than he liked.

But they'd started this together and they'd finish it.

She emerged from the shower less than three minutes later, wrapped in a towel, her hair twisted into a braid. Those dark eyes were still cool with anger. He'd rather see them hot. Hot was easier to deal with. That ice, she used it as a distance and he hated it.

"Look, I . . . I'm used to working with other Hunters," he said, watching as she paused by the bed, eyeing the black bag he'd brought in. It had been back at his place and he'd had Lindsey bring it up when she brought the van.

"I don't think you're used to *working* with anybody." Sylvia unzipped the bag and put her toiletry case inside before pulling out a pair of close-fitting black pants and panties.

Toronto was damn glad his kind weren't prone to heart attacks because he might have had one when she dropped the towel and pulled her panties on, then her pants. With her sleek, naked back to him, she reached back into the bag again, pulling out a bra—black—and a T-shirt—black again. In under a minute, she was dressed and turning to face him. "You have this *'it's my way'* deal going. We're working this together, but you don't ask for my input, my opinions—we just do what you think needs to be done. Is that how your kind works?" She shrugged and sat down on the bed, grabbed her boots.

"In a way . . . yeah. Discussing things down to the bare bones can waste a hell of a lot of time—today, it would have. We made it to Terre Haute last night—four hours. That's all we managed. While you were sleeping in the van, I got us to Toledo and I managed to catch an hour of sleep during the day, too. Doing it this way saved us time—we don't have any to spare." He stared at her bowed head, waiting for her to look at him. "I'm not trying to cut you out . . . it's just how I'm used to operating. I've done it for a damn long time, Sylvia, and if you think it through, it makes sense. You had to rest—you can't be in the sun. But we're losing time. I can drive while you rest, so why *waste* the time?"

"And you just turn my bike over to strangers?" She shifted her dark gaze to his, her face an unreadable mask. "You haul me out of a motel in the daylight?"

"I gave it to Lindsey—a woman I trusted to get it to my house," he snapped. Then, pulling the anger back in before it raged out of control, he said in a level tone, "I get that you don't know her. And I get that you're protective as hell over the damn bike. But do you want to find Pulaski or not?"

She gave him a withering stare and tapped her feet into her boots. Rising, she grabbed her bag. "Keep your paws off my things in the future, wolf. Got it?"

Paws—

As she turned her back on him, he rolled his eyes. "Sure thing, Sylvia. Whatever you say. I'm sorry I pissed you off." He could have said he'd try not to do it again, but it wouldn't matter if he tried or not. Pissing people off was his special gift in life. He'd tried to explain—and it hadn't done jack-shit, either. She was still mad at him. Having people pissed off at him wasn't anything new . . . so why did this bother him so much?

Fuck it, he told himself silently. *Fuck it, forget it, move on.*

Easier said than done, though.

Grabbing Angel's cloak, he tossed it in Sylvia's direction. "Here."

She snagged it, whipping it around her shoulders and not looking at him. Not speaking to him.

An ache settled in his chest, one he didn't like at all. Thirty minutes ago, she'd been wrapped around his dick and shaking with climax. Then she'd cuddled against his chest and held him. Now she was furious with him, wouldn't look at him or anything.

"So, would the mighty Hunter deign to share with me any information?" Sylvia asked as fastened the cloak.

Clenching his jaw, he debated between two responses. One was pithy and full of the temper she'd managed to spark in him. He went with the second response. "I recognized one of the scents in the house we were at. We're heading back to where I've scented it before."

"And that would be where?" She pulled the hood up, leaving it pushed back from her face.

For a moment, he was struck by the exotic, soft beauty of her. The dark velvet against her ivory skin, the soft tilt of her dark eyes, that pretty mouth. Fuck, he was so screwed . . .

"Ah . . ." Turning away, he grabbed his bag from the bed. He'd already showered, already packed. He was ready. "Back where they found me, after I was attacked. A lot of us have a habit of going back to whatever place held importance for us in our mortal lives. Guess this vamp isn't any different. I've noticed it before, off and on, but it's always faint, like I'm there weeks after he is. Since nothing's ever really tugged at me while I'm there, I never bothered to track it." He frowned, absently reaching up to touch the back of his head, memories racing through his mind.

Your darkest days are in your past . . . Nessa's voice. She'd told him that so often.

I told you he wasn't going to pull through. I'll put him down, Nessa. Put him down. Like a mongrel dog.

You'll do no such thing, Mary . . .

Shit. Shoving the memories to the side, he looked up, found Sylvia watching him, her eyes blank and remote.

"And where were you found?" she asked, one brow lifted.

Forcing himself to smile, he headed for the door. "Nobody knew my name, you know. They never found any family, even though they looked. They had to call me something. I ended up telling them to call me Toronto, after the city where they found me."

*T*ORONTO—
It hit her like a punch—nothing else could have hit her that hard, except maybe if he'd looked at her and told her he was going to let Alan Pulaski go free.

Toronto.

They were going to Toronto—*nobody knew my name* . . . Shit. Of all the cities. Why couldn't he have been found in Detroit? Albuquerque? Paoli, Indiana, for crying out loud. Anywhere but Toronto . . .

Get it together, she told herself. With a shaking hand, she pulled the hood of the cloak down over her face, made sure no sun would kiss her flesh.

"I pulled the van around to the front entrance. They've got a covered overhang and it faces east. No direct sunlight, so you'll be good," Toronto said as they entered the empty stairwell.

He might as well have been speaking Latin for all the sense his words made.

Toronto.

She had to get a grip on this, before he noticed.

Too late—

They hadn't even rounded the first flight of steps when he realized something was off.

So much for her poker face.

"What's wrong?"

She shook her head. "Now's not the time."

"Then when is?" He caught her arm and pulled her to a stop. But even as she tried to reach for some way to stall him, something saved her—on the next level, there were squeals of laughter, followed by raised, tired voices. Kids. Wonderful.

"Maybe when we're not trying to get out of here. Maybe when we're done with this job. Maybe never. I don't know." Averting her face, she focused on what mattered . . . putting one foot in front of the other. That was how she'd make it through this.

If she had to go to Toronto, then damn it, she'd go to Toronto.

But she sure as hell wasn't going to strip herself bare about why the thought of it terrified her so. The past was where it belonged. In the past. And it was *her* past, damn it. The monster who'd made her was dead.

Yeah, somebody had survived—the mirror was proof of that, but it had nothing to do with her.

She'd finish the job with Pulaski.

Then she was gone. Maybe even out of the country gone.

CHAPTER 21

H<small>E</small> didn't really want to do this.

You have to do it, though . . .

That quiet little voice had gotten louder over the past few days, and it was time he listened. He just needed to get it done . . . and go back home.

The casino's hotel was a busy one. Located in Detroit, full of people looking to get drunk, get laid, throw away their money in the hopes of winning more, they blended in.

Not quite as nice as some places, but it would work.

You can't be choosy. You need to hurry. This is fine . . . do it.

Not yet—not so fast. *Not so fast?* But . . .

He ignored the voice as he studied the people in the hotel. It was busy and it was loud. And better still? There was a wolf in hiding who worked the night shift at the local cop shop. Perfect. The wolf would be his messenger. He was being chased, and although the idea scared him, he figured if he gave them what they wanted, they'd leave him alone. He hadn't done anything, really. Nobody had died because of him, except Alan—and making him a vamp wasn't *really* dying.

Plus, he'd be dead soon. They'd want that, he knew.

He watched the taller man's back as they moved into the room, already seeing how it would play out. He had a plan, of course. It was one that had come to him as he rested.

As they went into the room, Alan was already stripping out of his clothes, his eyes glowing with two different kinds of hunger.

As Alan came to him and started to tug at his clothes, he let him. He'd already wanted another time—they had fun together. He'd miss him.

THE wolf in hiding was Sean Curtis.

He worked homicide. He'd been with the Detroit Police Department for going on twelve years now and he was considering a move. The sick work he saw in front of him made him wonder if he shouldn't go ahead and make that move.

But it would follow him. The sickness. The madness.

Because he couldn't get away from the kind of monsters that did this. Not any more than he could get away from himself, at least.

He smelled vamp in the air and he smelled madness, like something dying. It was the kind of madness that ate at one's mind slowly, over a period of years, eroding away any sign of humanity, any sign of decency, any sign of empathy or compassion.

It had taken a special kind of madness to do this, that was certain.

Madness . . . and strength.

The only recognizable part of the victim was the face. Every other part of him looked like . . . meat. Just meat. Slivers of bone. Muscles and tendons bared in a grisly display.

"This is some sick shit," his partner muttered, her face a chalky gray under the warm, smooth brown of her skin. Taya Mercer stood with her arms crossed over her chest and a grim look on her face as she studied the body. *Get a good look, Taya. You won't get another one, I bet.* "Look at that— tearing up the rest of the body, but leaving the face like that. Why?"

Sean had his suspicions.

He also needed to start making some calls. This sort of shit pissed him off. They were supposed to take care of their damn problems and when they didn't, it made trouble for those who tried to live their lives as normally as possible.

Like this piece of work. That was a dead vamp on that bed and Sean knew damn good and well a vamp couldn't go through an autopsy, couldn't have his blood tested, none of it. Which meant Sean was going to have to pretend to work a murder after the body "disappeared" as this one was bound to do. Once he made a few phone calls, that would damn well happen.

The body would disappear. Any blood samples would disappear. Nobody would be able to find a fucking trace, and everybody connected to it would get a new asshole ripped. Including Sean.

He'd be dealing with questions he couldn't answer and pretending to work a murder he couldn't actually solve.

Sorry, Lieutenant, but the man was murdered by a vampire. Yes, a vampire. I'm afraid that we cannot apprehend the vampire in the normal method, unless you want to arm the men and women of the DPD with silver bullets and stakes . . .

Dragging a hand through his hair, he stared at the body on the bed. That was one big-ass problem lying there in a pool of nasty, congealing blood—blood that was the wrong color to be human, too. The techs had already commented on that.

All sorts of big-ass problems for Sean, and that was just on the job front.

Since the nutcase who'd called it in had specifically requested Sean, it told Sean two things . . . the killer knew about him, and the killer wanted this vamp found.

It couldn't have been just a run-of-the-mill psycho.

Why me?

I T had been an hour since they'd left the hotel.

During that time, Sylvia hadn't said a damn word and with every minute that passed, the silence grew more brittle.

Toronto had the bizarre thought that she might shatter if

that tension got any worse. Even though the sun was just a memory now, she remained huddled in the back, all but clinging to the doors. Hell, he wouldn't have been surprised if she'd just decide to kick them open and take off, disappear into the night.

When his cell phone started to belt out "Freaks Come Out At Night," she flinched. It hurt his heart to see it.

She was afraid. Not just pissed—that, he could handle. He didn't like it, but he could handle it. But she was *afraid* and he really didn't like that. And he hated the fact that she wouldn't talk to him.

As the phone continued to shriek at him, he grabbed it. "Yeah?"

"Where are you?"

"Nice to talk to you, too, Rafe," he muttered, glancing out the window. "I-75 North, heading through Detroit. We're on our way to Toronto—and no, I'm not on a brood-bender or whatever your lady calls them."

"What's in Canada? You're supposed to be bringing Pulaski in." There was an edge to Rafe's voice, one that Toronto couldn't quite put his finger on yet.

"I'm not sure. But . . ." He sighed, cracked his neck. "I think whoever the rich fuck running the sex games was, is a vamp. Pulaski had something to do with them, I know it. Nobody has seen hide or hair of the sorry bastard, but—"

"We've confirmed that Pulaski has participated in some of the games," Rafe said, his voice neutral. "Nobody can give me an idea where to find him. Why do you think they are in Toronto?"

"Gut instinct." Toronto drummed his fingers on the steering wheel and shot Sylvia a look in the mirror. "Any news on this guy, Kit?"

"No." Rafe paused, and then said, "I do have news, though. Pulaski is dead."

Toronto almost slammed on the brakes. And Sylvia was in the seat next to him, as quick as that. "*What?*" she demanded, her voice hard and angry.

Toronto didn't bother echoing that. Rafe wasn't going to draw this out.

"You didn't do it, did you?"

Toronto snarled. "Shit." He resisted, just barely, the urge to slam his fist into the dash. He'd done that once—the car had ended up in the repair shop. Undriveable. "No, Rafe. I didn't fucking kill him."

"And the merc?"

Toronto slid Sylvia a quick look. She was staring at him, her eyes gleaming with that hint of silver, her fangs visible. "No. Sylvia didn't do it." He waited for Rafe to question him further, but nothing else came. "What's going on?"

"I got a call," Rafe said softly. "There's a loner up in Detroit."

Loners were the weres and random shifters that weren't affiliated with anybody. Not with a pack, not with the Council—they were just that, loners. But most weres preferred to have a pack, especially if they couldn't become a Hunter or work for the Council in some way. Loners . . . well, they ran alone. If they got into trouble, they had to fix the trouble. Alone.

"What's this got to do with us?" Toronto asked.

"He's a homicide detective in Detroit. Sounds like he's living very much in the closet—I did some poking around. He coaches Little League, goes to church on Sundays, has a house with a white picket fence even. No skeletons in the closet that I can find. He goes into work today and there was a message left for him at the station. He had a present for his people in a room at the hotel at the MGM casino. Gives the room number and that's it."

"His people?"

"I'm going to assume it's us. He gets there with his partner—a human—and what he finds is a dead vampire. Want to guess who it is?"

"Pulaski." Toronto wove in and out of traffic, making his way over to the exit ramp. He'd seen signs for the MGM. He needed to see this fucking body for himself. Talk to the cop. Something.

"Yeah. How long have you suspected he was changed?"

"Just since this morning. We left a house—it's why we're headed to Toronto. I smelled a vamp. I don't know him, but

I've had the scent before. And a new one was made there not long ago. That much weird shit happening close together, it's all connected." He clenched his jaw, helpless fury burning inside him. "I fucked up. He's gone, and those families won't find what they need. And *shit*, a vamp body was left where mortals could find it? What the hell?"

Rafe was quiet for a minute. "You find that answer for me. I want to know why some son of a bitch decided to go leaving a vamp body in the open—*none* of us want that kind of exposure. Doesn't matter which side of the line we walk. You get me that answer, Tor." Then he sighed. "I put in that call for a witch—if I get somebody strong enough, she can maybe track the bodies down. We're already working on getting Pulaski's remains and a cleanup crew is heading in to deal with any other evidence."

"That's going to be fun for the cop."

"No shit."

All too aware of Sylvia's hard stare, Toronto took the exit. "I need to talk to him. See what he knows."

"You can't do it in person—not now, at least. He's going to have his hands full making sure he's got his ass covered . . . he got yanked into this mess just because he's a wolf. He doesn't need to have his life ruined, and if you fuck with his job, it's going to happen. I've got his number, you can call him from the road."

Toronto swore. Fine. Shit. It made sense, but shit.

"Is that all?" Rafe asked. "You're not going to have a temper tantrum about it?"

"Oh, kiss ass," he muttered. "I want whatever info you have on this. I'm swinging by the hotel for a few minutes, but I won't be here long."

"Yeah, yeah—just *behave*. And leave the loner out of it. Find me the fucker who did this."

"H E's dead."

Sylvia stared at Toronto as he disconnected the phone. In the glow of the lights from the dashboard, his face looked remote, far more remote than normal. And those pretty blue eyes were icy.

"Yeah. Very dead."

"How?"

"I don't know yet. But we'll find out." He turned left and hit the gas, speeding down the street so fast that everything around them was a blur. "A vamp. He was changed. Somebody made him a vamp."

Sylvia closed her eyes and passed a hand over her face. "Shit. We'd already suspected that."

"Yeah." Up ahead, a light flashed to yellow. He hit the brakes.

A hand flew up, caught her before she could go flying through the window. "Shit," she muttered, grabbing at her seat belt. She didn't always mess with them—a car wreck wasn't likely to kill her. But then again, she rarely rode with somebody who drove like Toronto. His arm was a steady, iron weight across her chest and she ignored the bump of her heart at that touch. An innocent, innocuous touch . . . and it still made her burn.

"You drive like a lunatic," she muttered as she clicked her seat belt and tugged on it, just to make certain. "Who killed him?"

Now Toronto smiled. It was a slow, mean curl of his lips and his eyes glittered in the night. "I don't know . . . but it's a good bet it was the vamp who changed him."

"Why?" Sylvia shook her head. "It doesn't make sense. Why make him, help him stay underground like that and then *kill* him? It makes no sense."

"Yes, it does . . . if he knows we're hunting Pulaski; he wanted to throw us off the trail." The smile on his face faded. "There's a loner here—he found the body. Poor bastard, he's going to have a mess in a while."

"I heard. What's a cleanup crew?" She was still trying to absorb the fact that Pulaski was dead. Her job had abruptly been jerked out from under her. But the main thing—he was dead. He couldn't hurt anybody else. Toby . . . justice for Toby. Those bright blue eyes danced through her mind, that sweet smile. And the parents of the boy who'd hired her. She could let them know it was done. They'd just wanted him dead. How hadn't mattered. Dead was dead, right?

"When a non-mortal dies and there's a body that can be messed with, it's a risk. Our blood is screwy; vamp, were, shifter, it doesn't matter—we'd rather not have it on a slide in a lab. So we send a cleanup crew. They destroy the blood products, get rid of any other evidence."

"Any other evidence . . ." She slid him a look. "How do they get rid of a body?"

"They tend to steal them." He cut a sharp left.

She saw it coming and braced herself. Still, the seat belt cut into her skin. Up ahead, the bright lights of the MGM Grand Detroit danced. Casinos weren't her thing. She didn't see the appeal of throwing away her money. It was even less appealing right now. From inside the car, she could smell the stink of death.

Cops were all over the place.

"How do you propose we get inside?"

"I don't need to get inside." He rolled the window down as they drove around for a few minutes before settling in a lot just across from the hotel itself. "I just need to get the lay of the land."

S EAN caught the scent of the wolf even from inside the casino.

It made the edgy, territorial bastard inside him start growling, hackles raised.

But it didn't have him ready to spit nails and go for blood, nor did it set every protective instinct he had on edge. Blowing out a sigh, he checked his watch.

That was rather fast. He'd only sent the message twenty minutes ago. There was no way he could get away right now, either. If that Hunter came prowling around his scene, Sean was going to be pissed.

Hell. I'm already pissed. Squatting down by one of the techs, he pretended to be as thrown as they were by the damage done to the body. There wasn't much that could have surprised him, though, not once he'd caught the stink of crazed vampire.

Rising, he made a meandering path over to the window, gave an absent glance out. Saw the other were in a lot across the street.

Blond. Tall. Lean. Had a woman at his side . . . vamp. Pretty one. And it wasn't five seconds before they both looked up and saw him in the window. He could see the way the were's eyes narrowed. Felt the dominance rolling from him.

Sean curled his lip at him and turned away. He had a scene to work. If the wolf was still around when he finished, Sean would talk to him. If not, wasn't that what AT&T was for?

D ESPITE the restless, futile rage rolling through her, Sylvia was amused when she caught the way the were turned his back on them. She'd felt that silent roll of power come from Toronto. If she'd been a wolf, she would have been cowering at his feet.

"I don't think he's too impressed with you," she said mildly.

Toronto slid her a narrow look. "I wasn't really trying. If I wanted him down here, trust me, he'd be down here." He shrugged and started to pace, his head tipped back, nostrils flared. "The vamp was here—the one we're tracking. I'm still thinking he did this to throw us off his trail. Has been gone a few hours—some power, because I think he left before sunset. Did the kill earlier in the day, maybe when Pulaski was sleeping."

Sylvia had already noticed that, but she remained silent. He was working through the scent pattern or something. That required more skill than she had.

"He was clean when he left. No blood on him. Wasn't angry or anything, either. Not angry, not afraid." Toronto stopped, his eyes hooded as he stared off into the night. "This didn't mean much of anything to him."

"Maybe he's just good at control."

"No." Shaking his head, he continued to stare off into the

night as he picked the scent trail apart. "There's something else . . ."

"Like . . . ?"

"Well, he's fucking nuts for one. I smell the madness in him—it's like his brain is rotting inside." Then he shrugged. "Other than that, I'd need to be closer to the scene. Closer to where he was. And we can't do that with all the cops crawling around. This is enough for now."

Flicking one more look at the hotel, he headed back to the car. As he slipped into the seat, he grabbed his phone and sent Rafe a message. *At hotel. Not much for me to see here. Heading out now. Need to talk to that cop. Will call him from the road—number?*

It wasn't but a minute before the reply came back. *Just keep it at a phone call, Tor. And remember he's got his hands full and he's not one of ours, not one of yours.*

"Yeah, yeah." Toronto curled his lip and glanced up at the hotel. Wasn't like he'd been planning to storm in there and demand the other wolf start licking his boots or anything.

He sent a quick text. *I'd like a word when you have time, cop.*

He hadn't even pulled out of the lot before the reply came. *If this is the blond guy or the hot brunette, it will have to wait. Other things take precedence.*

Toronto narrowed his eyes as he slowed for a red light. That little pup had better watch it around the hot brunette . . . she was Tor's. *You don't want it to wait too long, cop. I just want details. You call me when you have five minutes, but you might want to do it soon.*

The next text came with a short response. Toronto snorted.

"You look amused." Sylvia gave him a narrow look. "I don't see too much about this that's amusing."

"That's because you weren't just told to go howl at the moon by a wolf you could break with one hand behind your back." He dumped the phone on the console. Something told him he'd have a bit of a wait before he got the call he needed, but that was okay. The vamp was already on the move.

"Where to?"

He shot Sylvia a look as he hit the gas and shot up the

ramp to the expressway. "Back on the road. We'll be in Toronto before dawn."

"But . . ." She glanced back toward Detroit. "We need to find out more about what happened to Pulaski."

"No, we don't," Toronto said quietly. "Other people have this. We need to find his killer, figure out why in the hell he did this publicly, make sure he won't do it again. Or at least that's what I have to do. I can't make you come with me."

"What, you're not going to take over again?" she muttered. Sighing, she shook her head. "We started it together. We finish together."

Then, as the night wind came blowing in through the open windows, he reached over and caught her hand. His thumb rubbed over the back of it. "Rafe already knows we're working this together. I'll call him. We'll get something to give to the family—they'll have peace."

Sylvia closed her eyes. "And what about the other kids he stole?"

"Rafe's working on that. We'll put a witch or something on it."

Sylvia closed her eyes. "It's too late."

"Not yet, it's not. Some of the witches, some of the psychics, they have freaky ass talents—some of them can pull memories from a fresh corpse, if they have to. Others can visit his home, maybe find something there that can lead them to his victims—what he did there is going to linger. Somebody will be able to untangle it and find answers." He twined his fingers with hers. "I'm sorry."

She was glad he didn't mention anything about how she'd tried to act as though those other victims hadn't been a concern. They had always been a concern. And now . . . *Stop it*, she told herself. *Just stop it.*

"Hell. He's dead. That's justice enough." Turning her head, she stared at him in the night. "It wasn't for me, though. Not really. One of the boys he killed . . . Toby. His name was Toby."

Toronto waited in silence, his gaze on the road. Good . . . if he looked at her, this would be harder. "Toby . . . he reminded me of somebody. Another kid who suffered because of a monster. I wanted justice because of him. That doesn't even make sense, does it?"

"Yeah, it does." Brooding, he stared straight ahead. "I didn't want to take the job. Rafe was going to give it to somebody else, but I didn't want anybody else near you. From the time I saw your picture, I was obsessed. But I hated that I had to stop you from killing Pulaski. The only thing that made it tolerable is that I knew how those families feel . . . living with unanswered questions. I've had them all my life. I wouldn't wish it on anybody."

Her fingers tightened on his. And she laughed, but it was a strained, unhappy sound. "Aren't we a couple of fucking badasses, Tor?"

"You bet we are."

CHAPTER 22

"It looks . . . different." Sylvia stared at the city, trying to take it all in. She didn't have much time. In less than an hour the sun would rise and she'd have to go to ground, find someplace safe.

He moved so quietly, just a whisper of sound before he was at her back. His fingers brushed through her hair as he said quietly, "You were made here."

"Yes." Arms wrapped around her middle, she gazed at the jeweled lights of the skyline. Nothing looked the same. At all.

"How long has it been since you've been back?"

"Eighty-four years . . . I came back to kill the one who made me." She blew out a breath. "I'd been living in California when he found me. He kidnapped me and dragged me across the country to this place . . . I *hated* this place, and I never wanted to see it again."

"What changed things?"

"A vamp tried to take my home." With a deep, shaking breath, she turned away from the city, met Toronto's gaze. "After I left here, I ran. So hard, so fast. Once I found someplace where I felt safe, I went into hiding—only left to feed and that was it. Then a vamp showed up at my place—he was running, too, and he needed a place to hide. *My* place. My safe place—my *home*. I was ready to run, ready to let him have it . . . I didn't want to die. Shit, I was such a coward."

"Not wanting to die doesn't make you a coward."

She held his gaze. "Running away? Letting him take what I'd earned? What I'd made mine? Not putting up a fight? *That* made me a coward." She shook her head and moved away from him. "He had a mercenary on his trail. A wolf . . . a woman. I'd gone and hid in a nearby barn, burrowed under the hay because the sun was coming. She found me—you damn wolves and your noses. There was this look in her eyes . . . she was so disgusted when she saw me. Disgusted. And sad for me. I saw it in her eyes.

"She didn't say anything. I think she knew what had happened. She just left me there. Went on to the house he'd stolen from me. Killed him while I lay hiding under straw and hoping I wouldn't be found while I waited for the sun to set." She blinked, a far-off look in her eyes. "It was the worst day I could remember since getting away from the one who'd made me. Then I woke up. And she was there. She asked me if I planned on living my entire life hiding like a mouse anytime somebody looked at me wrong."

"I take it you told her no."

She laughed weakly. "At the time, I was too damn terrified. But eventually, yes. That was the answer. And she was the one to teach me. It took me years to work up the courage to come back here." In a soft voice, she murmured, "By the time I came back, he was already dead. So I left. I left, and never looked back. Didn't plan on ever returning to this godforsaken place."

"And here you are."

She turned and stared at Toronto. "Yes. Here I am." Her gut was a slimy, nasty pit of fear, but here she was. A wave of exhaustion flooded her, and she looked to the east. It wasn't lightening yet, but it would. Soon. "It will be dawn before long."

"Yeah." He closed the distance between them again, reached up to toy with her hair. "I've got a place for us. It's small, quiet. Old. But it's the safest place I know. You'll rest easy there."

Sylvia nodded. "And you'll do what? I haven't seen you rest much."

"I grabbed an hour yesterday while you slept. I'll grab a couple of hours before I hit the streets."

Reaching up, she curled a hand over his wrist. Against her fingers, his pulse beat in a strong, steady rhythm. "And if you find him that fast? What then?"

From hooded eyes, he watched her. "You need to be a part of it, don't you?"

"Yeah." She swallowed, shifting her gaze away. "I need to know who was in that house. Why he had the mirror. I need answers, Toronto."

"Okay." He lowered his head, pressed his lips to her brow. "Unless I have to kill him, I'll wait until you're with me. But if he goes after somebody, if he's an immediate threat, I'll have to take him out. That's the best I can do, though. He's already proven he's a crazy fuck."

Weakly, she smiled. "Yeah. Leaving a vamp body the way he did was a good indicator."

H E'D asked for a witch.

And here she was, on his doorstep. The only thing Rafe could think when he saw the redhead was, *Hell. At least it's not Nessa.*

Not that Kelsey Hughes was much better.

"I heard you needed a witch." She smiled at him. Kelsey looked innocent and wholesome and kind . . . like a soccer mom. Like a PTA mom.

She could burn things with just a thought, could heal busted, broken bodies and could ferret out the nastiest of magics. Basically, she was perfect for what Angel had wanted her for, he suspected. Of course, she was also an active Council member. She could very well be here to bust his ass or kick him out.

Trying to keep everything locked down, Rafe just stepped aside.

"You heard right."

She sauntered in past him and took a look around the house before shooting him a smile. "I love what you've done with the place."

He scowled. Once upon a time, it had been her home. Now it was his. He hated feeling awkward, but he did. He'd fucked up—

"So, how are we going to play this?"

Meeting her green gold eyes, Rafe asked quietly, "We?"

"Yes." She slid her hands into her pockets and rocked back on the heels of worn, battered boots. "We. Your land. Your problem. You need to fix it . . . if you want to keep it. I'm just here for support."

Narrowing his eyes, he crossed his arms over his chest. "*If* I want to keep it?"

She smiled. "Nobody will kick you out if you prove you're capable of fixing the problems, Rafe. It's not like they don't happen. We can't be everywhere. So, again . . . how do we play this?"

"S o, two witches and a psychic walk into a school . . ." Angel said under her breath.

The woman playing Angel's mom—Tamara—looked tense, fine lines bracketing out from her mouth. Just meeting Kelsey had been enough to put the other witch on edge. Angel knew she probably wasn't helping, being sort of nervous herself.

Kelsey didn't look nervous. Didn't look worried.

And she kept that easy, calm veneer up the entire time Tamara handed the office staff a bullshit story about an extended trip—she had been offered a wonderful job, and Angie would be staying with her cousin, Kelsey. Kelsey, of course, would make sure she did all of her assignments, blah, blah, blah . . .

All of that shit might have been done over the phone, with a letter.

But they needed a legit reason to get Kelsey in the school.

Because once Kelsey walked in, she didn't leave.

Just an illusion of her, walking down the steps next to Tamara.

It was a damn good illusion, too. Even though Angel *knew* it had happened, her eyes, her mind insisted she'd seen Kelsey leaving.

A whisper of sound came to her ears, and inside her skull, she heard an amused voice, *So. How powerful is this psychic who walked into a school . . . can you hear me now?*

Grinning, Angel gave a minute nod as she made her way to her locker.

Good. You go about your business, Angel. I smell some nasty, nasty magic . . .

And then, Angel was alone in her head.

"*I* warned him, Sada."

She stared in horror at the still, pale child, hardly aware of the bastard in front of her. Harold stood near her, watching her with cruel amusement glittering in his eyes. "Why are you crying over him? He is the reason you are here, after all."

She blocked out that hated voice. The boy . . . that poor boy. He'd tried to help her. And this was what had happened. Reaching out a hand, she went to touch his chest, but Harold kicked him, sent the boy flying across the room.

He never made a sound.

Harold crouched in front of her, his green eyes glittering with curiosity. "Why do you care?" he asked. Catching a lock of her hair in his hand, he twined it around his finger, rubbing it with his thumb. "It is not as if that boy ever had anything to offer you, not as if he could have truly helped you."

She shoved at his hand. "Get away from me."

He caught the front of her shift and pulled her against him. "You forget yourself, Sada."

Pain lashed through her as he kissed her, his fangs slicing through her mouth when she wouldn't open for him.

She cared little. What had she done . . .

As she started to sob, Harold rose. "Tears already, Sada?

How . . . boring." In an almost absent move, he kicked her as well. Startled, she screamed, but it ended as she hit the wall and her head thudded against the solid rock. She slid, dazed, to the floor, her gaze locked on the boy's face.

I'll help you . . . even if it kills me . . .

Oh, you silly child . . .

"Get that waste out of there," Harold said to somebody out in the corridor.

Sada continued to stare at his still, pale face. His feeble, thready heartbeat was failing and he'd lost too much blood to survive. She could all but see the death on him. *My fault,* she thought woodenly. *This child dies because of me . . .*

"What—"

Still dazed, she lifted her head and stared at Harold, saw him holding the other boy. He hung in the air, dangling from Harold's fist by his shirtfront. Dirty hair hung in his eyes and he held a knife—a bloody one. *"You little animal,"* Harold growled, wiping the blood from his face. He hurled the boy to the floor. *"You could have made it through this, you know."*

"I'll gut you," the boy promised, his pale blue eyes glittering and angry. *"You're a fucking dead man."*

And Harold started to laugh.

"No, boy. You are. But since you're such a little fighter, I'll make you get the sort of death you deserve. A bloody one."

"No," she whispered. She shoved upright and lunged for the door. But the locked bars stopped her. Shoving her hand through the door, she grabbed at Harold's arm. *"Leave him alone. He has done you no true harm."*

He just smiled at her and walked away, dragging the struggling boy along behind him.

Moments later, she heard him scream.

*M*Y *fault—*
    Sylvia opened her eyes, staring at the exposed wooden beams overhead.

Light filtered in through the curtains—sunlight. Early in the evening, still. Turning her head, she stared at the windows.

The cabin belonged to a witch—Toronto had said her protections would keep sunlight from bothering her, and she'd trusted him. Apparently, the witch knew her business.

Kind of a shame.

Right now, Sylvia felt like a good, scorching burn would feel . . . well, right. She wanted to punish herself. That dream hadn't come on her that real, that intense in years. And the guilt was choking her. Two boys, both dead, because of her. One for trying to help, one for trying to avenge his fallen friend.

"Shit." Swinging her legs around, she rubbed at her eyes, then slid a hand around to the back of her neck.

A warm palm covered hers.

She held still as Toronto started to rub the muscles there, lowering himself to sit on the edge of the bed. He was still, so quiet. She'd known he was in the house, but hadn't realized he'd come into the room. He threw her off guard. That wasn't good.

"Are you okay?" he asked softly.

"Yeah." Keeping her head bowed, she opened her eyes and stared at the smooth, worn planks of the floor. There were throw rugs here and there, made by hand, she suspected, just like the quilt on the bed. A lot of history in this place. A lot of love.

And the power crackled in the air, even though the witch wasn't around.

"You're not a very good liar," Toronto said, pushing her hair over her shoulder and shifting so that he sat behind her. She groaned as he pressed his thumbs into her back, massaging his way down her spine. "I'm fine. Just . . . dreams." Memories. "I shouldn't be here."

"Why? Do you think whoever this is is going to have some pull on you?"

A vamp's maker could control a weaker vamp to some extent, as could others of his "family," but the connection had to be close. "No . . . it's not that." Brooding, she eased away from his talented hands and climbed off the bed, moving to stand by the window. She lifted a hand and rested it on the windowpane, amazed that she could do it. That she didn't burn. She could see the sun . . . truly see it as it sank closer and closer to the horizon. "I shouldn't be *here*. Period. Shouldn't be anywhere."

Swallowing, she leaned her head forward, resting her brow on the glass. "I keep remembering the weeks before he let me go. The way I killed that boy . . . I don't even remember how he came to be in there. I just remember the blood. The hunger. And then the hunger was gone . . . and I held a dying child in my arms."

"Don't do this to yourself, Syl," Toronto said quietly.

Turning, she stared at him. "Don't do this to myself?" she echoed. "Why the hell *not*?"

"If you don't remember how he came to be in there, that's because the fucker who made you probably had him bleeding and pushed him in there while you were asleep—he probably had you half mad with hunger and then put bleeding meat in front of you. What will a starved lion do when presented with food? It attacks, Sylvia."

"I'm not a *lion*." She shook her head. "I'm still capable of reason, of thought. But I acted like an animal . . . I let myself become one. That boy wasn't *food*."

"You were tortured. He knew what he was doing, and he did it damn well." Toronto came off the bed. "You didn't let it break you because you didn't go insane with it. If you were the monster you want to think you are, you'd be like those you hunt down."

He came to her, cupped her chin in his hand.

She resisted for a moment, wanting to do anything but stare in Toronto's blue eyes. It would be easy if she thought she could find condemnation there—she *should* see it. She wanted somebody to hate her as she hated herself. Wanted to feel that bitterness and hurt herself with it. But there was just compassion there. It broke her.

A harsh sob escaped her and she sagged against him, her hands coming up to fist in his black T-shirt. One of his hands cupped the back of her head. The other came around her waist, pulling her in close to him. His lips rested against her temple and as she cried, she heard the strong, steady beat of his heart.

* * *

"I found a place that feels off to me. It's all covered with a vamp's scent—his—but I can't pinpoint the place." Toronto braced his elbows on the table, watching her face as he spoke.

She looked up from the table, her face a pale, unreadable mask. She'd cried for nearly thirty minutes. And then, just like that, she'd cut off the flow of tears and pulled away. Without a word. Toronto wished like hell that he had some way of breaking through that wall of hers, but he was clueless.

Probably a result of living the past century stuck inside his own damn skull and not bothering to pay attention to the world around him unless it delivered a sharp kick to his ass.

She lifted a brow and said coolly, "And you're telling me this . . . why?"

"It's a lot of what it felt like when I was around you that first night. I should have sensed you long before I did, but until I actually *saw* you, I didn't even know you were there. It's a talent of yours, isn't it?"

"Yes." She shrugged. She reached into a pocket and pulled out a file, going to work on her nails. "That's my one shining accomplishment in more than a century—I can mask my presence from other non-mortals. I have mad skills, don't I?"

Toronto smiled at her, but she didn't smile back. "Hey, it's not a bad skill . . . pretty damn useful, if you ask me. I can keep people from picking up on how powerful I am, but hiding myself completely? That's not so easy. I spent nearly three hours combing through the city. Was like trying to find Hansel and Gretel after they marked their way with breadcrumbs. Pointless."

She shrugged, unimpressed.

"Can you sense him, do you think?"

Sylvia's gaze swung back around to him. Her eyes, darker than normal against her pale skin, widened. "Me?" She swallowed and looked down, focusing on the back and forth motion of her nail file.

"Yeah. If he was made by the same one who made you, there's a connection there. Can you use it?"

She continued to sit there, head bowed, focusing on her nails. He had the feeling her nails would be nothing but nubs if this conversation lasted much longer.

In the next second, she stopped, laying the file aside. "I don't know. I always knew when he was around. I felt like a rabbit, ready to dart into a hole to get away from him." She shoved back from the table and started to pace, her long legs scissoring back and forth, her gaze troubled. "It was a hot burn on my skin—the closer he was, the worst it felt."

"Did his other vamps affect you like that?"

"I felt them. They didn't make me want to bury myself someplace dark and deep and spend the next fifty years in hiding, but I could sense them." She stilled and shot him a look over her shoulder, a considering look in her eyes. "I don't know if that will translate to much, though. I haven't ever used my ability like that. I've never cared to."

"If you can use it that way, it's going to come instinctively." He rose from the chair, wondering if she'd start shying away from him again.

Sylvia held her ground, though, watching him with that careful, blank look.

"It doesn't mean it will come *easily*, even instinct can kick and pull from time to time, but it's got to be better than what I'm doing." He reached out to toy with her hair, but stopped himself when she flinched. "Sylvia?"

"Don't." She shook her head. "Just don't . . . okay?"

Closing his hand into a fist, he lowered it. "Sure." It was hard for her, he knew. Being here. He wanted to help, wanted to do all that stroking and soothing and patting . . . all that stuff he was fucking *useless* at. Giving her a tight smile, he turned away. It was hard for her to be here and she didn't really want his lousy attempts to comfort her.

He could understand that, too.

He just hadn't thought it would hurt so damn much.

Shooting a look outside, he saw that the sun was kissing the horizon. A few more minutes—still had a few more minutes before she should be outside.

"Toronto . . ."

Over his shoulder, he said tersely, "I need to go check a few things. I'll be back soon. We're going to do this on foot, so you need to be safe to travel outside."

He was out the door before she could say anything else.

There was a funny, heavy ache in his chest. Absently, he pressed his hand to it as he moved in a lope toward the far western edge of Nessa's land. Shit. Sylvia had really managed to figure out how to hurt him. And this wasn't the first time, either.

How was she able to do this to him, turn him into knots like this?

A second later, he almost tripped over his own feet as he figured it out. Through the rush and roaring blood pounding in his ears, he remembered being here just days earlier. When was it . . . a week ago?

Was it like wham, *some sort of click and you just knew? Did it take longer?*

Yes . . . and yes. There were all sorts of clicks . . .

Seeing that picture of Sylvia, feeling that strange little bump inside. The way he felt better when she smiled. The way he ached when he knew she was sad. How fricking *bizarre* it was to even know when she *was* sad . . .

"It doesn't happen like this," he muttered. "It just doesn't."

Why in the hell would fate throw something like this at him?

But then he realized the truth of it all—why shouldn't fate throw it at him?

The universe had gone and flipped him straight on his head, and it was likely just deserts for spending the past hundred years thinking about nobody save himself.

Now he had somebody else in his head . . . all the time, somebody he couldn't stop thinking of. And she was already doing her damnedest to separate herself from him.

The ache in his chest swelled until he thought it just might split him apart.

She might enjoy twisting on the sheets with him, but that didn't mean she had feelings for him. Hell, if she did, she wouldn't pull away from him when he tried to help, right?

Leaning against the wooden fence, he stared numbly off into the growing dusk. All these years of being an uncaring bastard had just caught up to him, in a brutal way.

Inside, his wolf shifted and started to pace. A long, hollow howl rose in his skull, aching to be released. He kept it quiet. When the job was done. He'd give into it when the job was done, and he'd managed to get some time away.

Just leave . . . a snide voice inside him whispered. *Leave now . . . That's what you really want, isn't it?*

He didn't, though.

He'd finish the damn job. Then he'd go back to Memphis, and do whatever else was needed of him, and he'd wait until Rafe gave him leave to go. Closing his eyes, he shoved away from the fence and straightened, staring up at the sky. "I get the point."

Rolling his shoulders, he forced himself to let go of the tension mounting there. As it drained away, he cracked his neck and then, slowly, he blew out a breath.

The wolf was going to come out and play sometime soon, but for now, he needed to get back to the house and keep a lid on everything. *Everything.*

Gathering up that fabled control he was supposed to have, he turned back and stared at the house. He was a fucking Master were. It was time to start acting like one. In all ways.

T HE man who came into the cabin looked a stranger. Remote. Contained. Controlled.

It was the Master were she would have expected to face, if she'd known she'd been dealing with one when she first hit Memphis, Sylvia decided.

And it wasn't the wisecracking, lovable bastard she wanted.

She'd meant to tell him she was sorry for pushing him away. She just needed . . . hell. Sylvia didn't even know what she needed right then. Her head was a mess and she couldn't think. Couldn't focus.

"Are you ready?" he asked, his voice polite.

Polite. She didn't *want* him polite. She wanted him

bossing her around and whispering dirty words in her ear . . . or wrapping his arms around her and not bothering to speak at all.

"Ah, yeah. In a minute." She'd already gathered her weapons. Knives. Check. Gun. Check. What to say to Toronto . . . that wasn't quite so easy to figure out. Swallowing, she hooked her thumbs in her pockets and said, "Look, I'm sorry if I'm . . ."

Toronto's blue eyes cut her way and then he shrugged, turned away. With his back to her, he said, "Nothing to apologize about, Sylvia. We're here on a job, after all, right? Just a job. Let's get it done so we can both get back to our lives."

She flinched. *Just a job . . .*

"Yeah." Shooting a look at the door, she said, "Let's get it the hell done."

CHAPTER 23

SOMETHING out there in the night was crawling around looking for him.

Kit felt it. He laid low, prowling through the lowest levels of his house, checking his escape routes.

He should run.

Except every now and then, he caught a scent that tickled something in the back of his memory. He couldn't quite place it, but it called to him. Made tears burn, made his throat ache.

And being here was worse, so much worse. The memories were stronger this time. Why? He didn't know.

He needed to run . . . but he couldn't.

Voices echoed in his mind, a blurred, mad cocktail and he couldn't quite separate one from the other.

Stupid little boy . . . you want to help her . . . fine. You'll help—I'll see to it.

. . . Can't help her. There's nothing we can do.

I have to save her—

Don't tell me you're sorry, boy . . .

Moaning, he buried his face in his hands and leaned against the wall. "Shut up," he said. "Shut up, shut up, *shut up!*"

The sound of his final, screaming words was still fading when he felt a prickle along the back of his neck, and a burn along the edges of his mind.

"No."

Close . . . too close.

S YLVIA stood staring at the house.
It was ridiculously modern. Shiny glass. Lots of metal.

And it stood in the exact spot where Harold's home had been all those years ago.

"Who owns this place?" She turned her head and looked at Toronto. He had been silent all night, trailing behind her like a silent shadow. "I can find out, but I'd have to spend some time researching. I bet you Boy Scouts have a network for just this sort of thing, don't you?"

She forced a smile, waiting to see that mirth light his eyes, but all he did was reach into his pocket and pull out a phone. His eyes sought out an address, dismissing her. She heard a voice come on the line. With a sigh, she turned away.

Apparently, wolves had a thing with being snubbed. *Get over it*, she told herself. So she couldn't do any touchy-feely crap right now. That was understandable, as far as she was concerned—she needed some space to process this, damn it.

He'd just have to yank the stick out of his ass. Before she did it herself, and beat him with it in the process.

Looking back to the house, she moved forward and lifted her hands, curled them around the posts of the wrought iron fence, searching the house. Something had pulled her here. Toronto had told her instinct should guide her, and she'd just started to walk. This was where she'd ended up, but that could have been because her memories had led her here . . . right?

Taking a deep breath, she closed her eyes.

It was a conscious thing, the trick she used to keep herself undetected by other predators. So it made sense that it was a conscious thing that would let her sense somebody else doing—

There was a burn on her brain.

Something nagging and small, but pressing against the edge of her subconscious, all the same. Small, and trying to make itself smaller . . .

I felt like a rabbit, ready to dart into a hole to get away from him.

And that's what this seemed to be, something burrowing itself deeper, trying to hide away.

Swallowing, she made herself open her eyes and stare at the house.

"We've got a name—apparently it belongs to a Harold Adler."

She managed to keep from flinching at the name. Harold Adler? The last name was a crock, but that wasn't any surprise. Most of them had a lot of fake names they used. Harold, though, why was he calling himself *Harold*?

"Harold was the one who made me," she said quietly. "And there's somebody here." Hearing a weird, whining sound, she looked down and realized she'd been twisting the metal. Hell. Sighing, she looked back up, focusing on the house instead of the strangely silent wolf at her side.

"Are you sure?" His nostrils flared and she knew he was checking the air.

"Yes." She'd already checked it herself and although her ability to scent-track was nothing compared to his, she hadn't really caught much, either. It didn't matter.

There was somebody in there.

Toronto moved closer and she shot a look up at him. Her heart managed to give one painful lurch in her chest, but all he did was focus his eyes on the house. He hadn't looked at her for more than a minute since they'd left the cabin, damn it. Why in the hell was he so pissed? *Was* he pissed—

"How do we get inside?"

Forcing herself to shrug it all off, she stared at the house. "The same way I always get into a house," she said, and she was damn proud to hear that her voice was about as emotionless as his. "We'll break in."

"He'll hear us."

She slipped him a look as she reached into her pocket for her lockpicks. "That's why you can wait out here. Regardless of what he's doing to keep you from sensing him, if he takes off, he's going to rattle his cover and you'll zoom in on him. This sort of ability works the best if he's hiding. If he takes off running, you'll get a better feel for him. It's why you sensed me so easily; I wasn't hiding."

She jumped over the fence and headed for the elaborate stairwell without another word. She had plenty of words she wanted to use—words like *I'm sorry, Why are you so mad? Are you really going to just walk away* . . . But now wasn't the time, and she needed to keep that in mind.

C LOSER.
  She was closer.

It *was* a she. He could smell her even better now, and it was so familiar. Kit shouldn't have come here. It wasn't usually so hard to think here, but ever since he'd killed Alan, things were worse. The voices louder. The blood brighter. He couldn't feed enough and the thirst was terrible.

It had been getting worse for a while, but it had never been this all-consuming—

T RYING to ignore the worry that was a scream in his gut, and the hollow ache that lingered in his chest, Toronto continued to stare up at the house. He could see Sylvia there, crouching in the darkness.

He didn't like this shit—her up there alone.

Didn't like it at all.

His phone vibrated in his pocket and he tugged it out, about ready to turn it off, but the name caught his attention. Josiah didn't text. He hated to even carry the damn cell phone.

Identified some of the chemicals from the house but be careful if you smell it again—get the hell away. The base is from a plant called pennyroyal—safe enough if you don't eat it . . .

Toronto scowled as he skimmed the next message.

This entire compound is a fucking disaster—there's shit

in here that's toxic to humans even in small amounts. It's poison. I'm also getting traces of cyanogenic glycosides and—

"Cyano what?" Toronto swore. Gibberish—it was all gibberish. He punched in a message. *Josiah? I'm not the chemistry freak. I'm not following this.*

A brief moment of nothing and then, a short, terse explanation. *Like most poisons, it's the amount you ingest that will get you. This isn't just one kind of poison, either, it's a shitload of poisons.*

I told Rafe he needs to get out there with a team and start looking for dead bodies, because any human around this shit for long was a corpse waiting to happen.

Humans are fucked. For us, depends on how big a dose you get and how strong you are. The shit is poison, though. Could drive one of us crazy—eat the brain right up.

"Drive us crazy," Toronto muttered. Lifting his gaze up, he studied the house. Sylvia had already opened the locks.

What if somebody was already on edge? he texted Josiah. *Then this would push them over hard and fast.*

He shoved the phone into his pocket just as Sylvia opened the door and slipped into the house . . . alone.

T HERE was another mirror. Hell. Did he have to use the same damn mirror? Sylvia caught sight of her ghostly reflection and even before she turned to face it, she knew what she'd seen.

The house appeared empty, but was anything but.

She could hear him, moving around somewhere below.

She could smell, too, that scent from the house in New Madrid. Beyond that, there wasn't anything familiar about it. She didn't like it, though. It smelled . . . wrong. Off. Like death.

This wasn't *exactly* like the smell of death; it was close, like rotten meat, hidden away, or forgotten about. It hung on the back of her tongue, clogging her senses until she could hardly smell anything past it.

Past *him*, she corrected. It was coming from the vampire.

She paused by the mirror and made herself block every-

thing out. She didn't need to breathe, so if she stopped rely-
ing on her nose, she wouldn't have to worry about having
that rotted stink in her head. Hearing a whisper of sound
behind her, she moved to the side, drawing a blade.

And then she stilled as she saw Toronto prowling his way
toward her. His eyes were glowing—swirling back and forth
between pale blue and eerie gold. *Wolf eyes . . .*

She lifted a brow and mouthed, *Outside.*

Shaking his head, he looked past her to the mirror. His
nostrils flared and a ripple of distaste danced across his face,
the gold in his eyes gleaming brighter, hotter.

Then he looked back at her.

So much for him waiting outside.

Turning back to the mirror, she reached up, sliding her
hand along it. This one was newer, she supposed. The mechanism was hidden differently, too, took a moment to find it.

But once she hit it, the door slid open with a whisper and
she found herself staring down a flight of stairs that were
horrifyingly familiar.

He'd built it right over the spot, she realized. Exactly.

As a fist wrapped itself around her gut, she rested a hand
against the wall. The smell was stronger now. Stronger. And
the vampire wasn't moving, either . . . waiting, she realized.

He was waiting . . . down there in that dungeon.

*S*HE'S *here . . .*
   Kit peered toward the stairs and wondered why he
didn't run.

I need to run. I should—

There was another smell, too, and it was one that struck
fear into the very heart of him.

But she was here . . .

I'll save you, Sada—

Even through the pain, he'd remembered that promise.
And he remembered how he failed. He also remembered
screams. Solomon's screams as Harold drug him away.

But he'd paid. Good ol' Harry. Kit giggled. He'd paid the
price, oh, he had.

*   *   *

THAT mad little giggle sent a shiver down Sylvia's spine as it echoed up through the stairwell.

Judging by the way Toronto aligned himself at her side, he didn't like it, either.

She wanted to remind him that he was supposed to be outside. Watching. Ready to chase . . .

Except some part of her didn't really want him gone, and another part of her suspected whoever was down there wasn't going to take off on them. If he was, he'd have done it already.

Swallowing the metallic taste of fear that had risen in her throat, she started down the steps. Memories slammed into her.

He'll pay you—
I'm so sorry—
He wouldn't listen—
I'll gut you—
I'll get you out . . . I'll get you out . . . I'll get you out I'llgetyououtI'llgetyouout—

"You got out . . ."

The voice tripped her up.

It caught her off guard so badly, she almost tripped and went to her ass.

That voice. Oh. That voice.

Stunned, she turned her head, seeking out the speaker. Shadows danced along the edges of her vision, distorting everything she saw. A hand touched her shoulder. "It's him. He uses shadows," Toronto murmured, his voice all but inaudible. "He's there."

Glancing back, she saw where he was watching and she followed that line, staring through the shadows . . . and just like that, the illusion of darkness faded. She saw . . . a ghost.

"No." She shook her head. "You . . . you're *dead*."

He stared at her, his eyes bleak, haunted. And mad. The light of insanity glinted there.

"You got out," he whispered again.

"You *died*."

He rose from his crouch on the floor, dragging his tongue

across his lip. And she saw the fangs. Fangs that seemed too large for his mouth. He had been a skinny boy, she thought distantly. A skinny, sad little boy who'd just wanted to try and undo a mistake . . .

Tears blurred her eyes. "I'm sorry, Christopher."

He flinched. "*Don't say sorry to me, boy*," he parroted, his voice mocking.

Then he cocked his head, looking puzzled and confused. "You got out, Sada. How did you get out? I kept coming back, looking for you . . . but he said he killed you. Just like he killed Solomon."

The pain in his seemingly young voice, the pain she saw in his insane eyes . . . it was real. "He didn't kill me. After he was done playing with me, he just let me go."

"He . . ." The man-boy looked down, thin shoulders stooped. A harsh sigh escaped him. "He let you go."

"Yes."

A harsh roar escaped him and he turned, driving one fist into the wall. The rock shattered under the impact, and Sylvia stared. Power rolled from him and she realized one painful fact. The boy she'd thought she'd killed . . . he was stronger than she was. He was insane. And he was strong.

"He killed Sol," Christopher whispered. "He told me he killed you. After he made me drink his blood, he threw me out on the street and told me that I'd burn."

Christopher turned a tortured face to stare at her. "All these years, I made myself pay for failing you . . . and he let you go."

Small, hard muscles bunched—Sylvia saw it coming. But she was still too dazed to move.

Toronto didn't have that problem. He moved her aside and she felt another ripple of power roll through the air.

When he moved in front of her, he wasn't the pretty, laughing blond, nor the brooding silent stranger of the past few hours.

He was a hulking thing from the depths of a nightmare—torn between wolf and man and towering almost seven feet in the air, the werewolf caught the vampire as it came for them.

* * *

It was disconcerting, Toronto had to admit, facing the illusive Kit. He'd been changed when he was still a teen, a young one, at that, possibly underfed. He didn't look much older than fourteen, with dishwater blond hair that hung in his eyes, a thin face and big, summery blue eyes that somehow managed to look innocent despite the depravity that lurked behind them, despite the wild light of madness.

This was no innocent child he faced—Toronto knew that. But it threw him for a moment. It wasn't until the vampire came for him, mouth open to reveal fangs, that Toronto was able to really get his brain on board with what his body already knew.

This was a killer.

A monster—one who was quickly losing any bit of sanity he might have once possessed. And Toronto's job was dealing with the monsters.

This one just happened to come in an innocent-looking package—a strong, wiry one. Toronto threw the strong, wiry little bastard across the room after he sank vicious fangs into Toronto's forearm, tearing it open. He went flying, crashing into the wall, and Toronto went after him. The boylike monster didn't stay down long—strong, and fast, he was up and moving before Toronto reached up.

Catching him, Toronto hurled him across the room again, this time in the other direction. He wasn't in the mood for a battering contest. He wanted the answers. He had to have those answers, and he wanted this over with.

Sylvia looked lost. He needed to get her away from here.

As he moved past her, he bent, grabbing one of the blades he'd dropped during his shift. It was a sleek piece of work—a mix of titanium and silver, one of his favorites. Custommade, stronger than silver alone. As the vampire surged to his feet, Toronto aimed and threw. It went straight through a thin shoulder and buried itself into the stone wall. The vampire screamed. As the shock of the pain and the silver hit him, Toronto grabbed another blade—a longer one, this time, and drove it into the vamp's belly, skewering him and pinning him to the wall. Peering down into dazed, pain-filled eyes, he growled out, "I take it you're the one called Kit."

The vampire spat in his face.

"That's a yes." He could speak in this form—the words weren't perfect, but they were understandable. Laying a clawed hand on the vamp's throat, he squeezed. "Know what I am?"

"A furry, cock-sucking bastard?" With a wild grin, Kit jerked against the silver blades pinning him to the wall. His eyes were half-mad. It wasn't just the pain doing it, though. It was more. Pain wouldn't leave him smelling like that . . . like something inside him was rotting away. He was crazy.

"I'll take that as another yes." Flexing his claws, Toronto let them scrape gently over the thin neck. "We can do this fast. We can do this slow. I don't really give a fuck. You know you're going to die. You decide how it goes. I'd like to know why you changed Pulaski, but that's a waste of time— you're an evil little bastard and that answers that. So let's get down to the big question—why expose us? Why did you leave a body for mortals to find?"

Kit panted. Then he coughed, a trickle of blood coming out of the corner of his mouth. "Well, it seemed like a good idea at the time. Fun and all. Besides, you wanted him dead, didn't you?"

Snarling, Toronto bent over and snapped his jaws shut, just a hair away from Kit's face. In this form, he could practically bite the vamp's head off. Not that he would—he didn't want any of that foulness stuck inside him. "Dead is one thing . . . publicly dead is different. Why?"

"Why not?" Kit smiled at him, and that mad glitter in his eyes seemed to increase for a moment before a fit of coughing seized him.

Disgusted, Toronto jerked the blades out of him. "Crazy son of a bitch. I hope you're ready to die—let's see how loud you can scream."

He jerked the longer blade free, ready to plunge it into Kit's heart and be done with it. He had the answer he needed to give to Rafe—the man was crazy. He was a powerful vamp, trapped in the body of a young teenager—spending eternity like that would be strain enough, but this guy's mental state was already unstable. Somewhere along the way, he'd just lost it or maybe he'd come through the Change like this.

Didn't matter. The madness had been eating at his brain for a good long while.

As he went to drive the blade into Kit's chest, Kit moved . . . Toronto was prepared for that.

What he wasn't prepared for was Sylvia, and as he went to catch Kit, Sylvia caught Toronto's arm. Kit reached up, grabbing the silver blade from his shoulder and swiping out, trying to get to Sylvia with it.

Snarling under his breath, Toronto pulled her back as Kit stumbled a few feet away, blood oozing from his wounds in a slow flood. Silver-wrought wounds wouldn't close easily and Toronto planned on killing him before he had a chance to heal up.

"Wait," she whispered, her eyes dark and tortured.

"Wait?" He shook his head. "He can't be left alive, Syl."

The boy-man laughed, the sound depraved and mocking. "No, no . . . we can't have that. Never mind that it's her fault I'm like this, right . . . Sada?"

Although he was watching the vampire, Toronto saw her flinch.

"It is my fault," she said quietly. "And that's why I'll be the one to finish it. And we're not going to play cat-and-mouse either, Christopher. Come on. Let's get this over with."

As she went to move, Toronto caught her arm. He saw the furred gray of his clawed hand and he swore. Grappling with the wild, angry power of the wolf, he called it back inside. It went reluctantly, the fur sinking back into his skin—the wolf wasn't quite done burning off his rage, either.

Bones realigned, shifted, broke and reformed. Toronto just couldn't stand to see his wolf's hands on her—those hands were tools of violence. Just violence. Setting his jaw, he said quietly, "You don't need to do this. Whatever happened all those years ago wasn't your fault."

"It was. In some part, whether I was completely to blame or not, it was my fault . . . he died because he tried to help me. And I mocked him. Threw his kindness in his face. This is my last kindness for him . . . he won't be tortured or played with, Toronto, and I don't want to listen to him scream. I've heard his screams in my nightmares already." She shifted her gaze back to Kit. "Come on, then."

With a sneer, Kit started for her, moving with lazy ease, despite the injuries he'd taken. He had enough years in him that he could function despite the pain. "Don't worry, Sada . . . I won't be too hard on you."

"I'm sorry I didn't accept the kindness you tried to offer, Christopher," she said softly. "Or the apologies. I accept it now, and I offer my own."

"It's Kit." He glared at her. "Christopher died the day you attacked me. The day he changed me. The day he killed Sol . . . and you can shove your apology up your ass, bitch."

He lunged for her. Sylvia met the lunge with one of her own. She'd been aiming for his heart—quick and simple, get it done. He needed to die—she knew that. And she wanted to tell him she was sorry. She'd done that. It was time to end it.

But he was fast . . . very fast, especially considering he was wounded. Dark, near-black blood trickled down his belly, his legs, leaving little streaks and puddles wherever he went. She couldn't hope for that to slow him down or trip him up. Whatever Christopher had been doing the past century, he hadn't just been lying around or changing murdering psychotics—the vamp knew how to fight.

He evaded each strike, moving away with ease, circling her. She didn't get the method of madness, though, until it was too late.

When Toronto had been at the cabin, he'd been loaded for bear. Or crazed vamp. He'd had numerous knives on that sleek body of his, although she didn't know why he bothered. His wolf form was a weapon in and of itself. When he'd shifted, the sheaths had ripped, as had his clothes, and all those weapons were now on the floor.

Idiot, idiot, idiot—

If she'd just let Toronto kill him, this would be done.

But now Christopher—Kit—had a blade in each hand. Sylvia always had one advantage over a lot of her targets—she was smaller and could use her body in ways they couldn't, despite their speed, despite their strength. Agility was a wonderful thing.

Kit had all her agility and more.

He circled around again, twirling one of his stolen blades. It was the one that was red and wet with his own blood. "Come on. Let's see how much *I* can make *you* bleed now. Will you bleed as much as I did, Sada?"

"Sada died that day as well," she said softly.

He sneered. "Don't make it sound like you're sorry. You kept throwing that in my face, remember?"

Don't tell me you're sorry, boy . . .

"Sylvia."

She didn't dare turn to look at Toronto. But the sound of his voice steadied her. "Just get it done," he said quietly.

Kit threw him an ugly look and then swung his head back around to look at her.

It was almost comical . . . the way he opened his mouth, that twisted look of hate on his face. And how it all froze as he looked back at Toronto, a cartoonish sort of double take.

It was so . . . strange that Sylvia found herself following his look. He took a step toward Toronto, one small staggering step.

What is this? She held herself ready, certain he was trying to set her up. But the rage had leeched out of him. And the glitter of madness seemed to be fading from his eyes, leaving what looked like nothing more than a lost, lonely boy.

"Your arm," he whispered, staring at Toronto, dazed. A soft, broken little sound left him and he sounded like the boy he had been. "You . . . you have a scar on your arm."

Toronto narrowed his eyes. "I don't have time for this. Sylvia, end it. Now. Or I'm doing it."

"Solomon?"

Toronto's lids flickered.

And Sylvia stared. Her heart kicked up in her chest and she found herself looking into those pale, silvery blue eyes. They were icy and distant now, as they had been all night. But always before today, when he had looked at her, it had been with humor or heat or hunger . . . or all three. Sometimes with a little bit of frustration thrown in.

No . . . She started to close her eyes, but Kit moved and she jerked up her blade. He wasn't coming toward her, though. Like a man caught in a dream, he shuffled toward Toronto.

"You get any closer, and I'm going to gut you," Toronto warned.

Gut you . . .

Unable to help herself, she shifted her gaze to the wolf, as well. Staring at those pale, silvery blue eyes.

I'll gut you for this . . . you're a fucking dead man.

No, boy. You are. But since you're such a little fighter, I'll make you get the sort of death you deserve. A bloody one.

She saw a face, one that swam up from the depths of her memory. She rarely thought of him. He hadn't been the one to take her to Harold. Hadn't been the one to lie, or the one to promise to get her free, or the one to die under her hands.

He simply hadn't mattered to her.

He had just been a sullen, silent boy who had been almost a man . . . and he'd been furious when he saw what had become of his friend. The face wasn't right. But it wouldn't be, would it?

I was a teenager when I was bitten. Five weres attacked me . . .

A teenager. Thrown to a pack of werewolves, by all logic, he *should* have died. Harold had promised him a bloody, painful death. He'd been thrown to a pack of feral wolves . . . did it get much bloodier? Much more painful?

"Shit," Sylvia whispered. The sound of her own voice jerked her out of her stupor and she looked up in time to see Kit taking another stumbling step in Toronto's direction.

He responded by twirling one of the knives he held. "Vampire, I'm about ready to cut you into ten different pieces. Come any closer, and it's going to happen—I'll start with your dick."

"Your arm," Kit babbled. It was like he didn't even seem to realize Toronto had said anything. "That scar on your arm. It's from when we broke into the warehouse—right after he dragged us here from San Francisco. I sewed you up, right and proper, don't you remember?"

A muscle twitched in Toronto's cheek, his lashes sweeping low to shield his eyes.

Swallowing, Sylvia said softly, "He doesn't remember his past, Christopher. He was attacked by feral werewolves here in Toronto over a century ago. He doesn't remember anything before his attack. All he has is what happened after."

"You . . ." Kit sagged, going to his knees. "Harold said he threw you to the wolves. That's what you deserved for trying to get him after what he did to me. He'd let you fight for your death."

Sylvia watched as something flashed through Toronto's eyes—shock. This . . . this just wasn't happening.

"Christopher, I—"

She never had a chance to finish her sentence. The blackish red blood was already spreading across the floor. Toronto lowered one of the blades he'd carried—the long one, nearly the length of his forearm, more a short sword than a knife, and wicked sharp.

Kit's head lay a few feet away from the toes of Sylvia's boots. "What . . . ?"

He'd just . . .

No.

Staring at Christopher's decapitated body, she closed her eyes. The image of it was burned on the inside of her retinas and she knew she'd see that for a good, long while. This not-boy had been a monster . . . she knew that. She'd spent a century blaming herself for his death, yet he hadn't died. Instead, he'd let himself become like the man who'd made them. Evil.

But still . . . once upon a time, he'd tried to help her. This had happened because he'd tried to save her.

Swallowing around the knot in her throat, she swung her gaze around to Toronto and found that he was doing the same thing she'd been doing—watching Christopher's lifeless body.

The odd, detached look on his face bothered her a hell of

a lot more than it should have, she decided. Especially since they were supposed to just walk away . . .

"Why did you do that?" she demanded. "He could have given you answers—he knew who you were, damn it!"

"I know who I am," Toronto said quietly. "I'm a fucking Hunter and I had a monster to put down."

"He . . ." She wanted to argue with him.

"He what?" Blue eyes flashed as he glared at her.

Sylvia stared at him, uncertain of what she was even going to say. Damn it, she knew how this would play out. She'd come here with the sole intention of making sure the man who'd made Pulaski a vamp would die. People who could turn serial killers into vamps were a unique breed of monster. She knew that. But this . . . shit. Turning away, she went to shove a hand through her hair only to come across the sticks holding it in a topknot. Pulling the sticks out, she tucked them into an inner pocket of her jacket and stared at the wall.

She could remember the strange expression on Toronto's face the few times he'd made any reference to his past. It bothered him, that emptiness. She knew it.

Turning back to him, she saw that he was still watching, still waiting.

"He what?" Toronto asked, his voice deceptively soft. "He wasn't a fucking monster? Is that what you want to tell me?

"No." Shaking her head, she held his gaze. "I get that."

Like she hadn't even spoken, Toronto said, "He was involved in the shit going on back in Memphis. Involved up to his neck."

"I understand." Swallowing, she shifted her gaze down to the ruin of a body on the floor and tried to think. "He was twisted. And he was sick—I don't know how anybody could survive under Harold and still be sane."

"You managed," Toronto said, his voice hardly more than a growl. "And don't *tell* me that you're a monster—if you can't see the difference between *you* and *him*, you're a fucking idiot. You don't strike me as an idiot, Sylvia—Sada. Shit, I don't even know what to call you."

"My name is Sylvia." She took a deep breath and focused on his face. "It's the name I chose for myself—Sada *did* die. I'm no longer who she was."

Still watching her closely, Toronto nodded. "I get that he had a rough time of it after he was changed. But so did you, and you didn't let it make you into a monster. A lot of us go through hell and come through it sane. Sometimes we do it on our own. Sometimes we have help. But he gave into the madness. Any shred of humanity he might have had, he gave it up long ago. And he fucking exposed us to mortals. We can't have that. He was dangerous in too many ways and you know it."

"I get it." Shit. She needed to think—had to think. Closing her eyes, she said, "It's not that. It's . . ."

"It's what, damn it?"

The temper she heard in his voice sparked her own and she lowered her hands, glaring at him. "He knew you!" She stared at him. "Damn it, the only time I've seen anything really seem to *get* to you was when you spoke about your past—he had the answers, he could have helped you piece together some of that past and you just killed him."

Toronto shook his head. "I've got a past, Sylvia. I've spent the past century making one. It just took me a damn long time to figure out that century is the part of my history that matters. That . . . and the future I make for myself. He didn't have any answers I needed to hear."

And then he stooped down, grabbed the head, lifted it up and stared into wide, dead eyes. "He was sick. You could smell it on him. He was sick and he was crazy. You said you wanted to show him a kindness for the one he tried to show you. The truest kindness you could show him was to end his life before he caused any more pain."

CHAPTER 24

Nasty, nasty business . . .

Kelsey sat in the back of the classroom, wearing a glamour—something she hated. It made her skin itch, made her eyes itch and if she messed with it for too long, the minor-level spell casting would fall apart.

Glamours were a very basic magic and most witches could cast them. The problem was they were easy to sense, unless the one casting them was a high-level witch.

Kelsey was.

But even a good glamour could fall apart if she didn't leave it alone—they were also a lot like high heels. A witch got used to them. Like the woman teaching the classroom. Kelsey suspected she'd been using that glamour for so long, it was like a second skin—it all but became a part of her.

Kelsey wondered how long the woman had been wearing it. It was good—*damn* good. If Angel hadn't mentioned that there was a teacher who'd made her eyes itch, Kelsey didn't know that she would have thought to look for glamours so soon . . . and it had taken a long, careful look at this woman to realize there was something not quite right with that smooth, polished look. She looked like a friendly, easygoing high school teacher. She looked pretty, and perfect . . . and she was so fucking foul, she made Kelsey's teeth hurt.

The glamour was good. It hid all of that. No wonder Rafe hadn't detected this. She'd been doing it a long, long time.

Angel was something the witch couldn't have planned on, though. Psychics had a way of screwing things up for non-mortals. They looked human, smelled human, acted human. They didn't give off the predatory vibe that vamps or weres did. They didn't crackle with magic like a witch did. They were, plain and simple, *human*. And although Angel was a bit more than human now, mortals with altered blood were a rare enough occurrence that unless the witch had ever actually come across it, she wasn't likely to realize anything was off about Angel. Especially if Angel behaved herself.

And Angel must have done just that, because this woman didn't seem to have any clue what was going down.

Kelsey smiled, happy to let it stay that way.

She wasn't here just for the witch, after all.

There were other people involved . . . and she wanted all of them.

I T was a pain in the butt to wear a glamour. Less of a pain to simply look . . . not there.

As the students moved in a wave out of the classroom, she manipulated the glamour she wore so that it looked like she was doing the same thing. The witch barely even noticed.

That was because she was . . . occupied.

Very occupied.

Kelsey had spent much of the afternoon using other high-level magics, thread by careful thread. They were passive spells, nothing aimed directly at the witch. It was just a shroud of worry.

She wanted the woman to worry. She wanted *all* of them to worry.

Fun things happened when people started to worry . . . a lot of them didn't do it well on their own.

Minutes ticked away on the clock.

Kelsey counted twenty-two before the door opened for the first time. The man who came inside was mortal. It opened again four minutes later. *That* man wasn't.

All in all, when it was done, seven people were gathered in the witch's classroom. Three weren't human. The others were. The humans, Kelsey would leave to the cops, if they could. There would be evidence somewhere; there always was.

But the others . . . they would answer to Rafe. He had to take control of this, and do it fast.

Knowing the temper he had, she suspected he'd do it in a glorious, bloody fashion.

R AFE didn't sleep much.
   He didn't need to. But he still avoided going outside before five or so, unless it was a dire emergency.

Or unless there were ferals who had been playing vicious little sex games right under his nose.

As he read the text from Kelsey, he realized he was going to have to make one of those early trips. Shoving the phone into his pocket, he called out, "Lindsey!"

She'd wanted a pizza party if she helped with Pulaski. Pulaski was dead, dealt with and hopefully rotting in some special level of hell for pedophiles. Maybe this would make up for not being able to help peel the skin off his hide.

As Lindsey appeared in front of him, her spiky black hair disheveled, wearing a T-shirt that read *Team Dracula* on it, he lifted a brow. "Want to go talk to a couple of sexual deviants?"

"What sort of talk?" She pursed her lips as she studied his face.

"The kind that ends with them bleeding on the floor and wondering why in the hell they decided to fuck around in our territory."

"Oooohhh . . . those sexual deviants." She smiled, and the grin had a decidedly mean slant to it. "Yes, Rafe. I would love to go with you."

"Cool. I might even buy you a pizza when we're done."

* * *

Toronto wasn't in the cabin when she woke. By the time they'd finished at the house, it had been less than an hour before dawn and she hadn't had much choice but to get ready to settle down for the day.

She'd hoped they could talk when she woke—they sure as hell hadn't said much during the night.

But he wasn't here. She was alone.

Sitting up in the bed, Sylvia stared around the cabin.

Her heart was an empty ache in her chest and the only thing she could think was . . . *he's not here*. Had he left? Already? The thought of it was enough to almost have her doubled over.

Then she looked around and saw his belongings piled neatly by the door. Shit.

Okay.

He hadn't left.

So . . .

"So what?" she whispered. Rising out of the bed, she went to stand by the door, touching her fingers to the long black coat. He'd be back, for long enough to say good-bye? Was that it?

They'd done what they'd set out to do.

Was there anything left? Any reason to stay?

Swallowing the knot in her throat, she turned around and studied the small cabin.

She guessed the answer was no.

He'd be back. But she'd be gone.

She'd let herself get too close to him. That was where she'd made the mistake.

The only way to fix it was to nip it right in the bud . . . starting now.

The moon was rising up as Toronto returned to the cabin. He wasn't surprised to find it empty.

If there was an ache in his chest, he pretended not to notice.

He'd known this was coming. From the time she'd started to pull away from him, he'd known. Better this way, he figured. If he'd had her around for much longer, it would have hurt even more when she walked.

Moving into the cabin, he walked around, checking each room, although he didn't know why. She wasn't there.

But as he lingered in each room, he found himself thinking back . . . and remembering. *You'll have to learn to control that . . .*

Control was something he hadn't used enough, he knew. Control. Discipline. Everything Nessa had pounded into him. Things he'd let go to waste.

I told you he wasn't going to pull through. I'll put him down—

Back then, it probably would have been the wisest thing. Hell, plenty of people probably still thought it would have been the best thing they could have done. Just ended him.

"My own fault," he muttered, rubbing a hand over the back of his neck.

You'll do well enough . . .

Nessa, though, she'd always had faith in him.

Shit. Maybe if he'd lived up to half of what she'd expected of him, he could have done better here. Maybe Sylvia wouldn't have been in such a hurry to leave. Maybe . . .

"Shit. Fuck maybe."

One thing was certain, though. He had to stop this. He'd spent a century trying to find some piece to the puzzle of his past, and now he had a few . . . and it didn't matter.

It didn't change who he was.

Toronto was who he'd made himself. And now it was up to him do a better job of it.

Turning his back on the bedroom, he strode to the door. His junk was there, waiting for him. He grabbed it and left without another look back.

It took him forty minutes to get out of the city, and this time, he knew he wouldn't be coming back. He was done chasing ghosts.

* * *

Sylvia had been prepared to bribe whoever necessary to get the pictures of Alan Pulaski's dead body.

Something to show the parents.

That was the first thing to figure out. Then she'd move. She should figure out how to get her bike back, but . . .

She rounded the bend to her house and saw moonlight glinting off chrome. Her bike.

If her heart could do it, it would have leaped right into her throat. Slamming on the brakes, she closed her eyes and turned off the car, listening. *Is he here . . .*

And almost immediately, the crack in her heart widened. No.

She was alone.

Gripping the steering wheel of the rental, she sat there and stared at the bike. She stared at it a good three minutes before she realized there was something on it.

Frowning, she climbed out of the car, pocketed the keys. It was an envelope. Automatically, she checked the air— she hadn't had too many attempts on her life after a job, but it did happen. No sign of explosives, though. Nothing that felt off.

Lifting it up, she held it to the sky and saw the faint outline of paper.

She should take it inside, check it out more thoroughly. But she just didn't care enough. Flipping it over, she used a knife to slice it open and reached inside.

Pulaski.

The photo was only of his face.

He looked peaceful. He didn't deserve to look that peaceful, that easy, Sylvia knew. But he did look very, very dead.

For a long while, she stood there, holding the picture. This was the last thing she needed to do before she could close the door on Sylvia James and move on to whoever she was going to be for the next few decades—finalize the job. Let Toby's parents know their son's killer was dead.

For some reason, the idea didn't hold as much appeal as it should.

* * *

"CRAZY." Rafe turned his head to look at Dominic only to have Kelsey poke him in the shoulder.

"Be still," she ordered, bent over the ugly wound in his side. She'd had to cut him back open.

Toronto started as the witch used a pair of forceps on the Master and stared working on pulling out the glass.

"Who shoved silver in you?"

A thin smile slanted Rafe's lips. "We rounded up the people responsible for the sex ring. We've got what's left of them locked up down in the isolation chambers. One of them is a witch—mean bitch. She managed to get this in me."

Kelsey grimaced. "She busted the glass while she was at it. I'll be digging glass out of you for the next hour, pal. Not my favorite pastime."

"Sorry." Rafe shrugged.

She jabbed him again. "I said be still."

He heaved out a sigh and looked back at Toronto. "So the bastard is crazy. I get that—figured that much out after he left a body where it would be found by *mortals*. You want me to buy that the only reason he did was because he was crazy?"

Toronto shrugged, moving to stare out the window at the half moon. "It's not as much of an answer as you needed, I know. You could all but smell the rot on him, though. I think it had been coming for a while. And if he got a heavy dose of whatever chemical crap Josiah was telling me about and it started eating what was left of his brain?"

"What else did you expect to hear?" Lindsey asked from the floor, busily munching away on pizza. She had a glorious black eye. Considering the fact that Toronto could still see it, he had to wonder how bad the damage had been earlier. "He went and changed a kiddie killer. That right there is a ringing endorsement of sanity, right?"

"I guess." Rafe didn't look at her, though.

Toronto could feel the vampire's gaze, boring into the back of his head. He wasn't overly surprised when Rafe abruptly said, "Can you all leave me and Toronto alone, please?"

Kelsey glared at him. "I'm in the middle of something rather delicate."

"It can wait ten minutes, right?"

Kelsey stared at him balefully for a long moment before she gathered up her supplies. "The only reason I'm leaving for *five* minutes is because I know you won't sit still if I don't do it. But that's all you've got."

Toronto waited in silence until the door shut behind Kelsey and he listened as the footsteps died away.

Although he was completely aware of Rafe's heavy stare, Toronto stood where he was, at the window. Watching the moon. It wasn't full, wasn't even close. He didn't have that heavy, burning urge to shift. Right now, the moon was . . . peaceful. It was peaceful to look at, and he sure as hell needed some peace.

"If you want me to head out, I can be gone within an hour," he said quietly, crossing his arms.

"Shit." Rafe was closer now.

Turning his head, he saw the vampire standing just over his shoulder, dark eyes flat, mouth unsmiling. With a short nod, he said, "I'm out of here, then."

"That wasn't a request." Rafe shoved a hand through his hair. "You did good. It wasn't exactly how I wanted to see it end—I wanted Pulaski here so I could torture him for a good, long while. But if he was a vampire . . . that was an unexpected complication. He was better off dead sooner, rather than later. We'll have to work on finding the answers for the families of his victims, but we can probably still accomplish that—I'll have Kelsey look into it. She's here anyway."

A weighted silence fell. He'd done good—what the hell, maybe after so many years of fucking up, he ought to feel pleased with that. But he just . . . wasn't.

Nothing felt settled for him.

He wasn't settled.

"I don't know if I can stay here any longer, Rafe." Lifting a hand, he laid it on the window, staring up at the moon. "I just don't belong here. Never did."

Rafe blew out a heavy breath. "I can understand that . . .

there comes a time when bastards like us just can't take serving, right?"

"It's not that." Toronto shook his head. "I'm not leader material—never will be. But I don't fit here."

"Don't fit?"

Turning his head, Toronto shrugged. "I'm a mean-assed square peg who's forced himself into a round hole, and I've made the lot of you miserable while you all put up with me. You deserved better. They deserved better. It's time I move on, I think."

"Where to?"

"Beats the hell out of me." Shifting his gaze back to the window, he focused once more on the moon. "I need to find something to do with myself that isn't a fucking waste, though. Find some way to not *be* a waste."

"You're not a waste, Tor." Rafe shoved him lightly. "The merc . . . Sylvia. Is she any part of this?"

He closed his eyes. Sylvia. Was she any part of this? "No." Because she didn't want to be any part of anything that had to do with him.

Turning around, he faced Rafe. "Sorry I caused you problems while I was here. And I'll hang around while we clean up the mess with the schools and shit. When you don't need me anymore, though, I think I'll head on out."

Rafe watched him with narrowed eyes.

Somehow, Toronto suspected the vampire saw more than he'd like.

CHAPTER 25

PACKING didn't take long.

Not at Rafe's, not at his place. He'd sold the house to the vampire, figured somebody else could use it eventually. The few things he needed to take—weapons and clothes—didn't take much time to pack up.

Sad, really.

More than a hundred years and all he really laid claim to were his weapons.

"Where do you plan on going?"

At the sound of Nessa's voice, he winced. Damn it. He'd wanted out of here before she made it back around. When she hadn't been in the house when he returned, he'd thought maybe he could avoid those all-seeing eyes. Apparently not.

Straightening up, he turned to look at her, giving her a smile that felt strained at best. Faked and frayed, worn around the edges. "Hey, old woman," he said.

"Harrumph. Old woman." She squinted at him and abruptly, a sad smile curled her lips. "Oh, Tor. You went and fell, didn't you?"

A dull flush climbed up his neck.

Turning back to his weapons chest, he continued making sure everything was secure. "I found a guy who claims he knew me—recognized the scar on my arm. Says I got it when we were climbing into a warehouse window."

"Hmmm."

Slanting a look over his shoulder at her, he said, "And what does, *hmmm*, mean?"

"Not much. What else does he have to say?"

"Dunno. He can't say much—I cut his head off. He was a vamp—a crazy one. Had to die. No time to chat with him before I killed him." Unable to pretend he was still inspecting the chest, he shut the lid and turned to face her. "How much do you know about what happened to me, Nessa? Honest—for once, be honest."

"I never was dishonest, Tor." She sighed and came into his room, lowering herself into a chair, settled on the edge. "You were covered in bites. You were near death. But there was a vamp's stench on you, too. I always suspected you'd been tossed out as a lesson of some sort. With that kind of history, how pleasant could your past be?"

Watching her closely, he tried to decide if she was being upfront with him or not. If anybody had more pieces of his past—other than Sylvia—it was Nessa. It didn't matter, though. He'd finally accepted it. It didn't matter.

Taking a deep breath, he blew it out and then grabbed the straps of the trunk, hefted it up. "That's probably exactly what happened—the vamp, I guess we knew each other. When he was attacked, it sounds like I went after the vamp who made him. He threw me to the wolves for interfering."

"And how are you with all of this?" Nessa studied him closely. "You always wanted answers—always searched for the pieces of who you were."

"Answers don't change who I was. Or who I am." He shrugged as he started for the door. "That's the one thing I finally figured out."

A hand touched his shoulder. Pausing, he looked into Nessa's blue eyes. They looked a lot like his own, he realized. She really did look younger than he did. This woman was both mother and sister to him. Yet she looked a good five years his junior. Except for those eyes . . . those wise, ancient eyes.

"Who you *were* never really did matter," she said quietly. "I always knew you could be something amazing. If you would just let it happen."

"It hasn't happened yet." He tried to smile, but couldn't. "I'll stop disappointing you, Nessa. I swear."

"You never disappointed *me*, love. You always disappointed yourself." She rose on her toes and pressed a kiss to his cheek. "Now . . . I've an idea of what you can do with yourself, if you're of a mind to listen."

He was tempted to just walk away.

But he couldn't. That was something he'd done too much of. "And what's that, old woman?"

D OMINIC found Nessa in the front yard, staring at the rapidly fading headlights of a souped-up van with a picture of the Death Star painted on the side.

She had a sad look on her face, and it pissed him off.

"What in the hell did he do to upset you?"

"Oh, hush." She reached up, patted his chest absently, all without taking her eyes off the back of the van.

"Hush?" He cupped her chin and drew her face toward his, until her gaze met his own. "You look about ready to cry, damn it. Look, I know you like that bastard, but—"

"I all but raised him, you know," she said softly. Blowing out a breath, she reached up and gathered some of her hair into her hands, absently started to braid it, something she did when she was distracted . . . or hurting. "We found him when he was a teenager—we came on him as five were-wolves were having themselves a lovely little snack . . . and taking their time with it."

Dominic, still riding the wave of what he'd thought was very righteous anger, went quiet, eyeing her with suspicion. "Did you say *five* werewolves?"

"Yes. It was a bloody, and I mean that literally, mess. Do you know Mary Kendall? I had her with me, and a witch,

Vax. He's not with us anymore—not a Hunter, at any rate, or a witch." She frowned, her eyes far-off and confused. "Sometimes, it all gets in a muddle, still. What was I saying . . . oh. Mary, Vax, they were ready to just kill him. It would have been a kindness, in a way. The virus was already working on him, healing him up as they went, keeping him alive so they could make him hurt even more."

She reached up, touched the back of her skull. "They damaged his brain—scrambled it. Like an egg. Fortunately, they'd already infected him so that the virus healed the damage, but his memories, his life . . . all of it was gone."

"Gone . . . ?"

"He doesn't know who he was. He found a few pieces, it seems. But he's lived all his life with a hole in him. And a memory." She glanced at him. "Do you know what one of his earliest memories is? Mary—saying she'd put him down. Like a dog. A mangy, rabid dog."

Nessa sighed. "I love that girl, dearly. But all of his life, he's lived with that in him. Feeling like not much more than a mangy, rabid dog."

"Shit." He scowled, and shot a look toward the van. It was out of sight now. "Look, I didn't . . . fuck. Screw that. He had a rough childhood, plenty do. He still acts like an asshole."

"Yes." Nessa started to laugh. "He does. And I love him. He's like a son to me, and I want to wring his neck for the way he lets everything trip him up. I think . . ." She paused and took a deep breath.

When she looked back at him, some of the sadness had lightened. It was still there. Just not so heavy. "I think he fell for the mercenary he was working with . . . and she walked away. Toronto just had his heart ripped out. Sometimes, it takes that to really wake up. He can start to heal now."

"You . . ." Dominic scowled, trying to follow her line of thinking. He couldn't. She had a few hundred years on him in the thinking department and he just couldn't keep up. "You're smiling because he had his heart ripped out. You're good with this."

"Oh, no." A light glinted in her eyes. "But he's figured out he's been holding himself back. And he's done with it. I'm good with that."

TWO MONTHS LATER

It hadn't been that long ago when Toronto had been facing another angry, pissed off non-mortal. That one had gone crazy.

This one was pretty damn close.

And he was expected to keep the kid on the sane side of the line.

As the young Alpha came at him, Toronto waited until the very last moment before he moved. When he did, he caught him by the scruff of the neck and hurled him to the floor.

Lifting his head, he stared at the small crowd gathered around. A few of them were shifting on their feet. Others were growling quietly, watching with rage flickering in their eyes. And fear. Baring his teeth in a snarl, he let some of the power inside him break free. Seconds later, the majority of them were cowering on the ground, whining low in their throats, their eyes swirling as they fought not to shift.

They were learning. A month ago when something like this had happened, they had all gone furry on him.

It was the Alpha causing the problems.

Crouching down by him, Toronto waited until the fogged eyes started to clear. He'd smacked his head hard enough that it took a minute. Blood was seeping out from under him—the kid had split his hard head open. Probably not enough to knock any sense into him, though. It also didn't do much to knock any of the anger out of him.

"I'm guuna keel yuu," he snarled, the words mangled by his altering form, his body heating, flowing under Toronto's hands as he shifted.

In response, Toronto whipped out a blade and plunged it through his shoulder. It was almost pure silver and enough to stop the shifter in his tracks. The youth lying on the ground wasn't a were. He was a natural-born shifter, and he reacted to silver differently than a were would. Silver would have pushed a were on the verge of shifting right *in* to the Change. For a natural shifter, it slowed it.

"You can't kill me," Toronto said quietly. Looking around what the pack called the war room, he studied their audience. "Leave. Nobody leaves the compound without my consent." Narrowing his eyes, he added, "If they do, I'll be the one tracking you . . . and you'll be dealing with me."

There were a couple of grumbles, a couple of swears. But even as the youth on the floor snarled out, "You're my fucking pack—stay *here*," they were heading out the door.

"I'll kill you," the kid said again. The words were clearly spoken—he'd reverted back to his human form and he couldn't think past the pain now to shift, although his eyes shifted from green to yellow and back again as rage swirled inside him. He had to be hurting, but he didn't show it.

"Matt, you don't have what it takes to kill me," Toronto said. With his hand curled around the knife, he peered into the shifter's eyes. Werewolves and natural-born shapeshifters weren't always the easiest of friends, but this kid needed to learn control and he had to do it fast.

A roaming pack of ferals had come and attempted to wipe the small band of shifters out, but they'd been hit with more resistance than they'd expected . . . and this kid had killed three of them. His father, the previous Alpha, had killed nine.

The boy was strong, and there was no denying he'd step into his father's shoes. But he had to get his rage under control or he'd become the very thing that had all but decimated his pack.

The shifter bared his teeth and despite the silver in his body, he managed enough power to make his face shift—a partial one, his face forming a muzzle, teeth elongating to fangs, fur spreading in a slow crawl over his skin. "I killed three weres . . . and I had fun with it. You're only one."

"Yeah. But I'm not a brainless, mindless murderer. You don't have the control it would take for a were like me." He wiggled the knife and watched as pain splintered through Matt's eyes before he managed to hide it. The partial shift he'd managed faded, melting away into his skin like it had never existed. "If you can't control yourself enough to shift even with the pain, then you can't control yourself enough to handle me. If you can't handle me, you can't handle the pack."

"It's my fucking pack!" Matt growled, and he swung out.

Toronto reacted by leaning his weight on the knife. "Yeah. And your fucking pack is losing its mind to your rage. Think back, kid. Your dad must have seen the signs in you—he knew what you'd be, knew who was going to take his place. What did he tell you about letting your rage color everything? What would it do to the pack?"

Matt's lanky, too-skinny body tensed. And then, Toronto watched as the rage drained out of him, replaced by grief.

"I never wanted to do this," the boy whispered. "It shouldn't be me. Dad should still be here."

"Yeah. You're right. He should. But he's not. He gave you the tools to handle this, though. It's up to you whether or not you decide to do it."

THAT night, they hunted as a pack.

Toronto stayed in his human skin, trailing along behind them and watching.

Matt kept his head, kept his cool, and for the most part, acted like the Alpha Toronto knew he could be.

It wasn't done. Most of the survivors were still kids—the few adults that had lived weren't strong enough to lead, but enough of them had lingering guilt or enough resentment to cause the kid grief.

It was going to be months, maybe even a few years before Toronto's work was done here, he figured.

Maybe that wasn't a bad thing.

If he was here, focusing on something else, he wasn't able to spend time wishing he was somewhere else. With someone else.

SYLVIA had moved to Miami, thinking the party city, the higher crime rate and the warm nights would do something to keep her occupied. She could find work—easily.

Even if she wasn't taking jobs, there was no shortage of people who needed to die.

She could spend the nights out by the pool in the back of the house she'd bought years ago.

And she could join the party crowds and have plenty of young, hot men who could feed any hungers she might have.

They did sate the most basic hunger—Sylvia had just fed off a musician who had already forgotten all about her. But nobody did anything to fill the void inside her.

He shouldn't have left such a big hole. It didn't make sense. But maybe that hole had already been there . . . and he managed to fill it. He'd fit into those empty, aching spots of her life that she hadn't realized she'd had until she met him.

Was that love?

Did it come that soon?

Sighing, she leaned against a bar, staring out at the mass of bodies and listening to the throb of music, trying to let it wrap around her and make her forget.

An unwelcome brush danced along her skin and she glanced up, met the gaze of a man standing under a streetlight, head tipped so that his face was in shadow.

A faint smile curled his lips and she caught a quick glimpse of his fangs, saw the sheen in the back of his eyes before he hid it. Bored, she looked away. She wasn't on anybody's formal territory. She'd made sure of that, and she was in a mean enough mood that she'd be happy to . . . *discuss* . . . things if he felt they needed to discuss them.

Turning her back on him, she met the gaze of the bartender. She wanted to get drunk. But there wasn't enough liquor in the world to do it. Sighing, she shouted for a beer over the crush of the crowd and tried to tell herself she was having a good time.

She was still attempting to convince herself ten minutes later when she heard the cutoff scream.

Nobody else would have heard it, not in this crowd.

Just as nobody would have scented the blood.

Sighing, she studied the bottle she held.

It wasn't really her concern, was it? She wasn't one of the

do-gooders, some altruistic Boy Scout—or Girl Scout—out to rid the world of every bad little shifter, were or vamp in the world.

So it's altruism?

Closing her eyes, she tried to block out the memory of how his face had looked when he'd stared at her, as if he couldn't completely explain it. As if he couldn't even understand it. *Somebody has to be willing. If it's not us, I guess it's nobody. And that's just not an option. Do you really want to live in a world where nobody stops the monsters, Miz James?*

Shit.

Slamming the bottle of beer down on the counter, she followed the trail of the scream . . . and the scent of blood. It was possible to feed without making them scream, damn it. She did it all the time. It was possible to feed without hurting them. She did that, too.

So why did she smell pain and terror in the air?

The woman was unconscious by the time Sylvia made it to the alley where he'd taken her. She'd already palmed one of the few blades she was carrying. As she sauntered into the alley, his eyes rolled up to stare at her over the woman's body.

He paused and looked up at her, smiling. "You're new."

"You shouldn't be so rough with your . . . dates," Sylvia said, skimming a look over the woman, snapping her fury under control as she saw the ripped dress, the bruises that were already forming.

He chuckled. "This? This isn't a date. This is a meal. When I'm done, if you like, you and I could have a date. You can tell me why you came into my city and why I shouldn't kill you."

"Hmmm." Sylvia studied him, weighing the age. He wasn't young, but wasn't old. Her age, she thought. And his power level was higher. She'd handled worse. Eyeing the woman, she listened to the heart, counting the beats. "You like taking so much blood you make them pass out?"

He shrugged, pulling a snowy white handkerchief out of his pocket to dab at the corner of his mouth. An affectation—

he didn't have a drop of blood on him. "Well, there's something about taking almost too much, you know?"

"Actually, no." She flipped her blade up, watched as his eyes dropped to it.

"Oh, now, come on." He dropped the woman, kicking her out of his way like she wasn't much more than a used hamburger wrapper or something.

To him, she probably wasn't, Sylvia realized.

Had he killed before, when he went just a little over that line? Probably. As he crossed the alley to stand in front of her, she found herself remembering that conversation again.

Do you really want to live in a world where nobody stops the monsters, Miz James?

No. She really didn't.

I T was nearly dawn before she let herself back into her house. She was dragging, too, although it was a mental weariness, not anything physical.

After a quick shower, she found herself staring at the mirror, searching for some sign that she'd changed. A month ago, she never would have bothered with what she'd done earlier.

If it didn't come with a paycheck, she only messed with those who got in her way. Or the rare monster like Pulaski.

So why had she messed with the vampire earlier?

She still looked the same—she looked like the young Japanese bride she'd been when she'd came to America all those years ago . . . just with a lot more knowledge in her dark eyes. The long black hair was the same, the pale skin, the unsmiling mouth . . .

Absently, she reached up and touched her lips.

Up until Toronto had come into her life, she couldn't remember the last time she'd smiled.

"Shit."

Spinning on her heel, she headed to bed. She was done mooning about this. It was over, right? They'd walked away. They had decided that was what they should do, right?

Halfway there, she stopped and scowled, shoving a hand through her hair. "Okay, we didn't *decide*. He just said it. I didn't argue."

Blowing out a breath, she tipped her head back, staring up at the ceiling. *Shit.* She wasn't going to get him out of her head as easy as that. She just wasn't. "Okay, fine. I'll call."

She even knew the number for the Enclave.

The phone only rang once before a bright, cheerful voice picked up. "Hello!"

Sylvia scowled. Shit, she'd hoped . . . no. It didn't matter. "I'd like to speak with Toronto, if he's available."

There was a pause. "Ah, is this . . . Ms. James?"

"Yes."

"Hold on a second."

She waited, feeling the exhaustion spread through her body. She stared at the clock by her bed, knowing even without its help that the seconds of night were burning away fast, too fast. Legs leaden, she made her way to the bed and sat down.

She heard footsteps, then the whisper as a hand took the phone—a woman's voice. *"I have that mercenary on the phone."*

That mercenary—

Her heart, that damn useless bit that reacted more to *him* than it did for anything else, leaped around in her chest. But then it crashed . . . the voice that came on the phone wasn't Toronto's.

"Hello, Ms. James."

She swallowed. "I imagine this would be Rafe."

"It would. You want to speak to Tor."

"That's why I called." She closed her eyes. If she was told he didn't want to talk to her . . . *shit.* No. She'd just kick his ass. He could be a man and tell her that on his own, right?

"Tor's not available," Rafe said softly. "I'm sorry. Can I—"

"Not available?" Her hand gripped the mattress. She heard fabric tear.

"I'm afraid not. He . . ."

Outside, the sun hit the horizon. She fought it, clinging to wakefulness with everything she had in her. "He *what*? Doesn't want to talk me? Get that fucking jerk on the phone, *now*. He can tell me that himself."

"No, he can't." Rafe's voice changed, became heavier. Harsher. "Tor's not . . . he's not with us anymore, Ms. James."

"Not . . ." Her tongue felt thick in her throat. She swallowed as her lids tried to glue themselves shut. "Not with . . ."

Sleep grabbed her, like a greedy, hungry monster and stole her will away.

The phone fell from a numb hand as she sagged backwards onto the bed.

NOT *with us anymore . . .*
       The words haunted her sleep.
What does that mean?

She dreamed they were in his house. She found him in the kitchen, standing bare-chested over the stove, cooking, of all things, a bologna sandwich. "That's not enough food for a full-grown wolf," she said. Her chest ached, even to look at him.

He glanced back at her, face weary, eyes somehow . . . dim. That wicked light, it was gone. A faint growth of stubble darkened his face. With a half shrug, he looked back at the stove. "I'll make four or five sandwiches," he said. "What do you want, Sylvia?"

She frowned, glancing around. "I just . . . I think about you. I called, looking for you."

"Did you now?" He stabbed at a piece of the deli meat and flipped it. "Too late. I'm gone. You didn't want to be around me, anyway."

She opened her mouth to argue, but his words echoed in her mind. *I'm gone . . . gone . . . gone—*

Swallowing, she closed her eyes and covered her face with her hands. This . . . this wasn't happening. "What . . . what happened?" She lowered her hands to stare at him as the ache in her chest spread.

"What do you mean, what happened?" He flipped the

meat onto a piece of bread and added another slice of bologna to the skillet. But just as it started to sizzle, a weird look came over his face.

"I mean *what happened*," she snarled.

"I . . ." He turned around, scratching at his bare chest. Then he shook his head. "I've got to go, Syl."

He padded toward her, a sad smile on his face. As he paused at her side, she thought she could almost smell him, and she thought maybe, she could almost touch him. But when she reached out, her hand passed right through him. "Take care of yourself, sweetheart."

From one blink to the next, he was gone.

W ITH a scowl, Toronto swung himself out of the small bunk he had tucked in a small room in the main house.

The dream about Sylvia clouded his mind. It wasn't the first one he'd had, but it felt different. He'd like to sit around and analyze it, think it through . . . brood . . . but he didn't have that luxury.

The bite of anger was in the air.

The entire fucking reason he was here.

There wasn't a clock in his room—there was barely room for a damn bed, but this was the only place for him. He grabbed his phone and checked the time. Past midnight. Shit. He was fucking *pissed*.

It was after midnight, he'd already been asleep, and there was no reason for anybody to be at the house, all chewed up with rage. It was there—the stink of it clouding the air even from here. And unless Toronto was way off base, he smelled booze. A lot of it. Which was exactly what it would take to get a shifter drunk—a lot of it. Hard, and fast, in copious amounts.

Slipping out of the room, he made his way down the hall, listening to the voices.

"You don't fucking *belong* here."

"Graham, it's late. You should go back home, back to your wife." Matt was in the office where his dad had conducted most of his business, and although he was hiding it, it was hard for the kid to be in there.

Poor guy, forced to be a man too early.

It wasn't going to get any easier for him any time soon.

He made himself stop in the doorway. Matt had to handle this. It didn't matter that the kid was only sixteen. It didn't matter that the other guy outweighed him, outreached him.

Matt was the stronger wolf and if he wanted to hold his place, he had to prove he *could*.

Toronto couldn't do that for him.

But he could damn well make sure the buffoon in front of him knew he was being watched.

It took him a few seconds to realize it, the knowledge having to work its way past the fog of alcohol and the haze of stupidity the guy wore like a shield. He half fell as he turned to glare at Toronto, eyes flashing with rage, glowing despite all the alcohol he had in his system.

Alcohol still depressed the body—it should make it harder to shift. Higher level shifters and weres could always find a way, though.

Great, so the kid had a stupid fuck with enough juice in him to make it interesting. And Toronto couldn't do jack but watch.

"What are you doing, you fucking moron?" The man glared at Toronto. "This ain't none of your concern, you mongrel dog. You shouldn't even be here."

Toronto bared his teeth. "If the kid had a halfway decent right-hand man, I wouldn't have to be. Don't worry, I'm just here to watch."

"There's nothing to watch." Matt gave both of them an equally derisive look, still slumped in the big leather chair behind the massive sprawl of oak that had been his father's desk.

He looked too small behind it, too young, Toronto thought. Another thing they had to work on.

"Graham, you need to go home," Matt said. "It's late, I'm tired and there's nothing . . ."

The sound of ripping cloth was a loud echo in the room. Too loud. Toronto shifted his gaze to the boy.

Matt was already on his feet. "I'm not fighting you in here."

Then you better move your ass outside, Toronto mused. The drunk idiot wanted to fight, and he wasn't going to leave until he tasted blood. Toronto wouldn't have minded giving it to him, but he was here to help the kid *find* control, and *get* control.

Not *take* control.

Hard-ass job.

I T only took Matt a few minutes. As he straightened up over Graham's prone body, the fur melting away into his skin, he had a look of molten fury on his face, one that whispered of madness lurking too close.

As he went to kick the still form, Toronto moved.

He caught the boy's arm and said, "It's done. He's had enough."

"He fucking challenged me—in the middle of the night. *Drunk*. I say when it's done," Matt snarled.

Toronto dropped his voice. "Look around. You're not alone. You want to be known for beating an unconscious follower?"

Matt trembled under Toronto's hand and he could feel the violence spurring inside him. Feel it burning through the kid. Toronto could understand that, but Matt couldn't lose it like this. For every step forward he took, he either fell backwards ten or was pushed twenty.

It had to stop.

And Toronto was damned well going to see it happen soon.

"Look at them," he said again. "What do you want them to remember about tonight—that somebody challenged you and you *won*? Or that you were beating an unconscious man?"

S HE'D just left Toronto's empty house—and she meant *empty*. There was nobody there, and more than that . . . his clothes had been gone, the few weapons she'd noticed the one time she'd been there. Maybe she shouldn't have looked, but Rafe's words had left a hollow feeling in her gut—an empty ache that just kept spreading and spreading until it felt like it was going to swallow her whole.

He's not with us anymore . . .

What in the hell did that mean, anyway? She could have called back. Demanded the information on the phone. But she wasn't going to have them stonewall her. Have them handing her empty answers, giving her the runaround or any of that.

Hoping against hope, she'd come here first. It had been a mistake, because she now had the image of his empty closet in the back of her mind, the empty dresser. And the weapons chest, that was gone, too.

With that knowledge adding to the ache in her chest, she blinked away the tears that tried to turn her field of vision red. She didn't have time for this. She had a Master vampire to deal with, and a Master werewolf to find.

He'd be there. That was the only way she managed to make the drive, by convincing herself he would be there, or that she'd find out where he was.

Yet in the back of her mind, she kept hearing, *He's not with us anymore.*

As she drew closer to the Enclave, she realized she'd picked up a tail. Several of them, actually. A couple running on four feet. Some just watching from the shadows. Fear tried to well inside her, but she shoved it aside. She wasn't breaking any laws being here—nothing to be afraid of.

Nothing.

Yet when she felt the buzz over her skin as she crossed over the official line of Rafe's territory, she had to yank herself under control. She wasn't going to walk in there stinking of fear, damn it. She had no reason.

She wasn't one of *them*, damn it.

But she wasn't one of the monsters, either—

Whoa.

That was . . . unexpected.

I'm not one of the monsters . . .

The road abruptly curved and she came around the corner, still wrestling with the knowledge reverberating through her brain; she didn't notice the house until she was almost on top of it. What caught her attention first was them. All of them.

That was when she noticed the house. Because there were even a couple of people up on the roof.

Oookay . . .

Slowing her bike to a halt, she met the dark gaze of the vampire who had to be the Master. Nobody else here quite carried the punch he did. He wasn't as strong as some she'd met and she suspected he wasn't too much older than she was, but he carried some serious power in him.

And he could kill her in an instant. She knew that before she'd even managed to turn the bike off.

"Hello, Ms. James."

She remained on her bike. "Everybody seems to know who I am. I don't much care for that."

"Sorry." He smiled, his teeth a bright flash in the dark. "What can I say . . . your reputation has just . . . preceded you."

Eyeing him narrowly, she tried to figure out how to respond to that. Then she decided not to bother. She didn't give a damn about her reputation. Swallowing around the knot in her throat, she asked, "I'd like to speak with Toronto."

Around them, people shifted, looked to Rafe, then to her. Then away.

"I already told you . . . he's not with us any longer."

Her heart shattered. It was like that organ had just been turned into glass, and then smashed with a hammer. Pain splintered through her and she wanted to scream, wanted to rail, wanted to cry—

Yet she just stared at him. Rafe held her gaze levelly, unflinchingly. He wasn't lying. And she didn't catch any hint of that scent . . .

No—

Convulsively, her hands gripped the handlebars of her bike while she fought for control. *Gone*. He was *gone*—

She started her bike. Fuck. She had to get out of there. *Now*. Before she lost it. Finding out what happened could come later and if whoever killed him was still breathing, they wouldn't be for much longer. It might take a bomb to do the bastard in, if Toronto hadn't been able to handle it, but still.

Shit. This wasn't happening.

A hand touched her shoulder.

Snarling, she shrugged it off.

When that didn't work, she whipped her head around and said, "Get the fuck—"

Angel's blue gaze met hers. "Rafe's an idiot some-times . . . Sylvia, Toronto isn't *dead*."

CHAPTER 26

A NOTHER day.
    Another dipshit.

"I just don't understand how much longer *he* has to be here."

Matt sat behind his desk. Still that solid, heavy oak that had been his father's. Toronto had asked him the other day to consider getting a new one. They could use the old desk in the library, if Matt couldn't part with it.

Matt didn't seem to see the point.

Telling him it made him look that much more like a boy trying to fill a man's shoes hadn't exactly made the kid like him more.

Still, as Matt faced yet another one of the adults from the broken pack, there was a little less antipathy in his gaze. It had been almost a week since the last fight, the one involving a drunken fool.

It wasn't much, but after more than two months, Toronto was ready for any sign of improvement.

"He'll be here for as long as we need him here," Matt said, looking bored as he hunched over a laptop. The spreadsheet held the information on the pack's finances. Toronto had been helping him get things back under control after they'd been left to float for just a little too long. They weren't in bad shape, but they weren't exactly ready to dance on the mountainside, either.

"Matty, look . . ."

Matt stilled and sat up, his eyes flashing from green to yellow. "Matty?" He lifted a brow.

The guy in front of him gave a cheerful, forced laugh, while behind him, Toronto pulled out his knife. The older wolf's eyes cut his way and Toronto smiled at him, nice and friendly. If only one of these bastards would just come up to him, they could have it out, but *no* . . .

"Matty is the kid who died the night I had to chase off feral wolves after they'd killed my father, Charlie."

A poker seemed to shove its way up good ol' Charlie's ass, Toronto noticed. His spine stiffened, hands clenched into fists. "We would have helped more, if we could have. We had families to protect."

"Yeah. You did." Matt shrugged. "I'm not disputing that." He paused for a moment, hit a button on the laptop and then shut it down. "You had families to protect, and you did it. But where were you when I was out there broken and bleeding, the next day? You were still protecting your family when I had to crawl back home?"

Charlie, wisely, kept his mouth closed.

Rising, Matt came out from behind the desk. "It was me and four guys my age out there. Two of us came back. The rest of you—*grown men*—were hiding in your houses afraid to come out because you were afraid of the other pack."

He glanced at Toronto, a faint scowl on his face. "Hunters were the ones to track down the stragglers who got away from us and kill them. A Hunter had to clean up the mess you all were too fucking chicken to clean up. So, yeah, he'll be here for as long as I want him around. You got a problem with me? We'll have a go, right here, right now." His eyes burned wolf-yellow now and he watched Charlie with a look that said he really, really wanted to hurt him. "If you got a problem with the Hunter, then maybe you should take it up with him. And spread the word—I'm not doing this every other day, damn it."

As the door closed quietly behind Charlie a few minutes later, Toronto looked at Matt. "You know, the Hunter has a name."

"Hell, you're lucky I didn't call you that fucking jerk," Matt muttered, returning to his spot behind the desk and staring at the computer with a look of abject misery.

"You wouldn't be the first." Moving to settle in the chair across from the desk, he said, "You know it's going to be a while before I can leave."

Green eyes stared into his. "I figured that out the day you stuck a silver knife in me. I'm stuck with you until I can function past that sort of thing, aren't I?"

"Yeah."

"I can get there, right?" He looked terribly young in that moment, terribly lost. "I can do it, can't I? They . . . they used silver on Dad, and he just couldn't . . ."

"Not all of you can. But you're stronger than a lot of the natural shifters I've met. You just have to find the control." Spinning in the chair, Toronto focused his gaze on the window. "And you have to survive all of them."

"I can handle them. The question is which one of them is going to push me too far." He propped an elbow on the desk, staring outside along with Toronto, eyeing the two men who'd met not too far away from the main house. Charlie was one of them.

The other was Graham—the drunken bastard who'd gone a few rounds with Matt's fists already.

"Graham's your biggest problem." Toronto hooked one ankle over his knee. "He mouths off, questions everything. You might need to kill him."

Matt curled his lip. "I was ready to do that. You stopped me."

"There's a difference between killing him in a fight and murdering an unconscious drunk." Toronto had thought about doing the man himself—something wasn't right with him. But this couldn't be his fight, not until it was forced on him. And Graham wasn't that stupid. He thought he could maybe handle a half-grown Alpha. He wasn't going to take on Toronto in a straight fight, though.

And Toronto had no grounds . . . Frowning, he spun back around and studied the kid. "Did your father have a second?"

"Yeah." Matt's lashes swept down. "Broderick Scott. He died first. Took a bullet for my dad."

"So your pack is used to having one around, right?" Not every pack used them nowadays. A few hundred years earlier, the packs had warred—often. But that had been brought to a halt, mostly thanks to Hunter interference—they couldn't have packs going to war over territory in this day and age. Bodies eventually got hard to hide and sooner or later, if they were burning them, they would be discovered.

"Yeah."

"Make me your second."

Matt just stared at him. Toronto smiled. "You realize when he came in here the way he did, he was insulting you. He didn't knock. He didn't announce himself. He used the same name for his Alpha that he'd use for a kid. They still treat you as a kid—you see some of it, but not all. Because you're used to it. It has to stop, though, and it won't, until you make them." Leaning forward, he braced his elbows on his knees and studied the boy. "I see it all. I see the conscious and the unconscious challenges. I can call them on all of those slights—if I'm made your second. As long as I'm outside the pack, they can ignore me. They can challenge me over it, but I'd hurt them—since I'm here to try and play nice, I'd try not to hurt them. Then they'd get ugly and decide to gang up on me. Once that happens, I kill. You make me part of the pack, they have to follow protocol and we all know it. They issue the challenge and follow through and when they lose, it's done, or they are outcast."

"I don't want a stronger bastard than me serving as my second," Matt muttered, rubbing at his shoulder, like he could still feel the silver there, although it healed days ago.

"I don't plan on living here forever and ever. Just until things are settled and you know what you're doing. Get a few years on you—and figure out who should serve as your real second." Toronto shifted his gaze out the window, studying the two men. They were walking away now, heads bowed. "You've got good people here. If you get the troublemakers out of the way, you'll be able to see them more clearly."

M ONTANA.
     He had come to fucking *Montana*?

Sylvia felt like she was in a different country—a deserted one. She'd been on this strip of highway for what seemed like hours, cutting through night-dark fields that were probably impossibly green in the day.

The mountains were dark shadows in the distance and if she had it pegged right, she should have another forty-five minutes to drive before she hit the city Rafe had directed her to.

After that, he told her, she was on her own.

Wonderful.

He sends her out in the middle of nowhere and then tells her she's on her own . . .

But hell, how was that any different from the past couple of months? She'd been living with a gaping hole inside her ever since the day she'd walked away from that cabin in Toronto. Leaving behind the one person who had actually made her realize she was . . . empty. Empty in her heart, in her soul.

Now she just had to figure out where to find him.

Although, seriously, once she got to the city, it wouldn't be that hard, she didn't think. All she really had to do was stop hiding herself so much, she figured. Do that, and just maybe he could find her . . .

R IDING a fence line wasn't what he'd planned when he'd come to Montana.

Riding a fence line and then having to fight off an attack

that came at his back was another thing he hadn't planned on—but he was more equipped to handle the attack than the fence line.

After he'd hurled Graham to the ground, he shrugged out of his leather jacket and threw it off to the side. "We don't need to do this," he said quietly. "You know you aren't going to win."

"You don't *belong* here." Graham shoved upright, staring at Toronto with rage burning in his eyes. It was an ugly sight.

"Yeah. You're right. But I'm not leaving until the kid is ready to stand on his own." He cocked a brow. "Deal with it."

"Deal with it . . ." Graham's voice dropped, gravelly rough. "If he can't stand on his own *now*, he shouldn't be the Alpha."

"You couldn't take him on your best day. Nobody in your pack can. But you think you've got a right to try and run him out? Because he's young?" Toronto shook his head. "We going to do this, or not?"

Graham sank to a crouch, his muscles already rippling as he started to shift.

Lucky bastard—it didn't hurt a natural shifter the way it hurt a were. Toronto kicked off his boots, keeping an eye on the stupid fuck. He'd seen the guy fight. He didn't stand a chance and had to know it—

As he rose from the ground, his body a meld of wolf and man, Toronto saw why Graham was so cocky—sunlight glinted off a glass vial in Graham's hand. Somehow, he didn't think it was just water in that little bottle. There was only one thing, really, that would do much good against a were. Silver.

Fury bit into him and he spun away halfway through his shift as the other wolf lunged for him.

Turning to face Graham, he said, "That's a dick move, bringing poison into this. When you go down, I'm going to make you eat it."

Graham's reply was a snarl. But there was fear in his eyes now.

The bastard had lost the edge of surprise and was now completely fucked.

* * *

Hᴇ had silver nitrate in his leg, eating its way through him, he had a dead body to haul back to the compound—Toronto was not happy.

Once he'd finally made it back, he saw several eyes cut his way before darting off without making contact. They'd already smelled the dead body. Lips peeled back from his teeth, he cut the ropes he'd used to keep Graham's body from falling. Hauling the corpse off the back of the three-wheeler, he turned and dumped it on the ground

Hearing a door open, he looked up.

Matt stood in the doorway, his young face rigid, eyes dark.

"What in the *fuck* did you do?"

Cutting his eyes to Charlie, Toronto said, "I dealt with a bastard who came at my back—one who decided he'd level the playing field with poison." Curling his lip, he looked down at Graham. The silver nitrate had burned and blackened Graham's face, his neck as it killed him. Toronto stared at him woodenly for a long moment before shifting his gaze upward and studying the people gathered around him.

"You murderer," Charlie growled, his eyes flashing to wolf-yellow.

"Murderer." Toronto lifted his gaze, staring at the other shifter. "He comes at my back, with poison, and you want to call me a murderer."

"He didn't have a chance against you, fucking monster."

"Then he should have thought of that before he attacked a Hunter," Matt said quietly.

All eyes turned toward the young Alpha as he came down the steps, striding toward Toronto. There was nothing hesitant on his face now, although Toronto saw something in the back of the kid's eyes. Regret, maybe . . . and resignation.

Charlie turned to Matt. "You can't tell me you're going to stand for this. This fucking *outsider* killed one of ours. He murdered him."

"No." Matt's gaze dropped to Toronto's leg.

Under the denim, he was bleeding. Thanks to the silver

nitrate, he wasn't going to heal until his body had managed to purge the shit from his system. And it *hurt*. Nothing hurt a shifter of any form, natural or were, the way silver did. He felt like something was trying to chew through his veins.

"You're injured," Matt said.

"He had two vials of silver nitrate on him. I've got one of them inside of me." And he meant the whole damn bottle, too. Graham had gotten one good hit in—using his claws to shred Toronto's leg and then shove the damn thing inside him, crushing it. He'd already been healing so that shit was now stuck inside him, broken glass vial and all.

A good healer could get the glass out. A good doctor could. The pack didn't have a healer but Toronto wasn't certain he'd trust the doctor here.

Eyeing Graham, Matt crouched down next to him and sighed. "I guess I don't need to ask where the other one is."

"No."

Charlie came storming up, bumping into Toronto. With a snarl, Toronto caught him by the shoulder and shoved, sending him flying facedown. He'd had *enough*—

The other man came back up with his fists bunched, muscles rippling under his clothes. "No outsider gets to do that to us," he growled.

"Toronto is no outsider." Matt blew out a breath and then looked at Toronto, gave a short nod. "He's my second, effective now. You want to fuck with him, do it at your own risk."

Toronto met Charlie's gaze and smiled.

"T HERE'S a vampire in Gallatin."

Toronto managed, just barely, to keep the growl behind his teeth when the wolf appeared in the doorway, head bowed. It was Jason, one of the kids who'd gone out with Matt the night their pack had been attacked. One of the two who had returned, while the adults were inside whining and whimpering.

Matt looked up over the table where his cousin Shelby was dealing with Toronto's leg. Heaving out a sigh, he said, "I'll head out there in a few. Tell Hank not to lose his calm."

"You can't." Jason shot Toronto a glance. "She's in the bar."

Matt rolled his eyes. "I'll just tell her to bring her ass out, then, so we can talk."

"Hank already tried to kick her out. She wouldn't budge. And . . . I . . ." The boy shifted from one foot to the other, nervous. "I think he's scared. Didn't want to sound that way, but he didn't sound right."

Staring at the mess of his leg, the skin still black in some areas, Toronto grabbed a towel. "I'll handle it." He looked at the doctor messing with his leg and she stopped almost immediately, dropping the forceps and gauze down by the scalpel she'd had to use to cut into his flesh.

"You need to let Shelby finish with your leg." Matt shook his head. "You're injured."

"And you're sixteen. You go into a bar in a town where the majority of the people are mortal, you're asking for trouble. At best, you'll get branded as a troublemaker. At worst, you get arrested." Toronto probed his leg—the resulting pain was less than it had been. She'd gotten a lot of the glass out and the poison was burning through him. A few days and he'd be good as new. "She can finish cutting the glass out later. For now, I'll deal with this."

"Toronto—"

"This is the job a second would do," he said softly. "You need to start figuring out how an Alpha is going to act, Matt. Otherwise, we'll be doing this again in a few months. You have to show them you're capable of this—show them you're able to do it, or they won't respect you, and everybody who resents you for being strong enough . . ." He shook his head. "You want another one turning out like Graham?"

Matt's silence was answer enough.

He let Shelby clean up his leg while Jason brought him some clean jeans. He was sweating by the time he got them on, but he had an hour's drive ahead of him. If he grabbed some food, he'd be good.

Although . . . considering the way his life was going lately, it wouldn't hurt to be careful. On his way out, he hit his room and raided his weapons chest. His Glock, loaded with the kind of bullets that would take down even some of the oldest vamps, went into a sheath under his arm. He slid a few knives into place and then grabbed a jacket.

Hopefully this wouldn't be anything.

It wasn't a Hunter, though—he would have sensed that, and he probably would have been called. So it was anybody's guess what kind of situation he was walking into.

A brief wistful moment passed through him . . . he knew who he *wished* it was.

But he figured he was as likely to find Sylvia in Gallatin as he was to find his memory. She'd walked away, as he'd expected. She was done.

He couldn't even say *they* were done, because there had never been a *they*. A few days . . . they'd only had a few days and he'd still . . .

"Shit, don't do this," he muttered, his voice hoarse even to his own ears. He'd spent more than two months working his ass into the ground to keep from thinking about her, to keep from wishing things could have turned out differently. Maybe . . .

Hell. Maybe he should have tried to find her. Talk to her.

You still can, a sly little voice whispered, that cunning, selfish bastard—the man he was trying to leave behind. He couldn't go back to that. Wouldn't. Although speeding down the highway in the dead of night, it was hard to remind himself of that fact.

Fate had given him a good, hard bitch-slap, showed him just how self-centered, how much of a bastard he'd been. If he couldn't be better than that, then he didn't *deserve* her. Until he could be better, he wasn't going to ask for things he knew he shouldn't have.

And the ugliest part of the mess . . . he couldn't be better overnight, couldn't become better by walking away from the responsibilities he'd agreed to take on. Right?

Shit, he'd feel better if somebody would just tell him he was right—that he was doing the right thing.

"No, you wouldn't," he muttered, checking the miles.

Gallatin was still a good thirty miles ahead. "It doesn't matter if you change or not . . . if you're doing the right thing or not, because it's not going to help with her."

And it wouldn't. If she'd wanted anything between them, she wouldn't have been so quick to walk away.

CHAPTER 27

"Look, lady. It's midnight. We don't stay open until midnight around here."

He gave her another nervous look, light glinting off his eyes. If he'd been human, he would have already called the cops. But then again, if he had been human, she wouldn't be there.

If Toronto was anywhere around here, somebody would know.

Sylvia hadn't been able to find any sign of him, so she figured the next best thing was making herself a pain in somebody's ass. Sooner or later, she'd find somebody who would tell her something.

But this guy wasn't that someone. She'd seen it on him the minute she walked inside. He was a midlevel shifter and he was freaked out just at the sight of her. A scared, nervous bastard who hadn't wasted any time in going to make a phone call about her after she'd refused his "polite" request that she leave.

She wasn't leaving. Sylvia was damn tired. She'd spent the day sleeping in the bathroom of her hotel, she hadn't fed in two days and water and alcohol weren't going to cut it for

too much longer. She was going to keep her ass in this bar for
as long as she damn well had to. If he'd called somebody,
there was a chance *that* somebody might have answers . . .
and a little more spine.

A ripple rolled across her skin. That presence of something . . . *other* . . .

The bartender's eyelashes flickered and he stared at her,
his pulse slamming inside his throat.

"Who did you call?" she asked quietly.

"My pack. The majority of them live out on the compound an hour away." He jerked his chin up, trying not to
look too nervous. "You come onto our territory, you really
ought to talk to the Alpha."

The Alpha. Shit. That twinge of hope withered away and
died.

This guy was a natural shifter. The shifters weren't like
weres—half the time, the two races didn't even get along. If
whoever she'd just sensed was the Alpha, if there was a local
pack, then what was she doing here? Toronto wouldn't be
here . . .

Carefully, she lowered her glass. Pushing her hand into
her pocket, she pulled out a twenty and tossed it on the
scarred surface of the bar. He wasn't here. She didn't know
what kind of game Rafe was playing with her, but Toronto
couldn't be here.

Head bowed, she slid outside. She needed to get to the room
and refocus. Replan. The Alpha could go fuck himself—

HE hadn't even hit the street when he caught that scent.
Shit.

This . . . what . . . no.

A job, he thought.

She was here for a job, he figured. For a half a second, he
wondered if one of the idiots back at the compound might
have hired her. But that didn't seem right. Although considering the burn in his leg, it wasn't an option he was going to
dismiss . . .

"Stop it. Get your head on straight." Swearing, he hit the

brakes and parked the car on the side of the road. He didn't give a damn if it was illegal—he needed to walk for a few minutes and think, make sure he had himself under control when he saw her.

Although each second seemed to make control even *less* likely. His heart raced, his mouth felt dry, his palms sweated and his entire body *ached*. The wolf in him whispered, *Want . . . find her. Want . . . want.*

"Can't," he muttered. He'd already had what he'd get from her.

And it wasn't enough . . . because he wanted everything.

*M*Y pack . . . *the Alpha* . . .
   Those words swirled through her head, but her heart was racing.

Because she *knew* that figure striding toward her. The long blond hair was pulled back from his face, and he was limping a little, but damn it, she knew him, even from this far off.

Sylvia wanted to run to him.

But she didn't.

Wouldn't. Not until she had . . . something.

So she kept her pace even, her hands in her pockets and schooled her face into a blank mask that didn't reflect anything she felt inside. Inside she was in agony—and ecstasy. Toronto . . . it was Toronto.

Shit, she'd missed him. The way he smiled, the way he looked at her, although the look in his eyes now was decidedly emotionless, the way he smelled . . .

She took a deep breath. She couldn't run to him, but she could . . .

Wait. What . . . ?

She didn't even remember running to his side.

But she was there—at his side and ready to kill, because she knew that scent. It was the acrid, awful scent of flesh dying—what happened when somebody poisoned a shifter with silver. Not stabbed . . . this was worse, a slow poison that ate away at the body, a slow, burning agony. "Who hurt you?" she demanded.

* * *

T HE silvery light dancing through her eyes puzzled him. Something tried to shift in his heart—it felt almost like pleasure, but he shoved it aside. "What are you doing here, Syl?"

"Your leg. It's your leg, isn't it? That's why you're limping. Shit, how did you manage to get yourself jacked-up like this out in the middle of nowhere? You having a pissing match with the local Alpha or what?" She crouched down by his leg, reaching up to touch him, but stopping with her hand just a breath away.

"Ahh . . . Sylvia, could you get up?" Toronto asked, shifting away.

She shot him a look and rose, her spine going rigid, but then she caught sight of his eyes . . . the way the blue started to swirl. *Ahhh . . .* not so emotionless, she realized.

"How did you get hurt?" Moving a little closer, she continued to watch his shifting, glowing eyes.

"A fight. What are you doing here? If it's a job, you need to be careful and if it's to do with the pack . . ."

"I'm not here for a job." She reached up, toyed with the lapel of his jacket. "I came looking for you."

I came looking for you . . . His brain stopped.

Just stopped.

I came looking for you . . .

She hadn't said that. He'd had all sorts of wishful thoughts on the drive in, and when he saw her, all of them had decided to dance through his mind again and now he was just having a temporary break with reality. That was it.

Clearing his throat, he caught her wrist and nudged it aside. "The pack is my responsibility now, so whatever the problem is, if it's a pack thing, we're going to have some issues and—"

"It's not the pack." Sylvia touched her fingers to his face. "Hey . . . you don't seem to want to look at me. What's the deal there?"

Shifting his gaze to her, he found himself falling. Falling into that dark, silver-flecked gaze. "I like looking at you just fine," he muttered. Reaching up, he curled a hand around her wrist. Under his touch, her skin felt like silk, soft, cool skin . . . wrapped around steel. Her strength amazed him, delighted him. He wanted her so damned bad. He could all but taste her mouth . . . no. Stop. Just no . . .

"Hmmm." She swayed closer, pressed her lips to his chin and whispered, "I like looking at you, too. Even if you are stupid enough to let some idiot get you with silver."

Tipping his head back, he fought the growl rising in his throat. "Sylvia, stop. Whatever you're doing . . . just . . ."

"Why?" She rubbed her cheek against his neck. "The silver is burning you—you've got a fever."

Fuck, no kidding. Her name is Sylvia and she's currently driving me insane. Breaking my heart. Reaching up, he rested his hand on her shoulder, eased back. "Baby, look, I can't . . ."

She stilled, her lashes sweeping down over her eyes. Then she took two careful steps back.

He'd hurt her, he realized. Fuck. He hadn't wanted that. But he wasn't going to be a fuck-toy. Swearing, he turned away and stared off into the night. Just a few buildings separated him from the open, cool night. He could shift . . . run. The injury to his leg wouldn't slow him down that bad. He could maybe try to outrun the ache in his heart.

But he couldn't escape this. What he felt for her.

"Why are you here?" he asked quietly. "If it's not a job, then . . ."

"You." She laughed, and it sounded hollow. "Shit, how dense are you? I came looking for you, but obviously that was a waste of time. I . . . I thought maybe . . . hell. You know what? Fuck it. Take care of the leg, Toronto. Have a nice life. I gotta—"

S HE threw the last words over her shoulder, intent on getting to her bike and getting as far away from Gallatin, Montana, as she could before the sun rose. She made it six inches before an arm came around her, hauling her against a long, lean body.

"Why?"

Jerking against his hold, she snapped, "Let me go, Tor. *Now*."

"No." With his other hand, he reached up, toying with her hair. "You . . . why did you come looking for me? You thought what?"

She wasn't doing this—

Abruptly, she sagged back against him. What the hell. She'd come looking for answers, she should at least *get* them, right? At least then she would *know*.

"I missed you," she said, her voice ragged. "I missed you, damn it. Yeah, you said we were walking away and everything, but . . ."

She stopped. The words froze in her throat and she stared off into the night, her heart aching. She felt stripped and naked and raw . . .

"But what?" He nuzzled her neck. "You didn't want to walk?"

"I never said I did." Closing her eyes, she held still. Okay. She'd said it. Now . . . what? She didn't even know. He wasn't saying anything, although she could feel his heart racing against her back, and—

The world spun. Then his mouth was on hers, one hand fisted in her hair, arching her head back.

Oh . . .

It was a damn good thing she didn't have to breathe, because she would have never been able to take a breath.

Then his hands were on her shoulders, pushing her back. "Wait," he demanded.

"Wait?" She reached up, touching a hand to her buzzing lips. Need, want and love ripped through her, but she couldn't do a damn thing about that . . . still, not with all of this unsolved between them. Peering at him, she tried to figure out what was going on. "Wait, what?"

"What do you mean, you didn't want to walk?" he asked. Shaking his head, he lowered his hands, backing up a few steps. "I . . . look, I don't want to be some sort of friends with benefits or whatever shit they call it now."

Part of her wanted to say, *Good!* That wasn't what she

wanted, either. But . . . damn it, she needed something before she kept throwing herself out there . . .

"I know this was supposed to be a short-term work deal," he said, shaking his head. He started to pace, looking very much like a caged wolf, even with the limp. "We didn't finish things up the way we planned, I know that, and yeah, we had a few good . . ."

"Fucks?" She smiled at him sweetly.

He stilled, and when he looked at her, it was with a wolf's gaze. "I've fucked enough women. What we had felt like more."

That ache in her chest, the one that had been lodged inside her for the past two months suddenly started to ease . . . *more* . . . ? She opened her mouth, but he was already pacing again, and talking, his words coming in rapid-fire bursts now.

"It was more, at least for me, and it's over. Okay. So it's over, but I'm not going to be a fuck-toy, friends with benefits, whatever. It's more than that for me and I'm too selfish to pretend otherwise and I—" He turned around and almost crashed into her.

"More, huh?" Slipping her arms around his waist, she tipped her head back and stared into his eyes.

"Yeah." Shit. He felt like an idiot. This is why it was easier just to avoid people, avoid relationships. Reaching down, he caught her wrists, untangled them from his waist and eased himself away. "You . . . you should go. I've got to get back to the pack, let them know there's no trouble. I'm . . ."

"So now I'm not trouble?"

She had that sly little smile on her mouth, that one that *meant* trouble. Toronto closed his eyes. Tried to steady himself. He needed to be calm right now. Calm . . . and rational, everything he should have been all these years, everything he'd been trying to convince himself he could be. And here she was, shattering that calm.

"You're all sorts of trouble." Opening his eyes, he met her gaze. Because she was so close, because he couldn't stop himself, he reached up, touched her lips. "But I don't think you're anything the local pack needs to worry about."

"No, the pack doesn't need to worry about me." She caught one of his fingers between her lips.

"Good. That's . . . that's good." He stared at her lips, swallowed the growl that rose in his throat as she bit him lightly. "I . . . fuck. I've got to go. You take care of yourself."

He made it two steps before her voice, deceptively light, stopped him in his tracks.

"You know, you say it was more than sex, but you sure as hell have an easy time walking away from me."

Spine rigid, he stood there. As she came walking up behind him, he didn't move, eyes locked on his car, parked a good half mile away. Her fingers brushed his arm. The scent of her flooded his head. And his heart . . . it ached. How could seeing her manage to both hurt *and* heal? She circled around to stand in front of him and he met that silver-flecked gaze and saw, for once, that she had no mask on, no walls.

She stared at him with her heart in her eyes . . . and it made him start to hope.

"Toronto . . . I'm not the one who decided we were walking away." She moved closer, until just a breath separated them—even that felt like too much. "I hadn't even gotten to that part, and I already knew it was going to hurt like hell if *you* decided to walk."

He wasn't saying anything, Sylvia thought. Not a thing. Slipping her arms around his waist once more, she told herself she wasn't going to let him pull back so easily this time. He felt something, damn it. She knew it—she saw it in his eyes. If he wanted her gone, he'd have to say it outright. Otherwise, they were staying right here until they had this worked out.

Rising up on her toes, she touched her lips to his. "I never realized I had a hole in me. Not until you came and filled it. Then you were gone and it was like . . . hell. It was hell. I don't want to be *friends*, Toronto."

And he started to shudder. Slowly, he reached for her, and that break in her heart started to heal. "Sylvia?"

"It was more for me, too," she whispered, pulling back and staring into his eyes.

The thick, golden fringe of his lashes swept down and he

went to his knees. "Shit." Pressing his face to her belly, he clutched her to him, almost desperately. "You mean it. You mean that . . . how in the hell can you mean that?"

"How can I not?" Seeking out the band that held his hair confined, she tugged it free. "You and me, we fit, Toronto. Haven't you figured that out yet?"

"No, we don't." He lifted his head and stared up at her. "I'm a self-centered asshole—but if you haven't figured that out, too bad. I'm not going to let you go without a fight now."

Sylvia laughed. Sinking down, she touched a hand to his face. "We're a match. Maybe you can be an ass, but no more so than me. And you make me smile. You make me feel. You make me want. I had a hole inside of me all of this time and I never even realized it until you came along. You made me feel whole and then you were gone. I don't want you gone again."

"Sylvia . . ." His voice hitched as he rumbled out her name. Once more, he pulled her against him, gripping her with the desperation of a man drowning.

Rubbing her cheek against him, she cuddled close.

They sat there like that, for long, silent moments, his heart beating too hard, too fast, his skin so hot, it almost burned. But she didn't care. Nothing mattered just then. She had him with her again and for now, that was all she needed.

This was real . . .

She was real . . .

This was happening—

Toronto stroked his hands up and down her back, kneading her flesh restlessly, his mind whirling, his thigh throbbing, and the silver in his blood still burning like a bitch. None of that mattered, he told himself. None of it—

Except something had to matter.

She came looking for me. She wants to be with me . . . that's all that matters, right?

Closing his eyes, he tried to convince himself that they could worry about everything else later. Much later. After he'd gotten her someplace dark and quiet and safe from the sun, so he could spend the rest of the night hours making love to her.

But . . . he couldn't.

"What's wrong?"

As she pulled back, he made himself meet her eyes. He had to explain. If she couldn't . . . or wouldn't . . . stay, he had to respect that.

He was bound here for now. Going back on his word would undo everything he was trying to change about himself.

"I . . ." He took a deep breath. Fuck, he had to move. Holding her tight, he rose to his feet, ignoring the scream of the slowly healing wound in his thigh. Putting her down, he started to pace. "I haven't spent my life very well, Sylvia. I break promises. I don't meet my responsibilities. I don't like who I am . . . when you . . ."

His voice cracked. Hell, he was a fucking mess. He tried again. "You left just like that, and I figured that was fate's way of kicking me in the face for the way I've spent my life. I'm *supposed* to be better than this . . . I wouldn't be a Hunter if I wasn't meant to do more, be more. And I'm the sorriest fucking excuse there is. Half the time, I can't even look at myself in the mirror. I may not remember who I was before this happened—and that kid doesn't matter. I've built a past and it's not one I'm terribly proud of. I promised myself I'd change that."

"Toronto . . . you act like you've spent all these years kicking puppies and stealing candy from babies." She came to him, touched his cheek. "And the boy you were . . . you weren't a bad kid. Harold did this to you because you tried to help your friend. I can . . ." She paused, memories and night-mares making her eyes glow. "I can tell you what I know."

"You don't need to. *He* doesn't matter. What I've done, what I've been . . . that matters. And maybe I haven't kicked puppies or shit." He gripped her wrist. Just touching her made him feel steadier. He could be better, be stronger. For her.

But he had to do it for himself, first.

"Why this happened doesn't matter, either." He stared off into the night, toward the compound where a kid waited—a young man who *did* need help. And Toronto knew he could do that. Could actually make a difference. He'd given his word. "I came into this life as I am for a reason, though. I'm supposed to do more. It's time I start doing it."

Shifting his gaze to hers, he said quietly, "The pack here needs me. They were attacked and their Alpha was killed. His son is strong enough to take control, but he's just a kid. He's sixteen and he's being challenged at every turn. He's swinging back and forth between losing control himself, and trying to do the right thing."

"You understand that better than some," Sylvia murmured.

"Probably better than most." He wanted to beg her to stay. Or at least wait. But he didn't have that right. She wouldn't be happy here, and she had her . . . life. And hell, how could the two of them even exist together? He *was* a Hunter. It wasn't just *who* he was. He'd finally figured out it was *what* he was. But would a mercenary—one who seemed to hate Hunters in general—want to tie herself to him? "I can't leave here yet. They'll fall apart without me. And I gave my word."

She continued to watch him.

The nerves, the need, the fear inside him spread, an ugly, twisting little mass. He wanted to tear it apart with teeth and claw, destroy it, but he couldn't. He had to deal with it.

"I know this probably isn't any place you would want to be—you've got your own thing that makes you happy, and I—"

Now she moved, covering his mouth with her hand. "Toronto . . . the only time I can remember being *really* happy are a few handful of moments with you." She grimaced and added, "Granted, those moments aren't many, considering you were either trying to piss me off, or we were chasing after Pulaski or whatever. But you've made me laugh. You've made me smile . . . and nobody else had done that in . . . well. A very long time. If I'm going to be happy, it's going to be with you."

Slowly, she lowered her hand, slid it around to hook over the back of his neck. "My own *thing*, as you call it . . . it doesn't exactly make me *happy*. There are a few jobs that satisfy me and I may still want to do those on occasion, but I don't do the job because it makes me happy. I did it because

I was good at it . . . and it was all I had." Rising onto her toes, she pressed her mouth to his. "I'd rather find something that really does make me happy."

"You . . ." He closed his eyes. She wasn't saying—no. He thought maybe she was. Reaching up, he curled his hands over her waist. Then he opened his eyes, studied her. "You'd stay? You don't mind staying here? And you're stopping?"

"Not only do I not mind staying, I'll tell you now they'd have a fight on their hands if they tried to make me leave. And yeah, I think I'm stopping. Not because you asked me." A wry smile came and went. "If you'd asked, or tried to tell me, I'd have probably told you to fuck off, no matter how miserable it made us both, no matter that I don't really love what I do. But I'm *not* happy . . . and I'm kind of tired of that. I think I've got a chance of being happy. With you. I don't want to mess that up."

"Yeah?" His voice hitched. This was real. It was happening.

Maybe fate wasn't giving him that kick after all . . . pulling her close, he wrapped her in his arms and buried his face against her neck. "You want to stay here."

"I want to be with you. Here, there, none of that matters." She pressed a kiss on the spot beneath his ear. Then she whispered, "Tor . . . I don't like the way the silver smells on you."

He started to laugh.

"Show me who did it. I want to kill him. Then I'll be nice for the pack. I promise."

He laughed harder. Then he lifted his head and pressed a kiss to her mouth. "You can't, sweetheart. I sort of shoved the rest of the silver nitrate down his throat and he choked on it."

"That shouldn't have killed him."

"No. Me breaking his neck finished him off."

She sulked. "That bites." Sighing, she rested her head on his shoulder. "So is this pack going to mind me hanging around town?"

"You won't hang around town. You come with me. And they'll learn to deal." Smiling, he pressed his lips to hers. "You're mine . . . and they'll deal with it, or deal with me."

"I fight my own battles, Tor." She tipped her head back,

watching him. "Maybe I could be useful. I'm good with knives and stuff."

"True . . ." He'd already thought about that. "A bunch of young wolves who need to learn how to fight, and need to get a lot of aggression out—you could have your hands full." Lowering his head, he whispered, "You really want to stay?"

"I really want you. And you need to do this . . . I just want to be where you are." She pressed her lips to his. "Somehow you went and became everything, Toronto. If you're here . . . then so I am I."

Everything . . . Smiling against her mouth, he let himself start to believe.

"You're everything for me, too."

Turn the page for a preview of
a romantic suspense novel by Shiloh Walker

THE REUNITED

Coming soon from Berkley Sensation!

"Now . . . if you'll just put your hand . . . right about
 there . . ."

Special Agent Joss Crawford stood to the back of the
group, his craggy face stoic, mouth unsmiling, eyes unblinking. And it took all of his willpower not to laugh. Keeping a
straight face through this shit was a rough gig, but he did it.
He wasn't sure why. He could get where he needed to go
without this joker's help.

"Do you feel it . . ."

Bored, he stared at the area the tour guide had indicated.
Nope. He didn't feel a damn thing.

"Yes, you feel it, don't do? Most of you can just *sense*
it . . ." the guide murmured, his skinny, ratlike face animated, dark eyes glinting in the lights of the flashlights.
"That *burst* of cold, feel how it radiates. All around. Almost
like a cold wind."

It was a cold wind, Joss thought, bored. A cold front was
projected to move through and he had a feeling that had
something to do with the sudden cool wind.

But he couldn't blame everything on the weather.

Plenty of weird, though, could be laid at the feet of the guide. If anybody with eyes had bothered to look, they would have seen the clues all over the place. At least, he had.

He'd seen where the dry ice had been used.

He'd caught it when the guide had signaled one of his co-workers, too, and not a second later, there had been *mysterious* banging sounds when they'd stopped in the middle of an open field where a battle had raged nearly a hundred fifty years earlier.

You can almost hear the soldiers, can't you . . .

All in all, he'd definitely gotten his money's worth. And he wasn't even at the highlight of the tour.

The Oglesby Cemetery. That was still a good thirty minutes away.

He just wished he knew what it was about that place that drew him so—well, he knew *what*. He just didn't know *why*. He was getting kind of tired of coming down here every couple of months and listening to this fake's spiel.

"**Y**ou, sir, have the aura of a man in need."

Joss looked down to see the psychic-wannabe standing in front of him, an anxious look on that skinny face, his hands clasped in front of his chest, his eyes hopeful, shining.

Aw, shit. He wasn't the target for the night, was he?

Then the man lifted a hand . . .

Yes. He was the target.

Each time he'd done this tour, the guy had picked somebody out of his group to focus on. He seemed to think it added something to the show, Joss figured. Hell, Joss could *really* add something to the show. But he wasn't in the mood to have some fake playing tricks on him, either, and he damn sure wasn't going to go along with the gag, either.

Instead of responding, he just stared at him.

"And you're so closed *off*," Larry "Cap" Rawlings said, his voice heavy and mournful as he peered up at Joss.

Joss stood six five. Most people had to peer up at him. Normally most people kept some distance but this guy was practically standing on his toes, so close that Joss could smell the garlic he'd eaten. It wasn't a pleasant experience. The guy had his head tipped so far back, one push against his chest and he'd be off balance enough to end up on his ass.

Joss amused himself with that image but didn't let it show on his face as he continued to stare at the con artist. "What is it?" Cap asked again. "Why are you here? What draws you here? What do you seek?"

Oh, that's a good guess.

But if this guy was a psychic, Joss was a prima ballerina.

And the last time he'd checked, he couldn't dance to save his life. He'd actually broken his date's toe at the senior prom. She never let him live that down, either. She was married to his younger brother now and when he went home on the holidays, she teased him ruthlessly. And fondly.

"Don't know what you're talking about," Joss said, keeping his voice flat, his face blank and his eyes shuttered. He also deliberately crossed his arms over his chest and looked away— *keep out, keep out, keep out*—the body movements said it all.

"Oh, yes. Yes, you do. You seek answers, but you don't even know if you believe in what you see before you. You don't believe in the . . ." He paused dramatically and looked all around. "*Gift.*"

Inwardly, Joss snickered. *The . . . Gift?* He wondered what this freak would do if he had any idea just what Joss's gift was. And Joss's gift was the freak of all freak gifts, because he didn't exactly *have* a set gift. He was a mirror—he mirrored the gift of whoever he'd last connected with—partnered with.

And the last person he'd partnered with had been one of the telepaths on the special tasks force. Eyes slitted, Joss stared hard at Cap and caught a rush of thought.

"*Shit, I should have picked the old broad. She just wants to hear the same shit old bitches always want to hear, but I get so tired of that shit. This guy looked like he'd be more fun, but he's not going to do a damn thing . . .*"

"*If tips are good tonight, I'm calling Candise—she's going to blow me so fucking hard to make up for shortchanging me last time.*"

"*Damn it, we need to get moving, if it starts to rain, half of these idiots will whine about a refund . . .*"

The wind grew sharper, colder. Lifting his face to it, Joss breathed it in. "Do we really need to stand around here while you try to play armchair psychologist, Cap?" Joss said. "I came out here to see the cemetery—I wanted to do the night walk through and the only way to do it is with you. If it rains before we get through it because you wanted to chatter, I'm going to ask for my money back."

Something ugly flickered in the man's eyes.

Joss stared him down and as the guide turned away, he let himself smile.

T HE phone in his pocket buzzed as he stood over the grave.

This was what drew him.

Joss didn't know why.

He didn't understand it, couldn't explain it, but *this* was what drew him.

> *Amelie Carrington*
> *Born April 1, 1910*
> *Died April 1, 1930*

Died on her birthday, twenty years . . . to the day.

Amelie.

The name was a song in his mind.

It whispered to him, called to him. And it had ever since the first time he'd seen it, nearly five years ago, when he'd been here working a case with the unit.

Off to the left, he could hear the rest of the tour group—they were all walking around carrying coat hangers. *Dousing rods*, that's what good ol' Cap had called them.

Joss could have told all of them that Cap was wasting their time in this part. There weren't any ghosts waiting for them. If there were any ghosts to be found, they were up in the newer part. Not here.

As the phone buzzed again, he pulled it out again and scowled at the message.

Instead of answering it, he hit ignore and went to text him.

Busy. What's up?

Not even a minute passed before the answer came up.

You're needed. And my wife wants to know why you're standing in a graveyard.

Joss scowled and lifted his head.

Cap came into his line of view, a tight frown on his face. "You need to put that away. Those are very disruptive to the deceased. Spirits don't like technology."

"Really?" Out of pure curiosity, he texted Taylor back. *Ask Dez if the dead care about technology.*

The answer was almost immediate. *Why in the hell should they? It doesn't affect them and the older ones aren't even aware of it.*

Glancing up at Cap, he smirked. "I have it on good authority that the dead don't care about technology." Then he scanned the perimeter of the cemetery. When he saw the car, he sighed. "I'm afraid I'll have to cut my tour short, Cap. I've been paged."

"Y**OU'RE** into ghost tours now?" Dez asked as Joss came striding up to the car. Up until three months ago, it had been Desiree Lincoln, but then she'd somehow lost her common sense and she'd married Taylor Jones. She was Desiree Jones now.

Joss tried not to hold that against her.

"Yeah. I wanted to do the real thing, but I figured Taylor would punch my lights out if I asked you out on a date to show me the real ghosts," Joss said, flashing her a grin.

Dez chuckled. "Nah. He's not the violent type."

Joss might have agreed with her—Taylor was normally a cold bastard and nothing affected him. Nothing and nobody. Save for Dez . . . He'd hidden it pretty well from most people, but Joss had spent too many times mirroring the gifts that let him read minds, read emotions, and when it came to Dez, Taylor's head and heart were anything but clear.

Speaking of the boss, he looked over the car and saw the man of the hour. "You know, I'm supposed to be off. For like the next five days straight. I haven't had many of those mythical off days lately and I specifically requested a few days of personal time."

"Yes, you did." Taylor shrugged. "Sorry, I just needed your particular talents."

Joss snorted. "My particular talents are nonexistent. I'm a fucking mynah bird. I mimic everybody else. Find whoever I mimic and stick them in."

"I can't . . ." He shifted a look at Dez.

It was just a bare glance—a quick flick and then his eyes were back on Joss's face. But it was enough. Okay . . . so Jones wasn't willing—or able—to send his woman into this? Was that it?

Dez sighed and flicked her hand through her hair. It was a little longer than she usually wore, falling almost to her chin. "He needs more than a ghost-talker on this gig, Joss. But if he sends in more than one person, we'll be made. And besides, I'm not exactly the . . . ideal . . . person to do this."

Joss had heard her. He had. But the one thing his mind focused on was *more than a ghost-talker*.

Shit.

Without even look at the man, without opening his mind, he knew. "You're going to head-fuck me again, aren't you?"

Silence stretched out between them.

Finally, Taylor sighed. "Joss, I don't have much choice. You're the only man I've got who can do this. Nobody else has the ability to pick up any needed gift at any given time; I need multiple abilities and I need them now."

"Where?" He didn't bother trying to talk his way out of it. There was no point. He was in this line of work because he had to be. He wasn't in it for fun, for kicks or for the money. If he was needed, then fuck it. He was needed. Shooting one last glance back toward the stone that kept calling him back here, he looked toward Taylor. The pull had been stronger this time . . . so much stronger . . .

"Here," Taylor said quietly. "It's right here. In Orlando."

* * *

From the penthouse, she could see the bright lights of the amusement park . . . and the castle. A bit of whimsy hit her and she wondered what it would be like, to be Cinderella and live in a castle, happy ever after with her prince.

Her heart skipped at little at the way the lights danced over it. That whimsical part of her, that little girl who'd yearned for that fairy-tale prince, melted inside as she stared at the castle and the longing in her heart just didn't want to let go.

But the more practical, cynical part of her was in control as she turned away from the window and made her way toward her bedroom. She wasn't here on a leisure trip and she wasn't here to stare moon-eyed at some child's pipe dream, either.

She was here to get married.

And it was going to be a debacle. Her prince charming didn't exist and she wasn't expecting that to happen now.

Drucella Chapman knew that much, even though she wasn't required to do much of anything. The bloody wedding planners were taking care of everything, from her one-of-a-kind designer gown, to the invitations . . . what the planners weren't doing, her fiancé was handling.

It didn't feel like her wedding at all.

But then again, her life didn't feel like her life, either. "Why should my wedding be any different?"

The knock at the door caught her off guard.

It could be one of two people . . . her father, and she hoped it was him.

It could be her fiancé. She suspected it was him and she rather hoped it wasn't.

It was a good thing she didn't let herself put much faith in her own hopes, because she was able to keep a smile on her lips as she opened the door and smiled at Patrick Whitemore, the man she was to marry in just under a month. It was going to be at the wedding pavilion, she'd ride in the silly carriage . . .

Her heart ached even thinking of it. Her father had mentioned to Patrick that she'd always wanted that fairy-tale wedding and here her men were, in the position to give it to her, so by God . . .

"Hello, darling," Patrick said, dipping his head to brush his lips against her cheek.

She resisted the urge to flinch and smiled at him. "Patrick, what a pleasant surprise. I wasn't expecting to see you so late."

"I just wanted to see you, see how you were settling in, Ella."

Dru looked down so he wouldn't see the way she frowned. She hated that name. She'd rather be called *Drucella* than Ella. Why couldn't he just call her *Dru*? Oh, yes. She remembered now . . . it was another way for him to remind her just how much he controlled her.

"How are your rooms?"

She smiled at him. "They are quite lovely, thank you." She missed her flat in London. Her parents had divorced when she was young and Dru had spent most of her childhood flying back and forth over the Atlantic—she'd gone to school in London, but she'd spent the summer months and most holidays in the States with her father.

Turning away, she glanced down at the sophisticated, elegant ring he'd given her a year ago. It weighed down on her heavier and heavier these days. She wished she'd never accepted it—wished she'd never accepted that first date. Wished she'd never laid eyes on him.

"I was thinking that I might fly back in a week or two, just for a few days, settle a few things with my flat," she said quietly, stroking a finger over the stone. *Get away from you for just a bit.*

"You were supposed to have all of that dealt with already." He lifted a hand, laid it on her shoulder. The touch was light. But there was no mistaken the threat there.

He didn't need to touch her to remind her.

But that touch . . . bile churned its way up her throat and images, bloody and dark, flashed through her mind.

"Yes. Most of it," she murmured. "I'm likely just nervous. I suspect it's just part of being a bride."

A bride who doesn't want to be one . . .

Plastering a smile on her face, she turned and faced him. "I'll just have a friend check on things for me, shall I? I'd feel better."

"You shouldn't worry so much," he said, touching a brow to her forehead. "It will give you wrinkles."

She only wished that were the least of her problems.

Wrinkles . . .

Marrying a man she hated.

She could always run away, she knew.

But if she did, he'd go after her father.

And worse, he'd track her down. And then, he'd kill her.

SHILOH WALKER

Chains

Three women seem to lead charmed lives . . . until one tragic night shattered their hopes for normalcy.

Now, fifteen years later, the women are returning to their hometown of Madison, Ohio, where three men await them—each dangerous in his own way. And if each of the women succumbs to her desire, they may also find the safety they've been searching for.

In the world of Breeds,
attraction isn't just human—it's animal.

• • •

From #1 *New York Times* Bestselling Author
LORA LEIGH

LAWE'S JUSTICE

Diane Broen is human, but just as much a warrior as
the Breeds she works with. But her new teammate,
Lawe Justice, may be more than she can handle.

penguin.com
LoraLeigh.com
facebook.com/ProjectParanormalBooks

M964T0911